PASSENGER 19

Also by Ward Larsen

The Jammer Davis Series
Fly by Wire
Fly by Night

The David Slaton Series
The Perfect Assassin
Assassin's Game
Assassin's Silence
Assassin's Code
Assassin's Run
Assassin's Revenge

Other Fiction
Stealing Trinity
Cutting Edge

Nonfiction
Thrillers: 100 Must-Reads (contributing essayist)

PASSENGER 19

A Jammer Davis Thriller

WARD LARSEN

OCEANVIEW PUBLISHING
SARASOTA, FLORIDA

ISBN: 978-1-60809-236-9

Published in the United States of America by Oceanview Publishing
Sarasota, Florida

www.oceanviewpub.com

10 9 8 7 6 5 4 3 2

PRINTED IN THE UNITED STATES OF AMERICA

To an unwavering supporter of Manchester United—
this one is for you, Lance

ONE

Bad news is rarely foreseeable. It can come in the middle of the night, as a knock on the door, or by a jagged ringtone. Sometimes it descends as a shocking television image, a thing that stamps forever in your mind where you were and what you were doing at that moment. The worst news always comes when you least expect it. For Jammer Davis it came at noon on a clear Sunday.

The morning had been tranquil, and he was right where he wanted to be. With the ink barely dry on his seaplane rating, a good friend had loaned him a J-3 Cub floatplane for an early morning solo. The weather was ideal, blue skies and a soft breeze, and for two hours he'd worked the finger lakes of Lunga Reservoir, which flanked Quantico Marine Base in Virginia, like a kid with a new bicycle.

He'd been hooked since the previous summer, when the same friend had taken him fishing in Alaska. Two weeks of flawless isolation, camping under the stars and casting for trout from the floats of a stout de Havilland Beaver. It was a new kind of flying for Davis. Seaplanes were not high performance aircraft—not compared to the fighters he'd flown in the Air Force—yet there was a fundamental freedom in being able to use two thirds of the earth's surface as a runway. So he skimmed across lakes and landed on still tributaries, a man without a care in the world, until the fuel gauge brought him back to earth.

Reluctantly Davis pulled the Cub up to a thousand feet, the highest he'd had her all day, and set a course for home port, a seaplane base near Chester nestled on the green shores of the Appomattox River. When the dock came in sight, Davis skimmed lower, gliding smooth and true over the mirrorlike water. He was a mile away when he noticed a vaguely familiar silhouette standing at the end of the pier.

Davis tapped the throttle and nudged the Cub down until he was no more than a wingspan above the water. He flew right at the slim man whose hands were in his pockets, and whose tight haircut and rigid bearing sealed the ID.

Larry Green had tracked him down.

Davis flew straight over Green's head before banking the Cub sharply. He transitioned into a lazy turn and set up for a final approach into the wind. That was one of the beauties of seaplanes—without the limitation of a concrete runway, you could land in any direction you wanted. The pontoons kissed the lake, twin trails of whitewater frothing the cobalt surface behind. When the aircraft settled, Davis steered to the dock with care. Legally speaking he was now driving a boat—and one without a reverse gear, meaning maneuverability was limited. He cut the engine before arriving at the mooring station, and Green grabbed a wing to help guide the Cub into the dock. Once fore and aft lines were secure, Davis was the first to speak.

"Larry, you gotta come up with me! I just finished my checkout the other day and I've been thinking about buying one of these, maybe something with a little more payload to—" Davis stopped in midsentence. Green was staring at him, a retired two-star general who hadn't lost his regulation two-star expression. He wasn't here to discuss airplanes. And Larry Green not talking about airplanes was like a bishop not talking about God.

"What is it?" Davis asked. "You need me for a job? Let me guess—an airplane crashed in Mongolia, and nobody in your office wants to spend six months camping with marmots."

Davis had worked for Green in the Air Force, and both were experienced aircraft accident investigators. Since retiring, the general had risen to head the NTSB's Office of Aviation Safety, and in recent years he'd called upon Davis to help with several problematic overseas crashes. Yet what Davis saw now was not the look of a commander preparing to issue a temporary duty assignment.

His gaze was intense, his mouth slightly parted, a man who knew what he had to say, but wasn't sure how to say it. In all the years he had known Green, Davis imagined he'd witnessed every mood and reaction in the general's catalogue. Never before had he seen indecision.

Green finally broke the silence. "We got a four-hour preliminary strip this morning. An ARJ-35 went down last night in southern Colombia."

The first blade of cold seized Davis' spine. He drew a slow, deliberate breath, and four heartbeats later said, "Colombia."

"The jet disappeared from radar near some high mountains and never reached its destination. There's an ongoing search, but no wreckage has been found. A passenger manifest was attached to the report."

When Green again seemed to struggle for words, Davis' senses went on full alert. His world became smaller, absolutely focused, like when a red warning light flashed on in the sky. "Larry, you're scaring me."

"Jammer . . . " Green finally said, "Jen was on board."

Davis took it like a punch, his gut lurching in a way his morning joyride could never have touched. On a dead calm lake the floating dock seemed to sway. "No! There's no way. You have to consider that Jen Davis—"

"I know, I know . . . that was my first thought too. Jennifer Davis is a common name. But you told me a few weeks ago she got an internship this semester, somewhere in South America. So I double checked the passport number, and—"

"*My daughter* called me yesterday from the airport in Bogotá!"

"What time?"

A simple enough question, but his mind seemed to seize. When Davis finally spoke his voice was tight, as if caught at the end of an exhale. "I don't know . . . late afternoon, I guess."

"What did she say?"

"I didn't talk to her. I was playing in a rugby match and . . . and Jen left a message. By this afternoon she was supposed to be taking soil samples from some damned hillside coffee farm. How could . . . " Davis turned away and put a hand on the wingtip of the seaplane, and when its floats dipped under his shifting weight, his agony translated to the physical as concentric waves swept out over the still water. "This can't be happening, Larry," he said in a whisper. "Tell me this is not happening."

Green put a hand on his shoulder. "I haven't had any updates since the four-hour, Jammer. The airplane is still listed as over-due—nothing's been found yet."

Davis was quiet for a moment, then he stood straight, which put him a full head above his old boss. "So maybe it only diverted because of bad weather. Or it could have been a mechanical issue."

Green was silent.

"Even if it went down, there could be survivors."

So disconsolate was Davis that it took a moment for him to recognize his arguments as the same ones he'd so often heard from the relatives of victims. He knew perfectly well what Green's response would be. *It's good to keep hope. But we have to trust the facts.* He also knew the underlying translation. *Not a chance.*

Green read him, of course. "Jammer, you and I . . . we do this for a living. You know the odds. Any of those things *might* be true. But when a small jet disappears over a big jungle, in the middle of the night, in mountainous terrain, there's usually only one answer. It's like we always tell families and the press—until the aircraft has been accounted for, anything is possible. But you of all people un-derstand the chances of a positive outcome in an event like this."

Event. Another word he'd often used. Davis gripped the wing tighter and forced his eyes shoreside where his car was parked. His phone was there, in the storage compartment between the two front seats. He had listened to Jen's message last night, but hadn't called back because he knew she was on another flight. A flight that never arrived at its destination. He tried to recall her exact words, but they escaped him.

Pain welled in his chest and he felt paralyzed, as if controlled movement was beyond reach. His daughter . . . *a crash victim.* Finally, Davis reacted in the only way that seemed to make sense. He pushed away from the wingtip and hurried up the dock, talking as he went. "I'm booking the first flight, Larry! When does the bank of South American departures leave Dulles? Evening? If I can catch the first—"

"Hold on, hold on! Just stop right there, Jammer!"

With all the self-control he could muster, Davis paused.

Green held out his hands, palms forward, and walked toward him cautiously. The way one would approach a drunk with a barstool poised over his head. "I knew you'd take it this way. I knew there would be no stopping you."

"And?"

Green let out a long breath. "This may be the dumbest thing I've ever done . . . putting a family member on an investigation. I can't think of any rule against it, but probably because it's such an *obviously* bad idea nobody ever thought it was worth putting on the books. At the very least this is an ethical lapse on my part."

"You're sending me."

"I already got it approved. You're on the investigation."

"Larry, I will never forget this."

"Well, hell—I had to send somebody. Turns out there were five Americans on that jet, so I'm obliged to send an observer. I've already got you a ride—there's a Gulfstream III out at Andrews, a State Department flight making a scheduled run to Bogotá. They leave in two hours. Do you still have your go-bag packed?"

"Always." The bag was an NTSB requirement. One week's worth of clothing to cover any climatic extreme, toothbrush, razor, and a few basic tools of the trade including a flashlight, camera, and handheld GPS.

"I know your passport is current, and we're working to expedite the visa."

Davis was already striding up the dock, trying to translate his anguish into momentum. "Send me the four-hour update and anything new you get. And babysit this airplane for me. The seaport office is over there, they'll tell you how to put it to bed." He pointed to a rustic shack that looked more likely to hold a cord of firewood than a flight operations department.

"I'll take care of it." Then Green barked, "But hold on, Jammer!"

The general's tone brought Davis to a halt on the wavering dock. Green closed in with a raised finger and stopped at arm's length.

"*Whatever* happens, Jammer, you promise me one thing."

"I'm listening."

"I am going way out on a limb sending you downrange in an official capacity. I'm doing it because I knew that's how you'd want it. That being the case, you will investigate . . . no matter *what* you find. If this gets too personal, if you can't finish the job, then you owe it to me to step aside. I'll send someone else to take over."

Davis squeezed his eyes shut for a moment, then nodded. "You're right, it doesn't get any more personal than this. That's why I'll get to the bottom of it, Larry. I swear to you I will."

The general's granite stare softened. "All right, then. Good luck."

* * *

Two minutes later Davis was steering his car toward the main road. The lane curved through trees, thick-trunked birch and cedar that were full and green at the height of summer, and the lake was intermittently in view on his right, a postcard-picture view. He saw none of it.

Davis drew to a stop where the gravel ended and waited for a car to pass. When it did, his foot seemed stuck on the brake pedal. His fists squeezed the steering wheel like twin vises, the faux leather handgrip grinding under the pressure. Davis leaned forward until his forehead was flat on the steering wheel. He shut his eyes and pushed everything away. Pushed until only Green's words plowed through his head.

You know the odds.

And there was the problem. He knew only too well.

Worse yet, he knew what came afterward. His wife had died in an automobile accident four years ago, a bolt from the blue that had left Jen without a mother. That had left him without a soulmate. Together they'd buried her on a steel-gray morning, the wind sweeping brown grass in undulating sheets. A fittingly foul day to mark the low point of their tailspin, a bottom from which he and Jen had eventually climbed out and recovered. Recovered. Could it ever be called that? Not completely. The worst was behind them, the ghosting about the house, preparing tasteless meals, neighbors whispering behind cupped hands at holiday parties. He and Jen had gotten through, leaning on one another as never before. In those dark days, they had grown closer than he'd ever thought possible.

Now it was happening all over again. If he lost Jen, where would he turn? For so long it had been the two of them, and even with Jen in college they talked every day. One of them made the three-hour drive every other week. His daughter was precious, absolutely everything to him. *You know the odds.*

Davis lifted his phone from the midseat compartment and scrolled to her last message. His thumb hovered over the playback button for a long moment before tapping the screen.

From two thousand miles away, her voice was effervescent, like sunlight on a new morning. *"Hi, Daddy! I made it to Colombia. One more flight and I'll be there. I've already met a girl who's going to be on the same project. By tomorrow she and I will be shoveling dirt—too bad you're not here to help! Love you, I'll call soon. And don't overfeed Captain Jack—bettas don't need much!"*

Then silence.

Davis couldn't say how long he sat staring into space, but when he refocused the first thing he saw was the green LED clock on the car's dashboard.

It was noon on Sunday.

The worst day of his life.

TWO

Five hours and twelve minutes. That was the air time between Andrews Air Force Base, Maryland, and El Dorado International Airport in Bogotá, Colombia.

They were somewhere over the Caribbean, and through the tiny oval window Davis saw azure-blue water and an island below. He was pacing the cabin aisle, his head bumping on the ceiling, a six-foot-two clearance that was two inches shy of his personal requirement. Like a zoo animal in a cage that was too small, his hips bounced between stitched-leather seats and his boots tripped over joints in the finely carpeted floor.

He had the jet all to himself. Aside from two pilots up front, there was only one other person on board, a demoralized flight attendant who'd listened to his story and tried to be sympathetic, but who knew this was one passenger whose flight she would never make more pleasant. She'd done all she could, coming round time and again with liquor minis, a bottle of wine, and prepackaged pita wraps. She gave up somewhere near the Florida Keys.

Davis wanted only one thing—to get his feet on the ground and *do* something. There had been one last message from Larry Green before leaving Andrews, a chime on his phone that caused his heart to miss a beat. Maybe two or three. He'd inhaled deeply before opening the message, acutely aware of how many times he'd been on the other end, acting as the sender of catastrophic news to be relayed softly to the next of kin. It turned out to be a false alarm.

Still no news. Good luck, Jammer.

Since then, three hours and twelve minutes of agonizing isolation, hanging seven miles above the earth in mind-numbing limbo.

For the twentieth time Davis reached the aft lavatory, and when he performed his about-face, the flight attendant, a pert and well-meaning girl whose name was Stacy, and who was not much older than Jen, stood in the aisle right in front of him.

"I wish I could do something to help. Your daughter sounds lovely." Her mouth crinkled at the sides as if trying to smile and frown at the same time. She was doe eyed and sympathetic, and wore something between a uniform and a dinner dress that was cinched in her favor at the waist. Not a blond hair was out of place, and her perfect teeth were an advertisement for whatever whitening agent she used.

Davis sank into the aft executive lounge chair, one of eight scattered in groups around the cabin. "She's everything to me," he said.

Stacy took the adjacent chair, an opposing basin of plump, cool leather, and between them was a rich wood table.

"Does her mother know yet?" she asked.

Davis hadn't gotten that far, and the question put him in a square corner—no way out. He explained about his wife, and Stacy's hand went to his arm sympathetically. Not the product of customer service training, but a gesture from the heart.

"You poor man. I'd be happy to—"

The goodhearted Stacy was cut short by a two-tone chime. She scurried to a panel near the front of the cabin and picked up a phone handset. She listened for a full minute, by which time Davis was standing next to her.

"What is it?" he asked as she hung up.

"The pilots want to talk to you."

* * *

It was entirely new for Davis: living in a state of dread. When Diane died it had been straightforward, a dour state trooper at his door with one crushing sentence. *There's been an accident, sir.*

This was altogether different, a metered process of torture. Every ringing phone and doorbell sufficient cause for a coronary.

"Up front?" he asked.

Stacy the Good nodded.

Davis knew it was against the rules for passengers to enter the cockpit during flight. He also knew that some captains still allowed common sense to rule. He had introduced himself to the pilots on the ground, and established that he and the skipper, a former C-130 driver, had more than a few friends in common from active duty days. The cockpit door unlocked and Davis pulled it open.

The flight deck was much brighter than the cabin, and he squinted as his eyes adjusted.

"Come on in," said the captain, whose name was Mike. "Take a seat." He pointed to a fold-down jumpseat behind the two crew positions.

Davis pulled and pushed the thing into place, and then wedged his wide shoulders between the port and starboard bulkheads.

"Have you heard anything new?" Davis asked.

"No," said Mike. "But we just sent that message you requested. We figured you'd want to be here if a reply came through."

"Yeah, I would. Thanks."

"Sorry about your daughter, Jammer," said Ed, the copilot. "That's gotta be the worst news a guy can get."

"Like you can't imagine. What's our ETA?"

"Two hours to landing in Bogotá. We'll go straight to Customs. We already called ahead to explain your situation—told them you were a special emissary of the United States Office of Foreign Aid. You know, like you might be delivering a big check or something."

Davis grinned for the first time in eight hours. "Thanks," he said, "that should get me through the gauntlet." He pinched the bridge of his nose. His back and shoulders felt knotted, like a shirt that had been twisted into a rope and left to dry in the sun. "So what are you carrying down below?" he asked.

"Below?" Mike queried.

"Well, yeah. You're clearly not moving passengers, so I figured you must have a belly full of diplomatic freight or mail. I was told this is a regularly scheduled State Department run."

The two pilots swapped a look. "State Department? Nah, those guys have their own air force, although we do run occasional contracts for them. This is a private jet, and today's load manifest is basically you."

Davis was surprised. "Maybe the return leg back to D.C. is a full boat."

Mike shrugged. "Could be, but you know how corporate flight departments work. They don't tell us anything. We just answer the phone, try to show up on time and sober."

A communications alert sounded, and on the navigation scratchpad a single word flashed to life: MESSAGE.

The pendulum of Davis' situation went on a hard downswing. He watched Ed call up the message, and they all read it at the same time: FROM LG AT NTSB. NO NEW DEVELOPMENTS. CONTACT IN BOGOTA COLONEL ALFONSO MARQUEZ.

Davis blew out a sigh, then combed his fingers through his short brown hair.

"They still haven't found any wreckage," Ed offered. "That's good. Maybe the jet lost an engine and diverted to some grass strip in the middle of nowhere."

A depressing silence followed. Captain Mike typed .89 into the Mach window of the flight computer. "That's as fast as we can go without peeling the paint off. Why don't you go back in the cabin and get some sleep."

"I will," Davis said, knowing perfectly well he would not.

THREE

Davis didn't sleep. Instead he stared out the window and checked his watch. He ignored a *Forbes* magazine in a sidewall pocket. He beat the hell out of his armrests. The coastline came into view an hour later, but it meant they were still four hundred miles from Bogotá. Positional awareness—the curse of being a pilot/passenger.

He had been to Colombia once before, a brief stay in Cali to interview the family of a pilot who'd been killed in a crash. As was often the case, that meeting had been awkward all around, Davis' carefully couched questions leading to nothing but agony and tears. He'd gained little useful information that day regarding the captain of the mishap flight, a man who had landed his jet half a mile short of a Bahamian runway. In the Bahamas, a half mile short puts you in the Atlantic Ocean every time, and that's where they'd found him, strapped neatly into his seat under thirty feet of emerald-blue water, a crustacean's jackpot. So Davis had sat in the parents' kitchen, turning a coffee mug by its handle, leaving unaddressed that their only child was suspected of flying for a drug lord, and that the six hundred pounds of uncut cocaine hydrochloride found in the cargo bay would likely result in a subsequent visit by the Bahamian police. On that day, the loss of a son whose confidence exceeded his skills was enough. Davis' last trip to Colombia had indeed been awkward.

This one had the makings of a catastrophe.

The view gradually changed, becoming a framed oval of green forest and rising mountains. This was the top of the Andes, seventeen-thousand-foot peaks that divided the Pacific Ocean from the headwaters of the Amazon. It was rugged terrain to say the least, and combined with the dense vegetation made for the kind of topography that could make a small jet disappear for months. Even years.

Davis wondered if he could handle not knowing for a prolonged period of time. Every day chipping away at hope and giving new false leads. He'd been drifting in no-man's-land for only eight hours, yet already felt like he was coming undone. He imagined himself hacking through the jungle with a machete in hand, tattered clothes and a full beard. If it came to that, he would do it. Anything to find his daughter.

As the Gulfstream slipped through the final miles, Davis' thoughts were not his friend. In a classic case of self-reproach he tried to recall his last words to Jen, and decided it had been a fatherly warning about the lamentable morals of young Colombian men. Characteristically paternal. Characteristically regrettable. He searched for something more positive, trying to remember the last time he'd seen her smile.

The engines throttled back and the descent began. Stacy the Good came back one last time, and was saying something about a seat belt when he found himself staring at a birthmark on her forearm. Jen had a birthmark on her right ankle. *Would it come to that?* he wondered. *Identifying marks and dental records?*

Davis was not customarily a reflective person, not prone to guilt or hollow regrets. Yet at that moment he felt himself spiraling into an emotional vortex, a death spin that seemed unrecoverable. He was rescued by Captain Mike's voice on the cabin speaker.

"Landing in ten minutes, Jammer."

* * *

Customs was indeed a gentleman's affair. The Gulfstream parked in front of a fixed-base operator, or FBO, where two uniformed officials greeted Davis and the crew, and went through the motions of an inspection. Davis presented his passport and expedited visa, and within ten minutes he was walking toward the FBO's executive lounge.

Waiting for him there on a red carpet runner was Colonel Alfonso Marquez.

He was a small man, perhaps five foot six and slightly built. There was a tightly trimmed mustache under a regal nose. He had olive skin and coal-black eyes. Give the man a metal helmet and a horse, Davis imagined, and he'd make the perfect conquistador. They introduced themselves, and the name "Jammer" seemed to throw Marquez off his stride. The colonel said it twice to be sure he had the pronunciation right, the first consonant something between a Y and a J.

The moment their handshake broke, Davis said, "Have you found anything yet?"

"No," said Marquez. "I have a car outside. Let's get underway, and I will tell you what we know on the way to headquarters."

The car was a Ford sedan, a standard-issue Colombian Air Force item with green lettering and official service emblem on the door. The emblem was drawn like a coat of arms, the main element being a burgundy bird that Davis thought looked like a turkey vulture. He supposed the artist had intended something more noble, a bird of prey as opposed to a carrion eater.

He took the front passenger seat while Marquez drove, which in itself told Davis something. A full colonel in a place like Colombia would typically warrant a driver. It could be that Marquez liked doing things himself. Or possibly he saw a driver as a waste of manpower. Those reasons Davis liked. On the other hand, the colonel could be a professional outlier, a senior officer stripped of his perks. In a small air force the specter of career politics had to loom large, so a billet in air accident investigations might be just the place for an O-6 who'd reached the top rung of his promotion ladder.

Marquez began an in-briefing in confident, albeit accented, English. "You may not be familiar with how we run investigations here in Colombia, so I should explain my authority. Most accidents fall under the watch of our Special Administrative Unit of Civil Aeronautics. In unusual circumstances, however, the air force can be asked to take over an inquiry."

"And this investigation is unusual?" Davis asked.

Marquez shrugged. "I can tell you I was surprised when the order came for me to take control . . . especially since there is no confirmation yet that we even have a crash."

Davis wasn't sure if the military's involvement was a good or a bad thing, but it did carry one implication: interest in the incident had reached a high level in Colombia. He envisioned government ministers and generals, all pushing and pulling. Favors given and markers called in. In the end, Davis knew there was one primary determiner of any investigation's success: the investigator-in-charge. For better or worse, the man sitting next to him was the most important person in his and Jen's world. "What can you tell me about the flight in question?" he asked, trying not to let his concern bleed through.

"The aircraft is a small regional jet, an ARJ-35, registration number HK-55H. On board were twenty-one passengers and three crewmembers—two pilots and a flight attendant. The flight departed from the passenger terminal on the other side of this airfield at 20:21 last night. It was a regularly scheduled flight bound for Cali. The proposed flight time was one hour, but after twenty minutes, on the far side of the Cordillera Oriental, what you would call the Eastern Andes, the aircraft began to lose altitude. Repeated attempts by the air traffic controllers to contact the flight went unanswered, and at 21:06 both the primary and secondary radar returns were lost."

"Simultaneously?" Davis asked. The primary return was a simple echo measuring range and bearing, while the secondary return was an electronic handshake, working through the aircraft's transponder, that included data such as altitude and call sign. The two returns could be decoupled, however, as proved in a number of incidents, including Malaysia Air Flight 470, if the transponder became inoperative or was disabled.

Marquez said, "Yes, early information suggests that the signals were lost at the same moment."

"Was a search initiated right away?"

"Of course. Our air force has begun an extensive campaign to locate the wreckage."

"Wreckage? Doesn't that assume the worst case?"

Marquez briefly locked eyes with Davis. "You have a daughter named Jennifer Davis?"

Davis turned his gaze to the window. "So they told you about that."

"You must admit it is irregular . . . taking part in an inquiry in which a close relative was on board." When Davis didn't respond, Marquez rubbed his chin with his free hand, resulting in a sandpaper noise that implied it had been a long day. "I must ask you, Mr. Davis—do you think you can pursue this investigation with a clear mind?"

"Honestly . . . no. But I can pursue it in a way that will get answers. Isn't that what we both want?"

Davis sensed the colonel eyeing him critically, in the way he might regard a corporal whose uniform was out of regulation. "Very well," said Marquez. "I will take you at your word."

* * *

The sun was a bronze semicircle on the hazy horizon when Marquez steered into the parking lot of what looked like an abandoned corporate flight department. In front was a simple two-story office block, square edged and colorless, and behind that lay a parking apron for small jets, the whole affair connected to the more vibrant tracts of El Dorado International Airport by an arterial system of service roads and taxiways. The parking lot was sprinkled with vehicles that looked familiar, six or seven sedans, each the same shade of green and with the same maroon vulture—probably half the staff cars of the Colombian Air Force.

Marquez parked next to the building's entrance, and said,

"Welcome to our headquarters. As you can see, we have already given it a name."

Davis saw a makeshift sign stenciled over the entrance: El Centro. No translation necessary. Inside would be people who'd been up since dawn, stirring and breathing life into a place that had been dead the day before. The colonel led Davis inside, and what he saw there supported his theory that the building's previous tenant had been an air taxi operator or corporate flight department gone to insolvency. A scuffed operations desk was backed by empty wall mounts where monitors had been, and next to these were a pair of empty whiteboards that would once have held schedules and notices. All of it was being resurrected by Marquez' crew. Davis saw a hastily arranged communications center, wires and transceivers and handsets, all nested haphazardly. Tiny green lights and a distinct electrical odor suggested most of it was working, and a young enlisted woman was busy making connections. Banks of bright fluorescent tubes hummed and fluttered, overpowering the workspace in a cascade of white.

Marquez led him to a large topographical map of Colombia that was tacked to a wall. He drew two fingers along a red-tape line. "This is the proposed route filed for TAC-Air Flight 223."

The line struck fifty miles west out of Bogotá, carrying over the rugged foothills of Sumapaz National Forest. Then, not quite halfway to Cali, the red line went to dashes and a green search box was drawn.

"This is isolated country," Marquez continued, "very mountainous. The terrain is severe, and on the other side of the range lies jungle, some of the most dense in our country—which is to say, some of the most dense in the world. As I'm sure you know, a small aircraft can disappear in a place like this with little trace."

"True," Davis said as he studied the map, "but it depends on a lot of things." He was relieved to be on familiar ground. For the first time in ten hours he was being productive, and felt an undeniable comfort in the mechanics of his job. "If the airplane was moving fast, or if it struck the forest at a low angle, we could expect a significant scar on the canopy. Fire is a near certainty, and that can be seen from satellites. Do you have any infrared imagery yet?"

"No," Marquez lamented. "I made a request through defense ministry channels this morning, but nothing has come. There is commercial imagery, of course, but that is expensive and often has poor resolution. Getting recent images could also prove difficult."

"I'll call Washington and see what I can do. What about pings from an ELT?" he asked, referring to the emergency beacon that would be giving off a locator signal if the airplane had indeed crashed.

"We've been listening, but there is nothing yet."

Davis thought this strange, but also comforting. "I think we should consider other scenarios. Is it possible the airplane diverted to an alternate airport and nobody has heard about it yet?"

Marquez eyed him steadily for a moment.

Davis waited patiently for an answer.

"There were no thunderstorms in the area last night to have caused such a diversion."

"They might have diverted for a mechanical problem. What about the aircraft's history? Have you checked the maintenance logs for discrepancies? Have there been any repairs recently or service issues?"

"We have people going over them now. There was an MEL for an inoperative anti-ice system on the port engine."

MEL stood for minimum equipment list. Commercial aircraft were designed with built-in redundancies, allowing them to be dispatched for passenger flights with certain inoperative components, although often with operational restrictions. Everything was spelled out in the airline's approved MEL manual for that type of aircraft. The anti-ice system Marquez was referring to was designed to counter buildups of atmospheric icing on engine fan blades.

"Engine anti-ice," Davis said. "That could be pertinent."

"As I said, there was no significant weather in the area."

"Significant doesn't matter. The CFB-22 engine is particularly susceptible to fan blade icing. I think there was an advisory circular sent out to operators last year."

Davis saw the colonel stiffen ever so slightly, but he relented. "Yes, it bears looking into. Our first order of business, however, is to find the airplane."

"I couldn't agree more."

Marquez crossed the room to a desk, and pulled a cell phone and charging cable from a drawer. "This is for you. A woman from the embassy stopped by and left it for you this afternoon."

Davis took the device in hand. It was a satellite handheld unit that looked inordinately expensive, exactly the kind of thing the United States government *would* buy. "The U.S. Embassy? They came and left this for me?"

"Your government can be very efficient."

"Is that what you think?" The phone was already powered, and Davis searched the contacts section but found nothing preloaded. It was either new or had been scrubbed clean. "Maybe I should give it a try," he said.

Marquez excused himself to an adjoining room, leaving Davis alone. He typed in Larry Green's number from memory and initiated a call. Twenty seconds later Green answered.

"It's me, Larry. I'm in Bogotá."

"Outstanding. Any news yet?"

"No, nothing."

"What about the guy in charge, Marquez?"

Davis cocked a half smile. It was uncanny how he and the general held the same outlook on things. "The colonel seems okay . . . so far."

"Thank God. You never know what you're going to get at zero latitude." It was a running joke between them—the closer you got to the equator, the greater the chance you'd end up as the de facto investigator-in-charge.

"Listen, I need one thing fast—some imagery. We're looking at a really big search box, mostly deep forest." Davis referenced the wall map and dictated the coordinates of a search area with plenty of slop built in. After Green read everything back, Davis added, "I also need IR pictures, and maybe some radar."

"Enough resolution to see a small fire under the canopy?"

"Exactly. And we need time contrast data for any radar stuff—pictures within the last twenty-four hours, then something older to compare it to. We have to look for changes in the canopy that can't be explained by logging or clear cutting by farmers. I think the DEA does some comparative imagery along those lines."

"They do, I've seen it before."

"Can you tell if this phone I'm using is secure?"

"I show a padlock on my end—but I never trust that kind of thing."

"Me neither. Speed, Larry, speed. We really need this yesterday, just in case . . . " Davis checked himself, not wanting to say the wrong words, "in case there are any survivors out there."

"I'm on it now. Bye."

FOUR

The general didn't waste time.

The first wave of images arrived at El Centro forty-five minutes later, infrared data blanketing the entire search box. It would take time to sort, so two junior officers from the colonel's staff were put under Davis' command. In a mix of English and broken Spanish he told them what to look for, and soon all three were scanning the images on a bank of computers that Marquez had ordered installed in the operations center. To Davis' eye, El Centro was running smoothly. There was no wasted motion, and nearly all the equipment seemed operational. So far, the investigator-in-charge appeared eminently capable, and at the very least was a top-flight organizer.

Finally having something to work with, Davis hammered the keyboard, working with the manic intensity of a condemned man searching for a lost pardon. After an hour he was blinking to keep his eyes focused. At the two-hour point, with night having taken a grip outside, he drafted two more technicians, a pair of enlisted men spotted idling near the entrance. It was nearly midnight when Marquez gave a shout from the adjoining room.

"I have something!" He emerged with two printed images in hand. "This came in from Washington moments ago!"

Marquez dropped the pictures on a table, twin radar images of the same plot of forest. One was dated last week, the other thirty minutes ago. The older image showed virgin forest, the more recent a two-thousand-foot-long scar of broken timber and disturbed earth. It was exactly what they'd been looking for. Exactly what Davis feared they would find.

The new development brought excitement all around. Davis straightened beside the table, subtly holding onto the edge. "Okay," he managed, "that's probably what we're after."

Marquez said, "We didn't see it sooner because this area is fifty miles south of our search box. The airplane must have drifted far off course." One of his lieutenants hurried forward and dropped a new photo on the table. He said in halting English, "Another is here, Colonel. Infrared, the same place."

Marquez cross-checked the reference grids. "The coordinates match." He pointed to a cluster of white blobs, obvious hot spots, and checked the time-stamp. "There was a very recent fire. Sections remain warm even now."

Davis stared blankly but said nothing.

"There can be no question," Marquez said. He turned to a lieutenant and issued the obvious order. "Give these coordinates to the helicopter crew on alert. Tell them to be ready in ten minutes."

Davis wasn't looking at the photos anymore. There was no need—the colonel was right. *There can be no question.* An aircraft had crashed in this isolated stand of Colombian rain forest, almost certainly TAC-Air Flight 223, wreckage that had been simmering for over twenty-four hours. During his flight across the Caribbean, Davis had tried to prepare for this moment. He'd wondered if he could keep his feelings in check. Then, after arriving in Colombia he'd become preoccupied, so focused on finding the airplane that he'd overlooked the end game. Ignored what would happen when their search succeeded. Now they had located the crash site, and the truth came down like a wrecking ball. What were the chances Jen had survived? He knew better than anyone.

One in a million.

All the same, he had to be sure. Had to see it with his own eyes. Davis pushed away from the table, checked that his Maglite was in his pocket, and was the first one out the door.

* * *

The helicopter swept fast and true through an obsidian sky. The craft was a Bell UH-1 Huey, and it rattled and shook as it sliced the Colombian night. The pilots struck out on a southwesterly heading, and for the first few minutes civilization ruled. Beneath them a sea of lights was blurred by the mix of speed and low altitude, until gradually the amber jewels of Bogotá fell away and the world beneath went to a void.

There was room for four in the chopper's cramped passenger cabin; Davis, Marquez, and two enlisted men riding shoulder to shoulder. Having ridden on many such birds through the years, he was accustomed to the noise and vibration. Less familiar was the way his hands clenched his thighs, and the way his back pressed rigidly against the metal wall. He shifted his hands underneath his legs, gripped the webbing on his seat and squeezed for all he was worth. Bile rose in his throat, and Davis choked it down as best he could. He remembered this sensation all too well—impending doom, just like four years ago when he'd driven to the morgue to identify his wife's body. Until this moment, the longest twenty minutes of his life.

Now he was there again, at that barren cliff, the last tendrils of hope snapping one by one. Long shots and slim likelihoods, all gone, sunk by a few irrefutable satellite images taken from a hundred miles above the earth. Images as cold and lifeless as the vacuum of space itself. The airplane carrying his daughter had crashed in a jungle. His and Diane's only child, the love of their life. Nineteen years old.

Nineteen!

The bile again. He gripped the seat harder, so hard that something gave in the tubular frame. Davis was seated next to the open door, strapped into a seat near an unloaded machine gun. The equatorial air rushed past a few feet away, a hurricane whose swirling wake buffeted his face and whipped his hair, asynchronously cool and bleak. But not nearly as bleak as his defeatist thoughts. Disjointed recollections of going through photo albums after Diane's death. Of giving her clothes to Goodwill and closing her account with the phone company. He would do it all again. Only this time he would do it alone.

His self-immolation paused when Marquez began shouting, a rapid-fire exchange with the pilots in Spanish. The colonel turned to Davis, his expression more somber than ever.

"We've received a message from the defense ministry command center. An army ground unit was working nearby, and they've already arrived at the scene. The crash has been confirmed. I ordered them to approach the aircraft and check for survivors. They will also set up a perimeter. I've given strict orders not to touch anything. We should hear back in a moment."

Amazingly, Davis shrugged it off—he could be no nearer the edge than he already was. He stared vacantly into the night, until minutes later when Marquez had a second exchange with the copilot. Then, with all the decency he could muster, the colonel gave one shake of his head.

No survivors.

Davis nodded back numbly, the first nine-inch nails of acceptance having already taken hold. Ten minutes later the crash site was in view, the headlights of two big army trucks trained on the area. It was a surreal scene. In a jungle violated by knives of white light, Davis saw the main section of fuselage, and around it far-strewn bits of wreckage. More than a day after impact, wisps of smoke still curled through the foliage, dissolving into darkness. He could make out a half dozen soldiers staking out the perimeter.

With irony that seemed almost divine, Davis saw a perfect clearing nearby in the light of the full moon, a grassy half acre that was made to order as a place to land a rescue helicopter. Only rescue was no longer the operative word. It was now a recovery operation. The Huey sank lower and dropped toward the clearing, the crash site gaining detail as the chopper's landing lights danced over debris. Davis unbuckled his seat belt, his hands finding new life.

If Jen is in there she needs me, he thought. *She needs me now.*

Davis rotated his body, putting one leg outside the open door and stepping onto the Huey's landing skid. His heart was racing as the rotor downwash snapped at his clothing and whipped his hair.

Marquez shouted something across the cramped passenger cabin, but Davis couldn't make it out. Or maybe he didn't want to.

The Huey's controlled descent paused ten feet in the air, and Davis' legs seemed to act on their own. He stepped out and rode the skid, the Huey rocking as two hundred and forty pounds transferred to the port side.

Marquez was screaming now, his voice clear above the roar of the engine. "No! Don't—"

Davis dropped into the night.

He hit the ground hard, rolled onto his hip, and quickly jumped to his feet. He broke into a sprint, the wreckage beckoning in its sickly yellow hue. He saw a shattered fuselage that was breached at its midpoint, the two halves clinging to one another at a noticeably odd angle. Davis was halfway to the wreckage when a soldier stepped into his path. The young man held out a flat palm, the way a traffic cop would to bring a car to a stop.

Davis brushed past him without a glance.

A second soldier, this one with a rifle on his shoulder, put out two hands. Davis put him on his ass with a stiff arm. He was running full steam, stumbling over vines and tree roots. After thousands of miles he was almost there.

He had to know!

More shouting behind him. Spanish? English? He didn't care. The entire Colombian Army couldn't stop him now.

One last soldier remained, a big man with a machine pistol hanging loose across his chest. He'd been inspecting the interior at the breach in the fuselage, and was heading back to join his squad. His eyes opened wide as he regarded the onrushing American who'd fallen out of the sky.

Probably on instinct, his hands went to his weapon, and he stood squarely in Davis' path. He was a considerable obstacle, a two-hundred-pound man dressed in fifty pounds of fighting gear. There was no way to go around him, so Davis didn't try. In the broken shafts of light, the soldier suddenly seemed to take flight, his wide frame sailing into the brush like a discarded rag doll.

Five steps later, Davis was there.

He thrust his head into the jagged breach at midcabin and stared in horror at the terrible scene inside. It was a sight he'd seen many times before, but never with tonight's perspective.

Davis was staring at the face of death itself.

A primal howl rose in his throat but was never delivered, because in the next instant everything went black.

FIVE

Larry Green arrived for work the next morning and went through the motions of his daily routine. Tall coffee in hand, he nodded to familiar faces in the lobby of L'Enfant Plaza, and took the stairs to his fifth-floor suite. In the anteroom of his office he said hello to Rebecca, his able assistant of five years.

"Good morning, sir."

"How was your weekend?"

"Great! Charlie and I got engaged!" She wagged an ice-laden finger at him.

"*Really?*" Green walked around the desk and gave her a heartfelt embrace. "I'm so happy for you! Charlie's a lucky man— let me know if you need any time off to plan the big day."

Rebecca gushed for a full two minutes about her fiancé's prospects—he was a junior attorney at the Department of Justice—and Green listened with all the enthusiasm he could muster. Only when he reached his office, behind a gently closed door, did his expression fall to reflect the grim mood he'd been battling all morning. He immediately checked his e-mail, but saw nothing new that would help Jammer. To the contrary, he found a message from his boss, Janet Cirrillo, Managing Director of the NTSB.

Larry, please keep me up to date on Cali crash of TAC-Air Flight 223. 2x a day minimum and any breaking developments. Sorry—heat from above. Bogotá embassy has issued Davis sat-phone: 011-57-9439220676.

Green took a long sip of coffee. For Cirrillo, heat from above had only two sources: the Office of the Chairman of the NTSB or the White House itself. On its face, neither seemed likely, and Green decided something else was at play. It wasn't unusual to get interest in crashes from outside the official food chain. It could come from a senator from the Midwest whose hometown built the hydraulic pumps used on the downed aircraft, or perhaps a manufacturer's lobbyist whose client had a big sale pending to China, and who didn't want bad press at a critical moment in negotiations. For Green it was a delicate dance—theories and evidence from investigations were privileged information. He supposed that in a day or two the source of the pressure would become clear, telegraphed when Cirrillo began asking more specific questions. He would respond as he always did, metering a few generic details, while gently reminding his boss that the integrity of the process was paramount.

He was disappointed to find no reports from Davis, but then the man had only arrived last night. He hoped the imagery he'd sent had been useful in locating the crash. Jammer had never been the best communicator, and given Jen's involvement, Green expected the information flow to be even more stunted than usual. With nothing new to report, he happily said so in a polite reply to Cirrillo and launched it into cyberspace.

He was tempted to dial the sat-phone, but then realized it was an hour earlier in Bogotá. Even so, he'd lay money on Jammer being awake. Given the circumstances, he doubted the man would sleep a minute until Jen was found—for better or worse.

Green decided a text best suited the situation: *Call with an update when possible. Hope all is going well.*

He paused, then hit send.

* * *

If misery on Earth kept an address, Jammer Davis had arrived.

His head throbbed, every heartbeat a systolic hammer, and his joints seemed rusted in place. Wretched as that all was, none of it touched the ache in his chest, a dull pressure without source that seemed acutely physical. A manifestation of lost hope.

The idea of movement was overwhelming, so with considerable effort Davis opened one eye. What he saw was confusing at first—the world, such as it was, appeared to be presented sideways. His brain processed the view, summed it with the rough texture grating against his right cheek, and he decided he was lying face down on a concrete floor. Not the most dazzling deduction of his career, but useful in that moment.

Davis took his time, an arm inching one way, a leg twisting another. It took a full two minutes to reach a sitting position, and from there he put a hand to the back of his head and felt a massive knot, along with the oozing warmth of coagulated blood. Everything came back slowly, frame by frame, like a PowerPoint horror show. Larry Green giving him the bad news on the seaplane dock. A five-hour flight from Andrews that seemed to take five days. Dashing over moonlit forest in a helicopter and jumping out before the skids hit the ground. Running for all he was worth toward the charred wreckage. It seemed like a nightmare, every wretched snapshot. Except for the final image that was stamped indelibly in his brain—the inside of the shattered jet. A sight so vivid and intense it could only be true.

Davis had seen the aftermath of crashes before. He'd seen blood and debris and unrecognizable human parts. He'd smelled the stench of rotting flesh days after impact, riding on air further desecrated by the vapor of melted plastic and spent kerosene. But never had he experienced it all on such a personal level. There was nothing explicitly damning in that picture in his head—he hadn't seen the birthmark on Jen's ankle, hadn't recognized a bracelet or a shirt he'd given her as a birthday present. Yet none of that was necessary. Not when the greater picture was so utterly overwhelming.

The crash of TAC-Air Flight 223 had been a typical impact—which was to say, a devastating event. A twenty-one passenger regional jet had struck the earth and been cast in a thousand directions. The results were predictable, and there could be no survivors.

He massaged the back of his head and tried to stand, but failed miserably. So, with his backside on cold concrete, he studied his surroundings. Four cinder block walls predominated. There was a barred window behind him, and a sturdy iron door in front with a slot at the bottom. Simple enough. He'd found his way to a prison cell, probably with good reason.

Davis was still on the floor, thinking about getting up but not really caring, when a familiar voice sounded from behind the heavy door. The lock rattled and Colonel Marquez stepped in. He stood with his hands clasped behind his back, scrutinizing Davis as if he were looking at a dog who'd bitten a neighbor. The guard gave him a look that asked if he should stay. Davis was sure the story of his crazed assault at the crash site had made the rounds, so perhaps he was considered dangerous. A threat to himself and others—even if he couldn't stand up.

Marquez dismissed the man.

"Sorry if I don't get up," Davis said.

"How are you feeling?"

"A bottle of ibuprofen would go a long way toward advancing relations between our two nations."

Marquez may have smiled, but he had the kind of face that made it hard to tell. "What you did last night did nothing to advance relations."

"Yeah, I know."

"An apology might be in order?" Marquez suggested.

Davis rubbed the front of his head, which throbbed less than the back. "Do you have children, Colonel?"

Marquez hesitated. "Yes, twins. They are eighteen years old, a boy and a girl."

Davis let that hang in the cell's thick, fetid air.

"All right," Marquez said, "I can only imagine what you are going through. But you must remember—we all have responsibilities, Mr. Davis. We all have our duty."

Again silence ruled, then Marquez came closer. He bent down on one knee until they were eye to eye.

"I received news this morning that perplexes me." The colonel cast this in a quiet voice, as if not wanting the guard outside to hear. "I have been coordinating things from headquarters while my team establishes a base at the crash site. They moved in quickly and have been working all night. This morning I received a report, and . . ." the colonel hesitated mightily, actually glancing over his shoulder before finishing, "and we seem to have an unusual situation."

"What kind of situation?" Davis asked.

"As I told you last night, the manifest given to us by TAC-Air listed twenty-one passengers and three crewmembers. I have personally reviewed the closed-circuit footage from the airport boarding area—in these days of terrorism, it is always one of our first orders of business, is it not? I can tell you without question that every one of those passengers boarded the airplane."

"So what's the problem?"

"I will put it to you as a question. What would you do, as an investigator, if you went through the wreckage and found two fewer passengers than are listed on the manifest?"

With those words, a barely discernible light flickered deep inside Davis. "You're two bodies short?"

"All the seats remain intact—none separated during the crash. Two, however, appear to be vacant."

"Which two?"

"I'd rather not say until things are more clear. We are still—"

Davis lunged and took a vise grip on the colonel's forearm. *"Which two?"*

Marquez jerked his arm away. "My people are still pulling bodies clear!" he snapped. "Identification takes time. You know this is something we can't afford to get wrong."

Davis looked skyward and closed his eyes. "Yeah . . . I know. Sorry."

"I realize this is difficult for you, Mr. Davis. When I have accurate information, I will let you know immediately. Until then, please answer my question. If you were missing two passengers, what would be your thoughts?"

Davis considered it and said in a monotone, "In a crash that was survivable it would give me hope. I'd think somebody made their way clear and walked off in a daze. I've had victims wander off and turn up in an emergency room miles from a crash site. I've had them take cabs and go home."

"But this is remote, the middle of a jungle. And you saw the wreckage."

Davis nodded, the hammer of despair swinging down again. "Yeah, I saw it. Nobody walked away from this one. The tail is gone, right?"

"Yes, we found the horizontal and vertical stabilizers still joined, roughly five hundred meters behind the main debris field in a stand of trees. It must have separated on the initial impact."

"So there's your answer. Somewhere in the top of a gumbo-limbo tree you'll find your missing bodies."

Marquez stood and began pacing, his small shoes silent over the naked concrete. Davis sensed his uncertainty.

"Yes," Marquez said, "you might be right. On a more positive note, I can tell you we've recovered both the flight data and cockpit voice recorders. Both were mounted in the tail section, yet appear to be in good condition."

"I'm glad to hear it. They'll go a long way toward finding out what happened."

"Let us hope so. There are a few other points I'd like your opinion on, Mr. Davis."

"Shoot."

Marquez gave him an odd look, his English evidently not going that far.

"Go ahead with your questions."

Marquez hesitated, as if in a careful decision-making process. "Actually . . . I would prefer it if you viewed certain evidence directly. I don't want to color your opinions. Are you feeling well enough to travel to the crash site?"

"Now?"

Marquez nodded.

His head felt like a split melon, and the idea of seeing the crash in broad daylight did not sit well. But his promise to Larry Green gave no alternative: he was on the hook to figure this out, regardless of what had happened to Jen. It had been an easy promise to make at the time.

He surveyed his malodorous surroundings. "I guess I can tear myself away for a few hours."

"Very well. But I must impose one condition," said Marquez.

"Condition?"

"Mr. Davis, you are clearly knowledgeable in our field. I need that kind of help. But you are also a willful man, and not formally under my command. Understand that if you play the cowboy again, I will send you home. This is my inquiry to run, is that clear?"

"Yeah," Davis said. "Crystal."

Marquez helped him stand, and new pain sites surfaced. Left shoulder, neck, lower back—the usual aches of a night spent semiconscious on damp concrete.

"By the way," Davis said. "I am sorry about last night. If we see the guys I pushed around, I'll say it in person."

Marquez nodded but didn't reply. He handed Davis a lanyard with rudimentary credentials—a stamped document with a picture that had been reproduced from his passport photo. As the colonel led to the door, Davis' thoughts were deflected by what Marquez hadn't said. They'd certainly identified *some* of the bodies by now, and if Jen had been among them he would have said so. It was the thinnest of straws, to be sure. But more than he'd had to grasp ten minutes ago.

Rubbing his neck, Davis said, "Colonel, let me ask you one thing."

Marquez stopped.

"Those two empty seats . . . were the seat belts fastened?"

"The seat belts? My photographer forwarded a few pictures,"

Marquez said as he considered it. "No. No, I'm quite sure they were unfastened."

Davis followed the colonel out, and he nodded to the guard as he passed the threshold. He tried to ignore the jackhammer in his head and the cement in his limbs. Yet as he walked down the hall, ever so gingerly, the ember inside flickered once more.

SIX

An hour later Davis was riding to the same crash site in the same helicopter. Through the open door he saw the same metal skid, and made a silent promise not to jump when they arrived.

A morning mist hung heavy, restricting visibility to no more than two miles. As the Huey clattered onward, the forest ahead resolved and everything behind disappeared, making it seem as if they were traveling in a bubble—a sensation that was both disorienting and isolating.

When they arrived, he saw that the grass in the clearing had been flattened by dozens of takeoffs and landings, and a new path had been worn through the jungle, connecting to the wreckage field. He'd been told the nearest town with a name was an hour away, more when the weather turned disagreeable. In the coming days trucks would begin to roll in over logging roads, makeshift thoroughfares that would prove indispensable as loads of debris were hoisted from the jungle and hauled away, the final inglorious journey of TAC-Air Flight 223. Until then, every bit of evidence would be plotted and recorded for future reference. The most delicate work, that of recovering remains, was already under way.

The Huey set down in a flurry of dust, and before the rotors stopped spinning, a lieutenant trotted up to the chopper and began a lengthy discussion with Marquez. He handed over a hand-drawn diagram before turning away.

The colonel studied the drawing, and announced, "We have recovered nearly all the bodies. They will be transported by helicopter to Bogotá and kept temporarily in a hospital morgue." He rattled the paper, his attention still divided. "This is a preliminary seating chart. We began with the assigned seating information provided by the airline, and then searched each body for documents—wallets, passports, boarding passes. Anything to confirm identity. Of course, we also cross-checked the basic information already on file, things like age and gender. All findings must be consistent."

The professional in Davis tried to be impressed. The father in him wanted to tear the diagram out of the colonel's hand. "Are you still two passengers short?" He didn't breathe waiting for the answer.

"Yes. And one of the empty seats *was* assigned to your daughter."

The weight of the world shifted ever so slightly—still on Davis' shoulders, but perhaps at a more comfortable angle. The odds were only abysmal now, one in a hundred thousand. It was progress, of sorts.

"You understand," said Marquez, "that seating charts are often misleading."

"I know," Davis said.

The colonel's acumen was again on display. Like Davis, he'd been born a military investigator, yet had acquired a working knowledge of airline operations. Commercial airlines were not as closely moored to precision or regulation, instead taking a more customer friendly, laissez-faire approach. When it came to seating, passengers freely traded places with friends and relatives. They might move to a vacant seat after takeoff to get a window view, or to avoid a captive conversation with a boorish seatmate. Flight attendants often reseated passengers to manage practical matters, such as language barriers in emergency exit rows, or weight and balance issues on small aircraft. Flight attendants also moved customers to suit their own objectives, shunting a drunk to someone else's serving section, or upgrading an attractive traveler to their own. The bottom line: people changed seats on airplanes like they did in church, and for nearly as many reasons. Which meant airline seating diagrams had to be taken with a grain of salt.

"How many passengers have you positively identified?" Davis asked.

"Of the twenty-one on record, twelve with a high degree of confidence. Four others are reasonably certain, and of course we have the two disappearances—if the seating chart is accurate, one being your daughter."

"That still leaves three."

Marquez handed over the diagram.

Davis saw a well-traced outline of the cabin, and depicted inside were seven rows of three seats. The seats were split by an aisle, arranged with two to port and one to starboard along the length of the cabin.

While Davis studied the drawing, Marquez said, "The front row of seats was severely damaged—all of the occupants were thrown clear. We found one body on the floor of the forward cabin, and another near the left wing root—both are in poor condition. We will sort them out in time, but judging by dress and build both are certainly male, which is consistent with the seating assignment for that row."

Davis nearly argued this assumption. He had once encountered a passenger manifest with one extra female, and a deficit of one on the male side of the ledger. That mystery went all the way to the medical examiner who settled things with one word: transgender. That was the thing about sudden death—it kept a recklessly intimate relationship with truth.

Davis decided to stay his objection. "And the third body from the front row?"

Marquez hesitated. "Seat 2A. This was also a man, however . . . it would be better to show you where he came to rest."

"What about the pilots?" Davis asked.

"Both remain in the cockpit. We are taking our time with their recovery—you will better understand when you see the circumstances."

"All right. And the flight attendant?"

Marquez pointed to an X outside the diagram. "The flight

attendant was thrown clear—she does not appear to have been strapped into the forward cabin jumpseat. Positively identified as Mercedes Fuentes, age twenty-six. She'd been working for TAC-Air for twelve months."

Davis nodded. "A hell of a way to end your probationary period. One more question—when your people removed the bodies from the seats, were all the seat belts cinched tightly?"

Marquez looked at him questioningly. "You seem very concerned with safety belts."

"Little things can tell you a lot. If all the seat belts were pulled tight, then the crew knew there was a problem. It means the flight attendant was screaming at them in the final minutes to tighten their belts and assume the brace position. The passengers would have done it, every last one. On the other hand, if you found all the seat belts loosened casually . . . it would suggest the airplane hit without warning."

"Yes, I see your point. I will ask my team for an answer. Earlier you asked whether the belts on the empty seats were latched. Why?"

"If the belts on that last row of seats were loosely latched," Davis hesitated for a long moment, "then I'd say those occupants were forcibly ejected in the crash."

"But they were *unlatched*. What do you take from that?"

"I don't know. This was a one-hour flight in an aircraft that had no lavatory. That doesn't leave many reasons to get up. If those two belts were truly undone, I'd say you're looking at two empty seats on an airplane whose paperwork shows a full boat."

"That is extremely speculative," Marquez said quickly. "The video footage was clear. Every passenger boarded that airplane. I must caution you again, Mr. Davis—if you raise your hopes too high, there is only one place to go."

"Nobody knows that better than me."

Marquez stepped down from the Huey, the chopper's stilled rotor blades sagging in the building heat. Davis followed, noting a lone vulture wheeling overhead on some unseen updraft—an apt marker for what he knew was to come. They came upon a soldier that Davis thought looked vaguely familiar. The man eyed him cautiously.

Davis stopped and said to Marquez, "Please tell him I apologize for my bad behavior last night."

Marquez provided the translation, and the corporal gave Davis an indifferent sideways nod.

"Tell him I'm going to send his squad a case of rum."

Marquez did, and the soldier lit a smile and slapped Davis on the shoulder.

That settled, Marquez set off toward the crash site. Davis stayed where he was, and called out, "Give me a couple of minutes. I'd like to take a look at the big picture first."

"Very well. Take as long as you need, but when you are done please come find me. I would like your opinion on what we've found in the cockpit." Marquez walked away on a freshly worn path through the knee-high grass.

Davis went the other way. He backtracked to the far side of the clearing and found a spot in the shade. He liked to begin every case in this same way, taking a distant viewpoint. He leaned against the trunk of a hardwood tree and pulled out a warm Coke and a bottle of Motrin—the restorative vitamin M—that had been given to him mercifully by the helicopter crew. He used one to wash down a handful of the other.

From that vantage point, in torpid jungle heat at the end of the earth, Davis went to work.

* * *

Not by chance, the vast majority of aircraft accidents take place within ten miles of an airport. The simple reason is that most mishaps occur during the business of either takeoff or landing. Such airfield accidents, on balance, present largely intact airframes, unfortunate vessels that have strayed from final approach, landed hard in a crosswind, or skidded off a slick runway during a rejected takeoff. In all these circumstances, the meeting of metal and earth takes place at a relatively low speed, and as Newton so elegantly proved, the force of any impact is a matter of mass multiplied by acceleration. Or in the case of air crashes, deceleration.

Unfortunately, deep in the south-central jungle of Colombia, Davis was looking at the other kind of crash. He was looking at the aftermath of a mid-flight interruption, one in which a reliable and tested airframe, for reasons undetermined, had fallen from normal cruise flight and struck the earth at a random point. It is the rarest kind of accident, and with few exceptions, the most catastrophic. To begin, there are no first responders. In many cases the loss is not even recognized until a flight becomes long overdue. The very location of such disasters can take days, weeks, even years to pinpoint. Some go lost for eternity. That they'd been able to locate this crash within a day put them well ahead of that curve. But as any investigator would tell you, such an accident site is to be approached with profound trepidation. You can end up staring at a hole in a swamp two hundred feet deep, or climbing the side of a mountain glacier. Even diving into the depths of a ten-thousand-foot ocean trench.

So as Davis stood leaning against a tree, a fizzing Coke in his hand, he knew things could have been worse. The jungle was the main impediment here, thick and impenetrable in sections, a high canopy of hardwood trees overlaying dense vegetation. Bits of wreckage would be embedded in the soft organic floor, snagged high in the upper canopy, and speared into softwood timber. Yet the very foliage that would bedevil recovery efforts had also done Colonel Marquez and his team a great favor.

Davis saw it from where he stood, to his left along the horizon—the point where TAC-Air Flight 223 had first clipped the trees, and then sheared off tops at progressively lower levels. This slanted pruning gave a good indication of strike angle. The jet had not been locked in a steep dive, nor had it been fluttering through a flat spin. It had been gliding in a shallow, controlled descent—still flying until the bitter end. From the clipped treetops, Davis could also infer the direction of flight, roughly to the southwest.

Precise heading and strike angle would be eventually calculated, confirmed by flight data recorder information and a survey using proper GPS equipment. But that would take time.

He next worked out distance, estimating that from the first sign of impact, at the crest of the canopy, to the spot where the main wreckage now rested, was roughly eight hundred meters. This gave an approximation of the energy state of the aircraft when it went in—essentially, a reflection of speed and weight—and Davis decided that the jet had been traveling at a moderate speed on impact. Not fast, not slow. Two hundred knots, two fifty at the top end. Again, an indication of an airplane flying within its normal performance envelope.

Surveying the debris field, his eye went first to the halved main fuselage, a shattered centerpiece to the fragments of airliner all around. Some of the strewn parts were recognizable, others less so. The tail was the most distant parcel, or so Marquez had said—Davis saw no sign of it behind umbrellalike stands of vegetation. The earth in that direction looked wet and swampy, suggesting a difficult recovery effort.

The tip of the right wing had broken off and was basking in full sun at the edge of the clearing. The left wing had separated completely—one of the few details he remembered from last night—and although Davis couldn't see it from where he stood, he knew it had been accounted for. Also not connected were the engines. The ARJ-35's twin turbofans were mounted aft, beneath the T-tail in a classic regional jet design. Both powerplants had separated on impact and pitched into the undergrowth. This was not by chance. Because jet engines are heavy, the most dense parts on any aircraft, engineers intentionally design fracture points in the mounts to allow them to separate in the event of a severe deceleration, thereby minimizing damage to the fuselage body and all that is precious within. Marquez, like Davis, would know where to find them—at the forward reaches of the debris footprint.

This was one of the things Davis had grown to appreciate

about his discipline. For all the apparent chaos and randomness, when airplanes hit the ground, they break apart with striking uniformity. A professor somewhere had once devised a model that predicted with 90 percent accuracy, or so he claimed, where any given subsection of an aircraft would end up after a crash. Davis thought it might be true, at least under laboratory conditions.

The problem was the other 10 percent. When a long metal tube careens through the air at hundreds of miles an hour, enough variables are introduced to implode any semblance of certainty. There are mechanical issues and weather, air traffic that ranges from jumbo jets to turkey vultures, and what safety specialists refer to as "human factors." This last variable was always the most difficult to derive from wreckage. It was also the most common primary cause. Everything from old-fashioned screwups to intentional acts of terrorism. Marquez had concerns about something in the cockpit, where the two most vital humans in this tragedy were seated in the critical moments thirty-six hours ago. As far as Davis was concerned, everything remained on the table.

He took one last look at his wide-angle panorama. In the surrounding jungle were a hundred yellow flags hanging limp in the stagnant air, makeshift headstones to mark the fragments of TAC-Air Flight 223. In time every piece would be mapped, photographed, identified, and ultimately moved to a final resting place. He saw fifteen men and women already working the site and a dozen soldiers guarding the perimeter. Guarding against who or what Davis couldn't say.

He drained his Coke and started off toward the site. The Motrin hadn't kicked in yet, and with the equatorial sun nearing its apex, brewing and pounding, Davis squinted as he left the protection of the shade. It was time to see the seat Jen should have been sitting in.

It was time to kill questions with answers.

SEVEN

Davis walked across the clearing, but it felt more like a swim, the air viscous and heavy. As he approached the wall of jungle, he encountered a soldier with a cigarette dangling from his lips. The smoke rose unbothered, a perfect straight line to the sky, and the young man smiled, causing Davis to think that his promise of a case of rum had swept through the ranks like wildfire.

He smiled back, as if to say, *Enjoy.*

Closing in on the wreckage, Davis got his first look in the light of day, and he was immediately struck by one thing—in a departure from most high-energy crashes, there was little evidence of fire. He saw a few singe marks, one wing root blackened by soot, but nothing like the usual inferno. No melted plastic panels or molten pools of aluminum. No trees or grass gone up like tinder. Fire required three things—fuel, air, and ignition. There was always ignition in a high-speed impact, tearing metal and arcing wires, and air was a given. So Flight 223 had gone down low on fuel. Possibly out of fuel. He made a mental note to check the flight plan, fuel truck logs, and estimated flight time. Somewhere in that chain, the aircraft had gotten critically low on Jet-A.

He arrived at the midpoint of the fuselage, where the hull was fractured, and Davis leaned his head inside much as he had last night. The bodies in the passenger cabin had been removed, a scant ray of light in his otherwise bleak day. Davis was sure the remains had been recovered with decorum, or at least all the decorum possible when working in the middle of a primeval jungle. If anybody was up to that job, it was the soldiers around him. All military units took casualties, and those in Colombia had seen their share. Narco-terrorists, paramilitary groups, the occasional border skirmish. Marquez and his squad would know how to deal with the aftermath of traumatic death.

Looking aft into the cabin Davis noted two smaller, secondary breaks in the ceiling that weren't obvious from outside. Just behind the last row of seats was the foot of a bulkhead, and behind that nothing but ferns and uprooted brush. This was the point where the tail had separated, the aft fifteen feet of jet coming to rest somewhere upstream in the impact sequence.

Owing to the dense canopy overhead, little light penetrated to the forest floor, and someone had strung a line of battery-powered work lights all along the shattered ceiling. The whole interior world was canted at roughly a ten-degree angle to port, which wasn't as bad as it could have been. Davis had worked before in completely inverted hulls, forced to wade over spilled carry-on luggage and crumpled beverage carts.

Comfortable with the general layout, he steeled himself to go inside. Davis had one leg through the jagged gap when someone said, "You want this one, *Señor*?"

Davis turned and saw the smiling soldier. He was holding out a cheap fabric respirator, the kind a house painter would use when spraying a bedroom wall. It was probably the only protective gear he was going to be issued. No gloves or booties. Certainly no hard hat or biohazard suit.

"Yeah, that's not a bad idea. Thanks."

He took the mask and snapped the white cup over his face. Davis stepped into the cabin carefully, planning each footfall and handhold onto the bones of what looked solid. A fall into jagged metal or razor-edged shards of composite could ruin your day, and of course it was always good form to avoid trampling evidence. He saw personal effects scattered across the floor. A half-knitted sweater and a pink tube of lip gloss—or was it lipstick? He'd never known the difference. A romance novel with the bookmark still in place, a story that would never reach its end.

There was never a question of where he would go first.

Row 7 was all the way in back, adjacent to the gaping hole where the tail had once been. The A and B seats were on the port side, and across the narrow aisle was the C seat. Set tight against the starboard window, 7C was the only seat in the row from which a body had been recovered.

According to the seating chart, Jen had been assigned the center B seat, and Davis felt an inner tightening as it came into view. The upholstery looked almost pristine, the seatback straight and unbent. Just as Marquez had said, the seat belt was unfastened. *Unfastened.* That was the tenuous thread from which his hopes had been hanging. Yet now Davis saw a second indicator that Jen had not been here at the moment of impact—seat 6B, directly in front, displayed minimal damage. His daughter weighed in at one hundred and twenty pounds—as she often reminded him, exactly half his own weight. In a crash as severe as this one, even a small unrestrained body would have hurled forward with devastating force. Assuming a typical thirty-G deceleration, without the constraint of a seat belt, a one-hundred-and-twenty-pound body became a projectile weighing nearly two tons. Davis, however, saw no sign of damage to the seat in front, no dents or misshapen frame.

He went down onto his hands and knees, and studied the bases of the seats. Each pair of port seats was anchored by six bolts, three forward and three aft on the frame. Davis pushed and pulled on Row 6 and found the aft anchors slightly loose. This was the classic signature of occupied seats that had pitched forward in a sudden deceleration, yet held fast because an engineer somewhere had done his calculations perfectly. Davis checked the aft anchors on Row 7 and did not find a similar looseness—a third indicator that this pair of seats had not been occupied at the moment of impact.

He pushed up off the tilted floor and, just as his spirits were rising, his gaze was seized like a magnet to metal. It was the smallest of details, barely noticeable amid the chaos and ruin. Hanging a few inches out of the seatback pocket facing 7B was a delicate white earbud. He hesitated, then reached carefully into the pocket and felt blindly. Searching for what he hoped would not be there.

Davis felt something and pulled it clear, and what he saw capsized his tiny lifeboat of hope. In his hand, stylish in its tiger-striped protective sleeve, was the iPod Touch he'd given to Jen last year for Christmas.

* * *

Ten minutes later Davis stood statuelike near the remains of the jet, Jen's iPod in his hand. He was staring at the device as if it were a lost relic, some kind of great archaeological find, when Colonel Marquez arrived. The Colombian stopped in front of him and said something, but Davis didn't hear. Marquez said it again.

"What is that?"

Davis blinked, then met the colonel's gaze. "It's an iPod . . . you know, for playing music."

"Where did you find it?"

"In the seatback pocket at 7B."

"Your daughter's," Marquez said.

Davis nodded.

The colonel let out a long breath as a pair of workers walked past. One held some kind of electronic device with a wand, its beeping tone guiding him into the brush. Even after the man disappeared behind the evergreen wall, the machine's chirp remained steady. Like a distant digital heartbeat.

"Then there can be no doubt," said Marquez. "She was in that seat."

As he'd been doing for the last ten minutes, Davis tried to think of an escape, a logical argument against the idea. There wasn't one. "Yeah," he said, more to himself than to Marquez, "she was definitely there."

Davis sat down on a log, a freshly snapped timber fully one foot thick that had come to rest where the port wing should have been. He wondered how much longer he could keep this up—one minute clinging to the idea that Jen had survived, and the next proving otherwise. He knew he was filtering every sight and sound and smell, first and foremost, through the lens of his daughter's fate. But in that process, what was he blotting out? What was he not seeing? Somewhere in the distance the chirping increased in frequency, rising until it became a staccato buzz. Something new had been located, most likely a piece of metal from an engine cowling or a separated wing flap, some fragment of marginal significance. It didn't matter.

How much longer can I go on?

Marquez sat next to him and put his hands on his knees. It was a markedly fraternal move, and after a moment's contemplation, he said, "You were once a military pilot?"

"Yeah, USAF. F-16s most of my career."

Marquez nodded. "Lucky you. I was doomed to fly A-37s, a version of your Air Force's old primary trainer. I am told it was referred to there as a two-ton dog whistle. A poor country like mine cannot afford the best, but we trained hard, and fought when the order came. I lost my share of friends to crashes over the years, and many times I was involved in the investigations that followed. That was hard to do."

"I've lost friends too."

"I'm sure. But losing a daughter . . . that is a very different thing. Fighter pilots assume a certain amount of risk. It is expected some will pay the ultimate price."

"What are you trying to say?"

Marquez cocked his head. "I think being so close to this inquiry—it will be difficult for you. I need help, expertise, and I am not sure you can give it. Perhaps it would be better if you went back home to grieve."

Davis shot back a hard look. "Is this your idea of a motivational speech? My daughter *was* on that aircraft, but counting the crew there were twenty-three other people involved. Each of them has a family and friends, decent people who are feeling exactly what I'm feeling right now. In the next few days they'll be identifying bodies, making funeral arrangements, and calling long-lost brothers to deliver the bad news." Davis paused for a moment, then continued in a level tone, "There is nobody on your team who will kick as much metal and stay up as late as I will to find out what the hell happened. If you want to send a message to Washington or throw me back in that cell, go ahead and try. But understand that I'll fight you every inch of the way. In my opinion, neither of us has time for that right now."

The colonel stared into the distance, his face a tight mask. He was not used to being challenged. "You know where she is," he finally said.

Davis didn't reply. In the pause, the jungle suddenly came alive with the sound of unseen birds scattering and squawking. A feral screech echoed as some creature in the distance succumbed to nature's way. It was a short-lived drama, and soon everything returned to what it had been. Steady beeping. The brush of wind through treetops.

Marquez nodded over his shoulder, toward the thickest stand of forest. "Your daughter was thrown clear when the tail broke off. It pains me to say it, but she is one thousand meters behind us in the swamp."

Again, Davis said nothing.

"As investigators we are bound by facts, however regrettable they might be. I have three people searching that area as we speak. It might take a day, or even a week . . . but we *will* find her."

"Find them," Davis countered. "There are two girls out there. And yes, you might find them. But I'm not convinced by your facts. Not yet. Until I am, I'm going to keep looking elsewhere."

A long silence ensued at the impasse. Davis turned the iPod in his hand, staring at it as if it were a talisman of some kind.

Marquez rose slowly, and when Davis followed suit, they exchanged resolute stares.

"I'll help you with this investigation," Davis said. "But don't ever question my motives."

"Very well," said Marquez. He backed away a step, and asked, "Have you seen the cockpit yet?"

"No."

"I think it's time you did. I should warn you, the bodies are still in place."

"Nothing I haven't seen before."

"There you are wrong." With that, the colonel began walking to the forward edge of the fuselage.

Davis fell in behind him.

* * *

As was his custom, Martin Stuyvesant sat in the first row of the bus, and through the front window he saw the sign he'd been waiting for: AKRON, 5 MILES. He sighed a vagabond's sigh. Would this place be different from all the others?

Of course not.

Stuyvesant was not a happy man. His stomach had been acting up and he was desperately tired. The burn in his gut, he supposed, was an ulcer, but he'd be damned if he was going to see any doctor about it. Ulcers were what you got when you had too many worries, and God knew, Stuyvesant had more than his share. He was effectively homeless, and drank more than he should. He also suspected he might be getting too reliant on the pain medication a friend had given him, but the old knee injury from high school wasn't letting up, and life on the road was as demanding as ever. Then there were his finances. He was nearly broke again, left with no choice but to tap friends and strangers "for the very last time." Everyone knew it was a lie. It had been that way as long as he could remember, walking through life with his hand out. Stuyvesant never hesitated when it came to begging for cash— he'd essentially made a career of it—but he needed a fresh angle.

If all that wasn't bad enough, a new problem was brewing, one he'd only learned about this morning. Somewhere in Colombia, deep in the godforsaken jungle, events were playing out that could land him in a great deal of trouble. Trouble of the criminal variety. There was never a good time for complications of that nature, but the timing couldn't have been worse. Stuyvesant had made a great many mistakes in his tempestuous life, yet this one he'd thought long dead and buried. One phone call had proved how wrong he was. Like a zombie, the most hideous crisis imaginable had mutated, stirred, and risen from the dead.

Feeling the familiar burn, he reached into a pocket, retrieved his last two antacid tablets, and stuffed them in his mouth. The bus veered onto the first Akron exit, and at the bottom of the off-ramp the brakes hissed as the big machine stopped at a red light. Stuyvesant spotted a man on the curb. Roughly his age—early fifties—he was limping as he ambled along with a cardboard sign that read: WILL WORK FOR FOOD, GOD BLESS.

Stuyvesant watched him sidle along the row of cars in the adjacent lane, pausing for a moment near each window. The man looked like Stuyvesant felt, old and weary, yet his clothes were more tattered, and his hygiene decidedly more repulsive. Stringy hair, yellow teeth, a week's growth of beard. Here was a man, Stuyvesant thought, who'd lost his self-respect. It was the eyes, however, that really drew his attention. They were cast downward, almost in supplication. *That's where you've got it wrong*, he thought. *You should look them in the eye, show them you're proud in spite of your circumstances.*

The light turned green, and as the bus accelerated Stuyvesant had an epiphany. He saw the driver's lunch cooler just behind his seat, resting in an open cardboard box.

"Excuse me," he said, leaning forward to be in the man's field of vision. "Would you mind if I took the flap from your box?"

The driver glanced at Stuyvesant, then at his lunch. "Uh . . . sure, help yourself."

Stuyvesant pulled the box over, removed the plastic cooler, and none too carefully ripped off a good-sized section of cardboard. He then put everything back as it had been, minus one brown corrugated flap. To the woman seated next to him, who was watching most suspiciously, he said, "Do you have a black marker I could borrow?"

She hesitated, but then opened her purse and after some digging pulled out a black Sharpie.

"Perfect! Thank you!"

Stuyvesant put some thought into his message, and after settling on the wording he scrawled it in thick block letters. Pleased with himself, he returned the marker to his bewildered seatmate, and then critiqued his creation at arm's length.

HOMELESS

NEED MONEY

GOD BLESS

The last line he had waffled on, religion always a touchy issue, but he decided it was safely non-denominational.

Now all he needed was a stage. The right corner from which to make his pitch. Stuyvesant thought he might know exactly where to find it.

He smiled inwardly.

And I'll look them right in the eye.

EIGHT

The cockpit of a twenty-one seat regional jet is a surprisingly small space. Smaller still after a two-hundred-fifty-knot collision into hardwood forest. That being the case, Davis and Marquez could not inspect the flight deck alongside one another. Access was gained through what had been the cockpit door, until recently a bulletproof Kevlar barrier, now reduced to a splintered six-by-two-foot panel clinging to its bottom hinge.

The aircraft's nose had come to rest disjointed from the main fuselage and canted at an angle. The cockpit was largely intact, albeit with significant impact damage. Aside from the broken door, Davis noted that a window on the left side had failed inward, and the forward windscreen center-post had buckled severely, a telephone-pole-sized timber winning that battle in microseconds. The flight instrument displays seemed in reasonably good condition, the wide flat-panel screens now dark from lack of power. Whatever chapters the instruments might add to this luckless story would take time to interpret. Microchips had to be recovered, analyzed, and eventually compared to flight data recorder information.

Two overhead panels had accordioned, both sides crumpled, although most of the switches and components were recognizable. The center console, where levers were mounted to manage engine thrust and flap extension, could have come straight from the factory floor. Davis shouldered inside the cockpit to inspect things more closely, and was immediately tripped by one very high mental hurdle. The ARJ-35 was certified as a two-pilot airplane. He was looking at three bodies.

"What the hell?" he blurted.

"My words earlier were in Spanish," said Marquez, "but much the same."

Davis leaned in further, snapping the mask back over his face to counter stale air that reeked of death. He saw two men in the left seat, stacked like a pair of burlap grain sacks. Both wore uniforms, the usual dark polyester pants, short-sleeve white shirts with epaulets, and black leather shoes. In the right seat was a man in civilian clothes, this body in the best condition of the three. None of it made sense.

Davis pulled back into the daylight and drew off his mask. "This airplane doesn't have a jumpseat, does it?"

"No," said Marquez, confirming that the third cockpit seat, common on larger airliners, was not an option here.

"The missing passenger from 2A—that's him?"

"Yes, we have made a positive identification."

"Who is he?"

"His name is Rodolfo Umbriz. He is a pastry chef from Cartagena."

Davis stared blankly at Marquez, opened his mouth as if to say something, then stifled it. His eyes drifted skyward. Of all the complications he might have imagined, this was not among them.

He returned to the cockpit. The three bodies, after much trauma and many hours without metabolic process, had reached the point of unpleasantness. He tried to decide which seemed more bizarre. A civilian slumped over the flight controls? Or the two pilots stacked next to him in the captain's seat?

Of the two pilots, the one on top seemed in better condition. The most obvious injury was a massive wound at the base of the man's skull. Dried blood, black and crusted, stained the back of his white shirt. Three stripes on his epaulets suggested this was the first officer. The body underneath had taken more of a beating. The head rested near the failed window, and Davis saw severe damage to the man's face and neck. He remained strapped in his seat, yet despite the heavy trauma there seemed to be less blood. In truth, hardly any blood at all.

Davis shifted to the other side of the cockpit and studied the civilian, a sixtyish Hispanic male in a blue madras shirt with wispy gray hair and crushed designer glasses. His seat belt was engaged, minus the shoulder harness that was mandatory on cockpit seats. The body had been driven forward on impact, ending slumped over the control column. Davis noted there was no radio headset clamped over the man's skull, nor any charts on the clipboard in front of him. Either might imply he knew how to fly an airplane.

He blurted out the obvious one-word question. "Hijacking?"

"There can be no other answer," said Marquez.

Davis stared at the colonel, thinking this an odd phrasing. He wrote it off to the language barrier.

"It explains everything," said Marquez. "The pilots were incapacitated at the time of the crash."

"Incapacitated? What makes you say that?"

A sigh from the colonel. Not impatience, but reluctance. "After a close inspection, I'm quite certain both pilots have bullet wounds at the bases of their skulls."

"Bullet wounds," Davis repeated.

"It is only my preliminary observation, but having battled the narcos in our country . . . I've seen executions before."

"That *would* be incapacitating."

"The pilots will be first in line for postmortem evaluations. We must confirm their cause of death as quickly as possible." Marquez paused. "A hijacking would also explain why the aircraft deviated so far off its intended course."

Davis nodded, but said nothing.

"Of course, there is more," said Marquez. He swept two fingers over the bulkhead where the cockpit door had been mounted. "The frame around this door is misshapen from the crash, but otherwise undamaged—except here." His fingers stopped at the electrically actuated deadbolt lock. "You can see evidence of forced entry. The lock is damaged and the frame bent severely near the bolt." Marquez next pointed with the toe of his mud-caked boot.

Davis saw a heavy steel bar on the cabin floor.

"That was also discovered last night," said the colonel, "exactly where you see it now."

"So you're suggesting this guy who ended up in the copilot's seat . . . he broke into the cockpit using that as a pry bar, then shot both pilots and took over?"

"It seems clear enough," said Marquez.

Davis stepped back and put his hands on his hips. He shifted his eyes from one bit of Marquez' theory to the next, settling on the crowbar near his foot. He thought, *Colonel Mustard in the study with the lead pipe.* What he said was, "It all looks pretty straightforward, doesn't it?"

"Tell me what doesn't fit. I want you to challenge this."

Davis didn't have to think about it for long. "In the post 9-11 world any would-be hijacker faces one overwhelming hurdle—how to gain access to the cockpit. And you're suggesting one guy did this? With a gun and a tire iron?"

"There are ways to slip weapons past security. The gun would keep the passengers at bay while he used the bar to open the cockpit door."

"Would it?" Davis countered. "There's a new mentality among passengers these days. Anyone trying to breach a flight deck will find themselves up against a mob."

"A mob of how many? We are dealing with a small jet. If he was able to work quickly, before anyone realized what was happening—"

"No," said Davis. "He might pry through the door in seconds, and he might shoot the pilots. But at that point the flight attendant and passengers would be overwhelmed by an instinct of self-preservation. They'd rush him like a crowd of medieval peasants, only instead of pitchforks and clubs they'd use coffeepots and fists. And in your scenario, the hijacker—who, by the way, is not a particularly intimidating individual—no longer has a viable door to protect him."

"That is where you are wrong. This door has a secondary

lock, a manual deadbolt that can be engaged from inside the cockpit. If he were to defeat the electronic bolt, I think he might have been able to isolate himself using the backup lock."

Davis looked quizzically at Marquez. "You've already researched the operation of this particular model of hardened door?"

"I looked into it this morning."

"All right—I've come this far with you. What's the motive?"

"In Colombia we have no shortage of desperation. Terrorism, narcotics, extortion. Or perhaps this man had psychiatric issues. We are looking into his history now. I would guess our suspect planned to fly to Panama or Ecuador, and from there demand a ransom."

"So now he's a suspect? And you're assuming our *chef pâtissier* could fly an airplane as easily as he could bake an éclair?"

Marquez ignored the jibe, saying, "It is possible he has some kind of flight experience. If so, there will be a record of it somewhere. We are already interviewing his family and coworkers, researching his background. By the end of today we will know a great deal more about Rodolfo Umbriz."

Davis said nothing for a time, then asked, "Have you found the weapon?"

"Not yet. But we will."

Davis sensed something beneath this answer, but it wasn't confidence. "So tell me," he said, "when will you go public with this theory?"

"*Dios mío!* To the press? We are nowhere near that point. I am only trying to keep you informed, tell you the road our investigation is taking."

Davis nearly blurted something about what kind of road involved a sexagenarian pastry chef commandeering a packed airliner. He held his tongue, and Marquez, as if reading his doubts, said, "We have not yet ruled anything out, Mr. Davis. As far as the press goes, our accident is drawing less attention than most. The aircraft was relatively small, and the crash site very remote.

There have been no photographs, other than a few dim images we released ourselves." His arm swept out in a smooth arc. "With our army friends on the perimeter, it will stay that way long enough."

"Long enough for what?"

"You should get to work, perhaps spend your morning in the eastern sector. Go see if you can find your daughter, Mr. Davis." The colonel patted his shoulder in a comforting gesture, which might or might not have been genuine, before turning away toward the clearing.

Davis watched him go, all careful steps and confidence. When the colonel was gone, he turned and looked again at the frame of the cockpit door and the crowbar at his feet. He took another long look at the bodies inside. In the end it wasn't the alleged hijacker that held his attention, but rather the two pilots. Davis leaned left and right, and he did see wounds near the bases of their brainpans. What bothered him about the picture wasn't that they probably *had* been executed. It was something more broad, something he couldn't quite pinpoint. A simple, one-word impression wedged in his mind.

Unprofessional.

His thoughts were interrupted when a pair of uniformed men arrived with three body bags.

"We clean up, okay?" the lead man said in strongly accented English.

Davis backed away. "Yeah, go ahead."

NINE

They call it rain forest for a reason. Moments after Marquez departed in the Huey the sky began to darken, and in a matter of minutes, the great slabs of cumulonimbus overhead reached their saturation point. It wasn't as much a rain shower as a regional waterfall. The treetops were barely visible, and gusts whipped foliage into undulating emerald curtains.

Rather too late, Davis took shelter under an open-sided tent. Thick raindrops peppered the roof, a thousand tiny explosions meshing into a low-frequency white noise, the overhanging canvas flaps snapping wildly in the wind. Davis was more wet than dry, and in the pulsing gusts he had the peculiar sensation of being hot and cold at the same time. He stood alongside a dozen Colombians, a mix of army enlisted men and the colonel's field technicians. There was also an exhausted powerplant expert from Pratt & Whitney, a man who'd flown in overnight from Miami and caught the first available chopper. Davis doubted the engines had anything to do with this crash—one of the few points he and Marquez agreed upon—but the big manufacturers always liked to have an ear to the ground while blame remained an open question.

There were three folding tables, and all had been turned into seating. Someone opened a cooler full of food and soft drinks, music began playing, and a spontaneous midday siesta began in earnest. Attacking a sandwich that might have been beef and cheese, Davis struck up a chat with the soldier standing next to him.

"How long is your duty out here?" he asked the *cabo primero*, or first corporal.

The young man smiled amiably. "We come last Friday. Stay three, maybe four days. More if our *jefe* say."

"It was lucky you were so close to the crash site."

"Two other squads were near, but we were closest."

"Sounds like a big exercise. What kind of training were you doing?"

"Training? I don't know about training."

Davis foraged in the cooler for a second sandwich. "So what . . . you were just out here waiting for an airplane to crash?" Davis' stab at humor was lost, the corporal only giving him an odd look.

"Sorry," said the soldier. "English no so good." He walked to the other side of the tent and began talking to a captain.

The rain began sweeping sideways, marginalizing the tent's usefulness. Nobody seemed to care, least of all Davis who had far more pressing things on his mind. Raindrops pelted his face as he downed his second sandwich, ham and avocado on thick-sliced bread. He was determined not to waste a moment. If field work was impractical, he'd use the time for sustenance and to organize his thoughts.

Davis tried to tear apart the hijacking theory, but to shoot down such a circumstantial premise was like firing an air-to-air missile at a ghost. Moving on, he rehashed the rest, and one detail tugged at him again and again. The jet had ended up well off course. What at first had seemed an oddity now appeared vital. Hijacking or not, someone had been at the controls of Flight 223, and they'd brought it here. But who had been flying, and what was their intention? He was virtually certain Marquez would find that their pastry chef, Umbriz, had no flying experience. If that was the case, there were only two scenarios in which the man would have killed the pilots and taken over the jet. One was a suicide mission, perhaps with a political agenda. The second was that he was flat out deranged. Neither seemed likely.

But what then?

He checked his watch to note the exact time of each clap of thunder that seemed near. On reaching the first ten-minute interval of silence, Davis headed outside. His example was not followed—the party kept going strong. It was undeniably irritating, yet he decided to let it play out. Davis knew his level of commitment was unique, and could not be expected of the others. The rain tapered quickly, falling to a steady drizzle, and the jungle acquired a new heaviness. He stepped over streams of fresh runoff, forded through puddles of muck, and soon his clothes were riding his skin like a suit of wet rags.

He circled the fuselage, ending near the tip of the aircraft's nose. An engineer would refer to it as station zero, the baseline longitudinal location. From that point, moving aft, the numbers increased, serving as reference units by which to gauge modifications, repairs, and weight and balance measurements. Davis would use station zero as his own starting point, thinking it the most methodical way to proceed.

He poked and prodded the radome, and under the cracked fiberglass housing he noted a damaged weather radar antenna. Climbing briefly onto the spine two feet farther aft, he saw nothing of interest. An unidentifiable piece of debris jutted from the ground along the port side, and Davis went down on his knees. With bare hands he dug through dirt and peat, and soon identified the part as a valve connected to a pencil-thin hydraulic line, almost certainly part of the nose gear assembly underneath. Not a noteworthy find, but one more thing to be logged and accounted for. That was how 99 percent of an investigator's time was spent—documenting what *wasn't* important in order to find what was.

An hour later he stopped for a water break.

After two, Davis stole a glance at his watch.

It was noon on Monday.

The second worst day of his life.

Which meant things were getting better.

* * *

The last helicopter to Bogotá from the crash site was set to leave at 6:45 that evening. Davis was given a ten-minute warning to be ready. He'd spent the entire day combing through wreckage, from nose to tail—or at least where the tail used to be. He'd found little to inspire him, and nothing to counter Marquez' theory that they were looking at a hijacking. But then, there was also nothing to support it. Bent metal gave little inference as to what might have distilled in one man's mind.

He reached the final row of seats shortly before the chopper was to arrive, and for the last time that day Davis stared at seat 7B. He'd been avoiding it, of course, like an elderly passerby might pretend to ignore a graveyard, yet he couldn't return to Bogotá without one last look.

The seat appeared much the same, unblemished upholstery and cushions over an unbent frame. He realized that after finding Jen's iPod he'd ventured no further into the seatback pocket. Davis slipped his hand in again, forcing the pocket wide, and behind an emergency evacuation card he saw something else. It was instantly recognizable—a dark-blue passport issued by the United States of America.

Davis made sure there was nothing more, then pulled the passport clear. It had to be Jen's, and on the second page he found her picture. The document was four years old, the photo taken in her early high school years. Davis saw a passport smile less muted than most, captured before her spirit had been flattened by the death of her mother, and long before she would leave home for college at that double-edged age of independence.

The sound of the Huey rattling overhead brought Davis back to the present. It was time to go, but on a sudden impulse he checked the pocket in front of the window seat, 7A. There was no iPod, but to his surprise he found a second passport. This too was an American-issued item, and inside he found a picture of a girl Jen's age. She had the same color hair and similar features. They could have passed for sisters. He remembered the final message Jen had left on his phone. She'd been at the airport in Bogotá and had already made a friend.

So here she was. Kristin Marie Stewart.

Feeling he was on a roll, Davis turned toward the aisle and regarded seat 7C. He slipped his hand into that pocket, and scooped out an old bag of peanuts and a plastic stir stick. Then something else caught his eye.

A crashed aircraft, if nothing else, is a study in contrast. Debris will range in condition from soiled to pristine, from ruined to unblemished. All the same, this was something he should have noticed. Amid the chaos all around, the aftermath of a frenzy of Newtonian mechanics, Davis saw one detail that didn't fit. On the back of seat 7C, square in the center, were two small holes no larger than a dime. He tested one with his little finger, and then the other. Both went clean through. There was a subtle stain on the upholstery below the holes, a discoloration that didn't catch the eye because something had spackled the remainder of the seatback, presumably mud from the crash sequence later flecked by rain.

But there *was* a stain. One that was dark and familiar.

Davis checked behind the seat, but there was nothing to see. The bulkhead was gone, and two feet farther back the shell of the shattered hull simply ended, presenting the forest like a jagged oval picture frame. He was staring intently, deep in thought, when someone shouted his name.

Davis was on the Huey three minutes later, rising into the fading orange twilight. Looking out over the scene, he saw a pair of dim lights to the east sweeping back and forth. At least one crew was still searching the wetlands for the last two bodies. *Still searching.* That was good, because it meant they hadn't found anything yet. An optimist's view, to be sure, and an outlook of which he'd rarely been accused of keeping. The chopper spun mercifully to a new heading, and the scene became more pleasant. Green forest under a painted sky, the sun playing its palette on a high deck of stratus clouds.

He pulled the two passports from his pocket and flipped open Jen's. Davis ran his thumb over the page with her photograph, the embossments and security strips rough under his touch, but strangely comforting. So tactile and true.

"I'll find you, baby," he whispered. "Wherever you are, I'll find you."

* * *

Davis arrived back at the Bogotá airport at eight that evening. He was told that Marquez had arranged a room for him at a hotel within walking distance of the headquarters building—probably a place that kept a running contract with the military—and the duty officer at El Centro provided an initial vector.

It was a ten-minute walk to the Hotel de Aeropuerto, a solidly two-star affair. He was given a room on the second floor that had a bed, a tiny table with one chair, and a painting on the wall of a bearded conquistador on a horse. The smell of cheap cleanser chafed his respiratory system, but the place met his most immediate needs—the sheets looked clean, and there was a restaurant directly across the street. Until Jen was found, little else mattered.

After ten hours in the field—enduring three thunderstorms, one landslide, and a near lightning strike—Davis looked more like a survivor of a plane crash than an investigator. There was algae and moss in his hair, his fingernails were black with topsoil, and the crusted mud on his pants and shirt would clog anything less than a commercial-grade washing machine. He took everything off, rinsed his boots in the tub, and threw the rest in the trash. He took great care with his best finds of the day—Jen's iPod and the two passports. The passports he would surrender to Marquez, as per procedure. The colonel already knew he had the iPod, and hadn't asked for it, so Davis reasoned that was his to keep.

He pulled a clean hand towel from the rack in the bathroom, got it damp under the faucet, and wiped the iPod clean as best he could. He removed the device from its case, pressed the power button and got a flicker, the screen only lighting long enough to blink a red battery symbol before going dark. Davis stared for a long moment, then set the iPod on the nightstand next to the bed.

He returned to the bathroom, looked in the mirror and was

met by a weary stranger. He'd been riding an emotional rocket, and spending last night on the floor of a prison cell, a minor concussion for company, had done nothing to brighten his mood. There had been little good news today, but all the same, he'd made it to sunset without hearing the worst news.

To the positive, his head felt better, and after a hot shower he put on fresh clothes, which meant his other khaki pants and a different drab cotton shirt. Like most former military men, he kept a detached sense of fashion, bordering on none at all. The clock by the bed showed eight thirty, and feeling revitalized, Davis knew what he had to do.

At the restaurant across the street he ordered the dinner special, which turned out to be a mountain of steak, chorizo, rice, and beans. In fractured Spanish, Davis tried to ask for it to go, and a bartender who'd studied accounting for two years at the University of Toledo laughed at him, and said, "No problem, buddy."

On the way to El Centro he came across a store that sold pirated DVDs and cheap electronic gear, and in a discount bin he found a knock-off charger for Jen's iPod Touch. The clerk asked for ten thousand Colombian pesos, which Davis didn't have, so he charged it to his MasterCard having no idea how much he was paying for a few feet of wire and a connecting plug that was made in China.

He walked into headquarters at five minutes before nine. Two newly installed window-unit air conditioners were battling hard, sponging moisture from the viscous air and cutting the heat that clung fast into the late evening. He took a seat at a vacant computer, pulled out his sat-phone, and checked for messages. There were none. Pulling in a long breath, he set the phone down next to the keyboard, and was soon spooning rice and beans from a cup as he caught up with the day's findings on the tragedy of TAC-Air Flight 223. He ate in the same deliberate manner in which he read, a physical manifestation of both thoughtfulness and fear. Davis didn't want to miss anything, but sensed that he already had. It was a confining process, to be sure, yet a straightjacket from which he made no attempt to escape.

Page by tedious page, he forged ahead.

* * *

The small room was in a nondescript building on G Street in Washington, D.C. Two analysts, a man and a woman, blinked simultaneously when one of their computers chirped an alarm.

"What is it?" the man asked.

The two sat facing one another at opposing desks, and it was the woman's machine that had alerted. "He just bought something with his MasterCard in Bogotá."

"What?"

"It looks like . . . a charging cable for an iPhone."

"An iPhone?" The man performed a quick cross-check. "He doesn't own one. Davis is strictly an Android guy, and the satphone he was issued Sunday is a standard Iridium platform potted with our special variant of the operating system."

The woman gave him a suffering look.

"Okay, okay—you knew that. Hang on."

As he typed, the woman shrugged a sweater over her shoulders. The room was dimly-lit and windowless, and the thermostat kept, strictly under lock and key, at a chilly sixty-eight degrees. Even at the end of August.

"December 15 last year. He bought an iPod Touch at the Best Buy in Manassas, Virginia."

"A Christmas gift?" the woman mused. "Or could he have bought it for himself?"

Thirty seconds later he had the answer. "During the last week of December someone downloaded nearly a thousand songs through his home computer."

"Paid or pirated?"

It was his turn to frown. "A thousand songs? Who pays for that much music these days?"

"Sorry."

"Hang on," he said, "let's be sure—I've got the playlist right here." After less than a minute, "No, this doesn't match the music on Davis' Spotify account . . . not even close. It's got to be the daughter's, a Christmas present. It's the only thing that makes sense."

"Okay. But why would he take his daughter's iPod, full of *her* music, to Colombia?"

"And then forget the cable?"

Silence as they both pondered it.

"I don't get it," he said weakly.

"Me neither, let's move on."

"What's he doing now?"

She looked at her screen. "We're getting every keystroke through his phone—he must have set it down right next to the damned keyboard. He's searching for performance data on ARJ-35s."

"Okay, at least that makes sense."

"What should we do about the iPod?" she asked.

"You know the orders." An extended silence ran. "Where is Stuyvesant?"

The woman had to check. "He's on another bus. Florida this time."

"They might reach out to him there—the South Americans are all over Florida."

"Maybe. But that's out of our hands. And you didn't answer my question. Are you going to send this little tidbit up?"

The man sighed. "Where is Strand now?"

She checked the schedule and told him.

"We can only use a landline there—even *he* has to turn his cell off."

"The number is listed right here on the schedule. He put it there for a reason."

The man relented, picking up a phone and placing the call. After two rings it was picked up across town in the Eisenhower Executive Office Building.

Right next door to the White House.

TEN

Davis found Marquez in a conference room preparing to go home for the night.

"You are working late tonight?" the colonel asked as Davis eclipsed the doorway.

"I don't exactly have a family to go home to right now."

"Did you learn anything useful this afternoon?"

Davis pulled the two passports and dropped them on a table. "One is Jen's. The other belongs to the girl who was sitting next to her, Kristin Stewart. I found them in the seatback pockets."

Marquez took both and flipped through the pages. "That is a strange place to leave them."

"I thought so too. Jen knows better than to put important documents where they might be forgotten. Now, the iPod being there—that doesn't surprise me. But for *both* girls to leave their passports in their seatback pockets. That's not right—there's a reason."

Marquez shrugged it off, a man already mystified by the teenagers he kept at home. He put the passports in a cabinet, locked it, and said, "I will keep them for now."

"What about you?" Davis asked. "Anything new to report?"

"Unfortunately, no. Nothing since we last spoke. Tomorrow morning I am going to the medical examiner's office. They will have the results of the postmortems on our pilots. Ten o'clock at Al Hospital Occidente de Kennedy. You are welcome to come."

"I think I might. Is that where all the bodies are being held?"

"Yes, for the present time."

"Okay. Before you leave tonight can you give me any information you have on the pilots?"

"Of course, we have a file on each man."

"I'd also like to see the video footage from the boarding area."

"I will talk to Rafael before I go. I can tell you I've watched it four times myself. Our suspect, Señor Umbriz, is only briefly visible as he gives his boarding pass to the agent. Apparently he arrived late—which in itself tells me something." Marquez looked at him as if expecting a response.

Davis didn't give one.

"If that is all," said Marquez, "I will see you tomorrow morning. Try to get a good night's sleep."

* * *

Rafael set up a monitor in a side room and gave Davis a quick tutorial, then left him alone. The video was black and white, a fish-eye view from a camera mounted near the jetway entrance, looking back across the gate area. Davis cued the video to a point fifty minutes before the flight's departure.

In the beginning there was little action, and he fast-forwarded liberally. Roughly twenty minutes before the scheduled push-back time passengers began lining up. They stood casually between twin rope-lined stanchions, waiting to board a doomed airliner. Davis imagined there had been a similar scene a century ago, when the passengers of an unsinkable ship boarded at a pier in Southampton, England. As ever, fate traveled as a quiet companion.

He studied the passengers one by one, and in shades of gray saw a mixed clientele, some dressed for business and others less formally. Sales meetings, in-law visits, second honeymoons. Summer internships. There were twenty-one good reasons why people were getting on TAC-Air Flight 223, and not a single person appeared to have reservations about the pending journey, including the pastry chef from Cartagena who boarded near the end and looked the most disinterested of the lot. There was no agitation in his manner. No sweaty brow or fearful, darting eyes.

One passenger, of course, demanded the bulk of his attention. Davis allowed himself that. He held steady as he watched, pushing away the chance that these sterile images might be the last ever captured of his daughter. She was near the back of the line wearing a familiar pair of jeans and a loose khaki shirt covered with pockets. She'd bought the shirt specifically for the trip, and he'd teased her that she looked like Indiana Jones—or at least the female, undergraduate version. She looked happy and vibrant, immersed in her big adventure. He watched Jen exchange a few words with her seatmate, Kristin Stewart, who responded in kind. Davis wasn't a lip-reader but he didn't need to be. *Where do you live? What's your major? How long will you be here?* The usual.

Again, he was struck by their similar appearance. Roughly the same age, same over-the-shoulder auburn hair and willowy build. He forced his eyes away and tried to pick out the last passenger in Row 7. Davis remembered the name from the seating chart. Thomas Mulligan. Mulligan—like an extra shot in golf. His attention settled on an Anglo at the end of the line, behind the two girls. A man whose busy eyes alternated between the terminal area and his phone. Not nervous. Alert was more like it. Watchful. Perhaps searching for an associate. He seemed to be alone, and by the way he was dressed—casual gray coat and pressed trousers—Davis fixed him as a businessman. A Yankee trader in South America selling drilling equipment or washing machines.

The most interesting frames were near the end of the video. They were all moving toward the gate, and presenting boarding passes to the TAC-Air agent. Almost imperceptibly, Davis saw Kristin Stewart turn and say something to Mulligan over her shoulder.

Davis played it back, and by the third replay he was sure. Aside from Jen, Kristin Stewart had made another acquaintance. At some point, she had also met Thomas Mulligan.

* * *

By eleven that evening Davis' concentration was ebbing. He'd moved on from the video to study a pair of manila file folders, the background on the pilots. The majority was government information pertaining to airman certificates, security and background checks, and medical licenses, all retrieved from records kept by the Colombian Special Administrative Unit of Civil Aeronautics—the local version of the FAA. The remaining information came from TAC-Air's corporate personnel files. These files each contained a photograph of the respective pilot standing against a wall, behind them the corporate logo of TAC-Air. That same photo would appear on the corporate ID each wore on a lanyard at work, and was probably on file in a half dozen government ministries.

Davis began with the second in command.

Hugo Moreno, thirty-one, had been the first officer on Flight 223. He'd worked for TAC-Air for four years, accumulating 2500 hours of flight time, including 700 on the ARJ-35. Moreno was a Colombian national and had worked his way through the ranks of aviation the old-fashioned way, flight instructing at a small government-run aviation school, followed by a three-year stint flying night freight over the Andes—a test of airmanship if ever there was one. He was married with two children and lived in a rented apartment on the outskirts of Bogotá.

Captain Blas Reyna, forty-five, was more of an enigma. Fifteen years with TAC-Air, he had 9000 hours of flight time, 4500 spent on the ARJ-35. His previous experience was simply listed as "corporate," with a half dozen types of business jets flown. He was divorced with no dependents, and his address of record was a postal box in Cali. Neither pilot had anything in their files about disciplinary action, and both appeared to have solid training records.

Before closing Reyna's file, Davis paused at the cover photo of the captain in uniform, and there struck the same mental stop he had this morning as he'd stood looking at the bodies. The word burbled into his mind once more: *unprofessional.*

But in what way?

He went back to Moreno's TAC-Air file and studied the photograph. There was no doubt about it—this was the man he'd seen this morning, the body on top of the stack with three stripes on each shoulder. The identity of Captain Reyna was less definitive due to the head trauma, but a long hard look at that photograph erased any doubts. It *was* another match. So what bothered him about it? He flicked through Reyna's file again and found an old background check. It looked like a standard government form, and while there was no photograph, Davis saw a thumbprint and signature at the bottom of a page of Spanish legalese.

The genesis of an idea surfaced. He dug deeper into Reyna's government records, and at the very back found an old and yellowed page—his original application for an airman medical certificate. He looked at the vital statistics, and finally found the problem. A very big problem. Of course, one mismatched number could be a simple clerical error. But it made no sense at all. Davis went back to the photographs of the two pilots and compared them to one another. Then he checked copilot Moreno's vital statistics. Together with what he'd seen at the accident site, it all clicked into one very disturbing scenario.

Davis sat for a moment with his hands clasped behind his head, ruminating on how best to deal with it. He considered the next day, his meeting at the hospital with Marquez, and decided it would present an ideal opportunity to sort things out.

He nearly shut the files, but paranoia got the better of him. From the government papers he extracted Reyna's old airman medical application and the background check form. He looked for a copy machine and found a brand new one in a side room. Better yet, it had paper, toner, and was already powered up. Not for the first time, he saw that Marquez was a good organizer. The man had El Centro running smoothly in little more than a day, not the usual chaos of monitors without cables, cameras with bad lenses, and an unreliable electrical supply. The crash site recovery effort was also gathering steam, and soon would begin the chore of moving wreckage to long-term storage. It would probably be housed in a nearby hangar or warehouse. Davis was sure the colonel had that under control as well.

He replicated the two documents and the photographs of both pilots, then folded all four copies to fit in his pocket. From a supply table he pilfered two cheap ballpoint pens and a pad of Post-it notes. Davis put the files back together just as he'd found them, squaring them neatly on the desk with his fingertips. He was energized by what he'd found, yet at the same time cautious. Fatigue weighed on his body. Part of him wanted to stay all night, digging and sifting, but he knew that at a point it became counterproductive. He needed sleep because he wanted to be sharp tomorrow. He bid a friendly *buenos noches* to a pair of soldiers manning the night shift, and as he reached the door the thought recurred and began looping in his head.

Marquez was good.

Almost too good.

He walked into the viscous night air and shook the notion away. He smelled the soot from passing cars and the tang of seasoned meat on a grill. The bar across the street was running a lively patio affair. The city glittered yellow in the distance, and above that he saw a bewildered sky, broken clouds reflecting urban light in some quarters, and elsewhere opening up to the stars. A night unresolved, looking for direction.

Davis picked up his pace.

It was midnight on Monday.

He had a great deal to think about.

* * *

Davis wrenched off his shoes and stretched out on the bed. The springs creaked under his weight, and a paper-thin pillow did little to cradle the knot on the back of his skull. His third dose of Motrin had done the trick—the headache he'd woken with was gone, as was the soreness from spending a night on a concrete floor. Unfortunately, the biggest ache of all was more acute than ever.

He closed his eyes and, as was his custom in any investigation, made a concise mental scorecard of what he'd accomplished.

The results were decidedly more troubling than usual. Escape from prison—check. Visit plane crash from which daughter's body was missing—check. The day's findings bounced in his brain like plastic balls in a lotto tumbler. He knew the problem. Every fact and facet, every theory and indicator, was colored by one insurmountable backdrop.

Jen.

His list of advances, such as they were, remained encouraging on one level—he had not yet visited the morgue to identify a body. Most of his findings were little more than negatives, things he'd proved *hadn't* happened. For all the effort, Davis was no closer to finding his daughter, or even proving that she was alive. He would give anything for one shred of proof, one phone call from a hospital or a reliable witness who'd caught a glimpse of a survivor. As it was, he was clinging to the same brittle hopefulness he'd arrived with.

On the nightstand he saw his most notable discovery: Jen's iPod. How many times had he given her that warning on a flight? *Don't put anything valuable in the seatback pocket. You'll forget it.* He was mildly discouraged she hadn't listened, but it proved she'd been on board. And he was buoyed by the tangible connection to his daughter.

Davis had begun charging the device as soon as he'd reached the room, and now he hit the power button and watched the cheerful little screen spring to life. He scanned his options and touched the music symbol, then scrolled through menus to a playlist called "Jen's Faves." He wondered what his daughter was listening to these days. He recalled posters of boy bands on her bedroom wall, but that was a long time ago. He scanned three pages of songs. A few he recognized, but most were a mystery, artless soul that he was. He wished she'd shared them with him. Wished he had taken the time to ask.

The earbuds were still attached to the device, and he unwrapped the wires from the case and stuffed them in his ears. Drowned out were the Bogotá traffic and the rush of an airliner taking off in the distance. The first track that flowed was an instrumental jazz piece by a group called Down to the Bone. It was good.

Davis listened and relaxed, the music sweeping his mind clear like a cool gust of wind. His thoughts drifted as another song began, misty jazz, vocals this time. *Since when did she listen to jazz?* He closed his eyes and succumbed to stillness.

As the miller told his tale
That her face, at first just ghostly,
Turned a whiter shade of pale

Davis drifted off in the middle of the fifth song, the time on the clock having lost all meaning. He slept surprisingly well, feeling closer to his daughter than he had in a very long time.

ELEVEN

"*Donde es hospital?*" Davis asked in butchered Spanish.

He'd woken late, thrown on his clothes, and rushed to the hotel lobby. The woman behind the desk, a smiling and bosomy matron who certainly had grandchildren somewhere, replied, "*Cúal?*"

Which one?

Davis said, "Kennedy."

She tapped a spot on the city map pressed under a sheet of glass on her counter. The map was colorful and dotted with cartoonlike drawings of museums and children's carousels.

She said, "*Taxi, a diez minutos,*" and held up ten fingers to be sure he understood.

"Taxi," he replied, nodding vigorously.

The merciful woman phoned him a cab, and Davis gave her a *muchas gracias* before heading outside. While he waited, he was happy to find an English-language daily at a corner newsstand, and happier still that the vendor didn't mind taking a U.S. dollar for it—he still hadn't found time for things like currency exchange.

Minutes later he was en route to Al Hospital Occidente de Kennedy, his life in the hands of a cabbie whose eyewear resembled shot glasses. If the man had a visual deficiency he didn't seem to care as he wove through traffic like a slalom skier. Thinking it better not to watch, Davis hung on tight and flicked through *The City Paper*.

He found five paragraphs relating to the crash of TAC-Air Flight 223, all of it on page three beneath a grainy photograph of the crash site—one that he was sure had been taken from Marquez' Huey. Yesterday the accident had been front page news, but interest was fading quickly. There were no scintillating pictures, no Hollywood celebrities or soccer stars unaccounted for. Better yet, more entertaining stories had found traction—the mayor had a new mistress, and a particularly nasty presidential race in the United States was heating up. Davis tossed the paper aside. He suspected that if Marquez were to make his hijacking theory public, the crash would quickly move back to page one.

He tried to steer his mind to positive thoughts, but it was hopeless. His daughter was missing and presumed dead, and so a visit to the city morgue could be approached with nothing less than trepidation. Davis forced his eyes outside and studied the city around him. He was reminded of Albuquerque, a blend of old and new, all trying to breathe in the thin air over a mile above sea level. Bogotá, of course, was on a larger scale, twenty million people living in a bowl carved by mountains, the biggest of these being Monserrate with its orange cable cars and moody cloud cover. Like so many cities, a place full of inviting corners, but one that collectively remained at arm's length.

On reaching the hospital he settled with the driver, and after fencing with a receptionist in broken Spanish, Davis was directed to the basement level. At the foot of a staircase he found bilingual placards on a stone wall listing a number of departments, including radiation oncology and nuclear medicine. With two minutes to spare, he found Marquez. The colonel was standing under a sign that was written only in Spanish, but one that even Davis could translate: *Depósito de Cadáveres.*

The cadaver depository.

Marquez was not alone. Standing next to him was a man in uniform, although not one issued by either the Colombian Army or Air Force. If Davis were to lay odds, he would say he was looking at a policeman. The two men looked tense as they conversed in hushed Spanish.

Marquez spotted him coming, and with a raised hand, he cut

the other man off in midsentence. "Thank you for coming," he said to Davis, shaking his hand with businesslike formality. "This is Major Raul Echevarria. He represents the Bogotá Region One Police, Special Investigations Unit."

Davis was inwardly pleased at the accuracy of his guess.

The two Colombians were standing next to an air-conditioning grate, probably an acquired behavior this close to the equator, and when Davis shook the man's hand it was cool and moist, like a wad of wet clay. Echevarria was a big man, almost as tall as Davis but padded in the middle, an effect magnified as he stood next to the smaller Marquez. His uniform was quilted with embroidered insignia, and thin wings of hair puffed from the sides of a blue beret. A Saddam Hussein mustache stood front and center, and most prominent of all was a set of coal-black eyes, frayed powder at the edges—it was like looking down a pair of gun barrels.

The major smiled, perhaps a bit more than he should have, and asked, "Is this your first time in Colombia, Mr. Davis?"

"I was here once before, a long time ago," he replied, suspecting this was something Echevarria already knew.

"Marquez tells me you are a good detective."

The policeman's decoupling of Marquez with his superior rank of colonel was not lost on Davis. He had seen such dynamics before, brusque interactions between military and police forces that typically functioned independently. In the best case it evolved to no more than healthy competition, committed individuals who answered to separate chains of command. In the worst case, careerist officers butted heads with corrupt government ministries, or even loosely tethered criminal elements. As a general rule, Davis stayed clear of infighting. If time wasn't critical, he might have left right then for the nearest place that served coffee and eggs.

He said, "If I was *really* good none of us would be here right now. We'd all be in our offices writing after-action reports." Echevarria almost replied, but Davis cut him off. "If there's something here to see, let's get on with it. I've got a lot on my plate right now."

Marquez said, "Yes, we all do. The medical examiner has completed her autopsy of the two pilots. Because certain findings suggest criminal involvement, the police must take part in our inquiry."

Davis didn't argue—there *were* criminal matters at hand. He did not, however, like this new trajectory. In certain countries, all air crashes were subject to mandatory criminal investigations. Police with zero knowledge of aviation plundered evidence and harangued witnesses, while attention-seeking prosecutors spouted cockeyed theories to the media. The United States took a very different approach. Air safety was considered paramount, and so NTSB investigators were given exclusive authority. They granted broad immunities to aircrew, mechanics, and air traffic controllers in exchange for the full and absolute truth. Barring willful negligence, the criminal justice system kept its big nose out. This latter model was widely recognized as the most significant advance to air safety since the seat belt, even if it did little to advance the careers of tort lawyers and prosecutors. Wishing he were in Kansas, Davis said, "Are we talking about a full criminal probe, Major, or are you here to observe?"

"Hijacking is a serious matter," Echevarria said in a light tone that was at odds with his words. "Here in Bogotá—"

"Here in Bogotá," Marquez interrupted, "we have an ambitious general prosecutor who cares less about victims than what he can do for himself. I think we will see a great deal of Major Echevarria." The two Colombians exchanged a look that discarded any pretenses of civility.

Davis thought, *I really don't need this.* He said, "Let's hear what the medical examiner has to say."

Echevarria led inside the morgue, no doubt familiar turf for an officer of the Bogotá Special Investigations Unit. The place looked and smelled like every other morgue Davis had visited. Clammy and cool, the schizophrenic lighting was eerily subdued in some quarters, and blazed like a supernova in others. The decorator had settled on gray as the dominant color, walls the hue of a battleship, a spalled concrete floor, and dull steel furnishings. At the far end of the room were two sheet-shrouded metal tables under harsh examination lights. A woman in scrubs was waiting. More greetings were exchanged with the medical examiner, a genial woman named Rosa Guzman, and she launched right into her briefing. Thankfully, her English was superb.

"All remains from the crash site have been brought here to our facility. Last night I performed postmortems on the two pilots. As requested by Colonel Marquez, this was our first priority due to the evidence of gunshot wounds."

Arriving at the first examining table, Davis recognized the copilot, Moreno. The autopsy had run its course, and he'd been stitched back together with all possible dignity and left in a restful supine pose. The body was very different from how Davis had last seen it, sprawled on top of the captain and wedged against a circuit breaker panel. Guzman launched into a detailed summary of her findings, much of which went over Davis' head. Professionals everywhere liked to impress laymen. The salient points for Davis: Moreno had been shot once at close range in the back of the head, and he displayed a host of other injuries that had likely occurred after death, all of these consistent with the trauma of an air crash.

When she finished, Marquez and Echevarria seemed satisfied.

Davis asked, "Can you tell what time he died?"

Guzman referenced a clipboard hanging from a hook on the examining table. "I set the time at nine o'clock on the night of the crash."

"One hour after takeoff," Marquez said helpfully.

Davis looked at Marquez, then the ME. "*Exactly* nine o'clock? That's pretty precise. Isn't there usually a window?" Davis saw an exchange of confused glances, and he realized his linguistic error. "I mean, isn't there a range?"

Guzman said, "There are always assumptions in such estimates. The postmortem interval, the time between death and when I examined the victim, was nearly two days, so, yes, there is definitely room for error. I would say plus or minus three hours is a certainty."

Davis nodded, and he asked no more questions. Neither did anyone else, and they moved on to Captain Reyna.

The captain's body was in worse shape. Same sutures, same restful pose, but bearing the severe cranial damage Davis had noted in the field. Guzman's second briefing was much like the first, and she looked directly at him when she said, "The time of death is roughly consistent."

"Roughly," Davis said.

"If anything, it might be a bit earlier." Guzman pointed to an advancing green hue on Reyna's stomach. "That is putrefaction, bacteria beginning the process of decay. It is more advanced in this body, but not significantly so."

Echevarria launched into an extensive line of questions regarding the bullet entry and exit wounds, which Guzman tackled capably. He then asked Marquez, "Have you found the slugs yet?"

Marquez replied defensively, "We are in the process of recovering an entire airliner from a jungle basin. It will take time to find and identify every small piece of debris."

"This shooting should be your most important task," the policeman countered with newfound gravity. "I am going to send my own team to the crash site. Clearly we are facing a criminal investigation."

"Do as you like," said Marquez, "but they will not be riding on my helicopter."

With that the floodgates opened. Marquez and Echevarria began a hushed argument that reverted to Spanish. Fingers jabbed the air, and soon they withdrew to an office to take turns using the phone—apparently cell reception in the basement was nil. When Guzman left to play referee, Davis saw his chance.

Still standing beside Reyna's body, he reached into his pocket and pulled out the ink pens he'd pilfered the previous night. Having already unscrewed the tops, he extracted one plastic ink sleeve and cracked it between his fingers. He rubbed the resulting seep-age of ink over Reyna's right thumb, and then pulled out the Post-it notepad. He rolled Reyna's finger over the pad, but there was too much ink and his first result was nothing but a blotchy mess. With a glance at the glass barrier between the examination room and the office, he discarded the top note and tried again. This time he got a crude but usable print.

Guzman reappeared and Davis pocketed everything, his fin-gers working blindly to fold an unused note from the pad over the good impression.

Guzman gave him a suffering look as the donnybrook con-tinued in her office. "Is there anything else I can tell you?" she asked.

"Actually, there is," he replied. "I'd like to take a quick look at another body—one of the passengers."

"You have the name or identity tag number?"

"Thomas Mulligan."

Guzman checked a board on the wall, found the name, and led Davis toward a row of holding drawers.

"Have you inspected this body yet?" he asked as she was reaching for a handle.

"No, a technician does our receiving, and I've been busy examining the pilots." She pulled out the drawer and looked at Thomas Mulligan for the first time.

Davis watched Guzman. He saw the recognition in her eyes.

Then the surprise on her face.

* * *

How the world around him worked had long been a mystery to Martin Stuyvesant. It was the simple things that most bedeviled him. His father, rarely present in his youth, had never taught him how to use a screwdriver or shut off the water to a toilet. His mother, rarely sober, had never taught him how to cook, although one of her less surly lovers, a tattoo-sleeved short order cook, had once given a rambling dissertation regarding the various grades of deep-fryer oil. Some years ago Stuyvesant had misplaced his wallet and left it at that—an imperceptible loss really, since he rarely had cash to carry in it, and because he didn't keep a driver's license since he didn't own a car. The everyday machinations of life did not exist for Stuyvesant, which at times simplified things. The downside was that it made him highly dependent on others.

Presently he was standing behind a cauldron of stew in a south Tampa soup kitchen, ladling a large helping of chipped beef onto a mound of mashed potatoes. The glutinous concoction spread a bit too far, slopping over the side of the plate, and from there onto the shoe of his customer.

"Goddammit!" croaked the man, a ruffian of no less than sixty who sported a week's gray stubble on his deeply lined face.

"I'm so sorry," said Stuyvesant, not that he really was. *Ungrateful bastard.*

The old man wiped his shoe on the opposite trouser cuff and moved on.

"Not such a large portion," whispered the kindly woman to his left who was dishing out the potatoes.

The line shifted, and Stuyvesant dropped another, smaller dollop onto the next mound of instant spuds.

"It's really quite tasty," Stuyvesant said to the woman. She was the lead volunteer, and the two of them had already shared an early lunch before she'd put him to work as a server. She was the usual sort one came across in these places, a well-meaning woman, perhaps slightly younger than Stuyvesant. He thought her attractive, in an oddly philanthropic way. During lunch she'd thanked him for volunteering, and told him she wished there were more people like him who were willing to pitch in and help, her entire sermon interspersed with lamentations about the shelter's lack of funds. Stuyvesant feigned interest while casting fleeting glances at the deep cleavage behind her earth-tone smock—made from recycled plastic bags—and by the end of the apple cobbler she had twice decisively brushed his hand from her knee. It was a silly fantasy, but one of the few pleasures Stuyvesant managed anymore.

He had a wife, somewhere, but the relationship had long existed only on paper.

Stuyvesant was about to deliver the next serving, targeting the oncoming mound of potatoes like an archer would a bull's-eye, when the man holding the tray abruptly grabbed his wrist. A surprised Stuyvesant looked up to see a downtrodden Hispanic man, perhaps thirty years old with tea-brown skin and a weary gaze. Both men stood still for a moment, frozen in a hesitant grasp. A large and alert man behind Stuyvesant, who was there for security, noticed right away and took a step forward. The Hispanic man chose that moment to smile and let go, and then he held out a small card which Stuyvesant took cautiously. He saw a biblical verse on the front: *For the wages of sin is death, but the gift of God is eternal life in Christ Jesus our Lord.*

Stuyvesant smiled, pocketed the card, and dumped half a pound of glutinous beef and gravy on the man's potatoes. The Hispanic shuffled toward the green beans, Stuyvesant addressed his next customer, and the large man behind him went back to watching.

The early bird lunch shift ended uneventfully, and not wanting to get stuck with cleanup duty, Stuyvesant bid goodbye to his coworkers, a group he would certainly never see again. He left by the back door, as was his custom, and paused outside to flex his bum knee. It hurt like hell, and he reached into his pocket for a newly acquired stash of Percocet. He swallowed two pills dry—a learned skill—and slipped the tiny bottle back into his pocket. His hand came back out holding the card he'd been given. He was about to flick it into a nearby trash can when he noticed something handwritten on the back, a message in English. It was brief and to the point. After reading through it twice, Stuyvesant closed his eyes and raised his face toward the heavens.

"Christ!" he muttered through taut lips.

Martin Stuyvesant's worst fears had just come true.

TWELVE

Thomas Mulligan was an Anglo male, late thirties with dark hair that was clipped short and neat, a cut that would have passed inspection in any man's army. Three days ago he'd been in excellent physical condition, something of a runner's build but more broad in the shoulders. The passenger list Davis had seen yesterday declared him to be an American citizen traveling to Colombia on business. There was little else to go on, other than the fact that he'd arrived on a connecting flight from Atlanta, the same connection four other passengers had made, including Jen and Kristin Stewart. That was all good information, but none of it explained what he and the medical examiner were looking at now.

Guzman pulled a small penlight from her pocket and inspected two wounds in the center of Mulligan's chest. Davis thought they correlated reasonably well with the holes he'd found in the back of seat 7C, and he was sure Guzman would find matching exit wounds on Mulligan's back. As if to confirm the thought, she rolled the body far enough to shine her light underneath.

"Gunshot wounds," Davis said. It wasn't a question.

"How did you know about this?" she asked.

"I didn't know—not for sure. I found two holes in the back of his seat, holes that I couldn't explain any other way."

Guzman shouted across the room, and the two querulous officers called a truce long enough to join them. Guzman explained what they were looking at.

Echevarria addressed Davis, "You discovered bullet holes in this man's seat? Why did you not mention it sooner?"

"I saw two holes . . . but I didn't know what made them. Any airplane that's been in a crash has a thousand new holes, caused by everything from fragmented turbine blades to hail impact. Bullets are rarely on my list of causal factors."

"In this case they will have to be," said Echevarria.

For once Marquez agreed with his rival. "Perhaps this man threatened our hijacker. Or Umbriz could have shot him as an example to the others. That would make sense—this man was the most fit passenger on the airplane, and therefore might be viewed as the biggest threat."

Davis stood very still. He felt everyone looking at him, waiting for a response. He gave them nothing.

Echevarria's glib tone returned. "This is only more reason for my office to undertake a full investigation. I will insist on full cooperation from both of you." Notwithstanding his words, the man was indifference itself in pressed fatigues.

Marquez nodded, and Davis sensed an unusual acquiescence—a colonel ceding command to a junior officer.

"Am I clear, Mr. Davis?" the chipper policeman reiterated. "I want your complete cooperation."

Davis only stared, and perhaps to end the impasse, Dr. Guzman pushed Thomas Mulligan back into cold storage. The drawer clunked shut with apt finality, and three detectives with widely angled agendas walked away in silence.

The light outside was blinding, and the heat had taken its sullen grip.

"Are you going back to headquarters?" Davis asked Marquez.

The colonel nodded. "I have a briefing this afternoon. Do you need a ride?"

"Yeah . . . and maybe a cup of coffee."

"Yes. I think I could use one as well."

They both looked at Echevarria, and Davis said, "Why don't you join us, Major?"

The policeman considered it before nodding. "Yes, I would very much like that." He edged away to make a phone call.

While he was out of earshot, Marquez said, "I have worked with Echevarria before. He's a bastard, that one."

"I don't doubt it," Davis replied, "but I'm forced to take the greater view. Right now he's an asset. If the Bogotá police can help find my daughter—I'll deal with the devil himself."

*　*　*

Marquez drove to a place called Calle Setenta, a string of shops and cafés in the financial district. Echevarria took his own car, so Davis sat in front with the colonel. The air conditioner was feeble, and Davis steered the vents to his face. The sun was higher now, beating the morning into submission and driving bystanders into narrow shadows.

Marquez spent most of the journey on the phone, but drove slowly and deliberately, making for a far different experience from the morning's cab ride. With the colonel doubly occupied, Davis withdrew to his own thoughts. He was increasingly uncomfortable with the way things were progressing. In most investigations time was on his side. Victims were either deceased, recovering in hospital beds, or seated in interview rooms. Wreckage was rarely perishable, and thus could be collected and analyzed at a leisurely, professional pace. To slow-roll reports and findings in the name of accuracy was commonplace, even encouraged. Here, however, patience seemed anything but a virtue. The primary difference was his daughter, yet Davis sensed something more at play, a niggling worry that some unseen clock was working against him.

Marquez parked on a street lined by colorful awnings, and they reconnected with Echevarria and walked into a busy café. The colonel asked for a table in the shade, and they were seated on the patio under a big red-and-blue umbrella. The three men made a triangle at a table built for four, Davis at the vertex. One American outflanked by two Colombians. Even so, he sensed that this wasn't any kind of two-versus-one scenario. It was more like the training scenario he would brief up, years ago, when leading a three-ship formation of F-16s. A one-on-one-on-one dogfight.

Every man for himself. He remembered those contests well, free-wheeling affairs in which the shifts from enemy to ally, and back again, were instantaneous and unpredictable. At least until somebody took a simulated missile up their tailpipe. At that point it became one against one. And nothing in the world was more clear than that.

Davis ordered white coffee, Marquez a double espresso, and Echevarria a latte, and when all of it arrived a certain measure of civility was restored. Couples in fine Italian clothes weaved between sidewalk planters, and hanging flowerpots all around them burst waves of color. Take away the equatorial heat, Davis thought, and they might have been in Milan or Barcelona.

"I have never seen such a case," Marquez reflected.

"Neither have I," agreed Davis. "We've got two passengers missing and three fatalities with gunshot wounds."

Echevarria asked Davis, "Have you ever dealt with a hijacking before?"

"No, and I'm still not convinced we're dealing with one here."

"How can you say that?" argued Marquez. "You heard the examiner's report. The pilots both died of gunshot wounds. What more proof do you need?"

"To begin with, I'd like to find the captain."

Davis watched both men closely. Echevarria wore wrap-around sunglasses, so all Davis saw were reflections from the street and the glint of the sun. Marquez simply froze, his espresso hovering over the table.

"What are you saying?" asked the policeman.

"I'm saying the man we saw on that gurney was not Blas Reyna."

Marquez' eyes narrowed, the tiny cup still hovering.

"I first noticed it at the crash site. Something about the captain's body didn't seem right. He had severe injuries from the crash, no doubt about that. But there was almost no blood. With that kind of trauma to the head and face, it should have been everywhere. And there was something else, although it didn't hit me until later—the guy's uniform didn't fit. Not even close. The pants were too long at the ankle, a good four inches, and his shirt collar was so tight the top button had to be left undone. I've seen circus clowns with better tailors. Very unprofessional."

Marquez set down his cup. "And on this you question his identity. That is loco, my friend."

"No, what's loco is that the body we just saw was measured out very precisely by the medical examiner to be five foot eight."

"What is wrong with that?"

Davis produced exhibit number one from his pocket. "In the back of Reyna's government file is an original airman medical application—I made a copy last night." Davis laid it on the table. "I think the Spanish word is *altura*. I'm American, so I had to convert from metric, but math was my best subject in school. According to that document, Blas Reyna is six foot one."

"That is all?" said Marquez. "You base this incredible accusation on one ancient piece of paper?"

"No, that's what made me look closer. Next I checked Moreno, the first officer, and he came out at five foot nine—again excuse my units. His paperwork matches perfectly with the examiner's measurements. Are you with me so far?"

Echevarria appeared relaxed, even entertained, and leaned back in his chair. Marquez nodded uncomfortably as Davis pulled out exhibits two and three. "These are the official photos of the two pilots. Of course, we can only see from the shoulders up, but I'm sure they're standing against the same wall. If you look at the TAC-Air logo in the background you can see that Reyna is significantly taller than Moreno. So unless Reyna decided to stand on a box for this picture . . . " Davis let his words hang.

As Marquez looked at the photographs his indignation subsided, and he went back to sipping his espresso. Behind his sunglasses Echevarria had gone blank, like the good poker player he probably was. Davis was sure he had everyone's attention.

"What about Reyna's TAC-Air ID?" Davis prodded. "Is that

what someone was about to ask? It was found on the body right where it should have been, clipped to his shirt pocket. As it turns out, Reyna was issued a brand-new company ID only a few weeks ago. It lists him as five foot eight."

The Colombians sat silently.

"Now, I know this is all confusing, but it won't be hard to find the right answer. Anybody who knew Reyna, a friend or a sister or a chief pilot, could tell you how tall he was. I'm betting six foot one is the answer. If I'm right, the three of us face a very uncomfortable question. Why was his corporate ID recently altered to match the physical characteristics of another man, one who would soon be found in the cockpit of a crashed airliner?"

Marquez thumped his empty cup on the table. "This is ridiculous! You can't really believe the body we found in the cockpit is *not* that of the captain!"

Davis pursed his lips and considered it. "Going into that morgue . . . yeah, that's what I thought."

"But now?" Echevarria asked.

Davis took a long draw on his coffee, then removed the last photocopy from his pocket, the Colombian Ministry of Transportation background check on Reyna. At the bottom right of the page was a clear thumbprint. He then pulled the Post-it pad from his pocket, which had the comparative print he'd taken from the body on the gurney. He set the two side by side on the table.

"These are from Reyna?" Marquez asked.

"Yes. One I just took from the body in the morgue, and the other is from Reyna's file. What do you think?"

Earlier, in a moment when the two officers were sparring, Davis had made his own brief comparison. He was no fingerprint expert, but the results were clear enough. He looked at the policeman, who would have the most knowledgeable opinion.

Echevarria confirmed the obvious. "I would say you have a solid match."

"I agree."

"So it *is* Reyna's body we saw this morning," said Marquez.

To which Davis replied, "It seems clear enough by these fingerprints. The one from Reyna's file matches the thumb on the body perfectly. But last night I noticed something about the background check paperwork. This form with Reyna's thumbprint, it was filled out fifteen years ago, the day he got hired. Only if you look at the bottom of the page, in very small print in the corner, this government form was revised last year." Davis let that stand for a moment before surmising, "Add that to the discrepancy in his height, and I'd say there's only one solution. While it pains me to say it, gentlemen . . . somebody is tampering with this investigation."

Echevarria and Marquez exchanged a look. Davis saw concern on the faces of both men, and in that moment he was struck by how widely varied their agendas were. He could almost see their thoughts brewing, see angles being measured. He also knew it was hopeless to try and read them. Davis could only go about his search with a newfound suspicion, checking and double-checking every new fact.

"We will get to the bottom of this," Echevarria said dismissively.

"Agreed," said Marquez. "If the body is not Reyna's, a family member can easily tell us."

"True," Davis said. "But if it's *not* Reyna, then it opens up two more questions. Why was this done? And—"

"Where is the real Reyna?" Echevarria finished.

Davis nodded.

With cautious words, they all agreed that settling the discrepancy was a top priority. Echevarria finished his drink and was the first to leave.

A subdued Marquez checked his phone for messages.

"Anything new?" Davis asked.

"No, there is nothing—other than the fuel you have thrown onto our fire."

Davis was contemplating a smart comeback when Marquez added, "I advise you once more to use caution with Echevarria.

He is the least trustworthy policeman I have ever dealt with . . . and here that is saying something."

"Caution noted. But like I said, right now he's just another guy out there looking for Jen." Davis pushed back from the table. "I need a ride back to headquarters. I want to head out to the crash site."

"I can take you."

Before they left, Davis went to the cashier's counter. He bought six cups of coffee and was given a cardboard tray to carry them in.

"What is that for?" asked Marquez.

"Your headquarters team."

"A display of kindness?"

"Not really. I just thought it might make everyone work a little faster."

* * *

"He just bought a gallon of coffee with his credit card," said the man.

The woman across from him in the G Street suite said, "The guy is huge. He could drink that much."

The man, noted for having a stunted sense of humor, frowned and glanced toward the open hallway door. "Should we tell them?"

An emergency meeting had convened down the hall, in the electronically swept main conference room. Neither of them had been invited because decision-making was not their realm. They were cyber-specialists, here to gather, filter, and forward raw data. Since there had been precious little of that so far, there was a serious temptation to pass along the coffee purchase.

Muted shouts rose from the conference room down the hall, the second outburst from a meeting that had been in session only five minutes.

"I'll leave it up to you," she said.

The man sunk back in his chair. "I've never seen them this

agitated. What do you think has got them so riled? Something to do with the crash in South America?"

She shrugged. "All I know is that I'd hate to be Davis. The guy has stumbled into a hornet's nest and doesn't even realize it. Whatever's happening," she cocked her head toward the hall, "it's making some important people very nervous."

They both heard a door slam.

"I think I'll log the coffee purchase with the afternoon brief," he said, dragging and dropping the electronic file into a slim group of findings that would be forwarded en masse later that day. His favorite capture was a cache of photos from the morgue at Hospital Occidente de Kennedy. The hospital's password protection for their security system had been laughable, but then imagination clearly wasn't a long suit in Colombia if they were naming their hospitals after dead American presidents. There was more, of course, including the exact times Davis' hotel room door had opened—indicators of when he'd returned last night and left this morning. They had already correlated those events with raw position data from the phone, which was pinging every sixty seconds.

The woman said, "Did you add in what he ran through the copy machine?"

"Of course. By the way—that was good. I never knew we could do that."

"Simple enough. The copier is wireless, connected to the network. Most are these days. But I don't know what to make of the stuff he copied. An old medical application from the captain, photographs of both pilots. What do you think he's on to?"

"I don't know. Davis is the expert."

"Let's hope."

"Should we try again for a voice stream from the mic on his phone?"

"No, don't bother, it puts too big a drain on the battery. As long as he keeps it in his back pocket the audio pickup is marginal anyway."

They began tidying up, their shift nearly over. The man had just finished the checklist for the afternoon changeover briefing when a two-tone chime sounded on his partner's desktop.

She held up a finger to tell him to wait. "Hold on . . . we might have one more thing to add. He's making a phone call."

THIRTEEN

Larry Green was slogging through his next year's budget request when the phone on his desk rang. He saw the caller ID and picked up immediately.

"Talk to me, Jammer."

"Hey, Larry. It's good to hear a familiar voice."

"Tell me about Jen."

Green heard a heavy sigh. "It's not bad, not good. We have two bodies unaccounted for, and she's one of them. They're searching a marshy area where the tail separated. The two missing passengers were sitting in the last row, so the standing theory is that they were ejected."

"What do you think?"

A pause. "I don't know . . . it's possible, but I'm not giving up."

"You never do. I'm glad you called, the chairman is getting pressure for an update."

"Chairman . . . as in the chairman of NTSB? Since when is an RJ going down in South America such big a deal?"

"Maybe things are slow. Then again, it's that time of year. Congressmen always get nervous around election time, not to mention all the agencies fighting for next year's funding. Maybe NTSB didn't have enough high-profile crashes this fiscal year to justify our budget."

"Speaking of budget, am I getting paid for this?"

Green chuckled. "Let me guess—you ran out of cash and you're getting hungry. Let's call it your usual consulting deal. I'll push the paperwork through. So what's the latest on the crash?"

"The latest is that our investigator-in-charge, Colonel Marquez, is convinced we're looking at a hijacking."

"Hijacking?" The retired general went stiff in his seat.

"The cockpit door appears to have been forced open. And the first officer was killed execution style, a bullet to the back of his head."

"Jesus. What about the captain?"

"His story is a little less clear. I'm working on it."

"Do we know who's responsible?"

"No idea. But one of the passengers was found in the copilot's seat."

"That's not good. The feds over at JTTF will want to know about this. Any idea who the alleged hijacker was? Any terrorist ties? Did he have any flying experience?"

"Marquez has just started looking into his background, but so far there's nothing of note. Before Saturday he was a sixty-two-year-old chef from Cartagena."

Green stared blankly at the wall. "A chef."

"Pastries, apparently. You know—éclairs and cream puffs."

"Cream puffs? That's my briefing point to the directors of Homeland Security and National Intelligence? I'm telling you, Jammer, for reasons I do not understand this crash is raising a shitstorm, and I'd sure like a little more than that when I dance on their carpets this afternoon."

"I could give you some lessons."

"No thanks, I've seen your moves and they're not pretty." Green blew out a long breath. "This hijacking theory—you say it's being put out there by Marquez. Do *you* buy it?"

The pause was too long.

"Jammer?"

"I don't know. Just trust me, skipper. I can tell you that Marquez is keeping the hijacking angle quiet for now. We need time to confirm some things. Oh, and one of the passengers was also shot."

"Do you have a name?"

Another hesitation. "No, there was some confusion in the seating assignments—you know how that goes. I'll pass the name along when we have a firm ID."

"All right," Green said.

"I should also tell you that the Colombian Police have gotten involved."

"That's never good, but I suppose it's no surprise given that bullets were flying."

"Right. Listen, Larry, I gotta get back to work. I'll call again when I have more."

"All right, Jammer. Good luck finding Jen."

"Yeah . . . thanks."

After the click Green sat still, his hand glued to the phone. Davis had told him a great deal, yet one sentence lodged in his head.

Just trust me, skipper.

Four words that could not have been more carefully crafted.

It took him back eighteen years, to a mission over Spangdahlem, Germany. Green had been a rising major, an instructor pilot, and Davis a green first lieutenant. They were flying a pair of F-16s, tearing through the sky on a five-hundred-knot low-level run, three hundred feet above the ground. The world was rocketing past, a Star Wars onrush in the front windscreen, nothing but a blur in the periphery. Green's job as flight lead was to navigate to the target, masking behind terrain and watching for obstacles. As the wingman, Davis had but one sacred duty—hang tight.

They were twenty miles from the target that day when the weather began to deteriorate. The ceiling above was a hard deck, a thousand feet over their heads at the beginning of the route. Yet slowly, insidiously, the clouds crept lower, and when their canopies began skimming the bottoms at three hundred feet, Green did the only sage thing. He rocked his wings, bringing Davis into close formation, and aborted the run, the two fighters climbing into the gray overcast as one.

It was a standard contingency plan—a weather route abort.
Everything pre-briefed and by the book. Davis was rock solid, his
wingtip two feet from Green's as they climbed at full thrust into
the soup. Then everything went wrong. Green became distracted.
He tried to raise air traffic control on the radio for a new clearance, tried to enter new navigation points in his jet's computer, all
while flying a smooth platform for his wingman. With so much to
do, he never noticed the problem.

In military aviation it is referred to as spatial disorientation,
or spatial-D. When the horizon disappears and clouds take over,
sight naturally becomes secondary to seat-of-the-pants sensory inputs. Vestibular and tactile responses try to take over, but they are
unreliable for orientation. That being the case, pilots are trained
to fly on instruments, exactly as Green had done that day. But
they are also trained to cross-check gauges, and in those very busy
moments Green had come up short. He didn't recognize that his
primary artificial horizon had failed—a one-in-a-million anomaly
the mechanics later told him.

Fortunately, on that morning, he had a one-in-a-million
wingman.

When flying close formation in the weather, a wingman has
but one inviolate duty—don't ding your multimillion dollar wingtip on the other only inches away. It is a time for absolute focus,
for constant small corrections and hand-eye coordination, allowing only the briefest of moments to glance at anything else in the
world. But Davis did glance.

The radio exchange remained fixed in Green's mind like it
was yesterday.

Davis in a calm voice, *"Bones 21, 22."*

Green replied with slight irritation. He was a busy man. *"Go
ahead 22."*

"I'm showing a ninety-degree left bank."

A lengthy pause.

Green remembered looking at his primary attitude indicator,
and seeing everything straight and level. But then a glance at his

standby instrument showed them turning on their heads. *"Uh . . . standby, Bones 22."*

There is perhaps no more sickening feeling in the world than to be rocketing though the clouds at four hundred knots, only to realize you have no idea which way is up.

Davis' voice again, as still as a mountain, *"You okay, Bones 21? We're nearly inverted, nose coming down."*

"My ADI is messed up!" Green recalled the terrible feeling, his head uncaged and spinning like a top as he tried to cross-check and correlate conflicting information. Airspeed, heading, rate of descent. *Big* rate of descent. And most important of all, altitude— the precise distance between two fragile jets and some very hard German countryside. A distance that was fast approaching zero.

"Give me the lead, Bones 21!" Not a fault in the mountain— but definite urgency.

"Bones 22, you have the lead!"

Davis' sleek fighter edged forward and the transition came. Green became the wingman, Davis his only reference to the misty outside world.

Later that night in a quiet debriefing in the squadron bar, and with both men less than sober, they talked about the recovery. Davis had referenced his instruments and confirmed they were screaming toward the ground. There was no time for calculation, no time to estimate the rate of pull-up necessary for survival. Davis could have pulled for all he was worth, a nine-G panic-yank on the controls that would have left a hopelessly disoriented Green alone and pointed toward the earth's mantle at just over the speed of sound. If he had done that, Davis would have saved his own ass, and no accident board in the world would have faulted him. He told Green after their third Jäger shot that he really didn't know the elevation in that area. The ground might have been twenty feet above sea level, might have been two thousand. But Davis, in his first ever maneuver as a flight lead, didn't leave his wingman for dead.

He'd gone for a metered pull-up, a smooth and steady

acceleration that began like a kid's roller coaster and finished like an orbital reentry. On the initial pull, with his orientation still sideways, Green had bobbled in formation for just an instant. That was when he heard the voice again. Steady and true.

"Just trust me, skipper."

And Green had.

They'd bottomed out that day at two hundred feet—Green knew because they briefly broke out underneath the clouds before climbing back into the muck for an uneventful recovery. If Davis had pulled just a bit harder he would have lost Green. If he'd pulled a little less they would have ended up as a pair of smoking holes in perfect formation.

In that critical moment, Jammer Davis had played it perfectly.

There was never any formal report of the incident. Aside from one maintenance write-up on Green's jet to have a faulty attitude system repaired, the events of that day remained between the two of them.

Now Green wondered what new fog he was flying into, wondered which way was up as he sat behind his desk at L'Enfant Plaza. Davis was walking a tightrope in Colombia, and Green wanted desperately to help him. Up against them were strange undercurrents. He was getting heat from above for information, and Davis' hesitation to provide it was obvious. Stuck in between, Green knew where his allegiance lay.

Just trust me, skipper.

Between the two of them it was a private message. An inseparable bond.

Larry Green would do anything for the man who'd saved his life on that bleak autumn day over Germany. Like most who attain the rank of general, he was an action-oriented individual, a Type A who didn't enjoy sitting on the sidelines while his troops engaged in battle. Sometimes, however, you had to do exactly that. Jammer had a daughter at stake, which meant

Colombia was his war. But if a time came when he needed re-inforcements, Green would be ready, because the bond worked both ways.

Jammer was trusting him as well.

*　*　*

At one that afternoon Davis boarded the hourly shuttle to the crash site.

Marquez demurred, remaining at headquarters in order to sling arrows at his latest targets—the identity of Captain Reyna, and the background of the accused hijacker, Umbriz. Davis knew he was useless for that campaign, his fitness for face-to-face inter-views handicapped by the language barrier. All the same, when Marquez encouraged him to head back into the jungle, he won-dered if that was where the colonel thought he'd be most useful, or if it was reflection of the vector their relationship had taken after the morning's accusations. On the surface at least, profes-sionalism ruled the day, but Davis sensed a new lens of mistrust between him and Marquez through which everything would have to be filtered.

On arriving at the crash site, the word that came to Da-vis' mind was *progress*. The first trucks had arrived to transport wreckage, and smaller sections of debris were already being load-ed up for their final journey. He saw two men in police uniforms poking through the fuselage, clearly Echevarria's contingent, and he wondered how they had gotten here so quickly. Certainly not by way of inter-agency cooperation.

Davis bypassed the main debris field and walked east into the wetlands, the area beneath the initial impact zone where the tail had been discovered. This was where Marquez had vowed to keep up the search for the two unrecovered bodies. When he arrived Davis saw no one on the task, and he was momentarily frozen by a terrible idea.

Had the search stopped because they'd succeeded?

Then, mercifully, he spotted two men leaning against a tree, smoking cigarettes, and his panic subsided. Davis approached the pair and launched into a broken conversation in which they confirmed that no additional bodies had been located. They also told him Marquez was going to end the search if nothing was found by the end of the day.

The cigarettes ended, butts went spinning into the wall of ferns, and both men got back to work. They pulled up hip waders, shouldered equipment, and in divergent paths began sweeping their probes left and right, like a pair of electronic lawn sprinklers. They set a loose pattern in the algae-topped water, stirring vegetation and parting thick stands of weeds. It was a primitive way to go about things, but Davis supposed it was effective to a point. A cadaver dog would have been better, yet he doubted there was one within a thousand miles. The marsh seemed exceptionally still, sound dampened by thick carpets of fungus and huge waxen fronds. Visually, it was a place more suited to dinosaurs than a wrecked airliner, a Jurassic topography that would grab things and swallow them, make them disappear for a million years. Davis had an urge to help the men, suggest better ways to go about their search.

But is that what I want? Success here?

His frustration level peaking, Davis decided he needed a little truth. A few fresh, hard facts he could trust and use to make some headway. Standing ankle deep in muck, and with a flying insect the size of a sparrow orbiting his head, he knew there was only one way to get them. Davis turned on a heel, his boot making a giant sucking sound, and began walking back to the main debris field. He would have to go over everything one more time.

FOURTEEN

After a full day in the field, Davis returned to Bogotá on what was becoming his regular flight, the last inbound chopper before nightfall. In his room he showered and changed into fresh clothes, preparing for an evening session at investigation headquarters. Before returning to El Centro, however, he allowed a few minutes of down time. He eased into the room's only chair and fired up Jen's iPod. Collective Soul was next on her playlist, a band he'd heard of, and a soothing track flowed through the wires to sweep clear his cluttered head.

It had been a frustrating afternoon, nine hours of stumbling through rain forest with no noteworthy finds. At least none that changed his outlook. Davis rose briefly to pull the curtains back from the room's only window, and for the first time since arriving regarded the second-floor view. Amber-hued lights played the cityscape of Engativá, the northern Bogotá district that surrounded the airport. The neighborhood was a mix of low-rise businesses, apartments, and a shotgun assortment of restaurants and churches. At this hour the buildings were no more than shadows, and in the valleys between, a vibrant midevening rush played out, the streets alive with traffic and bright-burning neon. Collectively it was like a visual static, light and movement with no cohesion, no common theme or purpose. Not when taken as a whole. But each element made sense in its own right. You only had to look closely, patiently to see the details.

He returned to the chair, earbuds still in place, and tapped his fingers along with the percussion. Davis closed his eyes and imagined Jen doing the same. He had seen it before, his daughter sprawled on the couch with her eyes shut, drumming to a beat. Then the vision dimmed and his fingers went still.

Try as he might, the approach that had comforted him last night was hopeless. Tonight Davis was beyond rescue. The melodies seemed broken, the warm images of Jen interrupted. Instead he found himself logging his paternal shortcomings, which wasn't hard to do. Not involved enough when she was young. Overbearing after Diane's death. If they'd only talked more. Just talked.

What anchored in his mind at the end was not a list of his failings, or even the issue of Jen's fate, which was a cyclone all to itself. Nor was it the burdens of a schizophrenic investigation. The menace that overshadowed everything lay farther afield. Farther to the north.

He felt as if he'd been standing at the edge of a cliff for two days, but was only now opening his eyes. He considered the executive jet he'd taken from Andrews. *A State Department flight making a scheduled run to Bogotá.* That's what Larry Green had said, and probably what he'd been told. Davis knew otherwise. The pilots were on-call contractors, and there had been no one else on board. *Nothing* else on board. No passengers or cargo or secure diplomatic pouches for delivery to the embassy. Someone had chartered a G-III, a *very* expensive bird, for no other reason than to launch him toward Colombia like some kind of guided missile. Next had come the satellite data to pinpoint the crash site. How many times before had Davis asked for such information through NTSB channels? It usually took weeks of infighting and interdepartmental memos just to get a request approved. The result this time—he and Marquez were buried in hard data in less than an hour.

Finally there was his conversation this morning with Larry Green, when his boss mentioned he'd been getting heat for information on the crash. It had been a trigger, causing Davis to do something he'd never done before—hold back the truth from a friend.

He removed the earbuds and walked to the bedside. Setting down Jen's iPod, he picked up the other device on the nightstand—the phone that had been waiting for him when he arrived in Colombia. His own mobile would never have worked here, but without so much as filling out a standard government request form, he'd been issued a replacement. *A woman from the embassy stopped by and left it for you this afternoon.*

Now *there* was some efficiency.

Jammer Davis had spent a career in the military, followed by an afterlife with the NTSB. By virtue of that background, he was a bona fide expert on labyrinthine bureaucracy and administrative ineptitude. He had taken part in dozens of investigations, and in every case made requests for information and equipment. Any fulfillment at all—set aside timeliness and accuracy—was cause for celebration.

And today?

Today he seemingly had the entire United States government at his disposal. A request for a pencil would get him a pallet-load within hours. Ask for a little flight support for aerial photos, and he'd probably get a carrier battle group. He was the beneficiary of a stacked deck, only the cards were being dealt by some unseen hand.

What the hell is going on?

He sat on the side of the bed, and for a long time stared at the room's deepening shadows. Like any detective, his goal was to shine light on things, to peel away layers of confusion and obfuscation until the truth became clear. Yet every time he made headway here, the world got darker. He sensed a greater cataclysm, something bigger than one airplane hitting a jungle. He wondered if Marquez or Echevarria knew anything about it.

Right then Davis reached a decision. He put on his boots and stood, then ordered his phone to check for e-mail. He didn't wait for the results. Leaving the phone on the nightstand, he pocketed his room key and closed the curtains. Davis slipped outside, closing the door softly and leaving the room light on.

* * *

It was seven that evening when Davis bypassed the restaurant across the street, postponing an urgent request from the well of his stomach. He took a cab downtown, asking the driver to drop him in an area where retail stores remained open late. Twenty minutes later he was delivered to someplace called Centro Comercial Andino. It was on the east side of town near the base of the mountains, a three-story mall whose directory boasted the likes of Pandora and Swatch, a place that would have looked right at home in Indianapolis or Atlanta. Davis settled with the driver in dollars and walked west along a wide boulevard, a four-lane affair that was busy in the early evening.

His countersurveillance tactics were rudimentary at best. Davis was not a trained spy, but he doubled back twice and watched for anyone who mirrored his movements. He drifted with the flows on the sidewalk, kept an eye out for recurring faces, and, perhaps in an ode to paranoia, even went to the trouble of stepping on and then off a municipal bus. Satisfied he was alone, he turned away from the mall, passing a busy faux British pub, and rounding a cemetery where every mildewed grave marker seemed to be topped with fresh-bundled flowers. After fifteen minutes of maneuvering he found what he wanted, a second-tier commercial strip. He steered into a family-operated convenience store that sold a little bit of everything, and emerged, one hundred and fifty U.S. dollars later, with two prepaid burner phones.

Walking back toward the mall, Davis activated the first phone. He boarded a busy escalator, and as he rose dialed one of the few phone numbers in the world etched into his private cloud memory.

On the third ring Anna Sorensen answered.

FIFTEEN

Anna Sorensen was blond, attractive, and had been immovably lodged in Davis' head for the better part of three years. They'd met while investigating a crash in France, Davis assigned to the inquiry by Larry Green, and Sorensen by her own government handlers. The truth behind that air accident had been both spectacular and combustible, as was the on-again off-again relationship the two of them had managed ever since. Their union was a tectonic thing—stable and hopeful for periods, but fracturing regularly along the fault lines of their professional lives. Davis was often on the road, and recently had been sidetracked by getting Jen out of the house and settled in college. Sorensen kept an equally unstable existence, one that had recently seen her move to the Far East, then back to Virginia in a matter of months.

For all their disconnects, however, the connects were worth it. Intimate highs outweighed crashing lows. Davis had not heard her voice in two months, after an awkward chapter in which he'd floated the idea of them sharing his suddenly too-large house. Sorensen had nearly accepted, but wavered over a possible reassignment to Europe. Three awkward dinner dates later, the new rift finalized.

Two months was their customary interval of separation— the point at which one of them generally found an excuse to call the other. Setting aside the sine wave of their romantic mingling, Davis felt he and Anna were increasingly close friends. Which was what he needed tonight. Someone he could trust, someone he could talk to.

And, if he were completely honest, someone who worked for the CIA.

Sorensen picked up. "Hello?"

"The caller ID must have shown an unknown caller."

A pause. "Hey, Jammer. How are you?"

Davis pulled a deep breath. It was nice to have somebody ask that. Somebody who cared about the answer. "I'm not good."

"What's wrong?"

He thought he might have heard music in the background, something soft and melodic. He told himself it wasn't any of his business.

"It's about Jen." He covered the purgatory that was the last three days of his life, and Sorensen listened in silence. At one point, he was sure he heard a male voice in the background.

When he finished, she said, "Dear God, I'm so sorry, Jammer. I know how close the two of you are."

An awkward silence fell, and he said, "Did I call at a bad time?"

"Oh, no. My sister and brother-in-law are staying the week." Davis felt a curiously strong wave of relief. Had it been more than two months since they'd talked? Whatever the interval, it was too long.

"So you're in Colombia looking for her?" she asked.

"The Hotel de Aeropuerto in Bogotá. Larry managed to assign me to the investigation."

"Any luck yet?"

"Yes and no. When I first got here . . . Christ, Anna, I thought she was dead. Now I don't know what to think. Twenty-one passengers and three crewmembers got on that airplane, but two are missing from the wreckage, Jen and another girl."

"So you don't even know if she's alive? That's got to be tearing you apart, Jammer. Are you okay?"

"No."

"What can I do to help?" Her sincerity was absolute, and Davis was glad he'd called. It felt good to have backup.

"I was hoping you'd ask that. First I should warn you that I'm not talking on the phone I was issued. I bought a couple of burners."

"Do you think someone is listening? The Colombians?"

"Somebody is very interested in what I'm doing here. Unfortunately, I think whoever it is lives closer to you." He told her about the first-class service he'd been getting.

"That doesn't sound like any government I know," she agreed. "I can't get a box of copier paper without the written approval of two supervisors."

"Tell me about it—I spent a career in the military."

"But how is that a problem? If you're getting too much cooperation, just run with it."

"Nothing comes without a price, Anna. I want to know who I'm running up a tab with, and for what reason."

"Maybe you could find out by putting it to a test. Call their bluff."

"How's that?" he asked.

"Ask for a bigger Gulfstream. If that shows up, go for a million in uncut diamonds. Sooner or later somebody's going to say no."

Davis came the closest to laughing he'd been in fifty-five hours. "That's not a bad idea—maybe I'll try it. But finding Jen is my priority, and that's going to take a little more subtlety."

"You? You're about as subtle as a concrete—"

"*Please*, Anna. I don't have much time. I need to find out who's so interested in this investigation. It's got to be somebody with a stake in the outcome, which should narrow things down. I need a name, an organization—something."

"And you want me to get it."

He sighed. "I don't know. Knocking on doors in D.C. when we don't know what we're up against . . . it has the potential to stir up a lot of trouble. Maybe if you could make it look like a standard dig. I don't want you putting your career on the line over this."

"I would, Jammer. I'd do that for Jen."

This caught him by surprise. "I know you would, Anna. And that means a lot. For now, I'd like you to concentrate on one thing—find out whatever you can on a guy named Thomas Mulligan." Davis spelled the last name.

"There's probably only about a thousand of those in the world."

"Five hundred if you don't count Ireland. He was on the flight with Jen, TAC-Air Flight 223. That should narrow things down. Only this guy didn't die in the crash—somebody shot him at point-blank range during the flight."

"*Shot* him?"

"Twice through the heart, nice and clean."

"That sounds like an execution."

"Could be. The investigator-in-charge down here is pushing the idea that this whole crash is a hijacking gone bad."

"If that's true, then the FBI would be all over it and I'd have seen something in the message traffic. Why haven't I heard about this already?"

"Because it's still only a theory, there are a lot of loose ends." Davis left it at that. "Mulligan—can you find out who he is by tomorrow?"

"If it can be done, I'll do it."

"Is there a different number where I can call you, one nobody would expect you to use?"

"Do you think that's necessary?"

"Yeah, I do."

Sorensen thought about it and gave a different number. She didn't say whose phone it was, and Davis didn't ask. He wrote the number with a pen and stationary he'd taken from the hotel.

"Is there a time I should call?" he asked.

"I've been working a pretty regular nine-to-five lately. Give me until lunchtime to work this."

"Right. Thanks, Anna, I owe you one."

"One what?"

"We'll figure that out when Jen and I get home. And like I said, be careful."

"I will, Jammer. You too."

* * *

The next morning Sorensen dumped her nine-to-five schedule, arriving at CIA Headquarters, formally the George Bush Center for Intelligence, a full one hour before most of her coworkers. On reaching her cluttered desk she undertook some basic housekeeping, deleting e-mails and scanning a few innocuous sit-reps, before launching her quest for Thomas Mulligan.

By virtue of her employment, she had access to a wide array of government databases. Unfortunately, even the CIA hit information roadblocks. The most sensitive material from other agencies required special authorization. Fortunately, the sources she started with did not exceed the classification of "confidential," and as such were there for the taking. She first screened Department of Homeland Security files, going through a list of U.S. travelers who'd flown to Colombia on the day in question, including those passing through on connections. There was no Thomas Mulligan.

Sorensen performed a secondary search by airline and flight number, and these results clarified why her original search had come up blank. Not a single traveler was listed that day from TAC-Air Flight 223. All information on the flight had been completely scrubbed. Sorensen wasn't sure how Homeland handled air crashes. Did they immediately sequester passenger lists after an accident? It seemed a reasonable explanation.

She tapped a fingernail on her desk and pondered how else to approach the problem. Customs and Border Protection was encompassed by Homeland Security, as was TSA, so either would likely have the same result. On a whim she accessed the National Joint Terrorism Task Force interagency server. She typed in "TAC-Air 223" and waited for the results. It didn't take long.

What appeared on her screen was a short event brief, one

paragraph carrying a relatively low priority. This meant, as Davis suggested, that the prospect of a hijacking had not yet been officially raised. There was one attachment, and Sorensen called it up to find a passenger list. Or at least a partial one. Davis told her there had been twenty-one passengers on board, yet the NJTTF list fell one name short. Jen Davis was there as clear as day. Thomas Mulligan was not. At the bottom, however, was a note related to the omission.

Passenger 21: DHS, USSS.

Sorensen pushed back ever so slightly from her desk.

Now she understood. Passenger 21 was an internal. DHS stood for the Department of Homeland Security. USSS was a well-known subsidiary of that agency, formerly administered by the Department of Treasury. Thomas Mulligan, in some capacity, was an employee of the United States Secret Service.

Feeling suddenly uncomfortable, Sorensen quickly cut the link by calling up an innocuous e-mail on her computer. Her screen filled with an interoffice memo heralding the new cafeteria menu. She stared with unfocused eyes at the price of chicken soup and beef brisket sandwiches, and thought, *What have you lumbered into this time, Jammer?*

To this point, her unsanctioned search had been superficial. If Sorensen went further she would have to tread carefully. From the main office you could find out pretty much anything about anybody. But to do so without raising flags or leaving a trail—that was more of an art. The United States Secret Service, she surmised, would not take kindly to intrusion.

There was likely a simple explanation regarding the mystery of Thomas Mulligan. He could be a Secret Service employee on vacation. If so, his identity might have been filtered from the report by some automated process. If he'd been in Colombia on assignment, there were any number of possibilities. Sorensen knew that most Secret Service employees served in the Financial Crimes Unit, combating money laundering, illegal funds transfers, and the counterfeiting of U.S. currency. Of course, there was also the

Secret Service's other mission, but that was a fence over which Sorensen had no desire to climb.

She left her desk, shouldered her purse, and headed for the door. There *was* one way around official channels. Her former college roommate worked in the Secret Service's Chicago office, on the Electronic Crimes Task Force. She was an expert in cybersecurity, in particular the detection and countering of network intrusions.

Best of all, three years ago Sorensen had introduced Melanie Schwartz to a really nice guy. Now Melanie Brown owed her a favor.

SIXTEEN

Davis was up with the sun, and his first stop that morning was at the restaurant where he was fast becoming a regular. He ordered a large coffee to fuel his walk to headquarters and to fight the fatigue he felt setting in. Davis paid with his diminishing wad of dollars, and he'd just stepped back into the blinding morning sun when his embassy-issued phone chimed with a message. Marquez was requesting his presence at an eight o'clock meeting that would include Echevarria. Having only a ten-minute walk ahead of him, Davis responded that he would arrive an hour early.

The building was quiet and his cup empty when he arrived and passed the bleary-eyed night duty officer who was just on his way out. Davis saw a new face by the main desk, and he walked over and held out a hand.

"Jammer Davis."

The man turned, and replied, "Pascal Delacorte." His accent could only be Parisian—Davis knew because he'd been there many times and spoke the language fluently. Delacorte was a big man, slightly taller than Davis, if not as wide in the shoulders. It took less than a minute to confirm that Delacorte was indeed French, and two more to discover that he also played rugby, which Davis took as a clear sign of a sound mind and virtuous character.

"I am a structural engineer for BTA," said Delacorte. "We manufacture two-thirds of the main fuselage on the ARJ-35."

Davis was well acquainted with BTA, a European consortium that supplied parts for nearly every airliner in the world.

On paper Delacorte would be here as a technical consultant. In reality, of course, he was much like the Pratt & Whitney man, an embedded corporate spy who would provide forewarning to BTA should any unwanted attention come their way. Unlike some investigators, Davis viewed the practice in a positive light. The people sent on such missions were generally top-flight engineers, so it was like having Oz available to explain his machine. Or at least some small part of it.

"I arrived last night," said Delacorte.

"Have they given you a status briefing yet?"

"No, I was promised one this afternoon. In the meantime, I hope to fly out to the crash site to perform a preliminary analysis."

Davis weighed giving Delacorte the condensed version of what they'd discovered so far, but decided it wasn't his place. On balance, the investigation was fast becoming a sinking ship, and the control of information was one of the last buckets Marquez had to bail with.

Delacorte said, "I did hear something about you, Monsieur Davis. Is it true your daughter was on board this flight?"

"She was listed as a passenger, but two bodies are still unaccounted for and Jen is one of them."

"Let us hope for the best, then," said the Frenchman, more with faith than conviction.

Davis nodded appreciatively. "Yeah, thanks."

Delacorte excused himself, explaining that he had to arrange for credentials. Davis turned to a computer and began scanning last night's logs. The system Marquez had adopted was a good one. Field teams, lab techs, and interviewers all transferred their raw reports into a central database, which was then correlated by staff and organized into a preset framework. Davis searched for anything relating to the interviews that were supposed to have taken place yesterday: one set to determine whether the body in the cockpit was Reyna, and the other to compile a background profile on their hijacking suspect, Umbriz. It took ten minutes to recognize defeat. There were no updates on either man.

He refilled his coffee cup from an industrial-sized pot—no crash could be solved without one—and was settling down again at the keyboard when Marquez and Echevarria walked in.

Marquez spotted Davis and beckoned him with a finger, and not a word was said as the two Colombians disappeared into the main conference room. Davis took a deep breath and followed.

"We have not found your daughter yet," said Marquez as soon as Davis walked in.

"That's good," said a hesitant Davis. "At least, I hope it is."

Echevarria said, "Good morning, Mr. Davis."

"*Buenos días.*"

A weary-looking Marquez unloaded papers from a satchel and began the meeting. "Major Echevarria and I attacked things using independent methods, and yesterday we both tried to resolve the questions surrounding Captain Reyna, and also our chef from Cartagena." Marquez stiffened as he looked Davis in the eye. "You were correct about the body in the cockpit—it was not Blas Reyna. This has been confirmed by family members, as well as the chief pilot at TAC-Air."

"Any idea who it *is*?"

"No," chimed in Echevarria. "My department is best suited to identifying unknown persons, but so far we have had no success. No fingerprints in our records match those of the man in the morgue, and we found nothing on his body or clothing to suggest an identity. We have good facial recognition software, but it will not help here due to the condition of the body. Dental records might be useful in time . . . but as of this moment, he remains a mystery."

"Any idea where the real Captain Reyna is?"

This, apparently, was Marquez' ground. "We interviewed eight family members and the last three first officers he flew with. He kept a small apartment in the Germania district, an address that was not on record with TAC-Air. We performed a thorough search but found nothing to shed light on his disappearance. Reyna was last seen there by a neighbor the night before the crash."

Davis rubbed his chin, and said, "Have you gotten TAC-Air involved?"

"In what way?" Marquez asked.

"It's a slim chance, but you have to rule out that the body we recovered is that of another TAC-Air captain. There might have been a last-minute change from crew scheduling that slipped past on the paperwork, or even two captains who swapped flight assignments without telling anybody. If Reyna got somebody to take his flight, he could be sleeping in right now at his girlfriend's apartment. Things like that happen."

The two officers exchanged a look. Marquez said, "I will make inquiries, but it seems too easy a way out."

Davis thought, *If I was you, that's exactly what I'd be looking for.* He said, "Okay, so we have a first officer who's been executed, and an unidentified captain who was also shot in the head. Any ballistics yet?" This was directed at Echevarria.

"No," he said. "If we include the passenger who was shot twice, we should expect to find four rounds, and probably the casings. Unfortunately, none have been recovered."

"Doesn't that strike you as odd?" Davis said. "I mean, I know this is a crash, and that strange things happen when metal meets the earth. But wouldn't you think at least *one* of these spent rounds would turn up lodged in a piece of insulation?"

Neither man answered.

"What about the weapon?" Davis looked at the two men in turn, but saw only blank stares. He addressed Marquez, his voice rising in frustration. "You know what, Colonel—I haven't been sleeping well lately. And when I don't sleep well I get difficult. No, that's not a strong enough word. I get irritable, which I think is the same word in Spanish. So let's take this apart. Your theory is that our methodical hijacker shot a passenger twice, then broke through the cockpit door, shot both pilots, and finally rebolted the damaged door before a mob could organize. Do I have this right?"

The colonel's face was set in stone. Echevarria regarded Marquez' discomfort with unveiled pleasure.

Davis went on, "If this scenario is valid, then I'd say there *has* to be a gun in that cockpit. Why haven't we found it by now?"

"The weapon could have been ejected in the crash," Marquez argued.

"Ejected?"

"The L-1 window failed on impact."

"You're saying this gun sailed on a perfect trajectory to the only place where the cockpit was breached and was thrown clear?" Davis paused and shook his head. "Putting aside that slim possibility, a handgun is a very dense piece of metal. With the detection equipment you've been using, scouring the jungle inch by inch—I'm sure you'd have found it by now."

Marquez said nothing, his flimsy theory wobbling under the tempest of Davis' words.

Echevarria broke the silence. "The medical examiner believes the same caliber gun was used in all three shootings. Dr. Guzman's best guess is that we are looking for a nine millimeter. If the slugs are recovered, my ballistics people can tell us with certainty."

The marginalized Marquez had gone still, a statue on his castered office chair. He was completely at sea, out of ideas, and drowned by facts. Davis had seen it before, investigators watching their neatly cobbled theories get shredded before their eyes. Yet there was something different here. Marquez' storyline had been riddled with holes from the outset, to the point that his very competence could be called in question. There had to be something else.

Offering no quarter, Davis looked squarely at the colonel. "Tell us what you've learned about your hijacker."

When Marquez didn't answer, Echevarria piled on. "It is a dead end. Over a dozen people who knew Umbriz have been interviewed, and each claims the idea of him being a hijacker is ridiculous. He was sixty-two years old and married for thirty years. Four children, six grandchildren, and he recently began caring for his aging mother. He's lived in the same house since 1980, and there is no evidence of fringe politics or financial difficulties—at least nothing he hasn't been dealing with his entire life. The man was a chef who made flan and pasteles—nothing more."

Davis almost felt sorry for Marquez, and having made his point, he decided to ratchet down. "Okay, maybe we should all go back to square one."

"I agree," Marquez responded, "a new approach is necessary. Each of us should spend the day going over the facts as we know them. If we independently develop theories, perhaps we can find new ground."

Davis nodded. "Fair enough."

Echevarria concurred.

They arranged to meet later in the day, and Davis was the first to leave.

He walked outside and looked across the tarmac. The Huey was departing, likely with Pascal Delacorte on board. Davis saw an ARJ-35 landing in the distance, gliding smoothly to a soft touchdown under cotton-ball morning clouds. Like much of the previous night, however, the oblique thoughts that skimmed through his head had nothing to do with airplanes. When did spring semester begin for Jen? Had she already talked to her advisor about a class schedule?

Davis had gone through it before, battled the malignant aftermath of an erased existence. A week or a month from now he would be home, and on a bright September afternoon find his mailbox filled with the usual junk advertisements. Most would be in his name, but Jen would get her share, the great machine of American capitalism being what it was. Student loan pitches, credit card offers, summer-in-Europe scams. Would he set them aside for his daughter with smiley faces drawn on? Or would he slam them into the trash crumpled in a bitter wad?

Davis had nearly lost his temper with Marquez. Almost done something stupid, which would surely have gotten him tossed off the investigation. Had he been rescued by reason, a rare display of self-control? Pity for the beleaguered Colombian? Would any of his efforts matter in the end?

After three days in limbo, the uncertainty of Jen's fate seemed suddenly overwhelming. Facts tumbled in his head without order or direction. Every investigation had its roadblocks, but typically problems that were sourced externally. Never before had Davis seized from within. That's what it was like—being frozen from the inside out.

He put his face up to the lifting sun, then checked his watch. Three hours until his call to Sorensen. Three hours to keep going.

SEVENTEEN

At three minutes past noon on Wednesday, Davis called the number Sorensen had given him from a corner table at a restaurant. The establishment was one he hadn't been to before, half a mile from his usual place. Three minutes past noon because it had taken that long to compose his fast-disintegrating thoughts.

His hard-won equilibrium lurched when a male voice answered, "Hello."

"Uh . . . hello. I was trying to reach Anna Sorensen."

"Oh, right. Here you go."

Sorensen's voice. "Hey, Jammer."

"Was that your brother-in-law?"

"Yeah. We all met for lunch in Manassas."

"Sounds like fun," he replied, not knowing what else to say. From where he sat, lunch in Manassas was like lunch on the moon. "Do you think this line is okay?"

"Best I can do for now," she said. "I'm stepping outside."

He was no expert in communications security, but a brother-in-law's cell phone from a sidewalk seemed marginal at best. Lacking any better plan, he said, "I hope you've got something for me. There's no news about Jen, and I feel like I'm beating my head against a wall down here."

"Too bad for the wall."

Davis said nothing.

"How are you really?"

A sea of clichés came to mind. He settled for, "I'm treading water—but barely."

"That's good, I think. I do have some news for you. I got a bead on your man Mulligan. Are you sitting down?"

He assured her he was.

"The guy was United States Secret Service."

Davis sank lower in his booth, staring at the empty plate in front of him that had fifteen minutes ago been piled with rice, beans, and chicken. He blew out a long breath. "Wow. I didn't see that one coming."

"Neither did I. Once I knew that much, I made some very discreet inquiries to find out what he was doing down there."

"And?"

"It's a little vague—I didn't want to put my source on the spot. Mulligan was on mission status, personal protection duty."

"*What?*"

"I know, I know. When I saw he was Secret Service, I figured he'd be part of some financial crimes task force—you know, chasing after laundered drug money or something. But that wasn't the case. Mulligan was on that flight to act as a bodyguard."

"A bodyguard for who?"

"That I couldn't find out. The Secret Service keeps information on principals at a *very* high level. My source went through some back doors to even discover that Mulligan was on mission status."

"Yeah, I get that part. But who *could* we be talking about?"

"Everybody knows these guys protect the president, but they also cover past presidents and certain family members. Then there's the vice president and his family. I've been told others can be covered in special cases—senators, department secretaries, foreign dignitaries. It's a bigger list than you might think. The problem is, only a handful of people know who's on that list."

"Okay," he said. "Anything else?"

"One more thing. These guys always travel armed, but it takes special authorization to carry on a commercial flight. Clearance is particularly complicated when traveling abroad."

Davis considered it. "Which means there would be people in Colombia who knew Mulligan was coming."

"They'd have known the time and date of his flight, and where he was going. They probably even knew his seat assignment. Which leads to something else." Sorensen paused to let him figure it out.

"They probably also knew who he was protecting."

"I think there's a good chance."

The gears in Davis' head ground to a stop, but he wasn't sure why. He let it go for the moment. "It opens up a lot of possibilities."

"What else I can do to help?" Sorensen asked.

"Let's take a pass on Mulligan. It would only highlight us to keep chasing that, and you've stuck your neck out far enough as it is. I might ask for one more thing, but I've got some work to do on my end first. Thanks for your help."

"She's out there, Jammer. I feel it."

"I hope to hell you're right."

Davis ended the call, but he didn't move. He sat at the table with the phone in his hand, Sorensen's last words ringing in his head.

She's out there, Jammer. I feel it.

For the first time since arriving in Colombia, he felt it too.

* * *

Davis used the ten-minute walk back to headquarters to assess his options. He considered calling a meeting to confront Marquez and Echevarria with the information on Thomas Mulligan. He wondered if one, or even both of them, already knew the truth about Passenger 21. His internal scales weighed against the idea for the time being—he just couldn't see how sharing that information would advance his cause.

Arriving at the El Centro he went straight to a computer, hoping to build on Sorensen's revelation. He called up the video he'd seen two nights earlier, the closed-circuit recording of the

TAC-Air boarding area. Cueing to the segment he wanted, he saw Jen and Kristin Stewart, and directly behind them Thomas Mulligan. Davis ran the video to its end, slightly short of the point where they all disappeared.

Mulligan was exactly as he remembered. Sport coat and pressed trousers. Busy eyes working the terminal and checking his phone. Davis had viewed the scene before, but his first interpretation was totally off the mark. If he'd been dropping a practice bomb on a training flight it would have rated unscorable—would have landed completely off the range. Davis had pegged Mulligan for a businessman here to sell some new line of products. When Kristin had turned and said something to the man, he'd taken it for a casual acquaintance.

He watched the video more closely. Not only did Kristin say something, but he saw Mulligan give a response. How had he missed that? Davis concentrated on a 1.2 second loop, and watched it over and over. In the end, he was reasonably sure he could lip read Mulligan's three word reply. *"No, Kristin, don't."*

He stopped the video.

No, Kristin, don't.

It was a response steeped in familiarity. And also a directive. Which was not at all how a thirty-something guy would address a college-aged girl he'd just met in an airline boarding area. With his elbows on the chair's armrests and his hands steepled under his chin, Davis ran the video back and carefully studied the minutes before those words. He paid particular attention to Mulligan's positioning, eye movement, and who seemed to hold his attention. By the third run-through there could be no doubt. Special Agent Mulligan was in the boarding area for one reason.

He was protecting Kristin Stewart.

Davis could have kicked himself. All along it had been right there in front of him. *Two* missing passengers. He'd been so fully focused on Jen that her seatmate seemed an afterthought. Now he realized it was quite the opposite. Jen was no more than an innocent bystander, swept into events beyond her control. Kristin Stewart was something else altogether. She was instrumental to everything that had happened on TAC-Air Flight 223.

Passenger 19 was the key.

* * *

"Seven million U.S.? Are they nuts?" asked the man named Evers. A characteristically dour man, his baggy eyes and creased jowls took on an unusually sour arrangement. In truth the number did not surprise him, but he thought it good form to make a show of displeasure.

"I don't expect any negotiation on the point," said the other man in the very private room on G Street. His name was Frederick Strand, and he was CEO of The Alamosa Group—the nicely indeterminate name of the company he'd founded six years ago, this after retiring from the Navy with twenty-four good years and the rank of vice admiral.

"That's your professional opinion?" asked Evers, his tone laced in sarcasm.

"It is," said an undeterred Strand.

"Where are we supposed to get that kind of money on short notice?"

"That's not for me to say, Mr. Evers. One source comes to mind, but there are obvious complications, the likes of which you would understand better than I. The deadline for compliance is noon this Friday."

"And if we fail to meet it?"

"You saw the message. If the transfer is not completed on schedule, they promise to—how was it worded? *Make the truth known to all?*"

"How would they make good on such a threat?"

The CEO cocked his head and pursed his lips, as he once might have done to consider which surface battle group to apply to an enemy's exposed flank. "I would use DNA, send samples simultaneously to a number of media outlets. That would guarantee a race to publication, with limited time for you to plan a preemptive public relations strike. The facts would run their course, and put you immediately on the defensive."

Evers closed his eyes, imagining that awful scenario. "What kind of samples?" he asked with clear discomfort. "They won't harm her, will they?"

"Is this a question from you . . . or your employer?"

"Me."

The admiral steepled his hands thoughtfully. "I doubt very much they would harm her. There's no benefit . . . and safe to say, in time, the possible downside could be significant."

"Do you see any chance of settling this by more direct means?"

Strand chuckled briefly, but held his bearing. "As in an armed intervention? Delta Force or SEAL Team Six? I don't see anyone authorizing that. And if you're thinking of a private venture—it would take a month to plan, and something in the neighborhood of the same seven million."

Evers wilted in his seat. "We're paying you a hell of a lot of money, and this is the best advice you can give?"

"We both face limitations, Mr. Evers, you know that. We have one asset presently in theater, the man the NTSB sent. It initially seemed like a good idea, to have someone in country and watching this investigation, but he hasn't gotten anywhere. The man might be capable in his field, but there can't be any thought about him getting the girl back. That would be way out of his league. For what it's worth, we were able to track down the old beggar who delivered the message to Stuyvesant in the soup kitchen. He's no one, a cul-de-sac. I'm sure there are at least three cutouts. These people are not beginners—they know what they're doing."

Evers fumed. "All right, I'll look into the funds. Assuming I can arrange it, what happens next?"

"If the message is accurate, the rest is simple. We send a man to Colombia to complete the transaction."

"Who?"

"I have someone in mind."

Evers stared, unsatisfied.

"His name is Kehoe, if you must know. He's my best man."

"All right, I'll be in touch. Please tell Mr. Kehoe to pack his bags."

The admiral smiled as the two shook hands. "Chief Petty Officer Kehoe has had a bag packed for twenty years. He uses it often."

* * *

Reinvigorated by his video session, Davis decided the next thing to attack was the whereabouts of Captain Reyna. He got up and found Marquez still in his office.

"Do we have a TAC-Air flight procedures manual?" Davis asked, his shoulders filling the door's frame. The room was utilitarian, one desk in the middle, a pair of wooden chairs, and a beaten couch against the wall. A file cabinet anchored one corner, and the walls displayed nothing more than puncture wounds from old nails.

Marquez looked up from his paperwork, none too happy. His uniform was wrinkled and he needed a shave. It was never a good sign in a unit when full colonels started letting themselves go. "Yes, somewhere." He scanned his office, and finally pointed to a binder on the couch. It was in pile that included an ARJ-35 maintenance manual and a copy of Colombia's aviation regulations.

Davis took the binder and began leafing through.

"What are you looking for?" asked Marquez.

"A little guidance."

Marquez frowned and went back to his work.

Davis guessed what he wanted would be in a chapter labeled *Regulaciones Piloto*. Pilot Regulations. He scanned over twenty pages of rules and company policies, all written in Spanish, before finding what he wanted.

He interrupted Marquez again. "Would you translate one part, right here—" Davis pointed to the section.

Marquez heaved a great sigh, and put on a pair of reading glasses. "All pilots will report to the aircraft at least one hour prior to the scheduled takeoff time. If conditions—"

"Great," Davis interrupted. "That's all I needed."

He tossed the manual back on the couch and returned to the computer where the boarding area video remained cued. Previously he'd viewed the recording as far back as fifty minutes before departure, reasoning that few passengers would arrive before that. But he was no longer looking for passengers. He took the video back one hour and ten minutes, and then let it run in real time. Twelve minutes forward—two minutes late by TAC-Air standards—Captain Blas Reyna and First Officer Hugo Moreno arrived at the gate.

Both pilots were pulling wheeled suitcases with their brain bags—thick leather cases packed with charts and manuals— hooked on back. The man in the captain's uniform matched the photo of the real Reyna. Using Moreno as a measuring stick, Davis decided the height was also dead on—six foot one. Definitely their missing captain. Not an impostor, and not another pilot who'd traded into the trip. Reyna had been right there at the gate, ready to fly.

"Yes, that is Reyna," said a voice from behind. Curiosity had gotten the better of Marquez.

Without turning, Davis said, "This puts him at the airplane one hour before departure. From that point, I can't see any way the flight pushes back from the gate without him. And we know it departed right on time."

"Which tells us what? That he is a ghost?"

Davis nodded, because Marquez had a point. "Maybe so. If Reyna began the flight, how could he *not* have been there at the end?" He could think of only one plausible answer. And one way to prove it.

He checked the time, and said, "I'm going back out to the crash site."

"We are to meet Echevarria soon."

"Give the major my regrets."

He had one foot out the door when he glanced over his shoulder and saw Marquez making a phone call.

EIGHTEEN

Davis jumped off the Huey as soon as it touched down and moved with nearly the urgency he'd had the first night. His short hair matted in waves and his shirtsleeves snapped under the chopper's pulsing downwash, and he set out toward the wreckage field at quick-time.

A thunderstorm had just ended, and by the time he reached the wreckage his cargo pants were sodden from the knees down. Davis was here to inspect the wings, and he began on the starboard side. That assembly was partially detached, rooted to the fuselage by a damaged main spar. Having come to rest upright, the underside of the wing lay flush to the ground, which didn't suit Davis' needs. He moved to the port wing, which had separated completely and come to rest near a fallen log. The underside was barely visible in a five-inch gap. Davis needed more than that.

He asked a crew working nearby if a hydraulic jack was available. Yes, he was told, but no one seemed to know where it was. This was the sort of complication often encountered during recovery efforts. Tools were handed from one team to another and invariably got left on a departing truck or lost in high grass. For twenty minutes Davis searched and got nowhere. Frustrated, he spotted a ten-foot section of four-by-four, stout construction-grade lumber, and decided it might do the job.

Aircraft structures are surprisingly light, and wings in particular are a marvel of lightweight engineering. The wings of most airliners are termed "wet," meaning that fuel carriage is integral to their design. When those tanks are empty, the baseline structure weighs only a fraction of the maximum load. Davis reckoned that the wing of this RJ—thirty-odd feet of aluminum and composites, maybe a mile of wires, two tires, and a dozen hydraulic actuators—would weigh in the neighborhood of a thousand pounds. Fortunately, since the wing was resting on the ground, he only needed to lever one edge upward a few feet, far enough to gain access to the underside. Yet even that would require help.

Davis hadn't had a chance to make good on his promise of a case of rum, so he ruled out asking the army. He recruited two men in Air Force field uniforms, part of Marquez' contingent, who were loading a truck with luggage extracted from the crumpled cargo hold.

"Can you guys give me a hand? I need to lift something." The bigger of the two, the one Davis needed, looked at him blankly, clearly not speaking a word of English. Fortunately, the second, a reedy kid in dire need of some dental work, said, "Sure, *señor*, we help you."

The ground was soft, the footing slick, and it took ten minutes for them to find the right rock to serve as a fulcrum, and to get their angles right. Davis and the big corporal leaned in with their combined weight, and watched the four-by-four bend under the strain. The wing began to rise, and as it did, the smaller man shoved a toolbox underneath in stages, raising the wing an inch on one heave, and another on the next. Twenty minutes later, with everyone sweating bullets, the leading edge of the port wing was wedged two feet off the ground. The toolbox was backed up by a cinder block taken from the truck, and Davis decided the job was done.

He thanked the two, memorizing their rank and the names embroidered above their shirt pockets. Davis would mention their help later to Marquez, although he wasn't sure if it would get them an atta-boy or a reprimand. Looking happy to be done, the soldiers walked off to finish their assigned detail, pulling the last pieces of luggage from the wreckage and hauling them off to the clearing where their truck was parked.

Once they were gone, Davis looked around and realized

he was alone. It was just as well. What he wanted to check was straightforward, but all the same, he'd be happy to do it without anyone from Marquez' crew or Echevarria's police contingent asking questions. He laid down on his back in front of the wing, and like a mechanic sliding under a jacked-up Buick, he pushed with bent legs until the upper half of his body disappeared under the wing. It was dark in the crawl space, and Davis felt cool mud on his back and moist grass against his neck, and smelled the earthen tang of freshly turned soil.

Three feet back he found the inboard landing gear door. A two-foot square piece of aluminum, it had been partially torn from its hinges and was hanging at a forty-five degree angle. A second landing gear door, the outboard, remained flush with the underside of the wing. Davis got a good grip and muscled that panel open, then curled a hand down to retrieve his flashlight from a pocket. Seconds later he had what he'd come for—a good look at the wheels.

The main landing gear on the ARJ-35 was a standard arrangement—one titanium beam supporting a twin-wheel assembly. The tires were similar in size to those of a midsize SUV, the main difference being a significantly higher speed rating. Davis could see the wheels clearly, as well as the brake and anti-skid hardware, and it all looked exactly as it should have. But there *was* something that shouldn't have been there.

It was woven into the valves and actuators. It was hanging from support struts and hydraulic lines like tinsel on a Christmas tree. Countless strands of long grass. There was also mud caked symmetrically around the tires and gear assembly. That symmetry was highly significant—it meant the dirt had not been acquired in the crash sequence, because when the airplane hit, the landing gear had been retracted, the wheels not turning. He shone the light up into the landing gear well, and on the metal ceiling Davis saw telltale splash patterns of mud and shredded grass. Two perfect longitudinal arcs on primer-green steel.

All exactly as he'd hoped.

Davis crabbed farther under the wing, until only his shins and feet were in daylight. He reached into his pocket to retrieve his phone, fumbled to select camera mode, and made sure the flash was active. He took ten pictures, and was maneuvering for a last shot when he sensed someone outside.

"What you are doing?" a raspy voice inquired.

Davis twisted his head far enough to see a black boot with a crescent-shaped scar on the heel. "I'm investigating," he shouted.

The boot spun a full circle.

Davis went back to his camera, and was angling it to take a picture when he thought about it. *Why turn a circle at a crash site?* He looked again. The boot was gone. Then Davis heard a thump on the wing over his head.

"Hey! Get the hell off—"

The wing rocked, and Davis barely had time to get his elbows to his side and his palms facing upward when everything over him shifted. The two makeshift supports toppled and the wing came crashing down.

NINETEEN

Davis locked his forearms at right angles to stop the wing's free-fall. The weight was crushing and drove his elbows into the dirt, but his arms held, a wheel hovering inches over his nose. His legs scrambled for purchase as he tried to extract himself, but he was pinned under the wing, immobilized like a weightlifter under twice what he could bench press.

"Hey!" he yelled. "Help!" Davis was trying to think of the Spanish word when the wing began to spring up and down. He envisioned the scarred boot and its partner dancing over his head, stomping and heaving.

The wing wavered like a demolished building choosing which way to fall. His arms felt ready to snap. How much had he guessed? A thousand pounds, add the weight of a man—he had to be supporting half that combined weight. Worst of all was the movement, everything swaying erratically.

Davis felt a surge from deep within. It wasn't a reaction to thirty seconds of desperate exertion, but rather three days of anger and frustration. A rage like nothing he'd ever felt rose within his chest. His arms began to move, slowly at first and then gaining momentum. The wing began to rise, but the boots only stomped harder, slamming down again and again. His arms began to quiver, and for a terrible moment Davis sensed a pause before his arms were locked vertically. He sucked in a quick breath, then heaved the last inches until his arms straightened fully. At that moment everything shifted. The burden suddenly became less, and he heard heavy footsteps running through brush. Receding.

Now what the hell do I do? Arms extended, the wing was frozen two feet over his face.

"Help!" he called again.

His arms began shaking uncontrollably, and Davis knew he only had seconds. He considered trying to roll free, but any movement would cause the death trap over him to collapse. If he lost his grip, even wavered for an instant, he'd be crushed like an egg under a hammer. His left arm began to buckle, and he shifted his shoulders to buy a few more seconds.

And then, salvation.

Someone outside was straddling his feet. Then a grunt, and the weight over him was suddenly halved. Davis kept his dead arms braced, but as the burden eased, he was able to shimmy until his hips were clear. He caught a glimpse of a man with a shoulder under the four-by-four. With a final heave, Davis pushed free and rolled away. His legs flew sideways, tripping the man above him, and the wing slammed down, grazing his scalp on its way to the earth.

Davis sucked in huge breaths, one after the other. Sprawled on the fern-clad forest floor next to him was Pascal Delacorte.

The Frenchman said, "Only a prop forward would find himself in such a *situation difficile.*" He was referring to the rugby position in which the most vital requirements were size, strength, and a particularly thick skull.

"Actually, yeah, that's where I usually line up."

"What were you doing under there?"

Davis almost said, *investigating.* He found himself staring at Delacorte's boots. They were brown. He spun a finger in a wide circle, and said, "Did you see anybody else around here in the last few minutes? Anybody leaving in a hurry?"

Delacorte shrugged. "No, I was getting a drink at the tent when I heard your call for help."

Davis nodded. "Thanks for coming."

The two men locked hands, and levered one another up as they would have on a rugby pitch. The wing had settled flush to the ground, and Davis stared at it for a long moment. "My phone is still under there—I was taking pictures."

"You should ask for help next time. You were in a very dangerous position."

"I sort of have a knack for that." Davis flexed his arms, and the feeling began to return. "Did you say there's water over at the tent?"

"It is even cold."

On reaching the canvas shade, Davis tried to cool down. He pulled a plastic water bottle from a cooler, cracked the seal, and began gulping. He worked his aching arms in circles. There was an abrasion on his scalp, and he ran a hand over it to find only a trace of blood. He looked around the tent and studied every face, looking for eyes that avoided his own. He listened to voices, searching for one that had minutes ago asked him what he was doing.

Investigating.

That had been his mission on arriving three days ago, a process that was in equal parts familiar and convenient. Solve the crash, find the daughter.

But it hadn't worked that way. Not at all.

Three days into the investigation he was no closer to finding Jen. He had only learned where she *wasn't.* He'd learned that someone in the States was using him, and probably also Larry Green. Playing them like tokens on a board game. To what end he had no idea, but it was apparently important enough that someone had tried to kill him.

Davis took a long, cool drink from his water bottle, and at that moment underwent a tectonic shift in mindset. His assignment in Colombia was no longer about an aircraft accident. Maybe it never had been. It was time for a new approach to finding his daughter.

He emptied the bottle and crushed it in his hand. On his way to the trash bin he registered six men under the tent and two outside. He checked every pair of boots. Davis didn't see the ones he wanted.

* * *

The photographs registered on the computers of the G Street

office within minutes of Davis taking them. The man and the woman called the CEO to their office, in line with a new directive that anything from Colombia was to get his personal attention.

Strand walked through the door seconds later. "What have you got?"

They all looked closely at the pictures, but no one knew what they were looking at. It was obviously *some* section of the crashed airplane, photographed from various angles. Sheet metal and tubing and dirt. A pair of grass-encrusted wheels.

"Is that all there is?" Strand asked.

"Yes, sir," said the woman. "The GPS link confirms that the pictures were taken at the crash site."

Strand gave her a withering look. "Well *there's* a nugget of brilliance."

That comment hung in the air until the man said, "He hasn't used his phone to make a call in nearly twenty-four hours."

Strand shifted his gaze across a table full of equipment and cables. In a more circumspect tone, he said, "Meaning what?"

"Well . . . he's using the phone to take pictures, so we know he's got it with him in the field."

"What's unusual about that?"

"Nothing on its face," said the man, "but yesterday we noticed he stayed in his room for an unusually long time in the evening. We didn't pick up anything on the open mic, and the camera was pointed toward the ceiling the whole time. We figured he was asleep. But . . . it *is* possible he went out."

"We don't know that," the woman argued, continuing their earlier disagreement.

"I thought we had his door logged."

"We lost that signal yesterday afternoon. Apparently the hotel's computer crashed. We had nothing to do with it," she added defensively.

The male tech said, "It's been a while since he used the phone to contact his boss at NTSB."

Strand thought about it. "Maybe because he's got nothing worth reporting."

Staring at the photographs of the wheels, the man said, "No. I definitely think Davis is onto something. These pictures prove he's making progress. But he's keeping the NTSB in the dark about it."

After a moment of silent contemplation, Strand asked, "Why would he do that?"

They all considered the question, and it was the woman who sighed as if relenting. "Only one reason," she said. "Davis knows someone is watching him."

* * *

Delacorte went missing, then showed up ten minutes later holding Davis' phone.

"You said you lost it under the wing. It took some digging, but voila!"

Davis took the handset. "Thanks." He used a wad of napkins from the makeshift dining table to wipe the case clean. When he hit the power button the screen came to life. "Looks like they gave me the hardened model—must have known I'd drop an airplane on it." He looked at the tiny camera lens, expressionless, before sliding it into his pocket.

"So what were you doing under the wing?" the Frenchman asked.

"I wanted to see the landing gear."

"You suspect a mechanical problem?"

Davis hesitated. "I'll explain later. What have you been working on?"

"The main fuselage is my area of expertise."

"The fuselage? I haven't heard anybody suggest a failure of the pressure hull."

"True," said Delacorte, "but there is still a great deal to learn. We design not only to avoid accidents, but also to ensure survivability in a worst case scenario such as this. The ARJ-35 is a relatively new variant with an updated design. The structural integrity relies

on composite fiber mated to a metal alloy framework. I've been analyzing the post-crash integrity of the hull, to see if it withstood the
crash as we hoped."

"Good luck with that. But it leaves me with the hard part—
figuring out why the airplane crashed in the first place."

"I do not envy you," said Delacorte. "So often these days it is
the human element, and that can be difficult to prove."

"Like you can't imagine."

"I should get back to work. I was going to take the next
flight back to Bogotá, but I've been told the helicopter is grounded due to weather at the airport. It will be hours before the next
departure, and by then there will be a queue—it might take two
or three trips to find a seat. Perhaps I will see you later tonight."

"Right."

Delacorte turned to leave.

"And Pascal—"

The Frenchman turned.

"Thanks again for your help."

Delacorte waved amiably before walking off toward the debris field.

Davis looked up at churning gray sky that was plotting more
afternoon mayhem. The idea of sitting in the jungle for another
four hours didn't sit well. He had what he'd come for, and with it
a new theory, albeit a theory that provided only a partial solution.
To make it complete he needed help, and he wasn't going to get it
here in the field, nor from the likes of Marquez or Echevarria. He
needed to talk to Anna Sorensen.

Which meant getting back to Bogotá as quickly as possible.

TWENTY

As Davis downed a second bottle of water in the shade of the tent, he found himself watching the luggage truck in the distance. The two men who'd helped him lift the wing were still there, levering the truck's tailgate into place. They had finished emptying the cargo bay, which meant the truck would soon be clattering back to civilization. He walked over and the men saw him coming. Davis stopped a few steps away and checked their boots. Satisfied, he said, "You guys heading back to the city?"

"*Si, con los equipajes*," the orthodontia candidate answered. His English seemed suddenly less fluent, and Davis guessed they were trying to get away before he put them to work again. Fortunately, he recognized the relevant word in the man's reply, having seen it before in airport terminals.

"Okay, you're leaving with the luggage. How long does it take to drive back?"

"Two hours, three. It depends."

It always does here, Davis thought. "Do you mind if I ride with you? The helicopter is delayed and I need to get back."

The two Colombians had a rapid-fire exchange that was completely lost on Davis. Then the English speaker said, "Yes, okay. But you must ride in back."

Davis thought the cab looked big enough for four, but a ride was a ride. "I'll take it."

The two men moved toward the cab, and Davis had one foot on the rear bumper when he paused. "Tell me one thing—"

The soldiers paused.

He thumbed toward the luggage. "Has this stuff been searched yet?"

"I don't think, *señor*. They bring dogs yesterday to smell for drugs, but find nothing."

Before Davis could ask anything else, the two disappeared into the cab.

He vaulted over the tailgate, landing in the cargo bed. A green canvas tarp was strung over the top on a steel-pole frame, a feeble effort to keep the sun and rain off whatever was being carried. The truck began to move, and after ten seconds, Davis wished he'd argued for a seat up front. The road was awful, the old truck's suspension seeming to amplify every rut, and the engine's rumble translated straight to his bones. Sunlight came and went as the road meandered through jungle, bordered on each side by dense walls of green.

The forward half of the cargo bed was taken up by two jagged pieces of metal—if he wasn't mistaken, the partial remains of the tail and aft fuselage spine. Behind that the floorboards were covered with luggage. Davis situated himself centrally in the knee-deep pile of suitcases. The truck swayed and bounced, but he got a rhythm and balanced himself with a hand on the side rail. He'd never before examined evidence in the back of a moving vehicle. It would not, however, be the first time he'd stood in a sea of brightly colored bags that would never be claimed—at least not by those who had checked them.

Davis was looking at roughly eighteen bags of various shapes and sizes. He started at the back and began checking claim tags. TAC-Air's luggage tracking system printed the name of each traveler on a fold-over adhesive printout, a common industry format. Davis correlated the name on each routing tag to the passenger list he'd memorized. He also cross-checked the TAC-Air generated wrap-arounds to the personal name and address tags he found on most of the bags. All matched except for one, and that had a common surname to one of the female passengers, suggesting a suitcase borrowed from a family member.

He found Thomas Mulligan's bag in the center of the pile. Davis set it aside and kept going. His gut wrenched when he reached Jen's bag—it was barely recognizable, covered in mud and the zipper torn. He bypassed it because his daughter's belongings would have little investigative significance. At least that was what Davis told himself.

He reached the front of the pile, and was satisfied that Mulligan had checked only one bag. He also did not find a bag for Kristin Stewart, which seemed curious. He went back and lifted Mulligan's suitcase, which was reasonably light, to the top of the stack and set it on its back. He pulled the zipper and threw back the flap, and on first glance saw little of interest. A few clean shirts, fresh pants, a spare pair of shoes. Reaching deeper with his hand, however, Davis felt a very distinctive shape. Beneath the tail of a button-down Oxford, cradled in the center of the bag, was a neatly folded shoulder holster and weapon. Davis had no doubt it was Mulligan's service-issued handgun, a Sig Sauer semiautomatic. There were also two spare magazines in a leather pouch, both fully loaded.

Davis left the gun where it was and rooted to the bottom of the suitcase. He found shaving gear, a travel iron, and deodorant—all the things any business traveler would carry. The truck suddenly bottomed on a massive pothole, sending Davis to the floor. He worked himself back onto a knee and considered his options. There was a fleeting urge to take the Sig and slip it into his waistband. He was quite sure there had been no previous search of the bag. If so, Marquez' crew would have found the gun, logged it into evidence, and put it in a secure place. Reluctantly, Davis jettisoned the thought of keeping the Sig. With the investigation going to hell at flank speed, arming himself with stolen evidence could do nothing but create complications.

The finding did answer one question. If Mulligan was on board to protect Kristin Stewart, why hadn't he done it? Now Davis knew. Mulligan had transported his weapon in a checked bag, probably because the Colombian authorities hadn't cleared him to carry it. This highlighted a more relevant issue—who had known Thomas Mulligan would be on board the flight? It was no coincidence that the only passenger shot was an unarmed Secret Service agent.

He zipped up Mulligan's bag and tossed it onto the pile. Davis leaned back and tried to get comfortable, but it was an exercise in futility as the truck battered over every rut. He forced his eyes shut and thought about Jen. He thought about mud and grass on a landing gear assembly, and a gun in a suitcase. He thought about a missing pilot and three dead people on a flight deck, one of whom remained unidentified. Yet most of all, as he bounced along in a two-ton troop carrier at the head of the Amazon basin, Davis found his mind circling back to one increasingly tall obstacle.

Who the hell was Kristin Stewart?

* * *

Davis arrived at El Centro shortly before six that evening. The driver parked the truck across the street, in front of a small warehouse that had been requisitioned to house wreckage. He thanked the two men for the ride and walked to the main building.

He found Marquez behind the desk in his office. Davis hesitated, then continued past the door and into the computer room. The only person there was a young woman in jungle fatigues who pretended not to notice him. Davis went to the copy machine, a big Xerox office model whose control panel shone a resolute green light, almost like an invitation. *I'm ready to go.* Davis ignored it. He instead took a firm grip on the trash can next to the copier and lifted it high.

The young woman got up and left in a rush.

For all its efforts to modernize, Colombia, or at least the city of Bogotá, had apparently not crossed the threshold of recycling. Davis turned the trash can upside down, and all manner of refuse cascaded onto a scuffed linoleum floor. Soft drink cans, food wrappers, Styrofoam packing peanuts—and most of all, paper. It was a big receptacle, and Davis suspected it hadn't been emptied since the beginning of the crisis. It didn't take a Holmesian deduction to know which documents would be on top of the inverted pile.

Davis began wrist-flicking pages aside, one by one. Inspecting the seventh, he found what he wanted. He went to Marquez' office.

"We need to talk," Davis said without knocking.

A visibly strained Marquez motioned for him to sit. "Did you find something useful at the crash site?"

"Actually, I need something from you. I want to see the flight data recorder information. Is it available yet?"

Marquez' expression clouded over. He stood, walked to the door, and pulled it gently shut. He looked different from when Davis had met him days earlier. He seemed frail, the countenance of a man who'd survived some kind of wasting disease, but who expected a relapse at any moment. A man living on borrowed time. "There is a problem with the recorders."

"What kind of problem?"

"I only found out this afternoon. Our technicians tell me the downloads are completely useless, both the flight data and cockpit audio."

Davis fell very still. "That *is* a problem." It had been in the back of his mind—they'd found the recorders early Monday, almost three days ago, yet no information had been forthcoming. An initial read usually didn't take that long. "Were they damaged in the crash?"

"No, both were recovered in perfect condition."

"Then how could you not have data?"

A sigh. "Apparently TAC-Air maintenance removed both boxes two days before the crash for a mandatory bench inspection. When the mechanics reinstalled them, they apparently did not reconnect the umbilical to either unit."

Davis thought this through, and ventured a guess. "So you've got perfect data for a flight that happened three days before our crash."

"Exactly."

"Aren't the pilots supposed to check for operability before a flight?"

"There is a self-test feature, yes. The pilots are required to perform it before the first flight of each day, according to TAC-Air's operating procedures. The test itself has no bearing on day-to-day operations . . . I have heard that some pilots ignore it."

Davis wasn't surprised. He knew pilots became rushed at times, and didn't always check every bell and whistle in the cockpit. When it came to black boxes, there was only one group of people who cared about operability—investigators like him and Marquez.

"That ties both hands behind our backs," Davis said in frustration.

"Yes," agreed Marquez. "The voice recorder would almost certainly have explained what happened on the flight deck."

Davis wasn't so sure. He was more interested in the flight data recorder, which would have shown the course the jet had taken to its final resting place. "Did you ever figure out why we didn't get pings? The emergency locator beacons should have gone off in this crash."

"That's something else I learned today. We inspected the ELTs, and apparently one had a bad battery. The other malfunctioned, although we are not sure why. In time the cause will be discovered."

Davis shifted in his seat. "Does this not strike you as extraordinary? Here we are, you and I, floundering around to explain missing passengers and pilots. Three people on that flight were executed, for Christ's sake. I've never seen an accident with such clear criminal involvement. And now you're telling me that right before the crash a mechanic inadvertently disabled our two best sources of information? On top of that, both ELTs malfunctioned simultaneously, making the crash more difficult to locate? What are the odds of all that?"

Marquez didn't reply.

"You know, I just took a long truck ride back from the field. It wasn't very comfortable, but it gave me time to think. And I wasn't dwelling on airplane wreckage or pilot profiles. I was thinking about you, Colonel."

Marquez remained motionless, his face a blank.

"I was thinking about how well organized this investigation is. Twenty-four hours after the crash you had a building arranged, equipment in place, computers up and running. That's very efficient. No, it's *incredibly* efficient. I could never have done that well." Davis leaned forward and put the page he'd retrieved from the copier room on the desk.

"What is that?" Marquez asked.

"I don't know. Some kind of procedure for troubleshooting a Windows network backup. It was probably downloaded and printed out because a technician was having trouble installing things on the first day."

"And that is important to our investigation?"

"Not at all. What's important is at the bottom . . . in little tiny letters and numbers. This was printed in that room last Friday night. The day *before* the crash."

Marquez stared silently at the paper.

"I've also been thinking about the army patrol that just happened to be training in the area when our jet went down. How lucky was that? They were looking for survivors and had the accident site cordoned off before a chopper could even get there."

"What are you suggesting?" Marquez said, his voice flat and expressionless.

"I talked to a few of the soldiers from that unit. They said they hadn't been training at all. There were also two other squads in the area, but nobody seemed to be on maneuvers. No tactical exercises or navigation drills. They'd simply been sent out into the jungle, like a camping trip . . . until an airplane crashed right in their lap."

"You are saying what—that I planned this crash?"

Davis shook his head. "I don't think you're that clever."

"Get out!" Marquez snapped, his words laced in venom.

Davis stood, but he didn't move toward the door. He hovered ominously over the colonel's desk, their bodies separated, in Davis' view, by the precise distance of one extended fist. "My daughter is out there, and I'm going to find her. Do not get in my way."

Marquez rose from his chair, the colonel's three stars prominent on his shoulders. "Pack your bags and go home!" he bellowed. "You are no longer part of this inquiry!"

"I don't answer to you, Colonel, so I'm not going anywhere. You can put in a request to dismiss me through official channels, but that will take time."

Marquez almost said something, his eyes going to slits. In the end he remained silent.

Minutes later Davis was walking through a sultry evening, his eyes level and his center of gravity forward. At one point a bystander backed out of his way, shouldering against a wall. So lost in thought was Davis, he never even noticed.

TWENTY-ONE

Davis stopped at his room where he exchanged the satellite phone for the second prepaid, which he had not yet used. Out the door a minute later, he set out on foot and left the airport behind, its terminal access roads choked by traffic on the evening rush. The sky was no better off, a string of white landing lights—lined up at precise three-mile intervals, Davis knew—stretching far into the night. An aerial traffic jam. Problems in the sky often had their terrestrial equivalents.

He thought a great deal about Marquez, how so many inconsistencies had slipped past him. It seemed careless, imprecise. Only Marquez wasn't that sort. He was the type of guy who would scramble eggs using a recipe, who would have the best-trimmed hedges on the block. So how had so many irregularities escaped his detailed eye? It made no sense whatsoever.

For the second time since arriving in Colombia, Davis found himself looking over his shoulder. It seemed an exercise in futility. Even if he spotted someone, he wouldn't know who to suspect of following him. Would they be tied to Marquez? Echevarria? An unknown assassin wearing a scarred black boot? The United States Secret Service? He could be on any of those radar screens, and possibly others he wasn't aware of. It was like flying through a great air battle in a neutral airplane, dodging and diving and trying to stay out of everyone's gun sights.

It was enough to drive a man to paranoia. Streetlights seemed to follow his every move, and the ubiquitous yellow taxis all had the same driver. He checked six after every turn, and backtracked twice. There was no chance of getting lost—the southern mountains were always there as a reference, dark shadows cradling the city in their interminable granite grasp. He passed an old church, bristling with crumbling stucco, whose door flyer invited those in need of salvation, then a fortresslike lending bank preferring those in need of solvency. Davis ignored all of it as he dialed the number—Sorensen's brother-in-law.

This time she answered directly.

"It's good to hear a friendly voice," he said.

"It's good to hear yours, Jammer. Any luck finding Jen?"

"Not yet, but I'm definitely making waves."

"That I believe. Did you learn anything more about Agent Mulligan?" she asked.

"I found his Sig Sauer a few hours ago. It was checked in his suitcase, presumably because he didn't have clearance to carry it on the flight. Does that sound right?"

"It does. Secret Service agents have carte blanche to carry on domestic flights, but foreign-flagged carriers are a different game. Depending on the principal he was protecting, Mulligan might have been forced to check. Or maybe it was a tactical decision— do you want to fill out a lot of paperwork in order to carry, or is it better to quietly check your weapon and not draw attention? I'm only thinking out loud here—I've never been on that side of the fence."

"It makes sense," he said. "And it probably made sense to Mulligan until somebody pointed a nine millimeter at him. Listen, I need another favor. This one's delicate too."

"Whatever—I'll do it."

"I haven't told you what it is yet."

Silence from Virginia.

"Thanks, Anna. Here's the deal—I think I know who Mulligan was assigned to protect. There was a girl on the flight sitting next to Jen."

"You said there were two passengers missing. Is this girl the other one by any chance?"

"Actually, yeah. Her name is Kristin Marie Stewart, a U.S. citizen." Davis took out his wallet and removed a slip of paper. "I wrote down her passport number—are you ready?" Sorensen said she was, and Davis read off the number and date of birth. "I think she was heading to the same internship program as Jen, but I'm not sure. That's all I've got. Does the name mean anything to you?"

"Nothing at all."

"It should be easy enough. She's twenty years old, and probably a college student. Try Facebook or Instagram."

"It won't be that easy, but I'll track her down."

"There's one more thing," he said. "Officially, I'm down here working for Larry Green at NTSB. I think I introduced you to him once."

"You did. I remember giving him my condolences."

"Well, I'm still driving him nuts. I want you to go see him and pass along a message." Davis told her what he wanted.

Sorensen considered it. "Jammer, I know how you operate. You won't be any good to Jen if you get in trouble yourself."

"I'll be careful."

A hesitation. "Okay, I'll do my best."

"That's exactly what I need, Anna."

* * *

The warehouse across from El Centro had once been the epicenter of a thriving air cargo business, a concern that fell abruptly insolvent when a raiding task force uncovered half a metric ton of high-grade cocaine embedded in shipments of aquarium filter cartridges. The owner of the company claimed to know nothing about the scheme, nor did the floor shift managers, and in the end the most expeditious path for everyone had been to simply shutter the place and sidestep blame.

That was the story Davis had heard, and it might well have been true. Heritage aside, the building across the street from El Centro was ideally suited to fill the investigation's most immediate need—ten thousand square feet of broomed concrete and a corrugated roof that didn't leak.

A guard at the door waved him through with only a glance at his credentials. Davis had been here twice before, and in the last twenty-four hours the room had begun to fill. Mostly it was the strays: antennas, wingtips, and sheet metal that had separated from the fuselage in the crash. The tail had been recovered largely intact, and now sat crookedly in one corner, the TAC-Air logo still sharp and clear on the unblemished white background. The most significant section missing was the disjointed fuselage and cockpit. Because the ARJ-35 was a relatively small aircraft, those pieces would likely be recovered as a whole, although the job would require a crane and a flatbed truck sturdy enough to handle a twenty-thousand-pound load—a matter further complicated by the condition of the roads and the remoteness of the crash site.

Davis walked straight past the wreckage. He was here with one objective in mind, and it had nothing to do with the metal on the floor. His footsteps echoed off the cavernous walls as he approached Pascal Delacorte, who was leaning over a bent horizontal stabilizer and taking a measurement.

"Glad to see I'm not the only one working late," said Davis.

Delacorte stood straight and stretched as if his back was sore. "I have not been in the field for over a year. One forgets how taxing it can be."

"You didn't come dressed for it, either," said Davis, staring at the Frenchman's silk shirt, pleated trousers, and Italian loafers. "How's the survivability of your airframe holding up?"

"From what I've seen so far, I would say the design carried the impact forces quite well. A few sections remain unaccounted for, but that is always the case, is it not?"

"It is."

"And you? Is there any news of your daughter?"

"Not yet, but I'm hopeful."

"Have you recovered from your near disaster under the wing?"

"I think so," Davis said, rolling one shoulder. "I've been practicing stiff-arms on the rugby pitch most of my life—I guess I finally found a practical use for it."

Delacorte smiled.

Davis said, "I'd like your opinion on something."

"I am glad to help. What is it?"

"Actually, I'd rather talk about it somewhere else, maybe over a beer. There's a bar down the street."

"*Très bon*. Are you buying?"

Davis nodded. "Now I know for sure you play rugby."

* * *

The bar was called La Pista, which Davis thought translated to The Runway. The place was darker than most and had a subdued atmosphere, which fit his mood perfectly. There were twenty square tables with chairs, ten stools at the bar. Half the seats were occupied by working men, and two young waitresses rushed deftly among them. The theme was predictably one of aviation. There was a wooden propeller bolted over the liquor rack, and pictures of old airplanes tacked on the walls. He caught the sporadic aroma of meat cooking on a grill and saw waves of smoke washing past an open back door. They took up station at one end of the bar, facing a picture of a DC-3 and next to a grizzled old man who nodded once, then went back to slurping soup from a bowl.

"I flew one of those once," Davis said, pointing to the picture.

"Was it challenging to land?" asked Delacorte. "I've been told tail-wheel aircraft require different techniques."

"I had my own technique," Davis said, thinking, *One that didn't involve the landing gear at all.* But that was another day and another place. He ordered *dos cervezas* from a curious bartender who probably didn't often entertain pairs of six-and-a-half-foot men from the high northern hemisphere. The beers appeared right away, reasonably cold in sweating bottles.

The two investigators exchanged a *santé*, and Davis' first draw went down like it always did, cool and dense. He hadn't had a beer in four days, which was some kind of record, but the usual gratification was missing. He made arrangements with the bartender to purchase a case of rum, and while he probably could have gotten a better bargain at a liquor store, the bartender was happy to take a credit card, and all Davis had to do to make good on his promise was haul one cardboard box across the street. That settled, he got down to his business with Delacorte.

"I have a theory about this crash, but I need some information about the ARJ-35 to back it up."

"What kind of information?"

"It relates to aircraft performance. Feel free to shoot holes in my idea. At the moment, Colonel Marquez and I aren't on the same page, and I could use an impartial opinion."

"You realize I am an engineer, not a fully trained investigator."

"All the better."

After talking to Sorensen, Davis had retrieved the sat-phone from his room, and he took it out now and called up the photographs he'd taken. "Here's what I found under that wing before it fell on me." He flicked through the pictures with an index finger and settled on one. "What do you see?"

"A landing gear assembly."

"What else?"

"Dead grass and dirt."

"Exactly. Now, BTA makes the gear doors for this airplane, right?"

"Of course."

"And can we agree that all the evidence we've seen so far confirms the landing gear was retracted when the airplane hit? The landing gear handle in the cockpit was up, the uplocks on this assembly are engaged, and there's no impact damage to the strut or support arms."

"Agreed," said Delacorte. "The landing gear was up when the aircraft struck. Are you questioning how this grass and dirt came to be in the wheel assembly?"

"I am."

Delacorte addressed his beer, adding a classic Gallic shrug.

"The airplane slid through a rain forest, so the landing gears doors could have jarred open momentarily, long enough to allow such contamination."

"My point isn't that grass and dirt are merely present—look more closely." Davis enlarged the photo. "That grass is *wrapped* around the wheel, and the gaps in the brake assemblies are full of debris. In a typical taxi-out, on an asphalt or concrete strip, those spaces would be scrubbed to a metallic shine by brake pressure. And up here," he pointed to the roof of the wheel well, "you can see a distinct splash pattern of mud and grass. Twin arcs, one above each wheel. The only way to get contamination like that is from a spinning wheel that's throwing muck."

Delacorte sat back on his stool.

Davis turned off the phone and slipped it back in his pocket.

The Frenchman said, "You are suggesting the airplane landed somewhere else? On an unimproved airstrip?"

"It would answer a lot of questions."

"Including what might have happened to your daughter?"

Here Davis hesitated. "It's possible."

"Where could it have landed?"

"That's where I was hoping you could help me. Tell me about the soft field landing capability of this airplane."

Delacorte's expression went sour. "It was not designed for 'soft fields,' as you put it. The engines are too low to the ground. On a grass or dirt strip there would be a high chance of foreign objects being ingested into the bypass fan."

"I know it wasn't designed for that—but is it *possible*?"

The Frenchman's mouth maintained its upside-down U. "An airplane is an airplane. If the landing surface was in reasonable condition, and if it was long enough . . . yes."

"Define long enough."

"One thousand meters minimum. Twelve hundred would be better."

Davis turned his bottle in his hand. It was the answer he'd wanted to hear, yet it widened his field of search considerably.

"Will you suggest this theory to Marquez?" Delacorte asked.

Davis blew out a long breath. "The colonel and I are barely on speaking terms right now."

"He seems competent enough."

"He's very competent. Only I think he's found himself between a rock and a hard place. The rock is the Colombian Air Force, which means his career is on the line."

"And the place that is hard?"

Davis grinned at the translation. "I don't know . . . it's strange. I don't think Marquez ever *really* believed this was a hijacking. But he kept pushing the idea, even after it clearly didn't work. It's almost like . . . like he was playing for time."

"Or trying to make everyone look away from the real cause."

"Maybe so," said Davis.

"What can you do?"

"I don't have much choice. I'm convinced this airplane landed somewhere before the crash. It fits everything we know. The evidence in the wheel well, the missing passengers, even the missing captain. I guess there's no choice—I'll have to go to Marquez and make my case."

They drained their bottles. The bartender was good, asking if they wanted refills as soon as glass hit wood. Both men declined. Davis paid for their beers, assured the bartender he would be back for his case of rum, and they headed for the door. Two steps from the entrance he heard the first sirens. Davis took a cautious step outside, and saw a police car skid to a stop in the gravel parking apron across the road. Two officers dismounted and ran toward a crowd of people. Their guns were drawn.

TWENTY-TWO

Sorensen drove back into work early that evening, passing through security after most of the day shift had gone home. The George Bush Center for Intelligence is necessarily a 24/7/365 operation, yet the vast majority of the workforce keep office hours as regular as any accountant or banker. That being the case, the halls were quiet, and there was no one else working in her section. It probably didn't matter.

On face value her inquiries were harmless. She needed only to identify a twenty-year-old girl who'd recently traveled to Colombia, which by itself put high odds on one of two scenarios— Kristin Stewart was either a college student on a semester abroad, or a young woman on a church mission trip. Sorensen figured she'd be able to write the girl's life story by eight that night, leaving time for a glass of Malbec before bed. The passport number was key. It would link a photograph and address to her subject, and from there the CIA's primary database would thread together driver's license information, school transcripts, and any recorded arrests. If necessary, Sorensen could go all the way back to a twenty-year-old birth certificate complete with tiny footprints.

She sat down at her desk, logged into the system, and had the research database active in less than a minute. The main page was essentially a questionnaire asking for all existing information on the unknown subject, including a facial photograph that could be uploaded and matched using disturbingly accurate recognition software. Sorensen entered what she had—full name, passport number, and birth date for Kristin Stewart—and then hit the send button. The computer hesitated longer than usual as it digested her request. The response that finally flashed to her screen was one she had never seen before. Indeed, one she didn't even know existed: UNAUTHORIZED ACCESS.

"What the hell?" she muttered.

She considered a second try, but hesitated over the input page where the fields had gone blank. Sorensen suspected a second request would end no differently. She'd seen the primary server go down before, and had more than once sent invalid requests upstream. That wasn't what she was looking at. *Unauthorized Access.* She had used this system to research terrorists, Wall Street financiers, foreign heads of state, and at least one philandering United States ambassador. Never had she simply been denied.

Sorensen pushed away from her desk and considered her options. During regular business hours she might have been tempted to call Melanie Brown, her Secret Service friend in Chicago. Melanie had already gone out on a limb for her once, however, and the name Kristin Stewart had obviously raised a flag. Sorensen was sure her denial of access had been logged and reported, and tomorrow would likely appear in a morning brief. But in which nearby office? Homeland Security? The Department of State? Internally within the CIA? It was bad enough she'd been locked out—but had she also unsuspectingly hit a tripwire?

Sorensen shut down her computer and minutes later was in her car. She cut through the nearly empty parking lot at an angle, and was almost to the front gate when her cell phone rang. She looked at the number and didn't recognize it. She sat through five rings, shrill and loud, before slowing down and taking the call.

"Hello."

"Hello, Miss Sorensen. I need to meet with you about your very recent request for information."

Sorensen steered to the curb at the edge of the parking area, coming to a stop at a diagonal against rows of empty white lines, her Ford Focus highlighted by a tall bank of sodium lights. She cautiously put the car in park before speaking. "Who is this?"

"That will become clear. We need to meet. Please be at Volta Park at eight thirty. It's near Georgetown University."

Sorensen looked at her watch. Half an hour. Her mind raced. "No. Nine thirty at the western path to the Washington Monument."

"Miss Sorensen—"

She ended the call and turned off her phone. Whoever it was, if they wanted to see her, they'd do it on her terms. It gave her a degree of control. It also gave her ninety minutes to figure out what the hell she was getting into.

* * *

From the bar Davis ran across the street, but nearing the parking lot he slowed. He saw a staff car like the one Marquez had been using, a small crowd gathered around it. Policemen were shoehorning in for a look, but nobody seemed in a hurry.

Davis recognized Rafael, the young man who'd helped him with the video two nights earlier. "What happened?" he asked.

"Colonel Marquez has been shot."

"Is he alive?"

A solemn look foreshadowed Rafael's answer. "I do not think so."

More police pulled into the parking lot, and when another pair of officers cut through the crowd, Davis fell in behind them. The staff car came into view, and he saw Marquez framed in the driver's-side window, just above the vulture coat-of-arms. The colonel was sprawled back in his seat, a massive splotch of blood centered on his chest and one ear resting on his shoulder. He was definitely not alive.

Being the tallest bystander, Davis looked over a sea of heads and across the parking lot. It looked no different than it had thirty minutes ago, when he and Delacorte had walked to the bar. The only changes: five police cars and a dead colonel. Davis found himself revisiting his earlier thought. *A man living on borrowed time.*

He backed away and said in a loud voice, "Did anyone see who did this?"

There were at least twenty people surrounding the car. Not one gave a reply. He spotted Rafael again, and asked, "What happened?"

"No one saw it. We were all inside."

"Did you hear gunshots?"

"No, there was nothing."

An ambulance arrived, and a pair of paramedics hustled to the car. With one look their sense of urgency abated. Soon one of the policemen began asking questions in Spanish. The second person he spoke with, an Air Force corporal Davis had seen regularly in the office, pointed a finger straight at him.

Davis stood his ground on the perimeter, making the cop come to him. He wasn't surprised at all when the man grabbed his elbow and said in English, "You come with me, *señor.*" Davis stared briefly at the cop, then at his accuser.

He was escorted to a quiet room in El Centro and told not to leave. Davis tried to tell the policeman he had better things to do, that he was investigating the crash of an airliner.

The door shut decisively in his face.

* * *

Sorensen had some years ago begun an MBA at George Washington University. She'd seen it as a career-broadening move, one of the square-fillers expected of those seeking advancement within the Company. With no small degree of irony, her good intentions were undermined when a foreign posting intervened. In a recurring theme, and one that extended beyond her professional life, she withdrew from the program after only two months. Yet even if she'd earned no credits, Sorensen had learned valuable lessons. Among them—the Eckles Library was open to the public, kept late hours, and offered computer access on the second floor.

She researched Kristin Marie Stewart strictly from public sources, and after approaching the problem from a number of angles, Sorensen narrowed her hunt to two possible suspects. One was a twenty year old who lived in Mesa, Arizona, a girl who had one arrest for possession of marijuana—less than six ounces— and was documented photographically as having participated in at least three swimsuit competitions at various spring break hotspots. She was a bottle blond who'd apparently undertaken her first boob job at a tender young age, and who looked smashing in a polka-dot two-piece with a T-back bottom.

The other prospect was also twenty years old, but cut from a very different bolt of cloth. This Kristin Stewart had graduated from her Raleigh, North Carolina, high school near the top of her class. She'd been active in a variety of extracurricular activities, including Spanish Club and lacrosse, and received a scholarship from the local Elks Lodge which, according to the blurb beneath a photograph, would advance her pursuit of a degree in soil science at the University of Virginia. She had dark, shoulder-length hair, and exhibited the buoyant smile of a young girl ready to take the world by storm. Also labeled in the Elks Lodge picture was her mother, Jean Stewart, presumably of Raleigh, North Carolina.

Sorensen was certain she'd found her girl.

She checked the time and saw she had twenty-five minutes until her rendezvous at the Washington Monument. With whom, Sorensen had no idea, but she wasn't particularly worried. The meeting had all the hallmarks of an inter-service turf war. Jammer had inadvertently crashed someone's delicate clandestine op, and now her parallel inquiries had trampled further onto the hallowed ground of some shadowy agency, likely a three-letter acronym she'd dealt with before. All the same, for a face-to-face meeting Sorensen thought it wise to keep things in plain view. She doubted she was in professional hot water. Not yet, anyway. If that were the case, the meeting would not have been arranged by an anonymous phone call. It would have convened in a Langley conference room by directive, a boulder rolling down the hill that was her lawful chain of command. No, she decided—this meeting under the stars was not on the record.

Sorensen nearly got up from the computer when a last contingency entered her mind. Whoever she was about to meet would likely try to intimidate her, and in the worst case she would get a phone call from her supervisor telling her to back off. If that happened, she would comply, at least on appearances. But she wasn't going to give up. Not as long as Jen was missing.

It took four minutes more on the computer to find what she needed. She scribbled down an address and stuffed it in her purse.

TWENTY-THREE

Davis waited in the room for nearly an hour, his only company a progression of sorry thoughts. A policeman checked on him every ten minutes, presumably to ensure that he hadn't chipped through the cinder block walls of the windowless room. Finally, the person he was expecting walked in.

"Good evening, Mr. Davis," said Major Echevarria of the Bogotá Police, Special Investigations Unit.

"Not really," said Davis, not rising from his folding metal chair to shake hands. "Certainly not for Marquez."

Echevarria pulled up the only other chair in the room, turned it backwards, and straddled it to face Davis with a Formica work table between them. The interrogation room—the only phrase that fit—was typically used for storage, and was littered with empty boxes, paper, and file cabinets. The air was laced in print toner and cheap cleanser.

"So what happened?" Davis asked.

"That is what I've come to find out."

"He was shot."

"Yes, three times. A very thorough job."

"Any idea who's responsible?"

Echevarria rubbed his forehead with a meaty finger, like a man at the end of a particularly hard and troubling day. "Where were you tonight?"

Davis smiled grimly, his head tipping to one side. "At the time of the murder? Are you serious?"

The policeman's silence said he was.

"I was across the street having a beer with an engineer from

BTA. His name is Pascal Delacorte. There was a bartender too, and I'm sure if you looked, you could find ten customers who'd remember us being there."

Echevarria nodded. "Actually, I already know that much. The trouble I am faced with is this—at least two of the workers in this building heard you and Marquez arguing not long before his death."

"We've been arguing for the last two days. You already know that, just like you know I had nothing to do with this."

"Then who is responsible?"

A shrug from Davis. "I'm sure Colombia has its share of hoodlums and thugs."

"And that's where you suggest I look? Hoodlums and thugs in the barrios? What would you know about such people?"

"A lot—I play rugby. But I'm not talking about the barrios. No petty criminal is going to shoot a military officer while he's sitting in his staff car."

"Organized crime, then?"

"You're getting closer. If I were you, I'd consider motive. Who benefits from his death? It could be someone respectable, somebody from the air force or city hall . . . maybe even the police department."

Echevarria remained steady, but his voice went cool. "Let me put it to you another way, Mr. Davis. Have there been developments in the investigation that might cause difficulties for Colonel Marquez?"

"I blew his hijacking theory out of the water today. That was probably difficult for him."

"Would it have been a problem for anyone else?"

Davis leaned forward and put his elbows on the table. "Now that's your best question yet, Major. I'd look into it if I were you. Who does Marquez report to?"

Echevarria hesitated, and Davis expected him to say that *he* would be asking the questions. Instead, he said, "He is attached to Comando Aéreo de Combate 2. General Suarez is in charge."

"So General Suarez is Marquez' commander of record. What about off the record?"

"I'm not sure what you mean."

Davis paused a beat. "I found evidence today that points to some very disturbing conclusions about this crash."

"Such as?"

"I can't say," said Davis. "It's privileged information relating to an ongoing investigation."

"If that's what you think," Echevarria said in a rising voice, "then you are not very well versed in Colombian law."

"So call a lawyer. Or if you really don't like it, put me up as a guest of the State tonight. I've already seen the accommodations, and they're not that bad." Davis straightened in his chair. "The way I see it, neither of us can afford to waste time."

"A serious crime was committed here tonight, Mr. Davis."

"True, a man was killed, one who had two teenage kids and a wife. The thing is, I'm investigating an even more serious crime. I've got twenty-one bodies and three missing persons."

Echevarria said nothing.

Davis stood and said in a calm voice, "A lot of people seem to have an interest in this crash. I don't know who or why, but I'll find out. When I do I'll share it with you, because the same people and motives are behind what happened to Colonel Marquez. In the meantime, I'm guessing this crash investigation will spin its wheels for a time. The air force will put a new colonel in charge, by next week if we're lucky. Unfortunately, he or she will have to start from square one. It'll take a long time to get up to speed, which means for the foreseeable future, the only person who's going to make *any* progress in this inquiry is me. I don't care if you like me, Major. I doubt we'll exchange Christmas cards this December. But right now—you should understand that I'm the best friend you've got."

Davis turned toward the door.

Echevarria spoke through what sounded like a clenched jaw. "You still have hope for your daughter?"

Davis paused at the threshold, and without looking back said, "Very much so."

"Then I wish you happy hunting."

* * *

Anna Sorensen was a trained CIA field operative. As such, she habitually arrived at clandestine meetings early in order to survey the field of play and take precautions. Tonight there had been no time.

She walked onto the west lawn of the Washington Monument at 9:33, three minutes late. There were actually two paths toward the monument from that direction—she hadn't been here in some time—and she opted for the nearest. To her left was The Ellipse, and beyond that the White House. Behind her was the World War II Memorial, and farther on the reflecting pool and monument where Lincoln sat eternal watch over the Potomac.

Even at this hour tourists were wheeling around the uplit monument and taking pictures with their smartphones, images destined to join tens of millions of nearly identical compositions in that web-based repository known as The Cloud. Sorensen was standing on one of the most highly monitored acres of land on Earth, which of course was why she'd chosen it. She saw the U.S. Park Police, U.S. Capitol Police, and along Constitution Avenue a pair of D.C. Metro squad cars were parked nose to tail. All that reassurance aside, Sorensen did feel a tendril of unease. Being so close to the White House, the Secret Service had to be near, quite possibly the agency she was here to meet. Had she put herself on enemy territory?

With no idea whom she was looking for, Sorensen paused a hundred feet short of the massive obelisk and pretended to admire it. Her confidence was rewarded.

"Miss Sorensen?"

She turned to see a man of medium height standing behind her. He wore a well-cut suit and tie, although he didn't look completely comfortable in it. Short hair and a square jaw made her think of the military.

"Yes. And you are?"

"Jones, ma'am."

Sorensen replied with a grin, and said, "Jones? Is that your last name or your first? Or maybe the only one—you know, like Pele or Bono?"

The face cracked briefly into a regulation smile, but it died quickly. He pointed a thick and noticeably bent finger to the east. "Would you mind if we walked toward The Mall? The crowds here can be difficult."

Sorensen allowed it, and they set off at a casual pace.

"Thank you for coming," he said as they paused at the 14th Street crosswalk.

"So who are you with?" she asked.

"I'm not sure if that's relevant to what—"

"My money is on the Secret Service," she cut in. "I performed a search on a young woman named Kristin Stewart, and was immediately locked out. I've never seen that before. Then a few minutes later you call and ask me for a shadowy meeting. A bit melodramatic on your part, if you don't mind my saying so. If I were to take this all to my supervisor, I'm not sure what she—"

"No," Jones interrupted, "I'm not with the Secret Service."

Sorensen stared at him, mildly surprised, and she thought he might be on the level. The crossing light changed and they began to walk.

"The name you just mentioned, Miss Stewart. She's a college student who's gone missing."

"Missing?"

"It's an age when kids tend to find trouble."

"You make it sound like she got caught skinny dipping in the university fountain. She was a passenger on an airliner that crashed under very suspicious circumstances."

Jones' gaze sharpened ever so slightly. "That situation is being handled. As far as you and your employer are concerned, Kristin Stewart should be left alone."

"Left alone?" Sorensen repeated. "That implies she survived. It makes me think you know where she is."

The two exchanged an awkward look.

"There's still a great deal of uncertainty," said Jones "which I think you already know."

Sorensen didn't reply, an admission he was right.

"You've been in contact with Mr. Davis, I think? I understand the two of you are friends on . . . some level."

Sorensen kept steady against the implication that Jones, and whoever he represented, knew about her intermittent relationship with Jammer. "He's down in Colombia looking for Kristin Stewart, and he asked for my help. I suspect you know that much. What you *don't* know is how close he's gotten."

"And you do?" he asked as they rounded a group of Asian tourists.

"Like you said—we've been in contact."

"I can promise you one thing, Miss Sorensen. Your friend Davis may eventually discover what happened to that flight—in fact, we hope he does—but there's no chance of him finding Kristin Stewart."

"You wouldn't be the first to underestimate him. His daughter was on that flight too."

Jones paused and gave her a peculiar look. "His daughter?"

Sorensen eyed the man critically. "I have you at a disadvantage, don't I? A little bit of knowledge—it can be a dangerous thing."

Jones seemed acutely deliberate in gathering his response. He stood silhouetted by the distant White House, which itself was pleasingly framed by dark, thick-branched chestnut trees in the warm evening air. He finally said, "Miss Sorensen, I can't tell you who I represent, but rest assured it is someone who doesn't forget a favor."

"Such as?"

"The easiest thing of all. Go home, have a glass of wine, and get a good night's sleep. Go to work tomorrow and forget all about this. If Mr. Davis calls, tell him you've hit a dead end in your search for the girl—which you did. Things are being managed at a higher level. Please believe me when I say it's best for everyone involved if you simply allow events to run their course."

"Best for everyone? Even Kristin Stewart?"

"*Especially* Kristin Stewart."

"And if I choose to ignore your sage advice?"

Jones heaved a sigh, a teacher weary of an unruly first grader. "Let me put it like this. If you didn't work for the CIA, Miss Sorensen, and if you weren't able to pursue any remotely related career on the civilian side—what would you do for a living?"

She stared at him in the half light. "I don't know, I never thought about it."

"Maybe you should."

And with that, the counterfeit Jones walked away. Sorensen watched him fade into the D.C. nightscape, a silhouette against a domed Capitol building struck in brilliant white light. She still couldn't say who the man worked for, and didn't understand the ties to Kristin Stewart. Sorensen was, however, sure of one thing. Whoever they were, they were running scared.

* * *

The call reached Strand at his G Street office minutes later. Not liking what he heard, the CEO of The Alamosa Group spent thirty minutes acquiring further information. Only then did he call Bill Evers.

"We made contact with the woman," Strand said.

"Will she do as we ask?" Evers asked.

"No way to tell. But this is clearly not an official CIA inquiry. She's only helping a friend."

"Davis," said Evers.

"Yes."

"Then that's good."

"The best we could have hoped for. If CIA were to blunder into this en masse we could have real problems. But there *was* something that took us by surprise." Strand paused, knowing Evers did not like surprises. "It seems Davis has a daughter—and she was on that same airplane."

"What?"

Strand said, "She's the second passenger who's missing. It does explain a few things. More of what we've seen in our surveillance of Davis makes sense, in particular the way he's pressing so hard. Just to be sure, I made a few calls. Davis works for a Larry Green at the NTSB, a retired Air Force general. Apparently, Green recognized the daughter's name on a preliminary manifest of crash victims. After verifying it was her, he put Davis on the investigation."

There was a long pause as Evers considered it. "Does this bother you? I mean, what are the chances of that—Kristin being on the same flight as an NTSB investigator's daughter?"

"Slim," said Strand, "but I've considered it from every angle. It's just dumb luck."

"Luck," Evers said, almost to himself. "But which kind?"

TWENTY-FOUR

It was nearly ten o'clock when Davis got back to his room. He arrived to find a note from Delacorte taped to his door:

I have information that would interest you. Room 302.

Davis climbed one flight of stairs, rounded the building and found 302 on the back side. The door was open and he found Delacorte sitting on a chair near the window. The room was much like his own, except the painting on the wall was of a mission-style church instead of a conquistador.

"I thought they put flankers up at the Ritz," said Davis.

"I would prefer anywhere but this room. My air conditioner has stopped working."

Davis saw a window-mounted air conditioner. The control panel had been removed, and wires dangled free like so much overcooked spaghetti. "Looks like you've already tried to fix it."

"The fan motor has seized—there is no hope." Delacorte fanned himself with a tourist brochure. "It does not get so hot in Paris."

"If you want to drag your mattress around the corner you can bunk with me."

"No, but thank you for offering."

"I got your note. What's the interesting information?"

"What you said earlier about landing on an unimproved field," he raised a finger to imply a revelation, "it caused me to think of other possibilities."

"Such as?"

"You have suggested that Flight 223 made an interim landing, after taking off from Bogotá but before the crash. We also have a dead copilot to consider, and another man dressed in a TAC-Air captain's uniform, but who has not been identified."

Davis nodded. "Not to mention the pastry chef who ended up as pilot-in-command."

"It will be a challenge, I think, to construct a scenario that brings all these things together."

"To say the least."

"I'm afraid I have—what is the term in America?—one more wrench to throw in your machine."

"By all means, toss away."

Delacorte pulled out a tablet computer and kept talking as he typed. "In studying the hull I have discovered that certain parts remain missing. Of course, this is not at all unusual in such a devastating crash. There was, however, one absence I thought strange." He turned the screen to show Davis a photograph of the forward side fuselage. "The main entry door is nowhere to be found."

Davis studied the picture. He had seen the opening before, even stepped through it once, yet he'd attached no particular significance to the missing door. "Nobody mentioned that it hadn't been found. I assumed it had broken off and was probably retrieved from the undergrowth."

"A reasonable assumption. You and I often encounter missing doors. It is usually the result of an evacuation, or sometimes they are removed and discarded in haste by firefighting crews."

Delacorte was right—doors were often absent. Such a normal occurrence, in fact, that he hadn't seen it as relevant.

Delacorte continued, "The cabin of an ARJ-35 has four access doors. At the front you have a port-side entry door, the one we are missing, and an opposing starboard service door that was undisturbed in the crash sequence. Aft of these are two small emergency exit hatches, one above each wing. In our mishap the evacuation hatches remained in place—they were never opened.

The two forward doors, of course, double as emergency evacuation points, although there are no emergency escape slides as you would find on a larger airliner."

"So the missing entry door—are you going to tell me somebody survived the crash and opened the door as an emergency exit?"

"Actually, quite the opposite. That door will likely never be found."

Davis looked at him quizzically.

Delacorte tapped the screen. "As you see, the door is a clamshell design, upper and lower halves hinged to the entryway frame. The bottom half contains an integral set of stairs, used at remote airports where no jetways or airstairs are available." Delacorte switched to another image. "I took photographs of the hinges—these are from the bottom half of the door."

Davis looked closely. Two heavy steel fittings had clearly failed, both twisted severely to the breaking point.

"I inspected them very closely," said the engineer, "and I can tell you that they failed very clearly in torsion."

"Torsion."

"A terrific force twisted the door and ripped it off the airframe quite cleanly. The top hinge is nearly identical. I also discovered two dents on the leading edge of the inboard port wing, and another on the number one engine cowling. All of this supports my theory."

Davis finally understood. "You're saying this door opened in flight . . . that it was ripped off its hinges."

A satisfied Delacorte said, "Almost certainly."

TWENTY-FIVE

Delacorte's finding changed the picture completely. It also created new complications.

"Okay," said Davis, "so we have a door that came open in flight. Could that have caused the crash?"

"This was my first thought as well, but I do not think it fits. True, the wing was damaged, but not in a way that would affect aerodynamic performance. This aircraft has no leading edge flaps on the wing, which would be prone to causing instability if damaged. The tail is a more critical surface, however, I see no damage there that correlates to door separation."

"The engine?"

"Yes, I considered this also. The outer cowling was dented, impact damage from the door, I would say. This led me to examine the engine, both the fan and turbine. I found no acute rotational damage—only the graduated distortions one would expect from an impact with the forest."

Delacorte allowed a moment for Davis to digest it all.

"Of course," he continued, "this is all no more than one engineer's opinion. With time, everything can be verified by way of laboratory inspections."

Davis shook his head. "That would be fine if we had time, but in my opinion you've already passed the most critical test—it makes perfect sense."

"What do you take from it? You realize what must happen for this door to be opened in flight."

Davis did know. Over the years there had been regular occurrences, often sensationalized in the media, of mentally unbalanced individuals trying to open aircraft exit doors in flight. What on the surface appears dramatic and threatening, however, is in fact a non-event. Passenger aircraft are pressurized to counter the thin air at high altitude, and among manufacturers the design specifications are more or less universal, the differential pressure being roughly eight pounds per square inch at service altitude. Simply put, a cabin door six feet high and three feet wide is held in place during cruise flight by an effective force of over twenty thousand pounds. Davis and his entire rugby team would never budge a fully pressurized door.

That said, there *was* a way to open a door in flight, a scenario that was problematic for one very good reason—it involved cooperation from the flight deck.

"The pilots could have depressurized the cabin," said Davis.

"It is the only way," agreed Delacorte. "But why would a crew do that?"

As Davis thought about it, disjointed details began to mesh. "Remember—we still have the issue of the disappearing Captain Reyna. Let's say Flight 223 landed on a grass strip somewhere, then took off again and flew to where it crashed. That requires at least one pilot on board to get the jet airborne and pointed in the right direction. We found three people in that cockpit. Two, as far as we know, weren't even pilots. The other was the first officer, and he was dead before the airplane went down. I'm guessing maybe a long time before, which would mean our copilot, Moreno, had no part in this scheme."

Davis watched Delacorte struggle to put it all together.

"If you think about it," Davis said, "there's only one person who could have made everything work."

"Captain Reyna."

"Exactly. I'm guessing he shot his copilot, probably before they even diverted to the remote airstrip. That way he gets no challenges about why they're changing destination. When they land in the jungle, the two missing girls are taken off, and the body we found in the captain's seat is brought on board. A John

Doe already dead and dressed in a uniform that didn't fit. That all works, but only if Reyna had help, somebody waiting for him on the ground."

"*C'est incroyable!*" said Delacorte.

"No less incredible than the paperwork I came across two nights ago. Captain Reyna's personnel file was altered so that his physical characteristics matched those of our mystery corpse."

Delacorte's gaze narrowed.

"I'm sure of it," said Davis. "Major Echevarria is looking into the details, but the very fact that he hasn't shot this down tells me we're on the right track. Somebody with official access has been altering evidence. The way I figure it, when Flight 223 made its second takeoff that night, the girls were no longer on board and Reyna was in the cockpit with two dead men, probably behind a locked door. The part I've been wrestling with was Reyna himself—what happened to him? You just gave me the answer."

After a long moment, an overwhelmed Delacorte said, "You are now going to tell me he used a parachute? Is that even possible?"

"D.B. Cooper thought so." Delacorte stared a blank, and Davis realized his reference to the legendary hijacker had fallen flat. "It was back in the seventies. A guy hijacked a Boeing 727, said he was carrying a bomb. The plane landed, and Cooper ordered two bourbon and waters while everything played out, even paid for them and tipped the flight attendant. Once he had his ransom and the passengers were deplaned, they took off again and headed out over the Cascade Mountains east of Seattle. Cooper took off his tie, put on a parachute, and ordered the pilots to depressurize the airplane and lower the aft stairs. Then he jumped."

"Yes," said Delacorte, "now I recall. He was never found."

"Nope. But if nothing else, D.B. proves our point."

Delacorte wrestled with the idea. "Reyna kills his copilot and flies to a remote airfield where the girls are removed? Then he takes off again, depressurizes the airplane . . . and jumps leaving no one on board to fly?"

"No one except his dead copilot and a corpse that was put in the cockpit while they were on the ground—that made the body count nice and neat, and it would have worked nicely if the crash had created the usual fireball. After Reyna jumped the passengers had one last hope, a pastry chef who broke into the locked flight deck and did his damnedest to save the day. He didn't quite do it, but he flew long enough to burn down fuel, and he probably guided the jet to strike at a relatively soft angle. That preserved a lot of evidence for us."

"You are suggesting that Reyna sacrificed an entire aircraft full of passengers. How could any pilot do such a thing?"

"Morally? I have no idea. The more pertinent question for us is *why* he would do such a thing."

Delacorte cast a critical gaze. "I have never heard such an outrageous theory in any investigation."

"Neither have I," Davis agreed. "Unfortunately, it's the only solution that lines up with the facts."

"Perhaps. But this theory you propose is convenient in one way, my friend. It allows a chance that your daughter is still alive. I must ask—could your heart be driving your solutions more than the evidence?"

Davis looked Delacorte in the eye. "I don't know, Pascal. I really don't know."

Davis got up to leave, and as he made his way back to his room the burden of Delacorte's question hung like a great weight. Which *was* leading? His heart or the truth?

* * *

At midnight Davis pulled off his boots at the foot of the bed. He was glad to have the Frenchman around. Even if Delacorte was an engineer by training, his instincts were good, and he had that flair of imagination found in all good investigators—the ability to ask with a clear mind, *What if?*

His own air conditioner blew like an Arctic wind, and he lay on the bed and tried for sleep. He plugged Jen's songs into his ears, and like the last two nights a tiger-striped iPod became his last tenuous link to his little girl. His last link to sanity. He flicked idly across the screen and saw a camera symbol. He'd never realized the gadget had a camera. Something else he should have known. His thumb hesitated. Was it a violation to look at her pictures? Of course it was. Davis rationalized that if he ever had to explain, he would say he was acting in an investigative capacity.

He hoped to hell he *would* have to explain.

He tapped the button and began flicking through pictures. There were none of him, but he didn't take it as a slight. He saw a selfie of Jen with her roommate. Jen with a pair of Asian boys he'd never seen. The oldest was from last Christmas, Jen with three of her old high school friends, all of them sporting Santa hats and shot glasses, a riotous party in the background. Davis held steady. The glasses were full, of what he could only imagine. He wrote it off for what it was—an inevitable rite of passage. Hadn't he done the same thing at that age? A year ago, certainly two, he would have blown a gasket at underage drinking. Now? Maybe he'd mellowed. More likely—since she'd gone off to school he missed her desperately. Somewhere along the road of adolescence, Jen had grown up, become as much a friend as a daughter. Then again, if he ever caught her drinking and driving he would back her against the nearest wall and do his best drill sergeant impersonation—which was *very* good.

Davis reached the end of the picture show, the last frame apparently taken from inside her back pocket—what happened when you sat down with the camera mode active. He lowered the Touch briefly, then did a double-take. The last frame wasn't actually a photograph—an arrow in the middle of the screen told Davis it was a video. He wondered when it had been taken, but there was no obvious date stamp. He hit the little arrow and the movie began to play. The video never changed, only a blank screen with a blurred tinge of brown on one side. The audio that came through the earbuds, however, nearly caused his heart to seize.

Jen's voice. *"I see men with guns outside."*

A different female voice replied, *"Don't worry. It'll be okay."*

Jen again. *"Is there an ambulance? They said the copilot is sick—maybe that's why we landed here."*

Shouting in the background, loud and authoritative in Spanish. Then two unmistakable cracks, sharp and loud. Even through the earbuds Davis recognized the sound of gunshots, and he knew where they had been directed—Special Agent Mulligan. As if to confirm his conclusion, hysterical shouts followed, and then a shriek of, *"Thomas! No!"*

Jen's voice came through, shakier now. *"Oh my God! They've killed him!"*

A man began shouting orders over the chaos: *"No te muevas!"* Don't move.

Things fell quiet. The invaders had made their point, had assumed control. Davis heard the second, distinctive female voice fall to a whisper. The words were spoken close to the microphone, which meant they could only have come from Jen's seatmate. The girl he'd seen her talking to in the boarding area video, and who Jen had mentioned in her final phone message.

Kristin Stewart.

Passenger 19.

"Jen, listen to me! If you want to get out of this alive do exactly as I say!"

There was a pause, and he imagined Jen staring at her seatmate, a look of consternation fused with dread: the man in the seat next to her was bleeding out, and multiple assailants stood brandishing weapons. But Jen had always been good under pressure, and in that silent gap Davis could almost sense her bucking up. He envisioned her making eye contact with Kristin Stewart, perhaps giving a deft nod.

Then another whispered command from Passenger 19. *"Get rid of your passport and any other ID!"* A hesitation. *"Do it, for God's sake!"*

He visualized both girls retrieving their passports discreetly and slipping them into the seatback pockets. Exactly where he'd found them.

"Whatever you do," Kristin implores, *"give them my name. Tell them you are Kristin Marie Stewart from Raleigh, North Carolina. That's what we both say and nothing else! Do you understand?"*

Next he heard a new male voice that was stunningly familiar. The words came in English, rumbling as if churned from a rock crusher. The same voice that had asked him what he was doing under a wing. Black boots with a crescent-shaped scar. *"Out of my way! Anyone who moves will be shot!"* Then closer to the microphone. *"Hands on your heads, everyone!"*

A last desperate whisper from Kristin Stewart, *"Say nothing else, Jen! Nothing! It's your only chance!"*

"Quiet!" the male voice ordered. His next words blasted full volume from the iPod's tiny speaker. *"Kristin Stewart! Which of you is Kristin Stewart?"*

There was no audible response, and the question was shouted again. Then Davis heard a sound that caused him to nearly crush the iPod in his hand—the sound of skin slapping skin, followed by the yelp of a young girl. He didn't know which, but it hardly mattered. Shuffling and grunting was followed by more commands in Spanish. Finally, he heard Jen's voice one last time. Her tone was matter of fact and cool. She could have been signing off from their daily dorm-room chat.

"Help us, Dad, we're—"

The last word cut off abruptly.

For three more minutes Davis sat still as the pictureless video ran, capturing the occasional distant shout, but little else. There were no muted conversations among the nearby passengers, which Davis took as evidence that at least one assailant had remained in the cabin to stand guard. The recording ended abruptly. He looked at the time bar and saw six minutes and ten seconds. That was when the iPod had given in. Davis didn't know why. Perhaps the battery had gotten low, or someone had nudged the off button.

He looked closely at the device to make sure there was nothing else. He saw no other videos or pictures. Further invading Jen's privacy, he checked her contacts, notepad, and calendar. Nothing held promise. He sat motionless on the edge of the bed, like a statue of carved marble. Jen *had* been pulled off the aircraft that night, abducted after an unscheduled landing by men who had come for Kristin Stewart. Lawless men who'd shot a Secret Service agent in cold blood. Here Davis paused. Had an unarmed Mulligan resisted? Had he tried to put up a fight against insurmountable force? No, he decided. There had been no sounds of a scuffle, no shouted warnings from Mulligan to Kristin. The bandits had burst aboard and shot him straight out. Shot him because they knew who he was, where he was sitting, and why he was there.

Davis imagined the rest. Two college girls getting pushed and shoved, possibly beaten. An image of pure conjecture, to be sure, and one that made him simmer with rage. As distressing as the recording was, however, it also came as a gift. He now knew with certainty that Jen had survived the crash. He knew she and Kristin Stewart were likely still alive. Somewhere.

All he had to do was find them.

TWENTY-SIX

Through the course of that night a reenergized Davis played back the recording fourteen times. In each run-through he registered fresh nuances, and he paused regularly to take notes. The only way to keep his emotions in check, he knew, was to be absolutely methodical.

On the second playback he isolated the sound of Flight 223's entry door being opened—the same door he and Delacorte had discussed earlier, and that was now missing—evidenced by the sudden introduction of white noise from the aircraft's auxiliary power unit, the small tail-mounted engine that provided power and conditioned air on the ground. He logged three male voices, including the distinctive gravel-edged baritone. Most of the words were in subdued Spanish, which Davis took for conversation between the assailants. It crossed his mind that one voice could also be that of Captain Reyna. With enough time, and in a proper lab, he could have the APU noise acoustically filtered out, the Spanish translated, and the voices analyzed. But those luxuries he didn't have. Jen needed him now.

On the tenth playback Davis drew a paper-and-pencil diagram of the airplane, sketching from memory where each passenger had been sitting. He traced the path the invaders must have taken: entry at the forward door, down the aisle, and ending at the back of the jet where the girls sat. He stopped and started the recording repeatedly, trying to place sounds one by one, and slotting each new fragment into his existing bank of knowledge. He listened closely to Jen's words. *They said the copilot is sick—maybe that's why we landed here.*

The copilot had not been taken ill, that much Davis knew, allowing that a bullet to the brain is not a common malady. All the same, Jen's comment meant an announcement had been made to justify what was happening. Most likely it came from Reyna, although it could have been relayed through the flight attendant. Either way, the intent was evident—the captain wanted to keep everyone calm during their unscheduled landing, compliant until his supporting cast of armed associates took control. Calm and unknowing was always the best mindset for prisoners, which was what the passengers of Flight 223 had become.

Davis wondered if anyone besides the two girls had been taken off the jet, even temporarily. He heard nothing on the recording to support the idea, and the fact that they were the only passengers not found in the wreckage cemented things. Minute by minute, his theory coalesced and gained definition: Flight 223 had diverted to a remote airfield, guided by a captain who was conspiring with individuals on the ground. The copilot had been executed, likely by his skipper during the first flight behind the protection of a hardened door. After landing, the two young girls were taken away. It also explained the unidentified body in the cockpit, a man who hadn't boarded in Bogotá, but who had materialized in the aftermath of the crash. He'd been installed as a surrogate for Reyna, a faceless crash-test corpse whose fingerprints had recently been inserted into the captain's files. It all made sense to a point.

But there the fall of dominos was interrupted.

Where had they landed? When the aircraft took off a second time, how were the passengers kept in check? And the most important questions of all: where had Jen and Kristin Stewart been taken, and why?

Davis could think of only one credible answer. Kristin Stewart had been the victim of a kidnapping, an elaborate scheme that was planned from the outset to sacrifice over twenty innocent lives. He knew kidnapping and extortion were rampant in this part of the world. Even so, in terms of scale and intricacy, this plot was in a league of its own, which meant the payday would have to be extraordinary. Was Kristin Stewart the daughter of a billionaire? Possibly, but the fact that she warranted Secret Service protection seemed doubly ominous.

Davis was consumed by a sudden sense of dread. Kristin Stewart had been clever. Realizing she and Jen were similar in appearance, she'd made a great call. *"Tell them you are Kristin Marie Stewart from Raleigh, North Carolina. That's what we both say and nothing else!"* In the confusion of the moment, the ruse had worked. The thugs, unsure how to solve that puzzle, had simply hauled both girls away. Kristin's quick thinking had saved Jen's life. But *why* had she done it? Any young girl would have been frightened, but it seemed a curious reaction to get Jen involved. With the level of planning Davis was seeing, the kidnappers were not unsophisticated—within hours, if not minutes, they would discover which girl was the real Kristin Stewart. *So why had she drawn Jen into it?* He could think of no logical explanation.

Davis rubbed his face in his hands and closed his eyes, trying to reboot his cluttered head. The reprieve was brief. There was no time for speculation or dwelling on shadowed motives. Now was the time for facts. The time to take Colombia, turn it upside down, and shake vigorously until his daughter fell out.

He set aside the iPod and began poring over his notes and diagrams. He kept working as the clock clawed into the lee of the night. Davis slept a fitful two hours. At the first glimmer of sunrise, he ignored the shower and his shaving gear, and struck out for El Centro at nearer a jog than a walk. He ignored the restaurant, and didn't even consider stopping for coffee. No boost was necessary.

He walked quickly because he was hopeful. He was hopeful because there was no other way. Amid all the uncertainty and angst, however, Davis allowed himself a trace of pride. The instigators of this conspiracy had hijacked an aircraft, not by the crude means Colonel Marquez had envisioned, but in a far more intricate scheme. He saw enough technical competence to divert an airliner, alter records, and arrange the disabling of black boxes. Yet whoever these geniuses were, in one moment at least, they had been outsmarted by a beautiful nineteen-year-old girl. Jen had sensed trouble, and after the unscheduled landing at a remote strip, she'd fashioned her very own voice recorder in the cabin of the aircraft. How brilliant was that?

As he walked down the dusty sidewalk in a waking quarter of Bogotá, Davis was buoyed by what his daughter had done. He only hoped she was maintaining that cool in whatever trials she still faced.

You did good, baby. Just hang on.

* * *

She bent over the putrid pot and vomited for the third time. When her stomach stopped heaving, she rocked back on her knees and expelled a rattling breath. Jen Davis had never felt so miserable in her life.

Dim light blushed at the gap beneath the door, introducing a new morning. She looked around the room and decided nothing had changed during the night. This had become her mental diversion, stamping every detail of her surroundings into memory. Four walls and one door under a warped ceiling. The mattress and the awful bucket, a stained brown blanket. *A blanket, for Christ's sake, on the middle of the equator.*

It was not the semester abroad she and her advisor had envisioned, that of guiding a tiny farming village through a soil improvement project. With reaching optimism, Jen made a silent pledge to enroll in creative writing next spring semester. She imagined a humorous essay in which she would contrast the conditions of her captivity to the dorms of Duke University. Last winter she'd been assigned to live in one of the school's oldest buildings, a famously dilapidated tenement known for its lack of heat, and one that was rumored to have been featured on the original 1924 recruitment brochure. The first two paragraphs of that essay were already composed word for word in her head, a feat she had never before attempted.

She had to do something to keep her sanity.

She'd slept poorly, even worse than the previous night. Jen was sure she had a fever—she was shivering and her clothes were moist with sweat. In the beginning she'd thought her ills sourced from the terror, but yesterday she began vomiting and suffering diarrhea, suggesting that a proper malady had visited to amplify her degradation and misery. She'd not left this room since arriving Saturday night with a canvas bag tied over her head, and she knew nothing of where she was or where Kristin Stewart had been taken.

More than once Jen had summed up the evidence from that night. The aircraft's sudden descent followed by a rough landing. The captain telling everyone to remain in their seats. At that point, perhaps with a suspicion inherited from her father, she'd hit the record button on her iPod. Seconds afterward, three armed men rushed aboard and, in the most terrible moment of the entire affair, shot the man sitting next to her. Fear and confusion reigned among the passengers. Then came the strangest part of all, the girl from the University of Virginia imploring her to assume her identity. Kristin, too, was shaken by the killing—Jen had seen it in her wide eyes and tortured expression. She'd recovered quickly, though, and when she became adamant about Jen taking her name, it seemed as if Kristin knew what she was doing. So Jen had followed her lead.

Had it been a mistake?

The rest was a blur. The two of them were bundled off the airplane, hoods put over their heads before they were shoved in a vehicle. The drive to wherever she was now had taken no more than fifteen minutes. At that point she and Kristin were separated, and Jen had been here behind a solidly bolted door ever since.

She avoided thinking of it as a jail cell, although that was effectively what it was. The lone window had been plastered over, and a feeble light bulb drooped from a wire five feet over her head, powered intermittently by a generator she could hear in the distance. The walls looked solid and impenetrable, and were painted an off shade of brown. Insects ran riot, and there was an ill odor about the place, not improved by the open bucket she was forced to use.

A bleak routine had been established by her captors. Each morning a man wearing fatigues and a black ski mask brought a tray of food—stale bread, thin soup, and a water bottle. An hour later he came for the tray and brought a replacement bucket—never clean, only empty. Then the same drill later in the day, right before sunset. Jen had tried to engage the man in conversation, politely at first, but more insistent with each passing day. She never got a word in return. Yesterday she'd stood up when he arrived, and he immediately pulled a truncheon from his belt and brandished it threateningly. Jen sat back down.

And there, in a nutshell, was her existence. She supposed Kristin had ended up in a similar room. But what was the point of it all? She wondered. Was this a kidnapping? Had Kristin gotten into trouble? Jen was not ignorant. She knew Colombia was notorious for its drug cartels. Could this abduction have something to do with narcotics? And where would she be now if she'd not taken her seatmate's peculiar advice, if she'd remained on board the airplane with the other passengers? Kristin seemed like a decent girl, intelligent and outgoing. All the same, there had to be more to her story.

In a small victory, Jen realized that her nascent college education was already coming in handy. Last semester she'd taken freshman psychology, and the lecturer happened to be an authority on the behavior of hostages and detainees. For an entire day the professor had led an open discussion on the subject, bits of which now clung in her mind like leaves to a gutter. She knew that captives held for interrogation, those with assumed intelligence value, were often subject to harsh conditions. They were systematically stripped naked, made hot or cold, and deprived of food and water. Any indicator of day or night was typically removed, and loud music, white noise, and bright lights were used to deprive the subject of sleep. Jen had endured none of these irritants, and she could easily differentiate day and night by referencing the gap beneath the door. Or could she? Might that be a manipulation designed to throw her off?

She sighed, not wishing to succumb to paranoia. What did these people want? If they asked, should she admit to *not* being Kristin Stewart?

Jen began to circle the room, turning the ten-by-ten square into her private exercise yard. On the third lap she heard voices outside. This was a first, aside from a few murmurings before and after her meals were delivered.

The door lock rattled and a man came in. He was medium height with thick black hair, a wispy beard and mustache. *A twenty-something Che Guevara.* The door closed behind him. She heard the bolt engage.

TWENTY-SEVEN

Jen was relieved to finally see another person. Less so when she imagined why he might be here.

"Good morning, Jennifer."

"My name isn't Jen—"

"Please, please," said the man, waving his hand as if shooing away one of the room's tenant flies. "We have known since you arrived who you are. However, it does cause me to wonder—why did you claim to be Miss Stewart?"

Having anticipated this question for days, Jen gave the only answer she'd come up with that would not implicate Kristin. "I don't know."

The man looked at her with marked disappointment.

Jen countered with outrage. "Why the hell are you holding me prisoner?"

"Strong language is unattractive in young girls. Didn't your father teach you that?"

Che, or whoever he was, spoke with a light accent. Jen took him for a Colombian who'd spent considerable time in an English-speaking country. He seemed educated and chose his words with precision. "Is Kristin all right?" she asked, battling yet another wave of nausea.

"Miss Stewart is fine. You, on the other hand, appear to be suffering." He nearly said something more, but hesitated.

"What?"

He cocked his head to one side, as if making a decision. "I suppose it won't hurt to say it. As uncomfortable as your circumstances are, you're far better off than those who remained on the airplane."

"What do you mean?"

"Soon after you and Kristin were removed, the airplane took off again. That second journey ended tragically."

"Tragically? You mean . . . it crashed?"

"Yes. So you see how fortunate you are."

Her nausea redoubled, and Jen crawled to the bucket just in time. She coughed up bile and the meager contents of her stomach. When the waves passed she kneeled upright, and with spittle on her chin she looked him in the eye, trying to show strength. Jen opened her mouth to speak, but he cut her off.

"No—I am not here to answer your questions, Jennifer. I am here to ask one. Very soon I will send a message, one that could lead to your freedom."

Jen felt suddenly dizzy, but tried to maintain focus. She wanted desperately to understand what was happening.

"What I need from you is a small bit of information, something that is known only to you and your father. It will serve to prove—"

"Prove that you're holding me hostage?"

Che grinned a disconcerting grin. "You're a smart girl. That is good for both of us. We must convince your father that you are here and safe."

Jen shut her eyes and tried to think. Part of her wanted to push back, to deny anything this man asked for. Had the airplane really crashed? Or was he only trying to manipulate her? If it was true—God, what her father must be going through. Then she extended that thought. Air crashes were his specialty. If the jet *had* gone down, would he find a way to get involved? Could he be in Colombia searching for her at this moment?

Absolutely.

The man shifted his stance impatiently.

Jen was buoyed by the idea that her father might be near. She tried to think of something clever, a coded message to tell him where she was. It was hopeless, of course, because she herself had no idea. There seemed but one option—do as her captor was asking, and prove to her father that she was alive.

"Two weeks ago he took me out to dinner at a nice restaurant, Reynaud's. He slipped me a glass of wine and told me how proud he was of me for taking this trip. Proud that I was coming here to help people. He said it was the kind of thing my mother would have done."

A pleased Che said, "Yes, that is good. Very good."

"So what are you going to do—ask for a ransom? My Dad doesn't have a lot of money."

The Colombian nearly said something, but then he checked his response and moved toward the door. With one last glance, he disappeared. The door closed and Jen heard the bolt slide home. She was alone once more.

She got to her feet and used a toe to push the stinking bucket to the far side of the room. Returning to the mattress, she laid down feeling tired and defeated. Her mood turned bleak, and she curled up on her side as a new worry arose—a thought more ominous than all of her other imaginings combined.

For the first time since arriving, she had seen someone's face. It brought back words from her hostage lecture of last winter. *"Only two kinds of kidnappers will show their face—amateurs, and those who know their victims will never live to talk."*

* * *

Sorensen drove through the night, and one large café Americano after sunrise she arrived on the outskirts of Raleigh, North Carolina. She was driving her brother-in-law's car, a midsize Acura with a GPS system, and by half past eight she was nearing her destination. If last night's search for Kristin Stewart had drawn blanks, locating her mother had been far easier.

Jean Stewart lived in a neighborhood called Eagle Preserve Estates on the north side of town. Sorensen didn't see any eagles, and nothing that looked like a preserve, but at the entrance there was an impressive wrought-iron gate attached to an unmanned guardhouse. She arrived right behind a school bus, and as soon as ten elementary-aged children filed on board, she piggybacked with a train of SUVs and crossovers to enter a well-managed community. With the sun barely above the horizon, landscaping crews were already hard at work on common areas, keeping lawns and shrubs in tight command. The houses were new and large, although not over the top. It was a comfortable place: safe, tidy, and indistinguishable from a dozen other developments she'd passed on the way here. She followed the car's GPS to the back of the neighborhood, and approached 1726 Saddleback Court with a measure of caution.

Kristin Stewart, for reasons Sorensen did not understand, had been issued Secret Service protection. There was no way of knowing if that protection extended to her mother, Jean, or anyone else who lived at this address. Sorensen saw no cars in the driveway, nor any drab sedans slotted carefully along the street or loitering in the nearby cul-de-sac. Just to be sure, she drove past the house, around a curve, and performed a three-point turn in the first driveway. Approaching from the opposite direction, she still saw nothing to raise concern.

Sorensen parked the Acura along the street in front of her targeted address, pointed toward the subdivision's only entrance. And only exit. She saw a light in a bay window, bright under the slow-waking skies, and another in what had to be a bedroom on the second floor. The home was loosely Colonial, four or five bedrooms, probably one and a half fewer baths. Sorensen hadn't had time to research whether Jean Stewart lived alone. She'd seen no mention of a Mr. Stewart, or any other children. All the same, it seemed a big place for a single mom who'd recently sent her only child off to college, so Sorensen reasoned there might be someone else.

The path to the front door was paver brick, and there were three garage doors that looked like they'd been taken from a barn, an element of style that had bloomed quickly and would no doubt wilt with equal haste. At the entryway Sorensen sank an elaborate doorbell button shaped like a horseshoe. The door opened a few beats later, and the woman from the Elks Lodge picture greeted her. Jean Stewart was fiftyish, nicely groomed with ash blond highlights and summer skin. She was brightly dressed for a dull Thursday morning in yellow slacks, whose fit could not have been off the rack, a cream blouse, and laceless therapeutic shoes. She was pretty in a manufactured way, the routine battle to subtract years wherein success fell inevitably in arrears to expenditures and effort.

"Yes?" she asked. "Can I help you?"

Sorensen had spent a long night behind the wheel preparing the answer to this question, along with subsequent options based on how things progressed. She quickly flashed her CIA credentials, two fingers loosely obscuring the agency emblem, and with precise wording said, "My name is Anna Sorensen. I've come about your daughter, Miss Stewart."

The use of "Miss" had been a gamble, but Sorensen saw that it didn't matter. The woman's smile collapsed. "Oh, God . . . did you find out something about Kristin? Is she all right?"

"Yes—at least, I don't have any new information. I'm sorry, I didn't mean to frighten you. This must be terribly stressful."

A heavy sigh, then, "Please come in."

Sorensen walked into a nicely appointed living room, and Stewart recovered quickly. "I've made coffee—can I get you a cup?"

"Yes, that would be lovely," said Sorensen, although she already had the jitters.

"You people never say no." Stewart disappeared into the kitchen.

"A little caffeine goes a long way," Sorensen called out as her eyes wandered the room. On a stone fireplace mantel she saw framed photographs of an abbreviated family. Jean and Kristin Stewart on a ski slope. Jean and Kristin Stewart on a beach. Another with what might have been a set of grandparents, and a candid shot of a younger Kristin with a friend—they were making silly faces in the front yard of a much smaller house.

"Is Agent Smithers off duty today?" Stewart called from the kitchen. "She's usually the one who comes."

"I'm not sure, I just go where I'm needed. But they did give me a briefing. Perhaps if you tell me what you already know, I can fill in any gaps."

The hostess came back with a tray presenting two cups of coffee, cream, and sugar. Sorensen took one, added cream, and began to sip, hoping Jean Stewart was the chatty type who enjoyed filling black holes of silence. She was in luck.

"It's been a nightmare—three days now since that airplane crashed and nobody seems to know anything. All I've been told is that Kristin is missing." Stewart sank into a plush sofa, the tray rattling as she set it down. Her hands began to grapple and she forced them into her lap. "I don't know how much more I can take. Kristin is all I've got—all I've ever had. Do you have children, Miss Sorensen?"

"No, not yet. But I'm hopeful."

"You always hear that there's nothing worse than losing a child. You nod like you understand when it happens to a friend of a friend, but let me tell you . . . " She rubbed one eye, trying to hold herself together. "You can never understand until it becomes real."

Sorensen was sitting on the couch next to Stewart, and she took her hand. As a CIA officer, she was well schooled in contrived gestures. This wasn't one of them. "You haven't lost her. There's still hope."

"Hope?" Stewart said, her voice breaking. "A tiny airplane goes down in a jungle and everyone is dead, only they can't find my daughter's body. You call that hope?"

"Remember, she's not the only one. There are two girls missing."

Stewart's eyes darted up. "*What?*"

"Nobody told you that?" Sorensen asked, trying to cover her mistake.

"No. I was just told that Kristin had gone missing, that they hadn't . . . hadn't found her in the wreckage."

Sorensen's first impression of Jean Stewart had been that of a shallow soul, a woman of vanity and appearances. Now she thought she might be off track. Perhaps this was a woman battling for sanity, clutching elements of normalcy in the face of a mother's ultimate horror. Looking into a pair of tortured blue eyes, Sorensen no longer had the will to keep up false pretenses.

"I should explain something," she said. "I'm not with the Secret Service."

The damp eyes fell puzzled.

"I'm here on the behalf of a man who—"

"Not—" Stewart stuttered, "*not* Secret Service?" In a transformation that took Sorensen completely by surprise, Stewart's pain went instantly to anger. *"You're a goddam reporter!"* she shouted. "Get the hell out of my house!" She jumped up from the couch and pointed firmly to the door.

"No! No, I'm not a reporter. I work for a different government agency. I—"

Stewart drew a cell phone from her pocket and placed a call. Two touches, like a number on speed-dial. "The number I am calling is *not* 911! Security will be here in less than a minute. For your own safety, you had better leave!"

"I'm with the CIA!" said Sorensen, pulling out her credentials and displaying them more openly than the first time.

Stewart held fast with her phone, and when the connection was made, she said, "I need help!" She lowered the phone and ignored Sorensen's ID. "Out!" she repeated, grabbing Sorensen's elbow and shoving her toward the door.

"All right!" Sorensen said, jerking her elbow away. "Just listen for thirty seconds, then I'll go if that's what you want."

Stewart stood back, venom in her gaze.

"Does the name Thomas Mulligan mean anything to you?"

A hesitation, but no denial.

"He was on that flight with your daughter, and he died. Did the Secret Service tell you how?" Sorensen saw the first crack.

"Thomas was a good man," Stewart said. "He was there to protect Kristin. But he died in the crash like the others."

"No, not like the others. Thomas Mulligan was shot twice through the heart."

Stewart looked at her, stunned.

"There are *two* girls missing from that flight," Sorensen continued. "I can't say that I know what's it's like to be in your position, to have a child who might be in mortal danger, or possibly already dead. But I know a man who is in *exactly* the same position as you—the father of the other missing girl. It just so happens he's an aircraft accident investigator, and he's in Colombia right now scouring the jungle for both of them. When he learned about Thomas Mulligan, he called me for help because he doesn't understand what the hell is going on. My friend is doing his damnedest to find his daughter *and* yours. But to do that he needs to know why your daughter is getting protection from the United States Secret Service."

A rush of footsteps on the pavement outside. Sorensen's eyes remained locked on Stewart as she said, "Jen Davis. That's the other girl's name. A nineteen-year-old student with a bright future and a frantic father. Help us, Jean! Help us find them both. Why is your daughter so important?"

Hard footfalls on the front porch. Then a commanding female voice. "Miss Stewart, it's Special Agent Smithers! Are you all right?"

Sorensen gave a final pleading look.

Jean Stewart made her decision. She leaned forward and began talking in a hushed tone. Sorensen tuned out the shouts from the other side of the door, and when it crashed inward thirty seconds later she stood motionless and stunned—for reasons that had nothing to do with the handgun three feet from her face.

TWENTY-EIGHT

While Sorensen was staring down a gun barrel, Davis strode along the shoulder of a mud-encrusted street. The sky tried to gather an early storm but only went gray, spitting a cool drizzle on the waking enclaves of northern Bogotá.

He was half a block from El Centro when the parking lot came into view. Marquez' staff car had been removed. Not surprisingly, there was no ring of crime scene tape circling the spot where it had been parked. He entered the building two minutes later, and saw not a single person on the phone or recording data. Echevarria was nowhere in sight, and the few people who'd shown up seemed shell-shocked and rudderless, chatting in hushed pairs and staring blankly at computer screens. It was all to be expected. The investigator-in-charge had been murdered—a first in Davis' experience—and that tragedy had driven the entire inquiry to a clattering seizure.

Which was, he thought, exactly what someone had intended.

He saw a newspaper on a counter, folded hastily to a second-page headline about the murder. Davis read three paragraphs, a reporter's speculation mostly, interspersed with cautionary words from the police spokesman, a certain Major Echevarria of the Special Investigations Unit, who promised to identify the guilty parties and bring them to justice.

For the next thirty minutes Davis attacked the previous day's summary report, but found nothing to bolster a case that was in serious need of bolstering. He considered asking if there was a skydiving outfit on the airfield, but dropped the idea when he realized he didn't know the Spanish word for parachute. It would likely be a pointless excursion anyway. The jungles where the air-craft had diverted, and subsequently crashed, were ruled by para-military militias. If that's who Captain Reyna had been working with, then a parachute could readily have been supplied by his co-conspirators.

Jesus, Davis thought, *am I reaching or what?*

The scheme he imagined was an elaborate one, and, if true, the question of who could coordinate such a conspiracy loomed large. Even more perplexing were the reasons behind it. He felt like a marathon runner who'd gone off course, plodding with am-bition but getting no closer to the finish line. One answer, how-ever, might put him back on track.

Who was Kristin Stewart?

Davis stared at the door to Marquez' office. Or what had *been* Marquez' office. It was open wide, like an invitation. Davis got up, walked over, and looked inside. The room had been sani-tized: file drawers emptied, bookshelves swept clean, dry-erase board on the wall wiped blank. It reminded him of the empty parking space outside. Every vestige of the colonel's presence had been quickly and quietly erased.

Had Marquez also been asking questions about Passenger 19?

Davis looked once more around the place, and saw a hand-ful of people going though the motions of an investigation. A few faces were familiar, people he'd gotten to know since arriv-ing. Even so, he'd never met a single one before last Sunday. Aside from Delacorte, who was probably across the street in the ware-house, was there anyone here he trusted enough to ask for help?

A disturbing corollary then came to mind. Which of these men and women had Marquez trusted?

The answer that arrived was a lonely one.

* * *

Sorensen was in the backseat of a dark-windowed Ford Taurus, her Flexi-cuffed hands secured behind her back. She remembered the car now, having seen it on her drive-by earlier—two doors north on the opposite side of the street, pulled sedately into a paver-brick driveway.

From the back seat she watched the two Secret Service agents work—they'd not yet admitted their affiliation, simply taking her into custody under the loose auspices of being "federal officers." The woman's name was Smithers, the man Shea. Presently, Shea was searching her brother-in-law's Acura, and Smithers was holding his cell phone while she talked to Jean Stewart. Sorensen wondered how she was going to explain to Dean that his car and Samsung had been impounded by the Secret Service.

To the positive, she was encouraged that after an hour no uniformed police had shown up. That meant the agents were trying to keep things internal, definitely in her favor. The two had to know who she was by now, and who she worked for. Sorensen also had little doubt that these agents were, at least loosely, tied to the "Jones" she'd met on the National Mall last night. She sensed fine lines being walked, messy jurisdictional overlaps being side-stepped. Best of all, she finally knew *why* everyone was treading so cautiously.

Jean Stewart had told her.

It left Sorensen with one pressing question. Had Jean Stewart told the agents what she'd confessed before they burst in? Once the car had been brought up, and a restrained Sorensen planted in its back seat, Smithers had begun interviewing Kristin Stewart's mother on the front porch, a long and animated conversation between a distraught mother who wanted her daughter back and a special agent seeking damage control.

Did you tell her why we're here?

That was the hundred-dollar question—or maybe the million-dollar question—that Smithers would ask again and again. But how would Jean Stewart answer? The Secret Service had been her daughter's protectors, tried and true until four days ago. Now, however, Stewart might view Sorensen and Davis as more relevant, because they were in a better position to help Kristin. If Stewart admitted having spilled the truth, Sorensen suspected they would all end up in the nearest field office for lengthy discussions. She didn't want that. What she wanted was to get in touch with Davis as soon as possible to warn him what he was up against.

Shea, a thick-necked silent type, was still turning over the Acura, and Smithers hadn't stopped talking. With both agents busy, Sorensen decided to be proactive. The Taurus was not a hardened agency model, but rather a stock vehicle—presumably a rental for two agents on a temporary duty assignment. Sorensen had been cuffed with her wrists behind her back, but not otherwise secured to the car. And, unlike a police car, there were no impediments to opening the door. She curled her legs and tried to wedge a toe under the door handle. Her first two attempts failed. On the third try she got it.

She kicked the door open, wriggled out, and began walking toward Smithers—Sorensen was sure she was the lead agent.

"Hey!" yelled Shea from behind. "Where the hell do you think you're going!"

Sorensen was halfway up the brick sidewalk when Shea reached her. He grabbed her arm but she shrugged it away—a move that wouldn't work more than once. She stopped short of the portico, and put all the indignation she could manage into her voice. "Agent Smithers, you've got some explaining to do! I'm here on assignment, and *you* are interfering with official business."

"And just what business is that?" Smithers asked.

"First of all we need to get rid of these ridiculous cuffs."

Smithers hesitated mightily before nodding to Shea. The big man reached into his pocket for a pair of wire cutters and snipped off the cuffs.

Sorensen made a point of rubbing the marks around her wrists. "We have a man in Colombia investigating an aircraft accident, and Miss Stewart's daughter was on that airplane. Understandably, she's worried sick. Her daughter is officially listed as missing, but last night our investigator told me he thinks she may be alive."

"And *that's* why you drove all night to get here from D.C.? To give hope?"

Sorensen regarded each of the agents in turn. "You obviously don't have kids."

Smithers replied with a seething look.

Sorensen said, "I'm sure you've verified my credentials by now." She held out an empty hand, and after a nod from his partner, Shea gave back her ID.

Sorensen said, "I'm going back to Washington now. I've got reports to file, and I'm guessing you do too. Let's not make them any longer than necessary. Oh—and I'd like my phone back as well."

Looking doubtful as ever, Smithers broke away and made a phone call. After a lively five-minute conversation, she pocketed her phone and gave Shea another nod. He handed back the keys to the Acura while Smithers offered up the phone. Her conversation with Dean had just got easier, but Sorensen had no delusions—she knew the car would be tracked and the phone monitored. A backlog of her brother-in-law's phone calls was probably already being analyzed in some distant cubicle. Jammer would call again, sooner or later, which meant she had to find a way to shift their communications strategy. But that could wait.

Sorensen shifted her attention away from the agents to Stewart who was standing by her damaged and very expensive front door. "If I hear anything new about your daughter, I promise to call right away."

"No," said Smithers, obviously not wanting to relinquish too much control. "If there's news about her daughter, you call *us* first." Shea handed over a business card with a phone number scribbled on the back.

Sorensen took it with a faux smile. "Have a nice day."

She was just turning away when she locked eyes fleetingly with Jean Stewart. If she wasn't mistaken, Sorensen thought she detected the most subtle of nods.

CHAPTER TWENTY-NINE

Sorensen drove briskly and stopped at the first ATM she came across. She withdrew three hundred dollars in cash, and asked a middle-aged man waiting behind her if there was a Walmart nearby. Yes, he told her, adding directions and a smile. Five minutes later she pulled into the parking lot. She went to the back of the store, and in the electronics department purchased an unlocked no-contract phone, along with a sim card that included data. She paid cash, and ten minutes later was online in the Acura's driver's seat. It took thirty seconds to find what she needed.

* * *

Miguel Hernandez was sleepy as he sat behind the front desk of the Hotel de Aeropuerto in Bogotá. His wife normally worked the night shift, but she had taken ill the previous evening, which meant he'd been sitting in the same seat for nearly fifteen hours. So when the phone in front of him rang he was slow to react, not picking up until the fifth ring.

"*Buenos días*, Hotel de Aeropuerto."

"Yes, hello. I am calling on an emergency. I must get in touch with one of your guests."

"*Una emergencia?*"

"Do you speak English?"

"A little. Who you want talk to?"

"Jam—Frank Davis. He's been staying with you for the last few days."

"*Señor Davis—un hombre muy grande, no?*"

"Yeah, that's him, *muy grande*."

"Two zero four. I will connect you to his room."

"No, no! It's hard to explain, but I don't want a connection to his room. Could you just go knock on the door, and if he's there have him come to the office?"

"*Señora*, I am the only one *aquí*. Is not so easy for me to—"

"One hundred U.S. dollars if you can find him and bring him to this phone. He'll pay you, I promise."

Hernandez' weary eyes edged open a bit wider. "Okay, maybe I find him. *Tres minutos*."

The proprietor set down the phone and walked outside. He climbed the steps to the second floor and rapped his knuckles on the fourth door. No answer. He rapped louder, and with the image of a winged hundred dollar bill in his head, he shouted, "*Señor Davis!* You are there?"

Nothing. As a last resort, Miguel took the master key from his pocket and ventured a quick look inside.

Back in the office he relayed the bad news.

"All right," said the voice from afar, "that brings us to two hundred and fifty dollars . . . "

* * *

Davis was studying the seventy-two hour dispatch on the crash of TAC-Air Flight 223, probably the final official act of investigator-in-charge Marquez, when someone called, "*Señor Davis!* A person here to see you!"

He walked to the entrance and saw a young boy of no more than ten. He was barefoot and smiling, and when he saw Davis he waved a piece of paper. Davis walked over and said in hesitant Spanish, "*Es para mí?*"

The kid smiled even more broadly. "Yeah, it's for you, dawg."

Davis sighed. Hollywood had indeed made the world a smaller place. He took the note, read it, and moved immediately toward the door.

"Hey, homie!"

Davis turned and saw the kid with an outstretched hand. He pulled out his wallet and put a ten in the kid's hand.

"That's it? I ran all the way here!"

"Yeah? Well take my advice—when you run back, make a stop at school and sign up."

* * *

Davis was breathless when he reached the hotel office. The proprietor handed over the phone saying there would be a charge to his account. Davis said that was fine, figuring he'd find a way to expense it to Larry Green.

Sorensen greeted him with, "The phone I was using got compromised."

"Compromised?"

"An hour ago the Secret Service had me cuffed in the back of a car."

"Damn . . . you okay?"

"Yeah, I talked my way out of it, but they'll be watching me now. The good news is I made some headway. I tracked down Kristin Stewart's mother. She lives in Raleigh, and I drove down last night."

"That's good. Did you talk to her?"

"It wasn't easy. I told her I was Secret Service just to get in the door."

"So there *is* a connection."

"A big one. She knew the basics of the crash, that the plane had gone down and her daughter was missing."

"She's been living with that for the last four days?"

"Just like you. She was definitely distraught, but then it turned weird. When she figured out I wasn't Secret Service, Stewart immediately assumed I was a reporter."

"A *reporter?*"

"Yep." Sorensen explained how the rest of the meeting had gone, and how she'd gained Stewart's confidence. "I think what won her over was when I told her you were down there searching for your own daughter. The agents were banging on the door when she decided to open up to me. Kristin Stewart has had Secret Service protection for over a year now."

"Why?"

"Because she's the illegitimate daughter of the vice president of the United States. The man who will likely be elected president two months from now."

CHAPTER THIRTY

It was a stage in every sense of the word. Rows of newly installed footlights were angled carefully upward, sure to cast the speaker in a glorious hue. A high-quality sound system had been tuned to match the venue's acoustic profile, allowing sage words to travel with pitch-perfect clarity. The chairs behind the podium were carefully placed, a squadron of congressmen, party hacks, and local politicians arranged in rightful pecking order—the most important sitting front and center, with certain deviations allowed in the name of social, ethnic, and gender balance. The rest—the hangers-on of the Cleveland establishment—were roundly relegated to the rear echelons.

The vice president began his speech in the middle of the luncheon's main course, preaching his stock spiel on foreign policy until everyone's genetically unmodified ducks were down to the bone. With the tiramisu and coffee delivered, it was time to come in for a landing.

"I say to you today that education and compassion will be the hallmarks of my administration. I have traveled this country and seen great need. I have traveled this country and seen even greater kindness. It comes by way of churches and non-profit organizations. It comes from well-structured government programs. Most of all, it comes from people like you. People who give time and money, and a helping hand to those facing hardships."

A polite round of applause broke the vice president's rhythm, and of course he allowed it. Happily, he saw the teleprompter pause as well. He'd stumbled there earlier, during the party convention. Rapturous applause had intervened once too often that night and the text ran ahead, mismatching his speech. He'd covered reasonably well, although on leaving the stage he had fired the media tech on sight. Today there were no such troubles.

He picked up again on a cadence that was almost musical. "My campaign for president is nearing the finish line. For almost four years now I have served as vice president of this great country, and I have fought the fights worth fighting. That record will serve as the foundation for the worthy programs I've outlined." A thoughtful pause to build anticipation. "In the course of my campaign, I've met a great many Americans, men and women, even children, who ask that most noble of questions—*How can I help?* By attending this fundraiser, each of you has already begun to do so. But I'd like to tell you about one man in particular whom I recently had the pleasure of meeting. It was in the Midwest, and his name was Thomas—not Tom, he was very insistent about that—and he was down on his luck. Thomas had lost his job in a company that manufactured American flags. That's right . . . American flags. His job had been outsourced overseas. We met in a soup kitchen, yet Thomas took no shame in that. He stood tall and proud, and he asked what he could do to help my campaign."

Another heavy pause.

"That's right—what *he* could do to help *me*. Thomas said he was homeless, and he jested that I was too—as you may know, the United States Naval Observatory, the traditional home of the vice president, has been undergoing extensive renovations. We had a good laugh about that before Thomas turned serious. He reached into his tattered jacket and pulled out one of his few possessions in the world, something he thought might help get my message across. He said he hoped it would raise money for my campaign, because if I was elected he knew I'd keep my promise to help others who found themselves in his situation."

The vice president reached under his lapel and extracted a large piece of folded cardboard. "So, for one night, ladies and gentlemen, I have a new fundraising director, and his name is Thomas."

He unfolded the cardboard sheet, and showed the audience a message drawn in bold block letters.

HOMELESS

NEED MONEY

GOD BLESS

Cameras flashed and the crowd went wild, normally sedate lawyers and bankers and businessmen cheering as if they were at a high school football game. It was a moment. It was *the* moment. Martin Stuyvesant, Democratic Party nominee for president, clasped his hands over his head and smiled like a candidate with a ten-point lead in the polls.

Which was exactly what he was.

He milked the moment for all it was worth, shaking hands with the mayor of Cleveland, two congressmen who were sweating reelection, and a man in uniform who was a something-or-other in the Ohio National Guard. Stuyvesant kept smiling all the way off stage, waving and slapping shoulders, pointing his finger occasionally as if recognizing someone special in the sea of strangers. As soon as he was backstage and clear of the cameras, his smile transformed—less broad and fewer teeth on display, but still in place. A more inward pleasure.

Roger Gordon, his campaign manager, sidled up and the two began walking. "We need to talk," Gordon said through the side of his mouth.

Stuyvesant said, "Did you hear that? They *loved* it!"

"You need to tell me before you do something like that. It could easily have backfired if—"

"If I hadn't set it up so well? Give me a little credit, Rog."

"Is there really a guy named Thomas?"

"Of course. Only he made me promise not to send any attention his way."

Gordon took his candidate by the elbow. He leaned in close as they steered through the exit and back to the campaign bus. "Marty, we are ten weeks away from the goddamn White House. A nine-point lead is good, but you can still screw this up."

"Ten points—CNN and Gallup both."

Gordon's voice broke to a whisper, "What's happening down in Colombia could flip that overnight."

Stuyvesant stopped short of the bus's stairs. "Is there something new?"

Gordon's gaze drifted to a group of reporters behind a barricade fifty feet away. They were shouting questions across the divide. "Wave and smile, then get on the damned bus. There's someone inside you need to meet."

Stuyvesant did exactly that, and soon the door shut behind them. The interior of the bus was plush, configured as an executive suite with meeting tables and couches arrayed in the forward salon, a small bed and study in the back. Stuyvesant saw three others at the main conference table: his chief of staff, Bill Evers, his top strategist, Maggie Donovan, and a coarse-looking, wiry man he'd never met.

Everyone rose as Stuyvesant approached, and Evers said, "Martin, I'd like you to meet Vincent Kehoe."

It did not escape Stuyvesant that Evers had ignored his title of vice president—it meant that whatever Kehoe was, he wasn't a wealthy donor. The man had snapped to his feet and stood practically at attention, the way the Marine guards did around the White House when the one-term outgoing commander-in-chief, Truett Townsend, ambled up the corridors. Yes, he thought, Kehoe was unquestionably ex-military—Stuyvesant himself had never served, but he'd seen plenty of the sort. The man looked like he was built from a series of coiled springs. Sinew and muscle, not an ounce of fat anywhere. Stuyvesant guessed him to be on the near side of thirty. He was clean-shaven with a receding hairline, what was left on top he cropped in a way that said he really didn't give a damn. The two shook hands, and Stuyvesant felt a firm grip, although one he suspected was being kept in check.

When everyone sat, Evers said, "We were able to arrange funding for the ransom to be paid—"

Stuyvesant cranked his eyes sharply to his chief of staff, who caught his look.

"Sorry. Mr. Kehoe is directly involved. He'll be the one going to Colombia to retrieve the girl. He works for a *very* discreet private company and has been thoroughly vetted. I won't bore you with his resume—suffice to say, he's done this kind of thing before."

"Does he know . . . " Stuyvesant searched for the words, "*why* we are so concerned about this abduction?"

Kehoe answered. "No, sir. I know we are dealing with the kidnapping of a young girl, and that I am to make a ransom payment and extract the victim with the greatest possible discretion. Those are my orders and it's all I need to know."

Stuyvesant grinned. "Good answer. What are the arrangements?"

Evers said, "Mr. Kehoe will be flying south later today, a private jet arranged by his employer."

"Is the Secret Service still involved?"

"We've come to an agreement with the director on that. They prefer to have no further involvement in this affair."

Stuyvesant wished he'd been in on that decision. "All right, we'll let the director back off. But I'll have his nuts in a vise come January."

Dutiful nods around the table, the usual reaction from staff watching a firing squad assembled for a colleague.

"What is the time frame for this mission?" Stuyvesant asked, liking the military sound of it.

Maggie Donovan, who in spite of her title as strategist was in fact more of a logistician, answered, "Mr. Kehoe will receive the funds directly after this meeting. If all goes as planned, Kristin Stewart will be back in North Carolina tomorrow evening."

"That will make her mother happy. How has she been handling it?"

"Well enough," said Evers. "We conveyed your message: we told her everything that *can* be done is being done."

"And it is," Stuyvesant said.

Everyone nodded. A few more administrative matters were discussed before they all wished Kehoe good luck and launched him to undertake his final preparations. When he was gone, Evers cornered Stuyvesant as the bus began to roll. "There *is* one complication. Someone's been asking questions."

"Questions?" Stuyvesant said. "About what?"

"About Kristin."

The vice president took a handhold as the bus rounded a corner. Outside, through a cracked window shade, he saw throngs of well wishers. He ignored them as Evers continued.

"A CIA officer made inquiries through official channels last night, a search on Kristin's name and passport information."

"*The CIA?* How the hell did they get wind of this?"

"We don't think it's anything official," said Evers, "and of course she got nowhere. All information relating to Kristin has been scrubbed from the official servers. We sent a man to speak with this officer last night in D.C. Apparently she's an acquaintance of the investigator, the man the NTSB sent to Colombia."

"Wasn't that supposed to be to our advantage? Having an insider on this crash investigation?"

"That was our intent. We've been monitoring him very closely, but for some reason our NTSB man—his name is Jammer Davis—sidestepped his normal means of communication and asked this friend at CIA for help. Davis has uncovered Special Agent Mulligan's identity, and we think he knows there's something special about Kristin."

For the first time Stuyvesant felt uneasy. "These two people know the Secret Service was protecting her?"

"They know there's a connection of some kind, yes."

"This whole damned protection scheme was a mistake from the beginning! We should have kept our distance like we always have."

"Once you got the nomination, Martin, we had no choice. Kristin was at risk of—"

"Of exactly what's happened! The Secret Service dropped the ball on this!"

"You know we tied a hand behind their back. They wanted a full protection detail, but we said no. We insisted they keep it small and discreet. They also warned us against letting her travel."

An agitated Stuyvesant banged his fist on a cabinet over the bed. "*That* was her mother's damned fault! The woman simply will not listen, despite everything I've given her. All right . . . this NTSB man, Davis. Does it do us any good to keep him in Colombia?"

"Not that I can see. The ransom is on its way, and Kristin will be on a plane home tomorrow."

"So pull him out. He's asking too many questions. We need to tie this up once and for all. Then we need to bury it for good."

Evers said hesitantly, "I agree, however . . . there might be one problem. Getting Davis out of Colombia could prove difficult."

"Why?"

"It's something that came out of the blue—a one-in-a-million coincidence. When the NTSB went to assign an investigator, the guy in charge—I think his name is Green—looked over the passenger list and saw a familiar name. Davis has a daughter, and it turns out she was also on that flight."

"*What?*"

"Apparently she and Kristin were headed to the same semester abroad program. Davis' daughter is the other hostage that was referred to in the ransom request."

"The one we ignored?"

Evers said, "I think 'secondary concern' was the phrase you used. My point is that getting Davis to leave might prove difficult. By all accounts he's a bull, and I don't see him leaving without his daughter."

The bus was gaining speed, heading for a barbecue to benefit wounded veterans. Stuyvesant sat on the mussed bed. "Is there any chance Davis can find her?"

"His daughter? Working on his own? Not a prayer. I've had

the full briefing from Strand. We've put a lot of effort into this, a lot of resources, and we still don't know who we're dealing with. It's not FARC, but probably someone like them, a splinter paramilitary group. There are dozens in the jungles down there, and they're all ruthless. Drugs and extortion are their bread and butter. They move constantly and are armed to the teeth. FARC lasted twenty years against the Colombian Army, and the others are just as persistent. I can't imagine one angry American dad is going to bother them. Honestly, if Davis pushes too hard—I wouldn't be surprised if he disappeared too."

Stuyvesant met Evers' gaze and saw discomfort. They were both thinking the same thing. If Davis *didn't* come back, their cleanup efforts would be greatly simplified. Evers was about to say something when Donovan poked her head around the corner. She handed Stuyvesant talking points for the veterans affair, and said, "Ten minutes."

As soon as she was gone, Stuyvesant took the lead. "All right—just get my daughter out of harm's way."

"And Davis?" asked Evers.

The vice president turned away and began to study his notes.

THIRTY-ONE

"The democratic nominee for president has a love child?"

"Apparently so," said Sorensen. "Jean Stewart worked on his first congressional campaign twenty years ago."

"Sounds like she worked more than the phones," said Davis.

"Do you realize how sexist that sounds?"

"Sorry. Look, I know Stuyvesant is married now, but was he at the time?"

"He was, but according to Stewart his wife never learned about the affair. They kept it very discreet until the inevitable hard landing."

"Thanks for putting that in language I can understand."

"I always try to keep things simple for pilots. Back then, Stuyvesant was a rising star politically. He knew the affair would blow him out of the water, so he ended the relationship in no uncertain terms."

"He was a jerk. That's not sexist to say, is it?" He heard Sorensen sigh.

"Then the complication came," she continued. "Stewart found out she was pregnant, but she never told Stuyvesant. Until last year he never knew he *had* a daughter."

"Last year? That's pretty awkward for a guy in the middle of a heated presidential primary. How did Stewart break this news to him?"

"She didn't have time to tell me that part, but I did notice she seems to be doing well. Nice house, furniture, clothes. I saw a few pictures on the wall of a different place, much smaller, a very different neighborhood."

"You think she hit him up? Demanded hush money?"

"Could be," said Sorensen.

"And maybe somebody else found out about Kristin—somebody in Colombia."

"That was my first thought. It could be even worse, though. What if somebody learned not only about Kristin, but about the payoff to Jean Stewart? It's one thing for a politician to find out he has a long-lost daughter from an affair that ended twenty years ago. That's awkward, but it's manageable. Throw in a hush-money scandal, maybe a kidnapping between now and the first Tuesday of November—it would be catastrophic for the campaign."

Davis thought it all through. "Okay, but how does this help me find Jen? Both girls have been kidnapped—that fits everything we know." He told her about the audio recording he'd discovered on the iPod. "The problem is, we still don't know who's taken them or where they are."

"I can tell you that Jean Stewart is as much in the dark as we are. As for the Secret Service, don't expect much help—we're not exactly on the same page right now."

"Which means any answers will have to come from my end."

"That's a wide net to cast. There are no end of suspects in Colombia—it's a haven for organized crime and extortion schemes. We have to narrow things down."

"If it *is* a kidnapping, there'll be a ransom demand," he said. "Who would they contact?"

"Stuyvesant, I suppose. Or maybe his campaign."

He heaved a long breath. "That's no help either." He saw the proprietor in a back room talking on a cell phone. When the man locked eyes with Davis he abruptly ended his call. Was there awkwardness in his gaze? Probably not, he decided. Even so, the readiness of his suspicion drove one thing home to Davis—he was becoming increasingly isolated.

"I need help," he finally said.

"I agree. Unfortunately, I can't just run this up the flagpole at CIA. Think about it—our next president getting blackmailed by Colombian drug lords right before the election? That's not a grenade I want to toss."

"Even worse," Davis added, "it might endanger the girls. Right now I'm the only one in a position to do anything."

"Like what?"

"I don't know. I'll have to be discreet."

"You? Discreet?"

Davis ignored this as an idea surfaced, and he ran it past Sorensen. She agreed it was the best course. "Thanks, Anna. I really appreciate everything you've done."

"Just bring Jen back safe and sound. Oh, and by the way," she added, "you owe the guy at the hotel desk two hundred and fifty dollars."

"Two-fifty? Are we married?"

"The way I spend your money—we might as well be."

* * *

Larry Green left his eleven-thirty meeting with a grim expression, one that anyone who'd spent time with him in the last few days would recognize. His wife certainly had, but generals' wives knew better than to ask.

The daily briefing had not gone well. His boss, Janet Cirrillo, had asked pointedly for updates on the crash of TAC-Air Flight 223, and for the third day in a row Green had given her nothing. The managing director was not an unreasonable woman, and she took in stride his explanation that contact with Davis had been intermittent. All the same, Cirrillo was feeling heat from above, and having spent twenty-eight years in the Air Force, Green knew the direction in which foul things flowed.

He rode the elevator to the first floor looking forward to his afternoon run. He was ready to blow off a little steam. In the name of hydration, Green purchased a water bottle at the lobby coffee shop. He was getting his change when he heard, "Hello, General."

He turned and instantly recognized Anna Sorensen.

"Miss Sorensen . . . hello. What a surprise to see you."

"Is it?"

He instantly understood her meaning, and Green scanned all around the busy lobby. "There's a courtyard outside—can I get you something?"

"That water looks pretty good."

The day was warm, and they found a bench in the shade of a maple tree. In front of them a fountain spewed water to the four cardinal points of the compass, gurgles echoing against the courtyard walls. One of the spouts was misaligned and water splattered over the southern edge.

"Jammer's been in touch?" he surmised.

"He called today. He needs help."

Green looked at her curiously. "Why did he ask you and not me?"

Sorensen held his level gaze but said nothing.

Green was fully aware that she worked for the CIA. Jammer had introduced them once, after he'd met Sorensen on an assignment in France. Although "met" was perhaps not a strong enough word. Collided was more like it. Sorensen had saved Jammer's life in France, and Green knew that he trusted her without reservation. So there was his answer.

"He thinks there's a problem on my end," said Green, staring at a skewed footprint of dampness aside the fountain's blue-tiled base. "He implied something like that the last time I talked to him."

"Jammer got suspicious a couple of days ago. That business jet he hitched a ride on—it wasn't any kind of scheduled run, in spite of what you were told. Somebody arranged the flight just for him. Later that night, you relayed a request for satellite information, and Jammer was buried within an hour. Then there was the high-end sat-phone he was issued. It was right there waiting for him when he arrived in Colombia, delivered by some unknown courier from the U.S. Embassy."

Green nodded. "I should have seen it myself."

"The sat-phone is compromised, so he and I have been using alternate means."

"I've been getting a lot of pressure for updates. Somebody near the top wants results."

"I know who it is."

Green studied her, took a long swallow of water. "Do I want to know?" he asked.

"Probably not."

He let it go at that. "How can I help?"

"First of all, Jammer wanted you to know why he's been unresponsive. He's making headway—maybe too much. He thinks Jen is alive."

"Thank God for that. But how?"

"Jammer is pretty sure we're looking at a kidnapping. He thinks the jet landed at a remote airfield in the jungle where the two girls were removed. Then it took off again, and the crash was somehow manufactured."

"*Two* girls," he remarked.

"Yeah—that's the part you don't want to know."

Green took a moment to consider it. "If this is true . . . it's a damned ruthless scheme. But I suppose the crash removed a lot of evidence."

"Neat and clean if you can make it all work. Jammer has been sorting through the details, but he's at a point where he needs help."

Green had been trailing Sorensen for most of the conversation, but all at once he went out ahead. "Actually, I suspected something like this . . . at least in a general way. I made a few phone calls yesterday that might give Jammer just what he needs."

Sorensen was studying the fountain too, in all its tranquil inefficiency. "I really hope you're right."

THIRTY-TWO

Davis left the hotel in a fog, meandering in the direction of El Centro. There was little conviction in his stride because he could imagine nothing there that would help his cause. He lumbered ahead all the same, operating on the same principle as a shark—keep moving or drown.

He'd come here on a mission to find his daughter, and as a secondary ambition, sanity permitting, to solve a crash. He now knew Jen wasn't the victim of an aircraft accident, but rather a kidnapping. And the crash investigation? It was unlike any he'd ever seen. The final report, if he even bothered with one, would have nothing to do with maintenance practices or pilot training or weather. This mishap was one hundred percent about people. In truth, it wasn't an air crash at all—more like a crime scene with wings. To top it off, an unbearable new stench was wafting in, seared by that most volatile accelerant of all—the acetylene torch of politics.

The vice president of the United States had fathered an illegitimate daughter. It explained a lot of things, including why Davis had been getting such focused help from Washington. He wondered if the president himself could be involved. Davis would bet against that idea. He'd met Truett Townsend, and everything about the man seemed aboveboard. The Montanan, fed up with congress, had declared he would not run for a second term unless the two parties found common ground. Gridlock continued, and Townsend kept his word. America's loss, in Davis' opinion. Now his apparent successor was being blackmailed by someone hiding in the headwaters of the Amazon.

With Jen caught smack in the middle.

When he caught sight of El Centro, Davis stopped on the roadside and stared. He'd already spent two hours there today, scouring maps and surveillance photos, asking searching questions and getting blank stares in return. The building glimmered under the high midday sun, but to Davis it suddenly seemed a dark place, an investigative black hole where evidence went in but nothing came out. Since arriving on scene he had pursued the standard practices of investigation, none of which had brought him closer to Jen. Marquez had done the same, and it had gotten him killed.

The sun beat down on his back. It pounded everything in sight. People, cars, airplanes landing on the nearby runway— all seemed to move languidly, as if time itself was overheating. A truck barreled past raising a cloud of dust, and El Centro disappeared in a swirl of brown. In that moment, Davis realized he needed a new direction. He studied the city around him, slow and observant, and then the mountains beyond. He considered a scarred plot of jungle eighty-nine miles south. Was that where the solution lay? Or was it in a plush D.C. conference room? He wondered if there was a military transport speeding south at this very moment, full of hard men and exotic weapons, prepared to settle a score for the man who would soon be king.

It dawned on Davis that the most useful piece of evidence he'd discovered was on the bedside stand in his room—Jen's iPod, which held an audible record of the abduction. Voices that could be analyzed. The gunshots that ended the life of a Secret Service agent. Kristin Stewart imploring Jen to act as her double. With fresh lucidity, he realized that Jen's recording was his best weapon. He turned on a heel and started back to the hotel.

By the time the weathered three stories of Hotel de Aeropuerto edged into view, he was breathing hard and his shirt was matted to his back. Davis was almost to the parking lot when he saw the door to his room. He scuffed to a stop on the road's gravel siding.

The door was ajar. There was no maid's cart parked along the railed balcony. No box of tools from the resident handyman. He was sure he'd left the *No Molestar* sign on the handle. Two men emerged from his room.

Davis edged into the shadow of a parked delivery truck and watched. The men were Hispanic, both beefy and rugged looking, a pair who would look right at home on a warehouse loading dock. One was wearing a soccer jersey and needed a shave. The other wore dark sunglasses and needed a gut-buster diet. They closed the door neatly, and Davis followed their progress all the way to the office. His suspicions about the hotel owner might have had merit after all.

The sunglasses went inside, and through a tightly angled window Davis saw him hand something to the proprietor. A key card? Cash? Maybe both. A few words were exchanged, and soon the pair headed out to the street.

They set out on foot, which was good, because a car would have forced Davis into a difficult choice—confront them here or let them go. He fell in behind the men, keeping a healthy separation, and watched them fall in and out of the shadows of high-rise apartment buildings. They tracked across a broad park, and twice disappeared behind foliage, but each time Davis reacquired them. They hit a good stride on a street called La Esperanza, a wide boulevard with a central tree-lined median and sided by retail shops. There were salons and brand-name clothing stores, practical *farmacias* next to extravagant emerald wholesalers. He was a hundred feet in trail, and working up a sweat, when the two men suddenly stopped. One pulled out a cell phone and had a very brief conversation. Then both turned and looked directly at him.

It didn't take countersurveillance training for Davis to realize he'd been made. They'd been alerted by a phone call, which meant there was at least one other person nearby, possibly more.

The two reversed course and started walking toward him, and Davis sensed a major shift in the odds. He didn't know how many he was up against or where they were. As he stood in the middle of a busy commercial district, there wasn't a cop in sight.

Never was when you needed one.

THIRTY-THREE

Davis spun an about face, and immediately spotted two more men with their eyes on him. They crossed the street quickly, taking an angle to cut him off. Davis made what he thought was the most unpredictable move—he dashed into the busy street.

Horns blared and tires screeched. He glanced left and right, and saw all four men in pursuit. He darted through the opposing lanes, dodging a motorbike, and on reaching the far sidewalk he found himself facing a five-story building with shops at street level. He turned away from the soccer player and his partner, and sprinted at top speed in an effort to outflank their pincher maneuver.

He failed.

The other two cut him off with fifty feet to spare. One white shirt, one green. Green reached under his shirttail and pulled a handgun, leaving Davis but one option—the store right in front of him. He burst through the entrance and sprinted down an aisle toward the back. Flashing past in his periphery were sets of dishes, Wedgwood and Mikasa, and along the walls he saw displays of silver flatware. The stunned sales clerk, a slim and well-dressed woman, stood at a counter in back, wide-eyed and speechless as she watched her new and only customer rush down the main aisle.

He aimed for an exit at the back of the sales floor, but as soon as he reached it Davis skated to a stop on the slick tile and cursed. The only rear exit was blocked, a sturdy-looking door secured by a thick iron bar and padlock. The only other opening in the storeroom was a high transom window, ancient glass scored to the point of being opaque and fortified by an iron grate. He heard the shop's front door open, then his pursuers shouting at the clerk in Spanish. No way out.

His head swiveled as he searched for a weapon. There was only one—leaning against a wall, a four-foot length of lumber. He grabbed the two-by-four, held it by one end and punched out the window. Glass shattered and light sprayed down through the opening, broken shafts playing the dim storeroom like a chapel nave under stained glass. Davis backed against the wall near the passage to the sales floor. He didn't have to wait long.

The gun was the first thing he saw, the barrel canted upward toward the broken window. Davis swung his club eighteen inches above that, and a head arrived right on schedule. The two-by-four connected, but not cleanly, and the man stumbled back. Davis' second swing was better, crushing his gun hand against the door-frame. The gun flew to the floor, and the man in the green shirt doubled over with a shout of pain. Davis palmed one end of the two-by-four and used it like a battering ram, a pivoting arc that ended abruptly under the man's chin. He collapsed in a heap. He'd barely hit the floor when the first shot rang out.

Davis threw his shoulders against the wall, hopelessly exposed. The only way out was the way he'd come in. He needed protection, and the only thing he saw was inside the showroom—an arm's length away, a massive silver serving tray. It was oval, the size of a manhole cover, and looked nearly as sturdy. Davis lunged into the open as a shot zinged past. He grabbed the tray by the handles and raised it, both surprised and heartened by its weight. With the white shirt ten steps away, Davis held the tray like a shield and bull rushed the man. Three more shots echoed, ricocheting off the thick metal. Glass shattered all around, and in the reflection of a wall-length mirror he saw the white shirt shift to one side. Davis altered his momentum and made solid contact.

Both men went down in a spray of crystalline shards. Davis was the quicker to roll, and he delivered his best strike of the day, an elbow to the forehead that sent the man cold to the floor. He scrambled to his feet just as the other two burst inside. Fortunately, neither man had a gun, but one was brandishing a black truncheon. When it came in a blur Davis moved too late, and took a painful blow to his shoulder.

It might have been the pain that set him off. It might have been so many days of frustration, not knowing whether his daughter was dead or alive. There was also a chance these men were tied to the abduction. Anger is never a strategy, at least not a successful one, but at that moment it swept over Davis like a breaking wave.

The nightstick came again in a backhand swing, but such blows were rarely effective. They lacked force and momentum. Davis diverted the strike easily before stepping in and dropping a weighted elbow to the man's collarbone. When he buckled, immobilized, Davis grabbed under his crotch, lifted the man, and sent him flying across the room like a Scotsman tossing a caber. The impact took out an entire row of display cabinets stocked with tea sets. The resulting explosion of ceramics might have been heard a block away. Before he could turn, the last man standing, the one in the soccer jersey, crowned him with some kind of vase.

It hurt like hell, but vases make lousy weapons because they have no density. With a broken ceramic handle in his hand, the man stood looking at his much larger opponent, obviously out of ideas. Davis started with a compact left, followed by a not so compact right. His fists arced down like a windmill gone amuck, and when the soccer player wobbled, Davis lifted him lengthwise, took a running start, and sent him headlong down a row of cabinets that stretched the length of the showroom floor. His head swept through sets of crystal goblets, two trays of figurines, before encountering the side of a very sturdy display case. One that held something called Baccarat. The big cabinet rocked back on its edge, hesitated for just a moment, and then crashed to the floor in a burst of glittering chips.

Davis fell still. He was battered and bloody. He was sucking air like a train at the top of a mountain. Four men lay motionless on the floor. Pretty much *everything* was on the floor. The carpet of glass shards and shattered ceramics was two inches deep in places. Behind the lone surviving counter, Davis sensed a presence, and the young saleswoman rose cautiously. First he saw her raven hair, then two wide eyes, and finally the rest as she stood straight. She looked at him dumbly, then surveyed what was left of her shop.

"Do you speak English?" he asked.

She nodded.

"You should call the police."

She looked at him questioningly, then set her eyes on the man splayed on the floor near her demolished Baccarat cabinet. The clerk pointed down.

Davis looked at the soccer player. He'd come to rest on his back, but was beginning to stir. Next to him on the floor was small leather wallet that had been thrown clear on the final impact. Only it wasn't exactly a wallet. It was a credential holder, and had fallen open perfectly to display a picture of what the man used to look like. Right next to that was his badge.

Davis heaved a long, heavy sigh. "Shit!"

* * *

"A china shop," said a dumbfounded Larry Green after hanging up his phone.

Sorensen looked at him blankly. "What?"

The two had met for dinner, intending to discuss options for helping Davis. Heavy plates of a Thai wasabi creation had just reached their table when the call interrupted.

Green expanded, "Jammer just waylaid four policemen and converted a Wedgwood factory outlet into a beach of ground glass."

Sorensen hung her head. She knew how much Jen meant to Jammer. She also knew it wasn't in his nature to wait serenely for the world to turn.

"He never has been the patient type," she said.

"That's all good and fine when you're turning over charred

airplane parts in a Kansas cornfield. This is different. From what you tell me, he's dealing with some pretty ruthless people who have high connections right here in the Beltway." Green shook his head. "I should have known better than to send him down there. It was a disaster in the making."

"Is he okay?" she asked.

"Jammer? He's indestructible, you know that. But he's definitely highlighting himself. That call was from my boss at NTSB, Janet Cirrillo, who has received some very specific guidance from the State Department."

"The State Department?"

"It seems their prevailing view is that Jammer is an embarrassment to our nation. She's been told in no uncertain terms to get him out of Colombia before he causes, in the Secretary of State's words, 'irreparable damage to a long and peaceable relationship with a vital strategic neighbor.'"

Sorensen looked at him doubtfully. "He won't come. Not without Jen."

"You and I know that."

"So you're not going to pull him out?"

He sighed. "I'll leave a message on his phone. He'll ignore it." Green watched her spin her fork aimlessly in her food. "Tell me . . . how are the two of you doing?"

"Jammer and I? As in personally?"

He nodded.

"Not as well as we should be—the usual."

"He's never been one for spilling his feelings, but I can tell he really likes you, Anna. Goes into a funk every time the two of you split."

"Does he?"

"I knew Diane. He was the same way about her when the squadron deployed. Send him to Italy, and he'd be fine for the first week. After a month he was miserable."

"Maybe that's one of our problems," she said. "Ghosts can cast pretty long shadows."

"And daughters?"

"No," said Sorensen. "I know how much Jen means to him, and I wouldn't want it any other way. In fact, that's what worries me now. Worst case, if she doesn't come back . . . I don't know if Jammer could handle that."

"Could any of us?"

Sorensen looked up plaintively. "You said you could help him."

"I said I was working on some options."

"Well, now's the time."

"Yeah, I think you're right." Green picked up his phone.

As he dialed, Sorensen kept playing with her food. In time her worry gave way to the slenderest of smiles.

"What?" he asked as his call rang.

"For real? A china shop?"

Green only shook his head.

THIRTY-FOUR

Prison cells, Davis had once mused, were rather like fine wine. Each has its distinctive bouquet, subtle flavorings and nuances that present a unique signature. As a full-bodied Merlot might have hints of red currant or blackberry, a robust drunk tank could allude to the bodily functions of the previous night's lodgers. If a Chardonnay reflected the essence of an oak barrel, the walls of a Third-World immigration lockup might offer scratchings and cranial imprints from vintage years past. The understated signatures were always there. All you had to do was look for them.

This particular hundred square feet was not the worst he'd seen. Three cement walls, and at the front a standard-issue iron grate with a hinged door. It wasn't old, wasn't new, and Davis could see three similar cells down the hall. Beyond these was a brightly lit office where uniformed policemen came and went. Though Davis had seen his share of holding cells, two in one week was a personal best. His other visits had been the result of minor transgressions, most fueled by alcohol. Rugby celebrations gone too far. The odd bar fight as a young enlisted Marine, the service in which he'd done a tour before gaining his appointment to the Air Force Academy. For all his proficiency, however, he had never spent two nights in the same week on ice. That was a record he desperately wanted to keep intact.

He sat on a stained cot as he contemplated his misfortune, and like suspects everywhere, tried to get his story straight. How was he to know they were cops? His daughter had been kidnapped, Colonel Marquez murdered, so he was understandably on edge. He'd witnessed two men breaking into his room and assumed the worst, that they were tied to Jen's disappearance. It never crossed his mind that they might be police. Not one of the four had identified themselves as such. He thought it best not to address the question of who followed who away from the hotel. He could rightfully claim that one man had tried to shoot him, and another took a swing with a club. Altogether, not a bad story, and one that would make a strong case for self-defense in most of the fifty States. But here in Colombia?

Not so much.

Davis knew he'd screwed up again, acted without reason. No, that wasn't right. His reasons were damned good. It was foresight he'd lacked. Given what transpired, he could easily have ended up in a hospital, or even on a metal table under Dr. Guzman's bright examining light. And if any of that happened, who was going to find Jen?

He stirred and began pacing his cell, feeling a host of new aches. He rattled the bars to get the attention of a uniformed guard down the hall. He asked for a phone call, and the guard yelled, "*Silencio!*" He demanded to contact the U.S. embassy, and two men in the adjoining cells heckled him in Spanish. Davis kept at it for the best part of an hour, making noise, trying to get a rise out of someone. It was well after dark, after floodlights snapped to life outside the window down the hall, and after a shift change at the guard podium, that the man he wanted to talk to arrived.

Major Raul Echevarria, Region One Police, Special Investigations Unit, walked up and stood in front of his door.

"I didn't know they were cops," Davis said, hours of pre-planned story crafting yielding to impatience.

Echevarria only stared at him, the oft-smiling mouth set straight under his bushy mustache. He looked tired, as if he'd been working all day. Even so, there were no wrinkles in his shirt, and his uniform trousers were sharply creased. Maybe a man who'd gone home after a long day, but who'd been called back to work overtime.

"Did I hurt anybody?" Davis asked.

"Most will recover. Officer Nunez has a concussion and is still seeing double."

"They should have identified themselves. And they definitely shouldn't have started shooting. What would you have done?" Davis knew any lawyer would tell him to shut up at this point. Except, perhaps, a lawyer whose daughter was being held hostage in a hostile jungle. "What were they doing in my room?"

"They were investigating."

Davis stiffened ever so slightly, remembering when he'd given a similar answer. *I'm investigating.* He looked again at Echevarria's shoes. Spit-shined black Oxfords, not a mark on them.

"Since when am I the subject of an investigation?"

"This crash is a criminal matter, Mr. Davis, there can be no doubt. And you withheld evidence." Echevarria reached into his pocket and pulled out a Ziploc bag containing Jen's iPod.

Any number of responses came to Davis' mind. He'd only recently discovered the audio portion, the element the police might find useful. He could argue he'd taken possession of the device as his daughter's personal effect, or even as part of the crash investigation. He didn't bother with any of that. He said, "This doesn't make sense."

"What are you speaking of?"

"Everything. The crash, the missing passengers. Gunshots and false identities. It's all too crude and obvious."

"Even a Colombian detective might realize that criminal forces are at work?"

Davis kept on track. "Whoever is behind this—they've practically advertised their crime." He explained his theory of the jet's diversion and the abduction of the girls.

"That is what you think happened?" Echevarria asked.

"It's not very subtle. The people who dreamed this up are confident of two things. First, they seem sure that only one person outside Colombia realizes what's going on."

"Who might that be?"

"Kristin Stewart's father."

Davis watched Echevarria cup a hand over his broad mustache and drag it down over his lips, a theatrical gesture of reflection. "And the second thing?"

"The people we're looking for—they seem certain they won't get caught."

The policeman shrugged. "Your ideas are entertaining as always, Mr. Davis. I will miss them." Echevarria pulled a United States passport out of a different pocket—Davis didn't have to ask whose picture was inside—and handed it through the bars. "Your time here has come to an end. Our foreign ministry forwarded a demand that you be sent home. We received an immediate response—from your NTSB head office, I think. You are being recalled immediately. The next flight to Washington is at seven tomorrow morning. Make sure you are on it. Until then, I will do my best to overlook these new troubles you have found yourself in."

Davis looked curiously at the policeman. "Do you have children, Major?"

No response.

"I'd guess not, because if you did you'd understand why I'm not going anywhere—not without my daughter."

"*Señor* . . . make no mistake. You attacked four policemen today in front of many witnesses. There is also the murder of Colonel Marquez to consider. That investigation remains in its early stages, and I *should* question you further. Take this as a once-in-a-lifetime offer—leave while you can. My influence is not endless. If you are placed on trial for these crimes you will likely end up in a far less accommodating place than this. And for a very, very long time."

Davis gave no reply.

"Rest assured that the investigation into the crash, and of course the fate of your daughter, will move forward. My department is taking over entirely until a replacement for poor Colonel Marquez can he found."

"That could take days, even weeks."

The policeman only shrugged.

"Your department knows nothing about aviation."

Echevarria once more reached into a pocket—he was beginning to remind Davis of a bad magician—and he handed over a small piece of paper. He said, "If my advice is not persuasive enough, perhaps this note will guide your decision. It was found in your room by one of the officers you assaulted."

The note was handwritten in block letters.

REYNAUD'S TWO WEEKS AGO—YOU ALLOWED YOUR DAUGHTER WINE. LEAVE THE COUNTRY NOW IF YOU EVER WANT TO SEE HER AGAIN.

Davis felt a clench in his gut. Every muscle in his body tensed as he glared at the policeman.

"I will find your daughter," Echevarria promised. "But if you stay in Colombia, I fear it might not be in the condition you wish." The major was silent for a time, then motioned to the jailer at the top of the hall. The man came with a set of keys and opened the lock.

"Goodbye, Mr. Davis," said Echevarria, beckoning him toward the wide-open door.

Davis felt like a soldier in an old war movie—being offered freedom, yet fully expecting to be shot in the back for attempted escape. He wanted Jen's iPod back, but knew it was pointless to ask. He walked past Echevarria into the long corridor.

Moments later Davis stepped outside. The night was deepening, a hard black punctuated by bright windows and passing headlights. He didn't know what part of town he was in, but he saw the lights of the mountain, Monserrate, to his left. He turned the other way. Airports in any city were set away from mountains, and Bogotá was no exception.

His shoulder hurt and his head was spinning, twin blows from very different truncheons—one hardened steel and the other a scribbled note in his pocket. *Leave the country now if you ever want to see her again.*

Davis knew he couldn't do it. He might end up searching a thousand square miles of jungle, or locked in another jail, but there was no decision to be made. He would find Jen or he would die trying. He was weighing the practical ramifications of this conclusion, grim as they were, when a voice called from an alcove, "Jammer Davis?"

He looked and saw a side entrance to the police station, a door that probably hadn't been used in years. Overhead was stenciled: PROHIBIDA LA ENTRADA. Out of the shadow stepped a scruffy Nordic-looking man. He was tall and strongly built, with long blond hair that fell to his shoulders and a bushy mustache. A seriously lost Viking in a loose cotton shirt and worn Levi's.

"Who are you?" Davis asked.

A thin smile, clear-blue eyes glinting under the stab of a streetlight. "I'm the guy who just busted you out of prison."

* * *

The stretch limousine sat motionless on black tarmac, blending with the quiet airfield that shouldered the Maryland-Virginia border. The ramp was lit in a sulfuric yellow mist, and parked nearby, like an ever-watchful bird of prey, was a sleek eggshell-white business jet. In the back seat of the limo, separated from the driver by an opaque privacy screen, Frederick Strand, CEO of The Alamosa Group, sat next to the vice president's chief of staff, Bill Evers. It was Evers, voice weary after a strenuous day of travel, who issued the final instructions to Vincent Kehoe.

"We still don't know who we're dealing with. If at all possible, we'd like you to find out, just in case this issue comes up again."

"Your boss will have more firepower in a few months?" Kehoe suggested.

Strand shot his man a hard look. "You are being paid for neither humor nor speculation, Kehoe. Put a sock in it."

"Yes, sir. Sorry."

Evers picked up, "Never lose sight of the immediate objective. First and foremost, get the girl out safely."

Kehoe promised he would, and two handshakes later he was stepping smartly across the tarmac, a large suitcase in hand. The two men in the limo watched him climb the boarding stairs and disappear into the big Gulfstream—in fact, the very same G-III that had whisked Jammer Davis to Colombia days earlier. The door shut immediately, and the twin turbofans purred to life.

"Will he be able do it?" Evers asked.

"Get the girl home? I think so. It's a lot of money, which in my experience equates to success. Also, I don't think they're fools. In a few months, Martin Stuyvesant will be the last man in the world anyone wants pissed at them."

"And the other? Will Kehoe be able to identify who we're dealing with?"

Strand hedged, "I'm not sure about that. It depends on how careful they are. But as long as we get the girl, the rest should prove moot. I think everyone will be happy at that point."

Strand's phone chimed and he looked at a message. He smiled. "Our Mr. Davis has turned into a complete bust. He can't even stay out of jail."

"Jail?"

"Apparently he beat four policemen senseless."

"Four?" Evers looked away from Strand and shook his head. "The man's a damned embarrassment. It's no wonder he hasn't gotten any results."

"It was worth a try. When you attack problems like this, you have to do it from every conceivable angle. Fortunately, the angle in the briefcase Kehoe is carrying is generally the most effective. You did well, raising that much cash on short notice."

"It cost us a great deal," said Evers.

"An ambassadorship?"

"Worse—a department head."

"Which one?" asked Strand.

"Treasury."

Strand studied Evers for a moment, then remembered that the Secretary of Treasury had announced her intent to step down at the end of the current administration. He was naturally curious who her successor would be, information being the currency it was in his town. A Wall Street hedge fund manager? A Goldman Sachs partner? Strand knew better than to ask, relenting that the answer would have to wait until spring.

The jet carrying Sergeant Kehoe began to move, and two minutes later clawed into the sky in a rush of tormented air.

"Kehoe did have a point," said Strand. "If Stuyvesant wins the election . . . he won't need the likes of me anymore. He'll have the entire United States military at his disposal."

"Worried about your job?" Evers asked playfully.

The retired admiral chuckled. "Certainly not. Midterm congressional elections are always right around the corner. Four hundred and thirty-five House members, one-third of the Senate, all coming up for reelection. With a crowd like that? I always find work, Mr. Evers. Always."

THIRTY-FIVE

"Where are we going?" Davis asked.

He was in the backseat of a Toyota SUV, and there were now two men, the Viking having been joined by their driver, a wiry dark-haired man with an ever-present grin. They'd told him their names were Jorgensen and McBain, and that they worked for the DEA, which was enough to get Davis into the Toyota—that and the fact that he was running seriously low on cash for cab fare.

McBain drove with abandon, blending perfectly in the demolition derby that was Bogotá traffic. The Toyota bottomed out on a pothole, and an audible crunch from the undercarriage widened McBain's smile. The vehicle seemed solid, in a mechanical sense, but the floorboards were littered with food wrappers and newspapers. Davis doubted the exterior had ever been washed, save for two arcs of clear glass on the windshield that could be credited to the wipers. A company car if he had ever seen one.

Jorgensen said, "We have an apartment nearby. There are some things there you should see."

An apartment, thought Davis. *One that probably looks a lot like this truck.* "So why is the DEA springing me out of jail?"

Jorgensen, who was in the front seat next to his partner, half-turned to face Davis. "We only follow orders, Jammer. By the way—is that your real name?"

"My birth certificate says Frank, but nobody uses it."

McBain said, "The guy in charge of our region, back in D.C., he's a retired Marine general. Apparently he got a sideways call from an old Air Force friend who said you needed help."

And there was the answer. Jorgensen and McBain represented the long reach of Larry Green, or more precisely, the old generals' network in action. That was what happened when you put a hundred or so high achievers together in the Pentagon for their last tours of duty before retirement. They formed cliques and had lunch, and when they all retired and moved on to corporate and government afterlives, they kept in touch and did favors for one another.

"Oh, and by the way," said McBain, "Semper Fi."

"They told you about that? That I did three years living in tents and eating MREs before trading desert camo for sky blue?"

"I won't hold it against you."

"Semper Fi, then. Where were you?"

"West coast, EOD, with two tours in the box. Got out ten years ago and ended up with the DEA."

"Defusing bombs and drug enforcement. What's next, parachute test pilot?"

Jorgensen whacked his partner's shoulder. "See, I told you this guy would be good!"

McBain grinned. This was the opening for him to say something more about his service. You could always tell who'd seen serious action—the rear echelon types boasted about their tours, amplifying every dust-covered step. McBain said nothing.

Jorgensen turned toward Davis, and said, "We heard about what you did to those cops. We deal with the police here every day. Some of them are great, but others will sell you out in a heartbeat. You never know who to trust. I've got to tell you—there's been a couple of times the two of us wanted to do exactly what you did."

Davis said at a near whisper, "I didn't know they were cops. It was dumb because getting locked up didn't advance my cause. Right now I'm only interested in one thing—finding my daughter." With his gaze fixed out the window, he stared at nothing. The truck jarred over bumps, and new sites of pain were realized. It was nothing compared to the empty ache in his core.

The Toyota pulled up to an apartment block garage. It was a notably featureless address, the building square-edged and bland, settled on raw concrete footings and finished in chipped stucco. Aesthetics aside, the place looked solid, which was probably the point. McBain produced a remote control, jabbed a button, and the sturdy parking garage door opened.

Jorgensen pulled into the spot labeled 16, and said, "We already got a briefing on your daughter, Jammer. From our office upstairs we can access pretty much every DEA asset in Colombia—and trust me, that's a lot. So don't worry, we're gonna get her back."

Davis could have kissed the man.

* * *

Apartment 16 was on the top floor, and it *did* look a lot like the truck. McBain said they'd been here for a month, but Davis would have guessed a year. There was takeout food on a dinette, half-eaten Chinese with the chopsticks still in place, and a cardboard box cradling two pieces of thin-crust pizza that had curled at the corners.

All the casual furniture—a couch, chairs, and an entertainment center—had been pushed to one side of the room to make way for a large table that bristled with computers, and two thick cables snaked out the main window, undoubtedly linking antennas on the roof.

"It looks like you guys keep busy," Davis said.

"Honestly, things have been a little slow," said Jorgensen. He explained that the DEA's Colombian footprint today was smaller than during the galloping drug wars, when the likes of Pablo Escobar and rival cowboy narcos pushed the country to the brink of lawlessness. "A lot of the coca production has pushed down into Peru this season. We'd like to call it a victory, but the cartels are resilient. It's a water balloon strategy—we clamp down on one spot and they move to another. Still, there's plenty to do. Our most recent op involved a small group of farmers on the steppe who decided that a downturn in coffee bean prices meant it was time to convert to a new crop."

"So how do you combat something like that? Go out and franchise a few Starbucks outlets?"

Both DEA men smiled. "I wish we could be that proactive," said Jorgensen. "But I like your positive outlook."

Davis said, "Whatever help you guys can offer is appreciated. I have to ask, though—is this an officially sanctioned event?"

"You mean will DEA Central be informed?" said Jorgensen.

"That's exactly what I mean."

"Let me put it like this. The best thing about our job is that we have a lot of autonomy—nobody in Washington is quite sure what we do down here. Not unless we tell them."

"Sounds like heaven."

"Pretty close, and we get a lot done. So tell us what you know about your daughter's situation."

Davis did, covering the abduction of the two girls and the subsequent crash.

"That's pretty brazen, even for this part of the world," said McBain. "Of course, the drug business *has* been slumping lately. It's possible some of the new entrants are focusing more on kidnapping and extortion."

"Even so," Jorgensen argued, "crashing an airplane to cover your tracks? I've never seen anything like that."

Davis said, "You've never seen the kind of hostage we're talking about. This isn't about my daughter at all—she's just caught in the crossfire. The primary kidnapping target is very high value."

"Bill Gates' kid?" McBain jested.

"Way worse."

The two affable agents exchanged a look, and their good humor dissipated. "Okay," said McBain, caution in his voice, "maybe you should tell us what we're getting into."

"I've been giving that some thought—whether you guys need to know. You sealed the deal a little while ago. Semper Fi." He paused, and then said, "But you should understand that just by knowing, you could be setting yourselves up for some difficult choices in the near future."

Again the two exchanged a look, and this time Jorgensen said, "All right, warning duly noted."

"The name of the other girl who was abducted is Kristin Stewart."

The DEA men exchanged a blank look. "So who is Kristin Stewart?" Jorgensen asked.

"She's Martin Stuyvesant's illegitimate daughter."

"Holy crap!" said McBain.

"Eloquently put, Marine. When they came to pull her off that airplane, Kristin seemed to realize what was happening. She told my daughter to claim that she was Kristin Stewart. The two look a lot alike, so apparently the thugs on detail didn't know what to do and took them both. As it turned out, it saved Jen's life. I'm sure the mastermind who cooked up this insanity has figured out who's who by now. That's what you're getting into. I need to find out where these girls are being held. Then I'm going to go get them."

"You? By yourself?"

"If necessary. Of course, a little help is always appreciated. Problem is, I don't trust anybody north of the Mason-Dixon line right now. Somebody in D.C. has been watching every move I make."

"Stuyvesant?" asked McBain.

"No way to tell. But I don't think we're talking about any kind of government-sanctioned surveillance. It all seems very shady and off the books, which makes sense in a way. And because this situation is a powder keg, politically speaking, nobody is going to authorize SEAL Team Six or an FBI task force to come down and rescue these girls. Bottom line—whatever help I *was* getting is gone. I'm on my own now."

"Wow," said Jorgensen. "You *are* screwed."

"Oh, it gets worse." Davis pulled out the note Echevarria had given him and showed it to the DEA men. "Someone is threatening Jen if I don't go home on the next flight."

"But you're not going," said McBain.

"Would you?" He looked at each man in turn, and got two head shakes. "That's what I thought. Help me find her, that's all I ask. I'll take it from there."

Without hesitation, McBain said, "Let's get to work."

THIRTY-SIX

The jungle is a black place on a moonless night, darker still when one is entombed in a thick-walled room during blackout conditions. That was one of many new thoughts coursing through Kristin Stewart's head as she lay in bed unable to sleep.

The blackout was taken seriously, evidenced earlier when she'd heard a soldier outside threatened with execution for lighting a cigarette. "The Americans can see that!" someone growled outside her door. *Was it true?* she wondered. Could spy planes and commandos be searching for her right now? Her father would not sit by idly—not when so much was at stake for him.

For a girl from the suburbs of Raleigh there were new sensations everywhere. If the jungle was dark, it was anything but silent. She'd tent-camped a few times in state parks back home, yet never had she witnessed nature in such primitive essence. For six nights she had lain awake to the call of birds, the keen of insects, frenzied cries from creatures under attack. She'd smelled the sweet scent of rain and the rich tang of decay, environmental cycles learned about in high school put vividly on display in her fern-carpeted surroundings. It seemed an impenetrable place, a living fortress of jade. But might that very imperviousness also serve in reverse? Could it not mask an assault should an elite Special Forces team arrive in the middle of the night to effect a rescue? Kristin was no expert in such things, which only made her imaginings that much more frightful.

She rolled to the side and pulled up a blanket to cover her naked chest.

"What is wrong, my love?" said the man next to her.

A light flicked on, a mobile phone screen called to life—who used a flashlight anymore? Against utter blackness the tiny screen cast the room in an unearthly blue-white hue. The meager furnishings already seemed familiar, as did the two square windows covered with plastic and duct tape. She saw their rations of food on the table, still in plastic shopping bags, and the teasing claw-foot bathtub in the corner that begged for a water supply. Finally, with a tilt of her head, she saw Carlos Duran.

In the dim light his long hair and beard were unchanged, the same as when she'd met him one year ago—seated in front of her in the auditorium on that first day of fall semester, twirling a yellow pencil nimbly in his hand. Psychology 1102, she recalled with amusement. A course he perhaps should have taught. He was twenty-six years old, or so he'd said. For reasons she could not discern, she often now added that caveat when it came to Carlos. *Or so he said*. Kristin thought he looked older now, and even in the dim, ghostly light she distinguished worry lines feathering from his eyes and a harder set to his jaw. A jaw that moved as he repeated his question.

"Nothing," she replied, "I'm fine."

His hand, the one not occupied by the phone, cupped her bottom, then moved up to find a bare shoulder. "You are shaking." He rubbed slow circles on her back.

"I'm frightened, Carlos. Everything has gone wrong."

He gave a weary sigh. It was not the first time they'd had this conversation.

He said, "Please believe me—I'm sorry about Thomas. My men got excited. They thought he was armed."

"I *told* you he wouldn't be. They made him check his gun in his suitcase, just as we expected."

The caressing stopped.

Carlos rose from the bed and walked to the bathroom. He was naked, and it occurred to Kristin that the body she'd come to know so well her sophomore year, the one that had educated her in the disciplines of pleasure, seemed strikingly different now. His face held deeper grooves, and there was weariness in his posture. Worst of all, on the few occasions when their eyes met she sensed a profound detachment. He was a photograph that had yellowed with age, and her feelings for him seemed correspondingly blurred and faded. Or was it only her perspective? She'd fallen in love with the passionate son of a revolutionary leader, a young man committed to reclaiming his country from a corrupt government, and steadfast in his support of the oppressed. *Or so he said.* The bathroom light clicked on, and soon she heard him using the toilet. Kristin rolled away to face the far wall.

"As for the airplane," he called out, "I can't tell you what happened. The passengers must have been frightened. Perhaps they attacked poor Blas, our pilot. What more is there to say? It is a tragedy, but I told you from the beginning—there is always risk involved when one reaches for great things."

"I know," she said, "but I thought the risk was on *our* part. I never realized others would be put in harm's way."

He finished, but left the bathroom light on. Kristin heard his naked footsteps pad across the stone floor, then the mattress shifted as he sat on the bed behind her. "It is almost over. The money is on its way, and in a few hours everything will be done. Your father will have paid a steep price for abandoning you, and mine will have the means to better the lives of many Colombians, good people who the government has cast aside. Schools and clinics will be built, children will be saved." His hand was on her again, this time finding a hip. "Soon you and I will be together again in Charlottesville, two poor college students attending class when we're in the mood and making love when we're not."

She turned back and met his eyes directly. "How long will we keep it up before taking our share?"

Carlos shrugged. "Maybe we should graduate—a year, perhaps two. Long enough for everyone to forget these unfortunate troubles. Long enough for the trails to go cold. The money will wait for us, and one day we will go where we please, raise children, and teach them the right way to live." He stood and pulled on his pants.

"What about my father—you don't think he'll pursue it? Won't he try to find out who was behind my abduction?"

"Your father will soon be president, my love. He will have far more important things to do than to turn over old rocks in search of dangerous things. He of all people will keep our little adventure a secret." Carlos reached down and kissed her on the forehead. "When this is done, it is done. It will be in everyone's best interest to leave the past alone."

"Won't I be asked about what happened when I get back?"

"By who? The police are not involved, nor is the FBI."

"The Secret Service? They lost a man in the line of duty—surely they'll want to find out who was responsible for his death."

"Their agent died in a plane crash. That will be the story, and if other ideas arise my father has sufficient connections in the Colombian government to make them disappear."

"When can I meet your father?" she said.

"Today. He will come for the exchange."

"What's he like?"

"He is a bastard, but unlike your father he puts it to good use."

"You said he helps people—I haven't seen that. Most of the soldiers outside are younger than us, and they don't strike me as very ideological. They act like thugs, smoking and drinking when Pablo isn't there to slap them around."

Carlos chuckled. "Pablo is my father's sergeant. He is a real soldier who does what he must to keep the men in line."

"He frightens me."

"He is big and ugly, yes, but Pablo understands who is in command. He has fought at my father's side for twenty years—I trust no one more."

Kristin closed her eyes. Trust on her part was an increasingly open question. She looked at the scratched dresser where she had, days earlier, discovered a passport while searching for scissors. Carlos' picture was inside, but the last name on the document was not Duran. *So who was he really, this student-lover she thought she knew so well?*

The fanciful plan they'd hatched over beer and wings in a Charlottesville pub bore little resemblance to what had played out. It had turned violent and dangerous. Innocent people had died, and she doubted very much that any of the ransom money would find its way to the underprivileged of the nearby villages, save perhaps for a handful of smiling barkeepers and prostitutes.

"What will I tell my mother?" she asked.

"Tell her the truth, that you were treated well." He slapped her naked haunch and laughed, then pulled on his boots. "I have to go outside and check on things. My father will arrive soon."

As he moved to the door, she said, "Carlos—there's one thing I want."

"What is it?"

"Let me see Jen Davis."

His head slumped lower. "We have been over this," he said, terseness in his voice. "It can only complicate things if you—"

"No," she said, standing her ground, "I want to see her!"

In the dim light she saw a stony expression come over his face. An expression she had never seen before. "You will see her in the morning. After the money comes, she can go back to America with you if that's what you want."

"What about you?"

"I told you earlier—I must join my father's little band of brothers when they vaporize into the jungle, but it won't be for long. Only until things are safe. For now we must keep Jen isolated. The less she sees and knows, the better it is for everyone."

"No, Carlos. I—"

"*Enough!*" he said harshly. Carlos took two strides toward her and spoke in a whisper, his words taking a slow cadence. "She should never have been part of this. I still don't understand why you told her to claim your identity on the airplane."

"I was frightened. I expected you to be there, and they'd just killed Thomas. I didn't know any of those men, and everything happened so quickly."

He heaved a sigh of exasperation. "All right, let's put it

behind us. But this is a problem of your creation. I will deal with it as I see fit."

"If I hadn't gotten Jen off that airplane she'd be dead."

She saw a flicker of something in his eyes, but it dissipated quickly. She'd seen it once before, in Virginia, when the meth-head who lived above his apartment came to the door with a gun in the middle of the night and accused Carlos of stealing his stash. She'd sensed a menace in Carlos' gaze that night, and gone quickly to call 911. While she was in a back room retrieving her phone, the situation had defused, ending uneventfully. Carlos assured her there was no need to call the police after all. And there wasn't—not until two nights later when the addict's drug-infused body was found on the concrete sidewalk beneath his fourth-floor balcony. It was the kind of accident that surprised no one, least of all the Charlottesville police whose detectives never so much as knocked on their door.

As she looked at him now, his features seemed to soften.

She said, "Jen will come with me tomorrow?"

"Of course."

A kiss on her cheek, and Carlos disappeared.

She fell back and put her head on the pillow. *Or so he said.* She took a deep breath, sensing vestiges of his musky odor. A scent she had once savored now struck differently, activating new synapses.

Much had changed in eight months, since that day during Christmas break when her mother had confessed, divulging the identity of her father. It explained the new house in Raleigh, and the sudden lack of handwringing over out-of-state tuition. Her mother had made a deal with the devil, a binding agreement that would guarantee them a comfortable life. *All we have to do is keep quiet.* That had become her mother's mantra. Kristin's own response, however, had been very different.

Why doesn't he want to see me?

That was the question she'd never been able to shake, ringing as loudly now as it had when she'd first put it to her mother on

Christmas Eve. Her father had always been characterized by her mother as an irresponsible drifter, a romantic mistake named Carl whose last name she'd never known. That blank slate in Kristin's mind, held lifelessly in place by a token name, had turned out to be something very different indeed—a man destined to be president of the United States. A man whose telegenic face was on the news every night, and whose eloquent words were quoted each day in the papers. A man featured on the cover of *Time* and *Rolling Stone* in the same month. A man whose campaign called their house asking for contributions.

All we have to do is keep quiet. How could anyone be quiet in the face of such lies?

There were times Kristin wished it had been the drifter. A vagabond ne'er-do-well would have been far preferable to a man who knew full well of his daughter's existence, yet who ignored her in the advancement of his own glory. Irresponsible she could understand. Ignoble she could not. She had cried herself to sleep time and again. It was some months later, when her fitful nights came to be spent aside the dashing young Colombian, that she sought solace in a wine-laden confession. She said nothing about *who* her father was—not then—but through welling tears Kristin explained her feelings of pain and abandonment.

Carlos had never been more caring or tender.

The next week he began asking questions. He took particular interest in the ever-present men who stood discreetly at the back of lecture halls, watchful and quiet. The following weekend, in the wake of a bleak sorority party and far too many margaritas, Kristin had told him who her father was. Carlos, thoughtful as ever, gave new insights, putting into words what she knew but had tried to ignore—that her mother's new home and car were a payoff for silence, even a contract of sorts, allowing her father to cling forever to his desertion. For Kristin, the pain was excruciating, but her lover understood. A man who listened and, unlike her father, who was there when she needed him.

It was a night soon after that Carlos had made his own

confession. His father was the leader of the Fuerzas Amazonas, a peasant militia fighting the Colombian government from the jungles. Carlos described his father as a tough but fair-minded man, a commander who had sent his only son to America for an education, quietly hoping he would return one day to carry on the struggle at his side. At the age of twenty, Carlos had but one desire—to escape the misery of war. Six years later, high on marijuana in a quiet and comfortable townhouse near the University of Virginia, the insurrectionist's son confided that the only product of his education had been guilt, a sense that he had abandoned his family and people.

It was Kristin's turn to comfort her soulmate, to arrest his shame and kiss his face. If there was any redemption in his years in America, a tearful Carlos had told her, it was that he had found her. More kisses were exchanged, and in the small hours of that morning, so many months ago, the young revolutionary had given rise to an idea.

An idea that had now gone terribly wrong.

THIRTY-SEVEN

No government organization on Earth, including those residing in Colombia, knows the jagged topography of the northern Andes as well as the United States Drug Enforcement Administration. The War on Drugs, advanced in earnest during the Reagan administration, had ushered in a new era in law enforcement, throwing the weight of the United States DOD, CIA, and State Department behind escalating drug interdiction efforts. High-tech surveillance, low-tech informants, and the aerial spraying of herbicides all became part of a master plan whose long-term results, when it came to supply-side interruption, were decidedly mixed. Less equivocal was the expertise gained by operators in the field.

While Jorgensen worked a computer, McBain gave Davis a briefing on the composition of Colombian rebel forces, some element of which would invariably prove to be their target.

"FARC used to pretty much own the jungle, everything south of Bogotá and east of Cali, which is the area we're talking about. It began during the sixties, and at their high point they controlled roughly one third of Colombia. Over the last decade they've morphed. The government came down hard a few years back, and FARC went into decline. They've made a recent comeback in the form of small cells—*pisa suaves*, which translates to tread lightly. These are company-sized units, about thirty men each, and they move constantly. Of course, it's not just FARC we have to consider. You've got your right-wing paramilitaries and fringe groups. They all make their living in roughly the same way—abductions, extortion, and acting as middlemen in the drug trade."

"Do they actually grow coca?" Davis asked.

"Not enough manpower. They let the peasants run the farms, and do like any legitimate government—tax the grower, tax the guy who harvests the leaves, tax the guy who processes it into powder, and finally tax the drug lord who hauls the final product through their territory to reach the market."

"Like we do with corn, but without the subsidies."

"Pretty much," said McBain. "Like most organized crime, these paramilitary groups have adopted a business plan based on multiple income streams, and kidnapping is high on the list. We're usually talking about the wives and kids of prominent business-men, though—nothing like the victim you're trying to recover."

"These company-sized units—do they operate independent-ly?"

"These days, yeah, most do."

"So if we can figure out which one is responsible, we'll have a good idea of the size of the force we're up against."

McBain raised an eyebrow. "We?"

"Well . . . I'm just sayin' . . ."

"Right. Let's see if we can find them first."

* * *

They worked through the night. Davis helped where he could, but mostly stayed out of the way. Just after sunrise he was dis-patched on a mission to a nearby Dunkin' Donuts shop, which seemed more prevalent here than in Boston. Davis returned with an assorted dozen donuts in a box and a tray of coffee. With an order like that, he decided this particular DEA safe house was not intended for deep cover work.

"I count fourteen airstrips in the area we've identified," said McBain, referring to a desktop computer display with exactly that many yellow circles. "A long time ago the big drug cartels were awash in cash. They flew in processing material and shipped out product using small twin-engine aircraft, so runways had to be cleared. Some were fairly long, because the guys in charge liked the convenience of flying in to visit their operations from villas in places like the Caymans and Panama."

"When you're grossing fifty million a month," expanded Jorgensen, "who wants to live in a tent in the jungle?"

McBain picked up, "Over the years we've surveyed every grass and dirt clearing in the jungle that could support an airplane. These airstrips come and go—a new one will get bulldozed now and again, while others are abandoned and the jungle takes over. There are only two official airports in this region, one in Neiva and one in San José del Guaviare. Both have asphalt runways, and at least a minimal degree of government oversight."

"No," said Davis, using a wrist to wipe glazed sugar off his chin. "Rule those out. I saw the landing gear—that airplane definitely landed on a soft field."

Jorgensen made the deletion on his keyboard, and two of the yellow circles disappeared. "How much runway would this jet have needed?" he asked.

"I've already talked to an engineer about some basic numbers. Landing is easy enough—the grass helps you stop. But our jet took off again, and that's more limiting. Let's say thirty-two hundred feet. That's conservative, the real number is probably higher."

Jorgensen did his magic and seven more circles disappeared. "Okay, we're making some headway. We have five unimproved strips that are at least thirty-two hundred feet long."

They all stared at the screen. It was a manageable number, but still too big.

"Where do we go from here?" McBain asked.

"Elevation? If any of these small strips are at high altitude there would be a performance penalty—jet engines put out less thrust when they run a mile above sea level."

"One's at six thousand feet."

"Strike it," said Davis.

Four circles stared back.

Davis lifted his coffee and took a long draw through the

plastic lid. "Let's draw a line. Take the last known position of the jet before air traffic control lost contact, then connect it to the crash." Davis pointed to both spots on the map, and Jorgensen drew a magenta line from one to the other. Two circles touched the line. The other two lay over fifty miles east.

"Our criteria are getting a little iffy," said McBain.

"Yeah, I know," replied Davis. "Fifty miles. The jet could easily have traveled that far in our time frame."

Everyone was silent until Davis said, "No, I think we're right. It's one of these. We need a way to take a closer look."

"What time is it?" McBain asked.

"Seven thirty," answered Jorgensen.

The DEA agents exchanged a knowing look.

"What?" Davis asked.

"You're gonna like this," said Jorgensen. "We have a drone that operates from a remote pad near Cali. It makes a run each night over the FARC National Wildlife Refuge, a preprogrammed route to log comparative imagery. Basically we look for changes—roads that have been traveled overnight, vehicles that have moved. This time of day the drone is nearly done, but there's a window for special requests before it gets low on fuel."

"So the drone can get us pictures of these two sites?"

"Even better—if we get it approved, we can watch them in real time."

"Who approves it?" Davis asked.

"The DEA regional manager for Colombia and Peru," said Jorgensen, his voice garbled as he bit into a vanilla-frosted with sprinkles. "Bert Collimore is his name, a real jerk. He works out of an office in Cali. Or at least he used to. Bert was fired last week, which means the decision goes to the acting manager, the regional chief operations officer."

"And who's that?"

Jorgensen smiled broadly. "That would be me."

THIRTY-EIGHT

The drone was a General Atomics RQ-1B Predator, formerly owned and maintained by the CIA. Long on the sidelines when it came to unmanned aerial vehicles, the DEA was desperate to get into the game, and had recently taken two aircraft on loan from its wayward cousin in Langley. According to McBain, the airframe was past its prime and had been destined for the scrapyard before being salvaged by the DEA—something akin to a brotherly hand-me-down on the federal level.

The Predator was controlled by two operators: one stationed near the runway outside Cali, and a second operational pilot connected to the aircraft via a Ku-band satellite link, and who worked from a nondescript bunker overlooking a gentle bend of the Panama Canal.

The letter R in the aircraft's designation meant this particular model was intended for reconnaissance—like most older airframes, the DEA's secondhand drone was a "looker," having no hard points on the wings on which ordnance could be mounted. Aside from takeoff and landing, the entire mission was flown by the operator in the bunker, and he was overseen by a single supervisor. Because no weapons were carried there was little else to the chain of command, this in direct contrast to combat versions which required a JAG, well versed in the laws of war and theater rules of engagement, to be in attendance during all flight operations.

Jorgensen and McBain let Davis choose which airfield to study first. He saw no difference, and selected the nearer of the two. The request was put through to Panama, and the drone arrived on station fifteen minutes later, just before nine that morning. Soon, pictures were streaming in from twelve thousand feet above their target area. Davis was awestruck by the clarity.

"The drone has three cameras," explained Jorgensen. "There's a nose-mounted color feed that's primarily used by the pilot. Then you have a variable aperture infrared for general use, and a synthetic aperture radar for looking through clouds and haze. Not all can be used simultaneously. Right now we're looking at infrared."

Alongside the clearing Davis saw a half dozen fifty-five gallon drums, discarded and rusting, and nearby piles of trash in which he could identify pipes, sheet metal, and an old tire. The airstrip was grass and dirt, and looked smooth from two miles overhead. In the infrared image, however, cooler splotches gave away large puddles that might be trouble spots—a pilot landing a jet would have to either steer around them or be lucky enough to miss.

"I see tracks where airplanes have landed," he said. "Is there any way to tell how long ago they were made?"

McBain replied, "It's hard to tell from this altitude, but there's definitely been activity—I'd say in the last two weeks."

"You guys have been to places like this. Would the ground be stable enough to support a forty-thousand-pound airplane?"

"It depends on the conditions," Jorgensen answered. "If the rains have been heavy, no way. This strip looks in decent shape, but it's impossible to say for sure without having boots on the ground. We have come up with one way to approximate." On a separate computer screen he added an overlay to the map, irregular blobs that varied from green to amber to red. Parts of the airfield were completely blotted out.

"What's that?" asked Davis.

"Rainfall," said Jorgensen. "Last year Colombia got a nice upgrade to its national weather radar—it was paid for by an environmental organization that wants to track rainfall in the Amazon. Good information, and open source."

"So, by quantifying how much rain you've had, you can predict how soggy a given patch of dirt is going to be?"

Jorgensen stepped the rainfall back one week and the blobs altered. "More or less. We've only been doing this for a few months, but it's surprisingly accurate. We were looking for a method to study road conditions. It should work just as well on unimproved airstrips." When the screen settled, he said, "There you are. This place got eleven centimeters of rain last week—about four inches. That's a lot if you're in Texas or Virginia, but here it's nothing out of the ordinary."

"I could take the drone lower to get a better look, but, like I said, without actually standing on dirt there's always going to be some guesswork involved."

"Actually," said Davis, "I don't think there's going to be any guesswork at all."

The two DEA men looked at him. Davis pointed to the screen that was still displaying a real-time feed from the Predator. They all watched a small single-engine propeller plane turn onto final approach, skim over the high tree line, and make a gentle touchdown in the clearing.

* * *

Kehoe got out of the Cessna Caravan and stepped squarely into a puddle of mud. Fortunately he was prepared, having worn jungle boots and waterproof hunting pants. The stewardess on the G-III had given him an odd look when he'd boarded in Virginia, being clearly more accustomed to Armani suits and diamond-clipped ties. Kehoe couldn't have cared less. He was a soldier, and soldiers knew the value of function over form. He'd stepped off the G-III immediately after landing in Bogotá, and walked no more than twenty steps to board the Cessna, a connecting flight arranged by whomever had brought him here. His new pilot's only words had been, "Kehoe?" and after getting a nod, "Come with me." Thirty minutes later, here he was.

It took ten full strides to reach dry land, a plot of crusted dirt and grass that looked surprisingly level. Behind him the pilot of the Cessna—the only other person in sight—stepped down from the cockpit, circled his aircraft, and kicked a heel into the soft earth. He gave Kehoe a woeful frown.

Kehoe called back in Spanish, "Will there be any problem taking off again?"

"No, is okay. The sun will be high soon and things get better. But we should not stay long. This afternoon will be hot. If big storms come . . . could be grounded for days."

Kehoe had no intention of staying that long. "I'll make it quick. Be ready."

The pilot waved to say he would, and Kehoe turned away without another word. He had long ago concluded that specialists worked most effectively when you let them do their jobs. Pilots in particular became unmanageable if you tried to tell them their business. They were also consistently rational when put in difficult situations—in no small part, because their lives were at stake too.

The forest was still on the breezeless morning, the only noise the *tic tic* cool down of the Cessna's engine, the only smell the faint burn of spent avgas. Ahead of him a lone dirt road curved away into the emerald wall, and he walked in that direction with the suitcase in hand. Kehoe had gone no more than twenty yards when a muffled roar broke the silence. A pair of jeeps rumbled into the clearing. Right on time.

So far, so good, he thought.

He made an effort to stand straight and tall, well aware of the delicacy of his situation. Kehoe had crossed the point of no return when the Cessna landed five minutes earlier. He was alone in the middle of a foreign jungle, about to engage a group of well-documented killers, and chained to his wrist was an oversized briefcase containing seven million U.S. dollars.

The odds of complications were, to say the least, significant.

He walked toward the jeeps through what felt like a steam bath, the early sun already torrid, sucking moisture from the ground and infusing it into the air. The jeeps looked identical, some kind of Chinese knockoff of the classic World War II U.S. Army Willys. He counted seven men—at least he guessed they were men, a point left in question as they were all wearing ski masks.

Kehoe knew instantly who was in charge. Lead vehicle, passenger side. He wore fatigues that were cleaner than the rest, and was the first to dismount. A stocky man, his long hair extended out the back of his knit mask, which had to be a miserable thing to wear in this kind of heat. By his build and movement Kehoe knew he was young, and he would say the same about the others. He also saw they were not well trained, written in the way they held their weapons and the fact that everyone's eyes were locked on him. None of it came as a surprise.

The armies here were like those in so many other jungles he'd seen, comprised of kids who had been recruited—if that word could be used—either at the point of a gun or, in the best case, because their families had taken fifty dollars for the contribution of an able-bodied young male. Seventeen-year-old kids, who should have been in school or plowing hillsides, were instead fed, given a gun and fatigues, and issued a few rounds of ammunition to shoot at a tree stump. Basic training complete.

And having sorted through all that, he knew there was only one man who mattered right now.

The commander approached him and drew to a stop. "Welcome to Colombia. I hope your journey was uneventful."

The first surprise—his English was good, nearly without accent. It made Kehoe think the man had a heavy hand in the scheme. He'd like very much to see the face behind the mask, since that was his secondary mission. All he needed was one glimpse. Tactical abilities aside, Kehoe had been selected for this op for one very specific reason—he had an astonishing memory, particularly when it came to faces.

"I'd like to do this as quickly as possible," Kehoe said, his eyes quietly snapshotting details as best he could. An old serial number on one jeep, a bracelet on the leader's wrist.

"I'm sure you would," said the commander.

"I don't see the girl," said Kehoe in the most casual voice he could muster.

"In time. There are preliminaries." The commander nodded to his men, and two closed in on Kehoe. The American assumed the stance, legs wide and arms outstretched, and took a head-to-toe pat down. They would be looking less for weapons than wires or tracking devices. Holding the briefcase at arm's length, an impatient Kehoe said, "Please hurry—this is a lot of money and it's very heavy."

The men stepped back, and one nodded to say they were finished. At that point one of the soldiers produced a black hood. Kehoe had been expecting it, so he made no protest as the man drew it over his head. He imagined everyone else ripping off their own sweater-knit masks with blessed relief. From this point forward, if anyone was going to be uncomfortable, it was him.

Someone took his elbow and guided him toward the jeep. He was pushed left and right, and could tell by the feel of the sidewall that he was being backed into a front passenger seat, almost certainly the second vehicle.

Sound became more important than sight. A pair of soldiers murmured, the words unintelligible, and rifle butts clanked to the jeep's metal floorpan. Waiting for the engines to crank to life, Kehoe thought he heard another faint sound, vaguely familiar, like the buzz of a distant insect. There was a hopeless urge to look up at the sky, and in a mischievous moment, as he sat baking in a black hood, he wondered if he could manage some kind of stretch that would appear as a wave from above. He knew it was a drone, likely under the command of some distant Air Expeditionary Group tasked to monitor his progress. Kehoe had been specifically briefed to expect no support, but it didn't surprise him that someone was watching. *Yes*, he thought, *the admiral leaves nothing to chance*. All the same, it wasn't much comfort. If things went badly, there was no chance of the drone facilitating a rescue—the cameras overhead would only record his demise.

If the Colombians knew what was in the sky above them, Kehoe heard no mention of it. As the Cessna pilot had noted on their arrival, the visibility in the valley was marginal, the low morning sunlight diffusing like a veil in the still, humid air. *Even if they heard the drone, they could never see it.*

The jeeps came to life, rattled into gear, and soon they were splashing with purpose into the heart of the jungle.

THIRTY-NINE

"Track them!" said Davis.

"I will," Jorgensen replied. "But the drone only has enough fuel to stay on station for another twenty minutes. Let's hope they're not going far."

"The guy who just arrived had something in his hand," said Davis. "Could have been a suitcase."

"What are the chances of us stumbling onto the payoff?" said a skeptical McBain.

"If the girl who could decide our next presidential election is being held hostage nearby? I'd say the chances are extremely high. We narrowed it down to two airstrips, and then we guessed right. If you think about it, the timing is perfect—a few days for Stuyvesant to worry, come to the right conclusion, and raise a lot of cash. This has payoff written all over it. Those jeeps are going to lead us right to the girls."

"Hang on," said McBain. "That little prop job didn't fly here all the way from the States. If this is the transaction, then the guy carrying the briefcase switched airplanes somewhere—probably right under our noses in Bogotá. If we maneuver the drone and get the tail number of that Cessna we might be able to verify where it came from. I'm thinking a jet landed at the same airport this morning after a long flight from the States."

"Maybe," said Davis, "but this is no time to overanalyze. We're too close, with eyes on target right now—I say we shadow the jeeps and nothing else."

All three men watched the display. The two vehicles disappeared under the jungle canopy, then reappeared a quarter mile later. The road was no more than a worn path through the forest that was lost occasionally under foliage. The hard part would be forks or intersections—if the jeeps made a turn under cover they could lose contact. Davis kept his eyes locked to the screen, his hands gripping the table every time they lost sight. Passive surveillance required considerable patience—never one of his virtues.

"Do you guys have an airplane?"

Jorgensen looked at him skeptically. "An airplane? We've got a fleet, but not in Bogotá."

"Do you have *anything* here?"

"Jammer, if you're thinking about—"

"I'm not thinking, I'm acting. If you don't have an airplane, I'll go to the airport and steal one. I only wanted to give you the chance to keep me from embarrassing our country again."

Jorgensen shook his head dismissively.

McBain smiled. He said, "There's a Twin Comanche we confiscated, keep it in a hangar we share with the government. It's nothing tactical, we just use it for shuttling personnel. No surveillance suite in the electronics bay, no hardened floor."

"Hardened floor?" Davis repeated.

"Certain farmers don't like airplanes nosing around their crops, for obvious reasons. They have a tendency to take potshots at anything flying low."

"But it runs?"

"Usually," Jorgensen said. "Unfortunately, we don't have a pilot. The guy who's checked out is on temporary duty in Panama."

"Do you have the keys?"

Jorgensen gave him a look that asked if he was serious.

Davis shot one back that said: *Stay out of my way.*

McBain broke the impasse. "Jammer's right, we need to do something. There's no telling how this will play out. We have to get *both* girls. They might or might not be released safely in the next hour, but this is our chance to get close, to have some insurance. If the exchange doesn't go well, this group is going to vaporize into the jungle. We got lucky once, but finding them a second time could prove way harder." He addressed Davis. "Have you flown a Twin Comanche?"

"Of course."

"That settles it," said McBain. "I'll come with you."

Both of them looked at Jorgensen, who relented. "All right, it's your funeral. I'll stay here and keep the surveillance for as long as I can. But like I said, we have less than twenty minutes of fuel—then the drone goes home."

McBain was already packing, stuffing a sat-phone and binoculars into a duffel bag.

"How long does it take for the drone to get back to its home station?" Davis asked.

"We fly it out of a remote strip west of Cali—about thirty minutes from where it is now."

"So you can stay on station for an hour, maybe more. There's got to be an emergency reserve padded into the fuel numbers."

Jorgensen, who was legally in charge and therefore responsible for the asset, said, "Are you suggesting we run this bird out of fuel and let it crash?"

"If that's what it takes to get this mission done," Davis said, "then, yes, that's exactly what I'm suggesting."

"We're talking about a three-million-dollar aircraft."

"No, we're talking about two young girls. Anyway, my boss will cover it."

McBain went to a closet across the room and pulled out a pair of lethal-looking weapons—black Heckler & Koch MP5s. "You ever used one of these?" he asked Davis.

"Hasn't everybody?"

McBain reared back and threw one of the guns at him from across the room.

"What the—" Davis reached with a long arm, but the throw was terrible and he barely touched the stock before the gun thudded to the floor. *Is that damned thing loaded?*

McBain laughed. "Easy, big guy. It's a fac."

"A what?"

"A facsimile, a training gun. We use them when we run exercises with the police and the army."

"I don't suppose you have any real ones?"

"Sure," said McBain, "in an armory on the other side of town. This time of day it'll take us an hour to drive there and back."

Davis picked up the faux MP5. Most of the training guns he'd seen before were blue, but these had the matte-black finish of the real deal—at least from a distance. "I guess it's better than nothing."

"That depends on which end you're looking at," said Jorgensen. "Down here, sometimes no weapon is better than one that doesn't work. It's situational, so be careful where you show them."

"Situational," Davis repeated. He slotted the training guns into a nylon bag. "Got any fake hand grenades? Maybe a paper mache howitzer?"

Jorgensen ignored this, and said, "Just so you understand—I'm not actually controlling this drone. I have priority for tactical requests, but that's it. I'm not sure the operators will give me more than twenty minutes on station."

"Use your emergency authority," argued McBain, already heading for the door with Davis behind him. "It's a legal move. Tell them blue-force lives are at stake and they have to comply."

"But there aren't any lives at stake."

"Not yet . . . " Davis said over his shoulder as he hit the threshold, "but give us half an hour."

* * *

Kristin Stewart stood in front of the villa where she and Carlos had been staying. Roughly half the soldiers were milling in the courtyard, chain smoking and agitated like expectant fathers. The rest had departed with Carlos to oversee the delivery of their eagerly awaited payday.

The idea that she was to receive a share of the proceeds had once seemed satisfying, a small retaliation against the father who'd abandoned her. Now it seemed more repulsive every moment. Thomas Mulligan was dead, along with an entire planeload of innocent people—all because she had tried to lash out in revenge. Kristin was desperate to bring it all to an end. She wanted only to get home, see her mother, and put this entire horrific week behind her.

God, what have I done?

Pablo Ramirez, Carlos' second in command, had been left in charge at the compound, and when his handheld radio crackled to life everyone watched him put the receiver to his ear. The message was a quick one-way burst, which, according to Carlos, was all that could be allowed—the government was getting better at homing in on their signals.

Pablo lowered the radio, and said to his men, "The courier is here. They will arrive in fifteen minutes."

Kristin scanned the courtyard, but didn't see Jen. She addressed Pablo. "Where is the other girl?"

The rough-hewn sergeant hesitated. She knew she was an enigma to the man, falling somewhere beneath Carlos in the hierarchy but above the rest of the soldiers. Roughly where he himself fit. When Pablo didn't reply, she decided to press.

"The girl! Go get her, it's almost time!"

Pablo's silence turned to confusion. "But . . . she is not to go, *señora.*"

Kristin looked at him tentatively. "What do you mean? She's leaving with me."

Pablo shook his head.

"Are you saying Carlos' father is going to demand a separate ransom for her?"

The sergeant shrugged. "I don't know, you will have to ask him."

With that, the big man retreated, heading for the warehouse on the far side of the compound. It was one of three buildings on the property, which, according to legend, was a hundred-year-old coffee plantation, some past settler's dream conquered by the

Amazon. Aside from the villa where she and Carlos had stayed, there was a main house whose roof had partially caved in, and a warehouse that drug lords had been intermittently repairing for years as a dry storage place for product. With ample floor space, and the only roof of the three that didn't leak, the warehouse was where Pablo and his men had bivouacked.

By process of elimination, Kristin realized Jen had to be in one of the two viable rooms of the damaged main house. She made her decision. Once Pablo was out of sight, she would set out to find her. She'd had no contact with her former seatmate since arriving, Carlos insisting all along that Jen remain isolated. Tentatively—and if she were honest, to keep her complicity in the scheme a secret—she had agreed. Now she sensed a mistake.

She was overwhelmed once more by reservations about her lover, not to mention the plot they'd concocted. What began as a backhanded swipe to frighten her father, and perhaps earn a little cash, had morphed into a deadly military campaign. More disturbingly, Carlos seemed perfectly at ease with it all. He had twenty men under his command here, and sufficient connections to deliver a ransom demand to the vice president of the United States. Someone—Carlos?—had even bribed the pilot of the TAC-Air flight to take up their cause. Kristin wondered what had happened to him. Had he perished in the crash? How convenient would that be? Eliminated along with a planeload of witnesses? She shuddered, wondering if Carlos and his father could be that ruthless.

Kristin saw but one certainty. The man next to her last night was not the same college senior who'd seduced her so many months ago. These soldiers were ostensibly part of his father's army, yet Carlos appeared perfectly at ease commanding them. Just as he was in answering her increasingly awkward questions. She finally relented to the facts: everything about the man was a lie.

Kristin looked over her shoulder, and seeing no sign of Pablo, she approached the remains of the old house. Only a few of the men were in sight, and none paid her any attention. She stepped through a doorless entryway and skirted what had once been a hallway, the outer wall no more than a collapsed heap of burnt brick. She reached the back, where two bedrooms remained largely intact, and found a lone guard posted at a door.

A guard. Something else Carlos had never mentioned.

Kristin steeled herself, and putting as much authority as possible in her voice, said in Spanish, "Open the door! Carlos wants me to question our prisoner." She held her breath, wondering if she'd gone too far. *Our prisoner.*

The guard, who was probably two years younger than she was, regarded her uncertainly. When he opened his mouth to speak, Kristin went all-in. *"Now!"*

FORTY

McBain had them at the Bogotá airport ten minutes after leaving the safe house. The Comanche was kept in a hangar not far from El Centro, and as they passed the familiar façade Davis yelled, "Stop!"

McBain hit the brakes hard enough to cycle the truck's anti-skid system. "What?"

Davis pointed to a familiar figure walking out of the building. "We need all the help we can get."

"Who's he?"

"A friend."

"Is he a Marine too?" McBain asked.

"No, he's French."

McBain looked less than impressed.

"But he's the next best thing to a Marine," Davis reasoned, "he plays rugby."

McBain relented, and two minutes later Pascal Delacorte sat shanghaied in the back seat. "Where are we going?" he asked.

"To an airfield like we talked about," said Davis. "It's a thirty-minute flight south of here, roughly fifty miles from the crash site."

"Your daughter is nearby?"

"I think there's a good chance. But there are also some people who might not welcome us."

Davis watched the engineer give this due consideration, as if running an equation in his head. The most subtle of smiles creased his face.

"Yeah," Davis muttered, "that's what I thought."

They reached the remote hangar, and while McBain went to retrieve the airplane's key from an office, Davis silently surveyed the place. Aside from the Comanche, he saw three single-engine props and a big Learjet, all bearing Colombian government markings.

Delacorte noticed his distraction. "Are you looking for something?"

"I was hoping there might be an airplane that's a better fit for what we need to do."

"You would truly steal an aircraft?"

"Until my daughter is safe, every aircraft, bus, and main battle tank in Colombia is fair game."

Together they kicked the chocks from under the Comanche's tires and pushed the hangar door open. McBain came back with two keys, one for the airplane ignition and another for a thick steel bar that was secured to the control column. It looked like an aviation version of the locking bars used to secure car steering wheels.

"A lot of airplanes actually do get stolen around here," McBain explained. He removed the locking bar and threw it in the back seat.

Minutes later they were all in place, Delacorte in back, McBain in the right front, and Davis acting as captain on the left.

Davis rolled his seat all the way back and stared blankly at the instrument panel.

McBain stared at him. "You *have* flown one of these before."

"Yeah, well . . . " Davis hesitated, "it's been a long time." He saw a leather pocket on the sidewall near his knee, and found what he needed inside—a normal procedures checklist. He ran a finger down the laminated card, past the exterior and preflight checks, and settled on a group of steps labeled "Starting Engines."

McBain watched closely. "What about all that other stuff— what you just skipped."

"Not important. You only do that stuff on checkrides."

McBain didn't look convinced. Delacorte was silent in back.

Davis talked himself through the pertinent steps.

"Master switch—on."

"Fuel pump—on."

"Mixture—rich, primed, cutoff."

"Magnetos—on."

"Starter—engage."

The starboard engine began to spin and quickly chugged into a rhythm. He adjusted the throttle and fuel mixture. When everything settled he cranked the port engine, and soon they were clear of the hangar and taxiing across sun-hardened tarmac. The next impediment, Davis knew, was air traffic control. El Dorado International was a busy place, and he was taxiing with no flight plan, no clearance, and no code in his transponder. The last pilot to fly the Comanche had left ground control frequency tuned into the primary radio, and on the overhead speaker Davis heard heavy chatter, most of it in Spanish—controllers worldwide had to be *able* to speak English, but they were free to issue instructions in their native language to local pilots.

The hangar used by the DEA was in a remote corner of the airport, half a mile from the main passenger terminal, and at the far end of the field Davis saw the dinosaur walk—a long lineup of heavy-metal departures, Boeings and Airbuses mostly, that would take thirty minutes to clear. He decided it was time to add a new qualification to his curriculum vitae—air traffic controller.

He pointed the Comanche away from the main terminal, and noted a service road that intersected the taxiway. There wasn't a vehicle in sight, no airfield operations car or facilities maintenance van. With one right turn, he'd have two thousand feet of black asphalt in a perfectly straight line. It was more than enough. He made the turn, checked the flaps were down, and shoved the power levers to the firewall. The little twin jumped forward with its relatively light load—seven hundred pounds of passengers and two fake guns in a nylon bag. Once airborne Davis kept low, clearing the trees at the far end of the airfield by no more than a few feet before banking into a valley between two apartment buildings. His maneuvers resembled those of last Sunday, only he wasn't flying a seaplane or skimming low for amusement.

This was the most important tactical mission of his life.

He heard no alarmed voices on the radio, so Davis was reasonably sure his departure had not been noticed. It wasn't particularly surprising—the air traffic controllers would all be looking the other way, concentrating on the big jets taking off and landing. Certainly a few local residents noticed his departure, catching a flash of white from their living room windows as he buzzed past apartments and skimmed over parking lots. Some of them would register complaints, and one or two might even snap a smartphone picture of a small twin-engine aircraft that was violating any number of rules. The Colombian authorities would look into it, in a day or a week, and the DEA might even get an official complaint, asking who had been piloting their Twin Comanche on this particular Friday morning.

As far as Davis was concerned, that could all be dealt with another day. The only important thing was the eighty miles in front of him.

He initially aimed for Monserrate, and just before reaching the mountain banked into a hard right-hand turn. He studied the navigation system, and after some trial and error managed to program the coordinates he'd memorized for the remote airfield. That done, he pushed the throttles up and flew a razor-straight course. In twenty minutes they would have decisions to make. All Davis wanted now was speed.

* * *

Jen was already on her feet when the key rattled in the lock. She'd been right—it was Kristin Stewart's raised voice she'd heard outside.

Kristin stepped through the door and rushed her with open arms. Jen stood rigid as she took a hug from a girl she'd met less than a week ago, one whose fate seemed inseparable from her own. In the days since being hauled off the airplane at gunpoint, she'd begun to think of Kristin as something of a sister, a compatriot suffering the same hardships. That myth ended moments ago when she heard Kristin give the guard an order.

With the browbeaten guard standing in the doorway, Jen pushed away and looked at Kristin. "What the hell is going on?"

"It's hard to explain," said Kristin. "But I'm going to get you home."

The guard said something that bypassed Jen's second-semester Spanish. When Kristin didn't answer, the guard shuffled away with his rifle drooping behind, like a dog with its tail between its legs.

"Home?" Jen said. It sounded wonderful, but things weren't adding up. There was no relief in Kristin's expression, no *it's almost over* sigh of exoneration. Jen saw only worry. Or even worse, fear.

"It's a long story," Kristin said. "There's no time to explain. Will you trust me?"

Jen looked at her doubtfully. "The last time you said that we were on the airplane together. You told me to say I was Kristin Stewart." She looked obviously around her containment room. "You see where that got me."

"It could have been worse. That airplane—"

"I know, it crashed."

Kristin looked at her pleadingly.

Jen stared at the open door. It looked a mile wide.

* * *

Pablo watched the guard rush from across the compound. The young man skidded to a stop in front of him and explained that Carlos' girl had insisted on seeing the other American.

"Did you let her inside the holding room?"

The guard said that he had.

"And then you left your post?"

A tentative nod.

Pablo's ham-hock fist swept out, striking the guard squarely in the jaw and putting him on the ground, stunned and sitting on his rifle. "Imbecile!"

Pablo pointed to two other men, and they fell in behind him

as he crossed the courtyard like a train gathering steam. At the entrance to the crumbling main house Pablo shoved aside a goat to reach the room where the girl was being held.

The door was open. The room was empty.

Pablo ran back outside and scanned all around. The only path of escape was the jungle, yet he saw no motion, no broken vegetation to mark the tracks of two American college girls. They couldn't go far, he reasoned. The nearest village was twenty miles away through walls of rain forest. They wouldn't even know which way to go.

All the same, Pablo felt a squirm of anxiety in his gut.

He turned and stared at the guard, deciding whether to execute the kid then and there. It would make a good example to the others, and might mitigate his own culpability. In the end Pablo decided against it. He needed every set of eyes because there was still a chance they could find the girls before Carlos returned.

He ordered his squad to fan out immediately. Twelve men went into the jungle with rifles at the ready.

FORTY-ONE

The girls were, at that moment, no more than thirty meters away. Jen heard every bellowed order, and in spite of her lack of fluency in Spanish, she caught enough to know that a search of the jungle was under way. That was where Kristin had wanted to run, but Jen had resisted the idea. To begin, it would have required a forty-yard sprint across open ground to reach the nearest cover. If they made it that far, neither of them had any idea which way to go. Jen had also thought the plan too obvious. She'd reasoned, correctly as it turned out, that it was the first place the Colombians would look.

She'd spotted the old cellar door under a pile of rubble, just out of view on the far side of the house. Jen guessed it was a basement of some kind, and together they quietly pulled aside timber and chunks of plaster. When they finally lifted the door it was a disappointment—there was no more than a crawl space beneath, two steps disappearing into an avalanche of soil and rock. It seemed useless at first, but when the shouting began—a man named Pablo, according to Kristin—the space seemed suddenly larger. The girls had scrambled inside, laid down shoulder to shoulder, and lowered the door, doing their best to pull bits of debris on top as it fell closed.

Now Jen was flat on her belly, Kristin crushed beside her and peering through their only window to the world—a narrow gap offering a tunnellike view of the compound.

"Can you see anyone?" Jen asked in a hushed tone.

"No. Not in the last few minutes."

"So you were actually dating this guy?"

"His name is Carlos. When I met him he was just a student like me. But he's completely different now." Kristin kept watch through the tiny gap, and at a whisper explained how everything had come to pass. She left only one thing out.

"Why did they kidnap you?" Jen asked. "Are your parents wealthy?"

Kristin sighed, and in the darkened shadows she twisted her head until they were face to face. "My mom and I have always been alone—I never knew who my father was. She told me he disappeared before she found out she was pregnant, and that she never tried to find him because he was a total loser. I guess in a way she was right." She glanced to make sure no one had wandered near. "Two years ago my mom lost her job. When I started college we really needed money. Then suddenly, everything changed. Last year, right before Christmas break, Mom told me she'd moved. I went home expecting a tiny apartment, but out of nowhere we had a nice new house. She wasn't looking for work anymore. She had new clothes and a new hairstyle. It was a good Christmas—tablet computer, gift cards, a car for college."

"The Dad who abandoned you is rich?"

"Not so much rich as . . . connected. There's seven million dollars in that suitcase out there. I can guarantee you not a penny of it is his."

Jen stared at her. "Who has connections like that? Is he a mob boss or something?" She saw Kristin smile for the first time since they'd been on the airplane.

"There are people who might put it that way."

Jen looked at her quizzically.

"My biological father is Martin Stuyvesant—the vice president of the United States."

"Holy—" A hand clamped over her mouth.

The silence outside was broken as footsteps scuffed nearby. The girls lay frozen with fear. Neither breathed, and through a slim gap Jen saw a pair of boots approach, then turn away until only one was visible. It was big and black, and had a crescent-shaped scar on the heel.

Kristin was watching too, and she silently mouthed one word. *Pablo.*

* * *

Davis had the engines pushed hard against the red lines on the gauges. The airspeed was pegged at 210 knots—painfully subsonic, but covering ground. He estimated they would reach the airfield in eight minutes.

"I've got Jorgensen on the phone," McBain announced as he jockeyed the sat-phone antenna to get better reception. "He says the jeeps got bogged down on a bad section of road—right now they're about three miles south of the landing strip."

"Ask him who got left behind at the airfield—I didn't take the time to look."

Moments later McBain had the answer. "He says the only person in sight is the Cessna's pilot." He gave Davis a tentative look. "Let me guess—we're going to land there too?"

"Why not?"

"We have no other choice," piped in Delacorte from the back seat.

Davis turned and said, "I knew I brought you for a reason."

"How do we handle the pilot?" McBain asked.

"There's three of us and one of him. We have imitation heavy weapons, he's probably packing something between a semiauto handgun and a Swiss Army knife."

"I doubt he's one of the bad guys. Chances are, he's only a charter pilot—probably got five hundred bucks plus expenses to retrieve this courier and deliver him to a coordinate set in the jungle. Tomorrow he'll go back to his usual gig. He'll fly a couple of movie stars to a high-end resort, or maybe give an eco-tour of the rain forest."

"By cruising over it in a turboprop gas hog?" Davis asked.

"Maybe he's got a Greenpeace sticker on the side of his air-

plane. My point is that we're not talking about a tactically oriented individual."

"Which means what?" Delacorte asked.

Davis reached into the same leather side pouch from which
he'd pulled the aircraft checklist and withdrew a cheap pair of
sunglasses. He put them on to ward off the brilliant sun, and said,
"Which means we can keep our toy guns in the bag . . . for now."

* * *

Kehoe sensed he was nearing the endpoint of his journey. He felt
the jeep slow considerably, and one of the men behind him muttered something about being hungry.

He was comforted that the briefcase full of cash was still in
his lap. Kehoe did his best to glean information during the ride,
but there had been little of use. Clattering valves from an ill-kept
engine, the occasional shadows from trees overhead, and enough
dust in his lungs to tell him he was riding in the trailing vehicle.
Not much to advance an understanding of his circumstances.

He was used to it, of course. Most of his jobs, by design, involved an acute lack of information. He'd been told there would
be seven million in the briefcase, and that much was true—he'd
opened it in a quiet moment alone on the G-III, because no one
can carry that much cash and not look at least once. What he
didn't understand was why the girl he was getting in exchange was
so important to Martin Stuyvesant.

Back in Cleveland, Stuyvesant's chief of staff let slip in his
briefing that the Secret Service was somehow involved. This was
not a complete surprise, given Stuyvesant's status, and Kehoe
was being paid well enough to know that the reasons were none
of his business. But it did pique his curiosity. He'd asked if the
money was counterfeit because he doubted he could spot a high-
quality forgery, and because there were plenty of people here
who could—Colombians had long been the world's most prolific
counterfeiters of U.S. currency. He'd been assured that the money was legitimate, and he thought it might be true. All the same,

the fact that the people he was meeting had brought him this far without inspecting the cash seemed doubly curious. Both sides, apparently, were highly confident of a straightforward deal, and if everything held together for a few more hours the transaction would be, in his experience, uniquely successful. It suggested that both sides had some kind of insurance, or perhaps a mutual interest in a positive outcome.

His inference that the end of his journey was near proved correct. The jeeps came to a rough stop and both engines fell silent. Under the black hood, Kehoe's senses heightened. He knew they were in the shade, and he felt the jeep rock as the driver and two soldiers in back dismounted. Someone ordered him to stay where he was. Kehoe was happy to do just that.

Then things got interesting. He heard a distant conversation in Spanish, the voices quiet but strained. Then he heard the man in charge, shout, "*Cómo pudiste dejar escapar a los dos?*"

Kehoe stiffened ever so slightly. There had been an escape. The girl he was sent to retrieve? *Los dos* implied two. A second hostage? That was news to him, but he supposed it wasn't out of character—they were, after all, kidnappers. *Get the girl back safe.* That was his objective, he reminded himself—aside from getting out alive.

He heard a command to begin a search, the voice of the man who'd spoken to him at the airport. Then another order, one that froze Kehoe to the worn upholstery. "*Ir a buscar el hacha!*"

Go find the ax.

FORTY-TWO

McBain was the first to spot the airfield. He pointed to a gap in the trees, and said, "Yeah, that one looks familiar. We did a joint raid with the Colombian Army—two, maybe three years ago. We showed up a day late and everyone was gone. Word of our arrival often precedes us when the army gets involved. At any rate, we got the enemy to pull up stakes. It's hard to run a processing factory when you're moving every two weeks."

Davis glanced at the airfield, but largely kept his eyes on the sky. There was a drone out here somewhere. According to Jorgensen it was loitering above their altitude, however, there were no air traffic controllers to sort things out, and a midair collision would ruin everyone's day. He was flying the Comanche much like he'd flown on his first-ever lesson—a small airplane, no autopilot, and operating on the see-and-avoid concept when it came to air traffic.

The sat-phone chirped, and McBain relayed the highlights of a message from Jorgensen. "The jeeps have stopped—we know where they're holed up. It's about five miles south down the airfield road. There are a few secondary trails, but we shouldn't have any trouble finding the place. It's an abandoned plantation we've had our eye on before, three buildings in marginal shape. According to Jorgensen there are four vehicles altogether, roughly twenty hostiles."

"Hostiles?" said the engineer in back. "That is not a word I like."

"And not a number I like," agreed Davis. He spotted the road easily because there were no others in sight—just a single brown

ribbon through the carpet of green. He flew over the airfield and
they all saw the single-engine Cessna that had delivered Martin
Stuyvesant's courier. It had fat tires and a big high wing, the signature features of an airframe built to operate on short, soft fields.
The pilot looked up at them. He didn't wave.

"Okay, Jammer, this is your rodeo. What now? Do we fly
south for a little reconnaissance?"

"No, that would only spook them—if I take this crate within
two miles of the compound they'll hear our engines. Besides, it
doesn't add anything. As long as the drone is overhead we've got
eyes on target. What we need is boots on the ground."

Davis sized up the landing strip, and what he saw wasn't encouraging. It appeared rough, certainly not the kind of surface
that the engineers at Piper Aircraft had in mind when they designed the Twin Comanche. But then, a few days earlier a Colombian named Blas Reyna had landed a regional jet here, and subsequently taken off again. Davis thought, *If he can do it . . .*

He tried to get a feel for the wind at ground level, but the
jungle air seemed to be only heating and rising, no measurable
vector in either direction. He made one last pass over the clearing, scouting for the smoothest surface and picking an aim point
for touchdown that was just beyond the most obvious obstacle—a
broad puddle that was one good downpour away from pond status. The pilot of the Caravan watched them closely, standing motionless under one wing. A good sign, Davis thought. It meant he
was more concerned with shade than issuing a warning with the
radio in his cockpit.

He set up on final approach and cinched his seat belt tight.
McBain noticed, and did the same without being told. Fifty feet
above the ground Davis spotted a pair of long grooves in the surface, likely made by TAC-Air Flight 223 days earlier. He adjusted
his flight path to straddle one of the tracks, reasoning that any
ground solid enough to support a twenty-ton regional jet would
hold up fine under the much lighter Comanche. If nothing else, a
comforting thought. His touchdown was reasonably smooth, and

as they coasted to a stop Davis sensed exhales of relief behind and to his right.

He did a pirouette at the far end of the field, a turn just wide enough to avoid bogging down in the soft earth. Davis shut down the engines as soon as the nose was reversed and pointed down the runway, a trick he'd picked up from an old Africa hand on an equally dodgy mission. *Be ready to go on a moment's notice.*

The propellers chugged to a halt and everything went quiet, the only sounds that of cooling fans and gyros spinning down in the instrument panel. Davis actuated switches to shut off the battery, and all three men turned their attention to the other airplane. The Cessna was fifty meters away, the pilot still standing under the port wing. He looked interested but not concerned. He'd parked his own aircraft close to the road, oriented to provide the shortest possible walk for his passenger. A pilot accustomed to clients who didn't want to get their shoes dirty. This reinforced McBain's earlier assessment. They were looking at a local charter pilot who'd been hired for a morning's work. He probably had no idea what he was doing here, who he was working for, and likely didn't care. He was just out flying a charter with one eye closed, somewhere south of propriety, a guy happy with a five-hundred-dollar morning.

"How do you want to handle this?" McBain asked.

"I don't see a lot of options," Davis answered. He outlined a simple plan, one born quite literally on the fly. There were no objections, and they all disembarked and walked casually toward the pilot. All three men smiled, and Delacorte even waved. When they were ten steps away, McBain greeted the pilot because he was the best Spanish speaker. Davis heard something along the lines of, *"Is this the road that leads to the Colombia Rain Forest Project?"*

Everyone knew it wasn't. It had been McBain's suggestion, an airfield and service road that did exist, but one they'd missed by forty miles. The charter pilot smiled condescendingly. He looked at Davis as if he'd just met the worst navigator in the world. The mood was easy and loose when the charter pilot began to reply.

Then Delacorte and Davis lunged the last few feet and trussed the Colombian firmly by his elbows.

* * *

Go find the ax.

Kehoe sat patiently with his hands crossed on top of the briefcase, perhaps subconsciously the one with the handcuff underneath. He hadn't liked the handcuff routine to begin with, thinking it amateurish and dangerous, but Strand had insisted. Kehoe didn't like to wear anything that restricted his movement—belts, ties, overcoats. Not in his closet. A Kevlar vest was the only exception, and that hadn't seemed appropriate for this mission. The key to the cuffs was in his shoe. Not particularly clever, but what the hell was he supposed to do?

His senses were still keen under the hood. He heard shuffling nearby, multiple sets of boots, and suddenly Kehoe was dragged off the jeep and thrown to the ground. The case flew from his grasp, and at least two men held him down. He saw little point in resisting—not until someone took his arm, the one chained to the briefcase, and forced it out wide. The briefcase was pulled until the chain went taut, and then everything stopped moving, his forearm pinned to the ground. The next Spanish command he translated instantly. *"Do it—cut it off."*

"Wait!" Kehoe yelled. "I have a key! Let me—"

His protest was cut short by a boot to the head. An instant later, he was sure he heard a whoosh of air as the ax swung down.

* * *

The Cessna pilot didn't bother to struggle, in Davis' view a display of sound judgment as he was outweighed by a hundred pounds on either side. The look on his face was one of intense concentration, the factors of his situation no doubt multiplying in his head. Delivering an American passenger with a heavy briefcase. Two jeeps full of paramilitaries. Another airplane with three men, also American, but who were clearly on a different team.

Men whose mission did not dovetail with his own. That fast, like flying into a box canyon, his easy money trip had disappeared.

McBain patted him down, but found nothing. The DEA man stood with his hands on his hips, a dubious look on his face. "No," he said. "Nobody flies to a place like this without protection." He went to the airplane, and in five seconds found what he was looking for under the left seat—a 9mm Beretta. McBain turned the piece in his hand and said, "Now we have a real gun." His expression of victory evaporated when he ejected the magazine and pulled back the slide. "One round," he announced weakly.

"*One?*" repeated Davis. He looked disbelievingly at the Colombian. "Don't you know there are dangerous people out here?"

McBain said roughly the same in Spanish, and the pilot only shrugged. He didn't look worried, which Davis took to mean that he either had faith that someone would come to his rescue, or that he'd been in difficult situations before. The latter seemed more likely.

McBain went over the airplane more thoroughly, but found nothing useful. "Now what?" he asked. "We've got one bullet, one gun, and five miles between us and twenty heavily armed soldiers."

"No," said Davis, "we've got five miles between me and my daughter. That's the closest I've been in a long time."

"So, how do we get her back?" Delacorte asked.

"We wait," McBain said. "That guy delivering the ransom will be back soon. His airplane and pilot are right here, which means he's leaving the same way he came in—delivered by two jeeps and a half a dozen guys. He'll have his girl, and maybe your daughter too."

Davis had already made similar calculations, only to hit a stop when it came to Jen. "I don't think so. If he's delivering a payoff, it's for the vice president's daughter. There's no incentive for these people to release Jen. And if that's the case, as soon as Kristin is clear, they're going to move. I say we go in now while we know where she is."

Davis looked at Delacorte, then McBain. Both nodded.

Delacorte said, "How will we do it? If we leave this pilot alone he might create trouble. He could make an unwanted radio call or disable our airplane."

"We have *one* bullet," said McBain.

Davis looked at him closely and saw the threshold of a smile. At least he *thought* it was a smile.

"Okay, just kidding," said McBain. "We don't have anything to truss him up with, and there's a chance somebody else might show up. One of us has to stay here to watch him, make sure he behaves."

They both looked at Delacorte.

"*D'accord*," the Frenchman replied. "It only makes sense that I am the one to stay."

"All right, tell him," Davis said. He released the pilot's arm and Delacorte did the same. McBain began talking, and pointed to Delacorte. The pilot looked at the Frenchman who was ten inches taller, twice his weight, and staring with a newfound menace. The pilot's expression said he wished he'd stayed home today.

Davis retrieved the canvas bag with the facsimile MP-5s, tossed in the sat-phone, and on a whim added the Comanche's government-issue survival kit. Finally, he took in hand the flight control locking bar and key. The Colombian watched closely as they went to the Caravan's cockpit and tried to secure the bar across the control yoke. Unfortunately, the design was different and the locking bar didn't fit. Davis backed outside, put his hands on his hips, and soon saw a better solution. The pilot protested vehemently as Davis secured the locking bar around a very expensive Hartzell propeller.

Davis said, "Tell him we'll be back in an hour with the key. All he has to do is sit tight and relax with his new friend from France."

McBain translated, and the pilot acquiesced by sitting on the ground.

"You sure you're okay with this?" Davis asked Delacorte.

"*Absolument!*"

With that, Davis and McBain moved out, the DEA man shouldering the canvas bag. The sun was getting higher, the temperature rising. Davis felt his shirt already clinging to his back, and sweat beaded his forehead.

"How far did you say it was?" he asked.

"According to Jorgensen, five miles."

"Sounds like about half an hour."

"Half an hour?" McBain repeated. "How the heck can we—"

Davis broke into a run before he could finish.

* * *

Kristin started to cry out when the ax came down, but squelched her outburst. The girls froze in place, as still and silent as twin toppled statues, fearful that their concealment had been compromised. They waited for a finger to be pointed in their direction, for a shout of alarm. None came.

After a full five minutes Jen, who was unable to see outside, asked what had happened. Kristin gave a hushed account, and Jen maneuvered onto one side, a tolerable position from which she could glimpse the scene outside. She saw six soldiers standing in a semicircle, all of them laughing. A man wearing a hood was seated on the ground, rubbing one hand over his opposing wrist where half a set of handcuffs dangled. She saw the other silver cuff and a severed chain on the handle of a suitcase. Carlos had it on the hood of one of the jeeps and was trying to pry it open with the ax.

"That's Carlos," Kristin whispered.

Jen said, "I've met him. He came to the room where they were holding me yesterday."

"What did he want?"

"First he told me about the airplane crash, probably to frighten me. Then he said he needed information. He wanted something only my father and I would know, details to convince him I'm still alive."

"And did you give it?"

"I did, but for my own reasons. My father is an aircraft accident investigator. If that airplane crashed, and my dad believed I was on it—I'm sure he's in Colombia right now trying to find us."

"Does he have a strange first name?"

"His name's Frank, but everybody calls him Jammer."

"That's it," said Kristin. "I heard Carlos talking to his father on the phone. There's a big guy stirring up trouble in Bogotá."

"Yep. That would be my dad."

They both watched the big soldier—who Kristin confirmed was Pablo—explain something to Carlos with a lot of gesticulating.

"Carlos looks furious," said Kristin.

"I think you put yourself in a bind by helping me."

Carlos looked around the compound, and as his gaze swept past their position, both girls instinctively dropped their heads. When they looked up again they saw Carlos double down on his mistake—he ordered everyone back into the jungle for another search.

Jen whispered, "That man sitting on the ground—do you know who he is?"

"No, I've never seen him before. My father must have hired him to deliver the payment. Or maybe he's with the Secret Service."

"Do you really think there's seven million dollars in that case?"

Kristin said, "According to Carlos, that was the deal."

"So the ransom is paid. They'll have to let you go."

Kristin hesitated. "I'm not so sure. Carlos wasn't happy when you showed up with me. I made him promise that you and I could leave together when the payment came, but today he changed his mind. He said only I would be released."

"Why? Do you think he wants a second ransom for me? My dad doesn't have that kind of money, he's only a retired military officer."

The two girls exchanged a long look in the dim light.

"He's not going to let me go," said Jen.

Kristin shook her head. "I don't think so."

"Is that why you came for me?"

Kristin nodded. "Yeah . . . I guess it was."

"Thanks for that."

A half smile from the vice president's daughter before she turned serious. "This whole damned thing is my fault," she said. "What happened to Thomas, the people on that airplane. You're my last chance to do something right. I'll get you out of here, Jen. I swear it."

FORTY-THREE

McBain was running twenty meters ahead of him, which aggra-
vated Davis to no end. The fact that the DEA man had a runner's build and was ten years younger meant nothing—it was *his*
daughter less than a mile ahead. He pushed his pace down the dirt
road, lungs heaving like twin bellows, and was right on McBain's
heels when he drew to a stop.

He pulled out the phone while Davis doubled over with his
hands on his knees.

"You're getting old, Marine," McBain taunted.

"I play rugby," he said, sucking a load of air. "That's where
you don't bother running *past* people. It's a little more direct."

After a brief conversation, McBain relayed the latest from
Jorgensen. "The jeeps are still at the compound, one klick ahead.
But we may have lost the element of surprise. The troops dis-
persed into the jungle a few minutes ago."

"Dispersed? Like setting up a defensive perimeter?"

"Can't say for sure," McBain said. "They fanned out with
their weapons and everybody is moving."

"That sounds more like a search."

"Could be. You think maybe the VP's daughter took a runner? Or your daughter?"

Davis considered it. *Yes*, he thought, *if Jen saw a chance to escape she just might try*. "Let's hope so. On the other hand, it's possible our Caravan pilot sent a warning before we landed. Or maybe there was someone back at that clearing we didn't spot."

"In which case," McBain reasoned, "they'll know you and I
are on the way."

The two exchanged a look. Both knew the answer. *No way to tell.*

McBain said, "They're trying to stretch the fuel burn on the drone, but it's getting critical. If the operators can approve an alternate recovery airfield it will give us a few more minutes. Jorgensen hasn't used his emergency authority card yet."

"Will that work?"

"I don't know, we've never tried it before." McBain looked up the road. "One thing's for sure. This road is the only way in or out of the compound, so it's going to be watched. We'll have to move into the jungle and make our final approach the hard way. Harder than usual because the red team is already in the bush."

"True," said Davis, "but there's still a chance they don't know we're out here. It would mean they're in the bush looking for Jen or Kristin, maybe both. They'll be expecting a couple of schoolgirls—not us."

This drew a grin from McBain. "Good point."

* * *

Kehoe decided he wasn't getting paid nearly enough. He was sitting in wet dirt, secured with heavy plastic zip-ties to the bumper of a jeep. The sun was beating down on his black hood, and he was sweating profusely in the equatorial heat. To make his morning complete, he had initially settled right on top of an ant pile, and his right leg was inflamed with at least fifty bites from some kind of stinging Amazonian insect. In spite of his shifting and rubbing, the buggers kept coming to life in his shoes and socks to deliver dying bites. Not for the first time, Kehoe weighed if it might be time to get out of field work. A vanilla consulting gig would be boring, but when nests of stinging insects came into play all you did was call an exterminator to spray the office baseboards.

His musings were cut short: footsteps approaching in the dirt, then pausing at his side.

"We've held up our part of the bargain," Kehoe said. "Can we finish this?"

"Patience," said the voice he recognized as the leader of this sorry pack. "I'm sure you speak Spanish, so you know the girl is unavailable."

Kehoe knew all too well. "Unavailable? That's a hopeful word from your point of view."

"And from *your* point of view I would hope she is found soon. Otherwise, my friend, there are few options."

Only one, Kehoe thought. He'd already made that calculation, and was displeased to find a contingency for which he had no plan. *What if the girl escapes?* He took a positive tack. "I should help you look. Chances are she's nearby, and she might respond to me. Call off your men and let me try. If I can collect her I'll be on my way—everybody wins."

The commander seemed to consider it. "Yes . . . but you've already been here longer than either of us expected. I don't think I'm ready to give you that kind of freedom. I'm sure you've been briefed to find out all you can about me and my team."

"Team? Is that what you call them?"

Kehoe heard a shuffle in the dirt and something hard slammed into his head. He saw stars for a moment, then the world slowly righted.

"Even wearing that hood you've heard enough to make our life difficult. If this problem is resolved soon, I will consider our business complete. You will be allowed to go, and we will take precautions to avoid reprisal. On the other hand, if these silly girls continue to—"

"Girls?" Kehoe interrupted. "I only paid for one." The boots shuffled again in the dirt and he braced for another blow. Nothing came, and he sensed he'd scored a victory of some kind. Someone else was being held, another girl. Who it was and why she was here was not formally his concern. All the same, Kehoe was a decent man, not the type to sit by idly and watch the strong prey on the weak. He was filing this all in his newly aching head when the morning calm was broken. He heard a distant *whoosh* followed by a pyrotechnic *pop*.

Birds fluttered from the trees, followed by shouts from all around. The voices were blended by the jungle, indistinct and directionless, reminding him of a crowd in a sparsely populated stadium. They all saw what Kehoe heard.

The commander ran off, barking orders as he went.

A second *whoosh*, perhaps on a slightly different angle, a second *pop*. This time Kehoe was sure he recognized the sound, at least in a general way. What he didn't understand was *who* it could be. The girls would be neither trained nor equipped, and he'd been specifically briefed to expect no help. Which meant the sounds were not the arrival of some kind of U.S. cavalry. And it was definitely not how the Colombian Army would approach things.

Another *whoosh*. Another *pop*.

Almost as if they were under attack.

Who the hell is out there? Kehoe wondered.

FORTY-FOUR

The signal flares, commandeered from the Comanche's emergency survival kit, were of the pen-gun variety—old, simple, and exquisitely reliable. McBain had circled west of the compound, keeping roughly one hundred yards from the perimeter, and was firing at random intervals. He loaded another flare in the hand-held launcher, straightened his arm at a new angle and thumbed back the firing pin. The fourth flare sizzled high to the west, penetrating the canopy and blossoming a red phosphorous star in the sky.

McBain ran like hell in the other direction.

Their tactical problem had been a vexing one. From the highest ground, Davis and McBain initially had a good visual on the compound. Yet they had no idea where the girls were. They saw a handful of soldiers come and go from the surrounding forest, and noted a luckless soul, who could only be the courier, sitting secured to the bumper of one of the jeeps. The operation to retrieve Martin Stuyvesant's daughter—certainly what they were witnessing—was not going smoothly.

Waiting things out was not an option because soon they would lose their biggest advantage—the Predator and its God's-eye view of the battlefield. The situation was complex and fluid, and time was working against them. There was a chance one of the girls might still be in the compound, and at the moment the bulk of the opposing force was distracted and distant. After a brief conference with Jorgensen, Davis made the call. They would make a play for the courier, reasoning that he might know where the girls were. At the very least, he would increase their troop strength by half.

With their objective set, the first step was to level the odds. According to Jorgensen, the soldiers were still in the bush, in search mode, the bulk of the force clustered to the south. McBain's job was to pull them west, deeper into the forest. He and Davis had actually blueprinted their plan using a stick in the dirt, like two kids playing sandlot football. Since the paras were searching for one or both girls, they reasoned that's who would be held responsible for firing the flares. At least, if one discarded the questions of how they could acquire such pyrotechnics and learn to use them.

It wasn't a perfect plan, McBain knew, but it was the best they had. So he ran deeper into the jungle.

Some distance away, Davis moved in the other direction.

* * *

He took the strategy of a fighter pilot heading into a close-quarters dogfight: stealth no longer matters, speed is life. Davis charged through brush like a bull elephant, the plastic MP5 held at arm's length to blade through branches and vines. Having waited ten minutes for McBain to launch his barrage, he was now circling clockwise to approach the compound from the southeast. According to the drone's imagery it was the best angle of attack, a place where thick jungle nearly abutted the largest building. Visibility was nearly nil, the foliage like liquid. Davis shoved one branch aside, and three took its place. He was moving fast, pushing and stumbling, when he ran into something solid. At first he thought it was a tree.

Only the tree had a face.

Not two feet in front of him was a soldier, a rifle hanging loosely from his shoulder—a cavalier way to carry a firearm in a low visibility environment. Davis was the first to react using his only weapon—the hard plastic stock of his knock-off MP5. The butt caught the soldier on the bridge of the nose, and his head snapped back like a waylaid bobblehead doll. When the head came back forward its mouth was open, prepping for a scream.

Davis targeted his second blow there, the result an instant dental catastrophe. When his adversary fell to his knees, Davis dropped his faux submachine gun, reared up, and lunged to put a knee in the man's temple. The guy dropped like his joints had disconnected and went completely still.

Davis went to ground with him.

He rolled away, completing two revolutions before pausing to listen. There was nothing at first, only the distant shouts of men responding to McBain's barrage of signal flares. There had been eight flares in the survival kit, along with the handheld launcher. By Davis' count, seven had been used. He lay stock still, listening and watching. Having come across one soldier, there was a good chance another was near. He guessed McBain was keeping the last flare in reserve—that's what he would have done. The far-off shouts subsided, and for a full two minutes he heard nothing more than the wind rustling through trees and the buzz of insects.

Then, finally, a sound that didn't belong.

It was very near, probably to his left, although it was hard to say in a jungle that muffled and reflected sound. He kept perfectly still and heard it again, a footfall on the soft, humus-laden forest floor. Then a clipped, baritone whisper, "Umberto! *Dónde estás?*"

With one cheek on the ground, Davis felt ever-so-slight tremors. The soldier he'd flattened was two steps away, probably unconscious. Possibly dead. Was the rifle still looped around his chest? Most likely, but Davis had no way of reaching it without creating a severe noise signature.

Another tremor, slow and cautious. Like a carnivorous dinosaur sensing a meal.

Davis realized he had a decent line of sight from where he lay. The ferns and waxen-leaved plants, all battling for scant sunlight, reached upward and out. At dead ground level he saw a wilderness of stems and roots, but between them he could make out fragmented details thirty feet away. It was like being at ground level in a parking lot and looking under the chassis of cars—better visibility beneath the clutter.

Davis turned his head slowly and spotted it right away. Moving branches twenty feet ahead. A worn combat boot stepping into view.

A black boot.

With a crescent scar on the heel.

FORTY-FIVE

He was as motionless as the earth itself, only his eyes moving to track the boot. A size twelve combat model, Davis guessed, standard issue footwear for every army. He watched it turn a quiet half circle. A soldier being cautious, looking and listening, wondering where his comrade had gone. Davis felt his chest rise and fall rhythmically on the damp forest floor. Silent intakes of moss-scented air. Controlled exhalations, warm and moist. He shifted ever so slightly, grounding to a position from which he could spring if necessary. His right instep found purchase, and the weight on his left elbow shifted to a hand.

There were no more whispers. The man had become wary—if they met it would be on level terms, neither surprised. A radio crackled to life, breaking the silence, and the second boot shuffled into view. A rustle of fabric as the man frantically tried to quiet the speaker. It was a mistake. And for Davis, information. A radio meant this was a commander at some level, probably a non-commissioned officer, or whatever the right-wing paramilitary equivalent was. It implied he was experienced, and by extension, that he knew how to fight at close quarters. More relevant for Davis—this was the man who'd tried to kill him.

He wanted nothing more than to launch at that moment. The problem was distance. The boot was twenty feet away and not getting closer. At that distance, any experienced soldier would sense his rush and bring a weapon to bear—the man wouldn't be here unarmed. A rifle, a handgun. He would pull the trigger before Davis covered half the ground. Of course, in the heat of the moment, there was a good chance he'd miss with the first shot.

Most did. But there was also a chance he'd have a gun capable of full automatic fire, and that Davis would be laced in seconds with more holes than an old shoe. So he forced himself to be patient. Jen was close, and *she* needed him to not do anything stupid.

The boots did a sudden one-eighty, and the scene quickly changed—now Davis saw one boot and a knee on the ground. The man had spotted or heard something, and he'd gone for concealment. Might it be Jen? Kristin Stewart?

His hand was forced.

Davis began inching forward, looking for every brittle twig and frond, trying not to disturb anything. He advanced ten inches, then twenty. The black boot and knee remained motionless. Davis edged closer, delicately, the only option when stalking a better-armed adversary. He was fifteen feet away when he heard a distant noise. A rustle of brush. Then everything went to hell.

The soldier jumped up and opened fire, a single blast that shredded foliage and scattered birds. Davis leapt to his feet and rushed forward, like a defensive lineman blitzing a quarterback. He saw the owner of the scarred boots for the first time, a massive bald-headed man with the stony eyes of a drill sergeant. A long-barreled rifle was close to his chest, and when he saw Davis coming he levered the bolt while shifting aim, going for center of mass. The center of *his* mass.

Davis flew the last five feet in a Superman pose, hands straining for the gun barrel. He swatted it at the moment of explosion, the gun's report obliterating the sound of their collision. Davis tried to wrap up his tackle while keeping a hand on the gun barrel. Someone's hand tripped the bolt, bringing a mechanical *click* but nothing else. The drill sergeant struck first, a stunning fist to the side of Davis' head. The Colombian immediately twisted behind him, a move that suggested he was a wrestler, and before Davis could react, a monstrous forearm was crushing his throat.

He tried to pry the arm from his throat, but couldn't wedge his fingers deep enough for leverage. He rolled to put himself on top, but even from underneath the massive sergeant held tight.

With his airway restricted, Davis was burning oxygen at a far greater rate than he was taking it in. He tried a backward head butt, but missed the mark—the man had seen it coming and angled his head away. With tunnel vision setting in, Davis knew all his adversary's weight and strength was going into one approach—a stranglehold.

He reached back with both hands, and on the left found a leg. With his last reserve of strength Davis split his own legs wide and pressed to standing position with the soldier on his back. Supporting five hundred pounds in a wobbling stance, he leaned forward and straightened his arm, flipping the man upward into an almost vertical position. Something had to give, and it was the arm locked across his throat.

The two men split, and both tumbled to the ground. When they rose, Davis was gasping for breath while the Colombian went for his weapon. The rifle's chamber was empty, so the man gripped the barrel end and swung it like a baseball player chasing an outside curve. Davis rocked back just in time, the stock whooshing past his nose.

The bald man cocked his high-caliber club a second time, and said, "I will not be so kind to your daughter."

He shouldn't have wasted his breath to begin with, because he had his opponent down and hurt. Those words, however, proved a calamitous choice.

Davis was instantly revitalized, reminded of what was at stake. The Colombian came again with his bludgeon, a coup de grâce aimed at Davis' skull. He was too close to miss if Davis backed away, which seemed the only defense. Instead Davis lunged forward, and the gun's stock thumped weakly into his left shoulder. They met chest to chest, and Davis kept the momentum. He drove with his legs and lifted the sergeant a second time, a horizontal drive that ended three yards later against the trunk of a big tree. Mahogany or Brazilian cherry. Some granitelike Amazon hardwood.

This time it was the Colombian who had the air driven

from his chest. The impact was cushioned for Davis, and he rebounded to one side, again keeping with the flow. With a hand locked to the gun stock he wrapped completely around the tree. The stunned drill sergeant tried to pull the gun back, and Davis allowed it to a point, the rifle ending flat across the Colombian's torso. Before the man saw the danger, Davis wrapped his free hand around the other side of the tree and found the gun's machined-steel barrel.

The two were locked on opposite sides of the tree, Davis with his face to the trunk and the sergeant backed against it. With a firm grip on either side the rifle, Davis pulled with both hands like a rower at a starting line. It wasn't a rhythmic stroke, but one long continuous draw, the pressure increasing mercilessly. With the gun barred flat across the Colombian's chest, the compression began.

The man realized his predicament. He squirmed at first and tried to duck underneath. Soon his legs were off the ground, but gravity wasn't enough, and the move only increased the pressure. He clawed for Davis' hands, yet with his own arms locked near the elbow, he only flailed and flapped, which did nothing to alter his dilemma. He was slowly getting crushed—a fate not unlike the one he'd tried to impart on Davis using an airplane wing.

Davis used the tree for leverage, working one knee upward and leaning back. The pressure increased markedly, and the first snap of bone rang through the forest. A rib most likely, though the sternum wasn't out of the question. A guttural grunt soon followed, liquid and uneven.

Davis kept pulling.

The motion on the other side of the tree turned frantic, boots kicking and hands grasping, finding nothing but air. A minute later the man suddenly went limp. Davis didn't buy it. He kept squeezing, levering all the strength in his legs and arms. That prompted a new flurry of pushing and pulling. Playing possum had been a gamble, but was probably worth a try. The Colombian finally got a foothold on something solid, and pried himself to the right. Davis felt his hands weakening, felt the gun sight cutting into the flesh of his palm. He didn't let go.

The man again went limp, this time in a slow and uneven way. A rasp of air was followed by another snap, and then a third, neither of which drew a reaction. No grunt of pain, no spastic lunge. Nothing at all.

His arms trembling from fatigue, Davis finally let go.

He did a brief self-assessment, making sure nothing was missing, broken, or leaking, before walking around the tree with the rifle in his hand. The sergeant was not a pretty sight. His eyes bulged in death and his chin was covered in blood. His upper body was misshapen, nearly cut in two. He'd come to rest on one side, folded in half with a crease that belonged on a cardboard box.

"Jesus!" someone said.

Davis turned and saw McBain. He was standing ten steps away with a hand holding his opposite forearm—there was blood where the sergeant's bullet had apparently found its mark. Yet McBain looked mobile, and there was a rifle slung over his good shoulder, likely taken from the first man Davis had encountered.

"I've been in the trenches," said the DEA man, "but I've never seen anything like that. You just—you *crushed* him."

Davis looked out across the jungle. "Happens all the time around here. You know, anacondas and the like. You okay?"

McBain nodded, still staring at the halved Colombian.

Davis said, "The good news is, we have three real guns now."

"Actually," said McBain, "I think it's only one. I tried the Beretta but it misfired." Then he pointed to the rifle Davis was holding.

He looked down, and for the first time recognized the gun as a bolt action Remington. Then he saw the problem—the barrel was bent like a steel banana. He dropped it to the ground. "Okay, one gun."

FORTY-SIX

"How many are out there?" Jen asked.

Kristin peered through the opening. "I only see one now. I know him—Manuel. He's only a kid, probably two years younger than me."

"Does he have a gun?"

"Of course, they all do."

"Then it doesn't matter how old he is," said Jen. "At least the gunfire stopped, if that's what it was. Is the Secret Service guy still there?"

"I don't know if he's Secret Service, but yeah, he's still tied down with a hood over his head. And his briefcase is still on the hood of the jeep."

Jen maneuvered and tried to get a look. "If we stay here they'll find us sooner or later. Right now most of them are in the jungle . . . I think this is our chance."

"Chance for what?"

"The guy chained to the bumper—he came here for you, so he's got to be on our side. If we can free him, the three of us could take the jeep and make a run for it before the others get back."

Kristin thought about it. Finally she nodded. "Okay, but how do we get past Manuel?"

Jen drew a blank, facing the kind of problem never addressed in university—how to overcome an armed guard and release a captive. She looked around their crawlspace, desperate for inspiration. In the end, Jen asked herself a question she hadn't asked in a very long time. *What would Dad do?*

She was surprised by what came to mind. When she explained

her idea, it brought a look of disbelief from her new partner. But then Kristin relented. "It's crazy—but yeah, it might work."

* * *

As he stood guard duty next to the jeep, Manuel Rivas wished he were anywhere else. He was homesick and lonely, having not been back to his village in ten months. The tiny settlement on the steppes of the Andes had been his home for sixteen years, until that autumn day last year when the paras came to town.

He wasn't surprised when he saw them—not really. They had taken his older brother four years earlier. Eduardo had made it back home, a victory in itself, and now spent his days learning how to repair farm equipment, an ambitious undertaking for a young man with one leg. The Colombian army had shot the other one off, and for his troubles Eduardo was imprisoned for a year before being repatriated to the village. No one seemed to mind. In the end a misguided young man was reunited with his family, a burdened penal system acquired a needed vacancy, and a village was blessed with a new one-legged mechanic. Such was the course of life here, and Eduardo, always a positive person, considered himself lucky to have made it home at all.

Manuel, on the other hand, had never been blessed with his brother's optimism. Nor his luck. He always lost the football pools with his friends and invariably fell one card short in poker games with the other recruits. Still, like gamblers everywhere, Manuel clung unwaveringly to long odds. Which was why, when Carlos guaranteed a month's leave to any man who found the girls, he thought he might have a chance. Then he'd been assigned guard duty. By Pablo's order, he was left behind to watch their new prisoner, not even given an opportunity to search. Luckless as ever, he would not be going home. These were Manuel's thoughts, alternately angry and defeatist in the face of his chronic misfortune, when he saw a vision only God could grant.

Carlos' girl was running toward him with her arms outstretched. Her shirt was ripped open at the front, giving fluttering glimpses of skin from neck to navel. She was wearing a brassiere, but her breasts bounced heavily inside, the lovely white cups straining at the seams. She looked terrified, and her body language was that of a woman desperate for help. Manuel took his hip off the jeep's fender and blinked his eyes. The vision was still there. It was a rush of sensory inputs like nothing he'd ever experienced—sex and hope and fear all rushing toward him on a dead run. It never occurred to him to raise his weapon. He had talked to the girl a dozen times—her Spanish was quite good—and she'd always treated him kindly and with a smile.

As she came closer she yelled breathlessly, "Manuel! Help me! The other girl tried to take me away—she's hiding in the barracks!"

With all the self-discipline he could muster, Manuel turned and looked at the place he and his squad had called home for a week. It seemed quiet and still. Then it occurred to him that it was one of the few places they had not searched. In a matter of seconds his luck had changed. He'd found both girls, which meant *he* would be the one going home to see his family. Carlos was a bastard, but a bastard who kept his word.

Staring at the barracks, he heard the girl stop behind him— none of them knew her name—and as he began to turn, Manuel admonished himself not to stare at her chest. She might take exception to that, even if she *was* a depraved young American. And so, in turn, might Carlos.

I must do nothing to change my luck.

That was Manuel's last thought before the brick struck him in the head.

* * *

Kehoe heard someone approach, then the hood was ripped off his head.

He blinked against the light, and when his eyes adjusted he saw the girl he'd come to rescue. She looked just like the pictures in his briefing: dark shoulder-length hair, wide-set brown eyes. What hadn't been in the picture was the open shirt, which she was buttoning from the bottom up. Kehoe saw the guard on the ground, the brick lying next him, and of course he'd been listening. It was simple enough to put together what had transpired.

"Good work, Kristin."

"It wasn't my idea," she said, thumbing closed the last button on her dusty blouse. "Who are you?"

"My name's Kehoe. Your father sent me to bring you home."

"My father is a spineless bastard who doesn't have the decency to—"

"Stop right there!" he interrupted. "I don't give a damn who or what your father is!" He was in no mood to play counselor to whatever righteously screwed-up domestic calamity he was cleaning up. "We are leaving right now! Find something in the jeep that will cut these." He gestured to his plastic-cuffed wrists.

She scurried to the jeep and began searching.

Kehoe said, "Wire cutters, bolt cutters, anything to—" he spotted a knife in the downed soldier's belt. "There! Use that!"

Kristin looked where he was pointing and saw the knife. She knelt down and pulled it from its sheath, revealing a toothy, eight-inch-long Rambo special. The moment she pulled it clear, Manuel began to stir.

"What do I do?" she asked, clearly horrified at the thought of hitting the soldier again.

"Slit his throat," said Kehoe.

She looked at him incredulously.

Kehoe rolled his eyes. "Just give me the knife." She did, and Kehoe worked the blade between the bumper and the plastic band. It snapped on his first pull. The soldier was moving, but barely. Kehoe quickly confiscated his AK-47, made sure it was loaded, and then searched the man for other weapons. There were none.

"Transportation is next." He slid into the driver's seat and saw the key in the ignition. Not all military vehicles had keys, but Kehoe knew this one did—from under the cloth hood he'd heard the rattle of the chain, and click of an ignition cylinder when they'd left the airfield. You could learn a lot by listening.

"Get in here!" he ordered. "Do you know how to get to the airfield?"

"The only road leads straight there. But we can't leave without Jen!"

"Who?"

"My friend, Jen Davis. She's—"

Kehoe heard shouts in the distance, near the road. The road that was their only way out. Kristin waved toward one of the buildings, no doubt to signal her friend to join them. A gunshot rang out and a bullet pinged off the jeep, and Kehoe thought, *Consulting, that's really where I need to be.*

"Get in now!" he shouted.

She ignored him, and he saw the second girl running toward them.

Kehoe turned the key and the diesel engine rattled obediently to life. The briefcase was still on the hood, and after a very short internal debate, he snatched it and threw it on the seat next to him. By the time he had the jeep in gear both girls had vaulted into the back seat. He decided introductions could wait. They had advanced no more than twenty feet when Kehoe's foot slammed on the brake, the jeep skidding to a stop in a squall of dirt and gravel. Two men with raised semiautomatics were blocking the way out, positioned perfectly where the road funneled to the forest. A third soldier approached from the side, armed with a Steyr machine pistol and looking very sure of himself. Kehoe pondered the AK between the two front seats. Then he considered the two young girls behind him.

"Don't do it!" said the man to his left.

Kehoe stood down, his hands going open palmed on the steering wheel. The voice was familiar, and he got his first good look at the man in charge. He was short and thick, dusty fatigues over sun-etched skin. A thick beard and lively, intelligent eyes. A street-smart ranch hand.

"Carlos!" Kristin said. "I'm so glad you came back to—"

"Be quiet!" he snapped.

Now Kehoe had a name to go with the face.

Carlos looked at the girls, then at him. "You have all made a serious mistake."

Kehoe watched the two men a hundred feet ahead edge nearer. They were closer together than they should have been, he thought, limiting their lines of fire. Unfortunately, there were times when sheer numbers and firepower compensated for a lack of training. Carlos reached into the jeep, pulled out the AK and tossed it into the dirt. He seized a handful of Kristin's long hair and wrenched her out of her seat.

Kehoe sat still. His tactical situation was not good, but he knew the value of control. Waiting for a decent opening, he watched the man named Carlos push Kristin to her knees, and then whisper something into her ear. She shuddered visibly as he nodded to his men, and then gestured toward the second girl. When Carlos pointed the Steyr directly at his chest, Kehoe realized the chance he was waiting for might never come.

Nothing to lose, he inched his right hand between the seats. The prospect could not have been more slim, but it was all he had left. Kehoe was all concentration, preparing to instigate what might be the final conscious act of his life, when the most implausible thing happened. A massive form came flying out of the brush.

In a blur a man crashed into the soldiers in front, clotheslining one with an arm and tackling the other to the dirt. Three seconds and two haymakers later it was done. Both soldiers lay sprawled on the ground, motionless.

Carlos, as stunned as anyone, whipped the barrel of his gun toward the new threat. That was Kehoe's cue. In one fluid motion, he rotated in his seat and flung his weapon.

The world went on pause.

Two soldiers lay unconscious.

One man stood over them.

Kehoe's attention was fixed entirely on Carlos. He watched as the bearded Colombian seemed to hesitate, the Steyr curiously silent. Then he spun a lazy half turn, aimless and wobbling, and

everyone saw the reason—the massive combat knife was embedded to its hilt in his back. When Carlos eventually fell it was a
slow thing, like a felled tree clinging to its roots. The look of surprise in his unblinking eyes was absolute as he lay motionless on
the ground amid a fast-spreading pool of red.

Kehoe was the first to recover. "Who the hell is that?" he ex-
claimed, staring at the hulk who'd burst out of the jungle.

It was the second girl who answered. "Dad!"

Jen jumped out of the jeep and ran.

* * *

It was just one word, but it made Davis' heart leap like nothing
he'd ever heard.

"Dad!"

He saw Jen running toward him. Full of joy. Full of life. *God,
so full of life!*

Standing frozen, Davis realized that in nineteen years he had
never before worried about his daughter. Not really. Not like the
mind-numbing fear that had consumed him since last Sunday. After five days of dread and anxiety, five days of never giving up . . .
it was here. This was the vision that had filled his dreams.

He opened his arms as wide as the sky.

Jammer Davis, who had stood tall and strong against four
hardened soldiers in the last five minutes, was knocked flat on his
ass by his hundred-and-twenty-pound daughter.

Jen was in his arms.

He would never, ever let her go.

FORTY-SEVEN

The overloaded jeep careened wildly with Kehoe at the wheel, and everyone took a handhold to keep from being tossed into the jungle. Davis sat in the back of the jeep with an arm around each of the girls—he hadn't let go of Jen since she'd jumped into his arms.

McBain was in the front passenger seat talking on the satphone, struggling to keep the handset in the vicinity of his ear as the jeep bucked over massive tree roots and bottomed out on potholes.

"I knew you'd come," said Jen.

Davis pulled her even closer. "We're not out of the woods yet."

She rolled her eyes at his awful joke—like she always did.

He said, "We have an airplane a few miles from here, the same dirt strip where you and Kristin were pulled off that flight."

"Is there a pilot too?" Jen asked.

He gave his daughter a pained look. "What am I?"

"Well," she hesitated, "it's just that I've seen you fly through rough situations. Like that time in Egypt when you nearly crashed into the—"

"Trust me," he interrupted, "I'll get you out of here. The worst is behind us."

"We can't assume that," Kehoe said over his shoulder. "We aren't the only ones with communications gear."

Kristin said, "Carlos' father was supposed to come today. He must be nearby, and I've been told he never travels alone."

"His father?" Davis asked. "Who's he?"

The jeep hit a massive rut and everyone went airborne in their seats. Shouting over the engine noise, Kristin gave a rundown of her relationship with Carlos, explaining that his father commanded a paramilitary force, but also had close ties to the government.

"Any idea what the government connection is?" McBain asked.

"I don't know, but Carlos talked to his father every day on the phone, and he always had good information. He knew all the details of my flight, including that Agent Mulligan would be on it. He also knew a lot about the crash investigation."

"Does Carlos have a last name?" McBain asked. "His father might be somebody we've tracked at DEA."

"I always thought it was Duran," said Kristin. "That's what he used at school. But a few nights ago I saw an old passport with a different name—Carlos Echevarria."

"Echevarria?" said McBain. "That's a pretty common name."

Davis was only surprised by his lack of surprise. "Not as common as you might think," he said, without bothering to explain.

McBain went back to his sat-phone, and soon was relaying bad news. "Kristin is right. Jorgensen says reinforcements are heading our way. There's a group of four vehicles less than a mile away on an intersecting trail."

"Which direction are they coming from?" Davis asked.

"East. We're going to pass a junction any minute on the right."

"What about the airfield? Is it clear?"

"Right now it is. Delacorte is still there with their rent-a-pilot." McBain locked eyes with Davis, and said, "You realize the Comanche is a four seater. How the heck are we all going to fit?"

Davis was well aware of the seating limitation, but he'd once seen a Comanche rigged for six passengers. At least he thought it was a Comanche.

"What about the other airplane," said McBain, "it's bigger. Could you fly that one?"

"I could fly it, sure . . . but it would take a few minutes for me to figure things out. Same goes for convincing the other pilot to switch to our team. There's no time for any of that." He tried to sound confident when he said, "It's okay, the Comanche will work. The girls can squeeze into the cargo area behind the seats."

He made no mention of weight and balance calculations—something he would have considered if they weren't being chased by an enemy platoon.

"There's another problem," McBain added unhelpfully. "Our drone is nearly out of gas—if it doesn't leave soon it's going to turn into a glider. Jorgensen played the emergency authority card, so there's not much more he can do. We're about to lose our eyes."

At that moment the intersection came into view, and everyone went eyes-right like a squad marching past a reviewing stand at a parade. Sure enough, the reinforcements were there, less than a hundred meters away. In the lead was a light troop carrier, and it made the turn with two men in firing positions at the roof of the cab. To their credit, they didn't waste ammunition—it would take a miracle to hit anything given the speed they were all traveling and the condition of the road.

"This isn't going to work," said McBain. "Two miles to go, and they're right behind us. We've got a one-minute lead, but it'll take five for us to climb into the airplane and get airborne."

"Three," said Davis, already going over the Comanche's start procedure in his head. "But you're right—it's not enough time."

Kehoe was completely focused on the road, but he diverted his attention long enough to say, "I saw three vehicles, so I'd say we're up against twenty-five men. We don't have the firepower to suppress a unit that size, let alone stand and fight."

With the airfield just ahead there seemed no way out. An extended pause drove home the drought of ideas as the jeep's tiny motor strained and its suspension rattled. It was Davis who broke the silence. "We might have one more round to fire than we think—a pretty big one, actually." He explained his idea to McBain.

"No!" said the DEA man. "There's no way they'll approve that!"

Davis snatched the sat-phone from his hand. "Jorgensen, you there?"

"*Yeah, Jammer, I'm here,*" crackled the voice over the phone.

"I need you to patch me through to the guys controlling that drone. Tell them operational command of their asset has just been chopped. They are now taking orders from General Jammer T. Davis, Commander of United States Southern Command . . . ”

* * *

The bunker in Panama had been dead quiet at the beginning of the shift. But then it always was. The soft hum of cooling fans from the computers was barely audible, as was the gentle hiss emanating from an overhead speaker, perpetually tuned to a little-used radio frequency. Until two hours ago the biggest disturbance of this early shift had been the coffeemaker at the back of the room gurgling to the end of its brew cycle. Then came the call from Colombia.

There were three workstations in the command center, each with a driver's seat—triple multifunction displays, a flight control joystick on the right, and a throttle on the left. Only the center station was in use tonight, the lone operator glued to his colorful screens. The largest of these displayed essential flight information and a moving map, while the others offered sensor feeds and secondary flight data. An old-fashioned dry-erase board, nailed to the wall near the operator, confirmed that there was a single mission on the schedule today—one that had actually begun yesterday. Aside from the pilot, the only other person in the bunker was a supervisor standing behind him. Both were frowning. All systems on the Predator were functioning perfectly, but it had been a trying morning, and they now faced two critical problems. One was the aircraft's fuel state, highlighted in red on the secondary flight display. The other was the level of confusion in the bunker.

“General *who*?” said the drone operator, his hand briefly coming off the joystick as he turned to look over his shoulder. He was a retired Air Force pilot, twenty-two years under his belt flying six different types of aircraft. He was one of the few among his commissioning year-group to have spent his entire career in a cockpit of some sort. The last four were spent in the same seat he was in now—controlling an unmanned aerial vehicle from a great distance.

"Jammie Davis?" questioned the supervisor. "Is that right? Southern Command is a goddamn four-star general!"

"I've never heard of the guy," said the operator, pulling one side of his headset away from his ear. "But that doesn't mean much. When I retired two years ago I could have told you my wing commander's name, and maybe the guy who headed up First Air Force. Four star billets were never in my future, so I didn't bother to keep up with them. I do remember that there was a change of command at SOUTHCOM a few months back."

A brief silence ensued.

If unmanned aerial vehicles were new to the DEA, they were quickly making their mark, undertaking previously impossible surveillance missions, and guiding interdiction efforts over the jungles of South America. Yet the Predator, like any new system, was not without growing pains. Chief among them was that little consideration had been given to operational decision making. Since the DEA's drones didn't carry weapons, little guidance had been drawn pertaining to command authority or rules of engagement. As for what this team had just been asked to do— that wasn't in *any* manual.

"Where did that message source from?" asked the operator.

"It was the secondary secure line, the regional chief operations office."

"Which means what—that Jorgensen's got a four-star sitting next to him?"

"Could be," said the supervisor, "or maybe he's patched through to the guy. This is obviously some kind of black op we're watching."

The men stared at the big screen where a jeep with five confirmed friendlies was being pursued by truckloads of unconfirmed hostiles.

"I don't know . . . " the supervisor hedged, "we've been watching this whole thing spin up for hours. My guess is we're looking at a Special Forces team that's working with DEA. The bottom line is that known friendlies on the ground are requesting help."

"Normally I'd say run it up to headquarters," said the operator, "but I don't think there's time." He slewed the view forward and back, measuring things out. "Two minutes max—after that they'll be at the airport and we won't have any decision to make. Honestly, I'm not sure we have enough fuel to do it anyway."

"Terrific," said the supervisor. He had an all-civilian background, thirty-one years with the DEA. He was also a GS-13 on the cusp of retirement. He'd arrived in country five days ago for a six-month temporary duty posting—his stroke of genius, figuring that a winter in Panama had to beat one in D.C. He was now revisiting that choice.

A new voice boomed in, patched over the secure link. *"This is General Davis! We need that support now, dammit!"*

The two men in the bunker looked at one another. The operator keyed his microphone. *"Archer one copies, we are working on authorization."*

"Authorization? Did you not hear me? Look at your infrared! Lives are on the line . . . at . . . this . . . moment!"

The operator kept to his flying, and said in a hushed voice, "I'm glad this is your call."

The supervisor snatched up the hotline to DEA headquarters and on the fifth ring someone answered and put him on hold. "Dammit!" He slammed down the handset. "Well, we're gonna earn one of two things here—a medal or prison time."

"I vote we do it," said the pilot.

"*Can* you do it?"

"Never been tried as far as I know. But if I switch to the nose camera . . . yeah, I think I can make it happen."

The supervisor closed his eyes for just a moment. "All right, you're cleared in hot. And for God's sake, make it count!"

FORTY-EIGHT

Davis told the girls to stay low in the backseat, and covered them as best he could. The convoy behind them was losing ground, though only slightly—the jeep was lighter and more nimble, yet its speed was hampered by the condition of the road. As far as he could tell, no one had started shooting, but the men with rifles remained ominously behind the rocking cab. Davis was reasonably sure he recognized Major Raul Echevarria, a distant but steady presence in the passenger seat of the lead truck.

Echevarria's involvement made perfect sense. It explained why the Bogotá police had so quickly become engaged, not to mention the quality of information Kristin Stewart's kidnappers enjoyed. The note Echevarria had delivered, warning Davis to go home, was the most transparent clue. Less obvious, though every bit as certain—the murder of Colonel Alfonso Marquez in the parking lot of El Centro. Echevarria was behind everything, the keystone in a very unstable wall.

Riding shotgun in the lead truck, Echevarria knew the tactical situation as well as Davis did. There was no need for the Colombians to close ground, because in minutes they would all be at the same end point, and the hundred-yard gap would disappear in seconds. Davis looked up to the sky. He saw nothing above the high trees lining either side of the road. General Jammer T. Davis, apparently, had not made an impression.

Just then a piece of paper swirled up and slapped his cheek. He looked down. Kristin and Jen, bent low for cover, had the briefcase open on the floor.

"What are you doing?" Davis asked as another piece of paper

shot skyward. This one stuck to his shirt and he recognized it as a U.S. Treasury bill wrapper.

"Something that will get them off our backs," Kristin said.

Kehoe cast an eye over his shoulder. "Hey, wait a minute! You can't—"

Before he could finish, the girls together lifted the suitcase high over Davis' head, and seventy thousand hundred-dollar bills flew into the air like so much confetti. Everyone watched the flurry of Benjamin Franklins rise up into the air and flutter into the path of the oncoming trucks. The convoy plowed right through the cloud.

"*What?*" said an incredulous McBain. "You thought they'd just stop to pick it all up?"

"Okay . . . " Jen said, "maybe it was a bad idea."

"No, it was a great idea," Kristin countered. "The last thing I want is to give that money back to my deadbeat father."

Kehoe rolled his eyes. "I can't wait to file that expense report."

"The girls are right on one count," said Davis. "This is no time to give up." He picked up the empty briefcase and heaved it backward. It bounced once, twice, and struck the lead truck squarely in a headlight.

"There's only one solution," said McBain. "When we reach the airfield, we'll park the jeep to block the road. Jammer, you and the girls make a run for the airplane. Kehoe and I will hold them off."

"Hold them off?" Davis questioned. "With what? You've got an AK with a partial mag, an empty Beretta that misfires, and a pair of rubber MP-5s that don't even make good clubs. How long are you going to make a stand against two dozen armed men?"

"Hopefully long enough," said Kehoe, "unless you have a better plan. They don't know what we've got, so they'll be cautious. It might buy enough time for you to get airborne."

"What if I stayed and—"

"No!" argued McBain. "There's no time to debate. You're the pilot, Jammer, so *you* have to take the girls."

Davis looked at Kehoe, who didn't hesitate a beat before saying, "It stinks, but he's right. That's how we do it."

From a tactical viewpoint Davis knew they were right. It was the only way to get the girls to safety. He also realized that McBain and Kehoe were prepared to risk their lives to make it happen. In times like this you learned a lot about people.

The airfield came into view in the distance, and Davis was about to give the plan his okay when his eye caught a glint in the sky. He searched above the horizon until his view was interrupted by a pair of towering trees. When the sky opened up again, Davis definitely saw a black speck. It was getting bigger, gaining definition. Soon he could make out a central body and two long, thin wings.

"There!" said McBain, who saw it as well.

Everyone watched the drone. It seemed to be coming right at them, no more than a few hundred feet above the treetops. It didn't appear to be flying fast, but drones weren't built for speed. Davis saw distinct oscillations in the aircraft's path, jerky corrections that suggested it was flying above V_{NE}—the "never exceed" speed. He watched the aircraft pitch and buck, and he wondered if it had run out of gas. For an instant it steered right at them, then the Predator lurched upward and screamed over their heads. The powerplant was loud and clear at full power.

Everyone, Kehoe included, turned to watch the drone as it leveled for an instant, then pitched down in a violent maneuver aimed squarely at the lead truck behind them. The driver swerved, and Davis was certain he saw Echevarria duck in the final milliseconds.

None of that made any difference.

For all his experience in investigating air crashes, Davis had never witnessed one from such an intimate perspective. He knew jet fuel was an accelerant, and that it was at its most deadly form in what brewed in the nearly empty wing tanks of the Predator— a vast reservoir of fuel vapor waiting for a spark.

The initial explosion was immense, and the aircraft and

truck both disappeared in a cloud of fire that boiled above the tree line. Davis saw the next truck in line veer sharply to avoid the inferno before toppling on its side and skidding to a stop in the middle of the road. The third truck T-boned the second, and any subsequent disasters could only be imagined as a thick cloud of black smoke enveloped everything. Next came the secondary explosions—ammunition in the burning vehicles detonating like firecrackers. There were plenty of survivors, and they ran and crawled away from the flames like vermin from a burning building. A hard-core pair stumbled forward out of the cloud, as if trying to keep the chase alive, but gave up when the trailing man's camouflaged trousers caught fire.

With half a mile to go they were nearly in the clear, but Kehoe's foot stayed hard on the accelerator. They broke into the airfield clearing to find Delacorte and the charter pilot staring at the cloud of black smoke in the distance. Both had something in their hands. Davis couldn't tell what it was at first, then Delacorte took off at a run toward the Comanche, and a fistful of playing cards fluttered to the ground.

The overtasked Comanche lumbered down the airstrip three minutes later. Even with the disaster a mile away, no one wanted to wait to see if the survivors had the wherewithal to organize a last-ditch assault. Davis used every bit of dirt to accelerate before milking the overloaded twin into the sky. The Comanche climbed out slowly, clawing at the heavy air, and Davis made one lazy orbit over the airstrip. The key to the chartered Cessna Caravan was still in his pocket, and Davis instructed McBain to tie it securely to the pitot tube cover of their own aircraft, which had a long red streamer and block lettering that read: REMOVE BEFORE FLIGHT.

Davis cracked open his side window, and when they were directly over the Cessna he dropped the key with the streamer outside. It was nearly a hit, landing a few feet behind the Caravan. They all watched the pilot—whose name, Delacorte had learned, was Segundo, and who was a damned good poker player—run to recover the key. Before they lost sight of the airstrip, Segundo had the propeller spinning and the airplane moving. In Delacorte's words, "A man who definitely knows when to fold."

There were six people crammed in the Comanche's tiny cabin, and for a time no one spoke. Davis looked at McBain, who was seated next to him, and exchanged a nod. He then turned toward the others who were shoehorned in back. The girls were the farthest away, sitting cross-legged on a grease-stained plot of carpet. They looked exhausted and happy. Like kids at noon on Christmas day.

He locked eyes with Jen for a moment and sensed her relief. Then he saw her mouth something.

Davis went back to flying with a weary grin. He made the first turn toward home, and thought, *I love you too, baby.*

FORTY-NINE

The G-III landed at 3:02 a.m. that Saturday morning, and taxied directly toward a massive hangar on the southwest side of Andrews Air Force Base—the very place Davis had begun his odyssey less than a week earlier.

Vincent Kehoe was the first one off, and stepping down to the tarmac behind him was Kristin Stewart. On the long flight Davis had learned a good deal about Kehoe. He was an Army Ranger and ten-year Delta Force veteran. No surprises there. But Davis was more impressed by what he'd seen. Kehoe had been ready to put himself in harm's way in order to save Jen and Kristin, no hesitation whatsoever. In truth, almost with relish.

Davis watched Kehoe escort his charge into the big hangar, which was encircled by a phalanx of Secret Service agents. Nearby was a motorcade of limos that stretched around the corner, at least three that he could see. There were no flags flapping from fenders, however, and no police motorcycle escort waiting to lead a parade. This was low-profile, high-value security. It didn't take a rocket scientist to figure out who was inside the hangar. Someone with access to the most sensitive corner of Andrews. Someone with a very good reason to be here.

Martin Stuyvesant was finally going to meet his daughter.

Davis stepped down the stairs, Jen following, and two men walked up to greet them. One wore a nice suit, had a tight haircut and a wire in his ear. He might as well have had Secret Service stamped on his forehead. It was the second man who addressed Davis, a rotund, wonky type with droopy eyes behind wire-rimmed glasses.

He held out a fleshy hand, and said, "Mr. Davis, my name is Bill Evers. I'm—"

"I know who you are," Davis cut in. He kept his hands at his side.

Clearly put off, the vice president's chief of staff said, "Mr. Kehoe wasn't supposed to share that kind of information."

"Mr. Kehoe is a good man—something in painfully short supply around here."

With Evers at a loss, Davis turned to the Secret Service man and said, "Sorry about Agent Mulligan. The girl really liked him."

The agent seemed surprised to be brought into the conversation, but his expression turned solemn and he nodded appreciatively. "Yeah, Tom was one of the good ones."

Evers began to recover. "I realize it's very late, and that you've traveled a great distance, but we want to debrief both of you. A lot has happened in the last few days, and everyone must understand what's at stake."

Davis cocked his head ever so slightly. *Everyone must understand what's at stake.* At that moment, he saw where things were going. Candidate Stuyvesant was not surrendering. He was doubling down.

A dark sedan pulled up on some unseen cue, and Evers guided them toward the backseat. Jen was already inside when Davis heard a distant yell. He looked over his shoulder and saw Kristin Stewart bolting from a gap in the hangar door. She was in tears, and from fifty yards away he heard her scream, *"I don't ever want to see you again, you bastard! Just leave Mom and me alone!"*

Davis watched her run to one of the limousines. A middle-aged woman emerged from the car, her arms open wide. The two embraced, burying their faces in one another's shoulders. He was sure he knew the woman's name—Sorensen had told him two days ago. Jean Stewart.

Mom.

Davis could hear them sobbing from where he stood.

Evers tried to urge him into the limo, putting a hand on his lower back. Davis didn't move. Jen's sadness was evident as she watched Kristin and her mother console one another. He remembered the somber expression that came over the Secret Service man when he'd given his condolences about Mulligan.

Evers gave another shove, but he might as well have been trying to move an oak.

Davis turned slowly and looked at Evers. He gave a half smile, and said, "Look, I know how things will go down here, and I'm okay with it. Really, I'm on board."

"Tell me about it," said an interested Evers.

Davis did, and when he was done Evers nodded thoughtfully. "I'm glad you can put the good of your country above all else, Mr. Davis."

"Very much so," said Davis. "But I do have just *one* request . . . "

* * *

Martin Stuyvesant stood in the middle of the hangar. Designed to hold a Boeing-747, the place was nearly empty, yet the man walking toward him seemed to fill it up. He studied Jammer Davis under bright fluorescent light as he plodded across the floor between two Secret Service agents. The man was exactly as he'd imagined. Big and brutish, not a trace of sophistication. He might be a savant when it came to deciphering air crashes, Stuyvesant thought, but he clearly had no idea how to carry himself with style. He moved stiffly and his clothes were ill fitting. He hadn't even bothered to shave or comb his hair for a meeting with the vice president of the United States—the G-III had all the necessary toiletries, so there was really no excuse.

The good news was that Davis was on board with the plan— at least that's what he'd told Evers. He would maintain a strict silence regarding everything that had happened in Colombia. All he wanted in return was one face-to-face meeting with the soon-to-be president. Stuyvesant was accustomed to such requests—he practically expected them. Davis would ask a favor, most likely a promotion to a more senior position at NTSB. That would be

easy enough, and mutually beneficial. Of course, he would probably want a mantel photograph as well, all handshakes and smiles,
but Evers had already explained that wasn't going to happen. Security was the best excuse. With the crisis finally over, it was all
down to damage control, something Evers excelled at.

Smooth as ever, Stuyvesant began walking as Davis neared.
That was always the best way to meet physically imposing men,
although Stuyvesant was more accustomed to scions of industry
and Hollywood moguls. He thrust out his hand and beamed his
best campaign smile. "So glad to finally meet you, Mr. D—"

So heavy was the right hook that met his jaw, it was the last
time in his life Martin Stuyvesant correctly enunciated the letter D.

FIFTY

At least it wasn't another jail cell, Davis mused. Not really.

The meeting room adjacent to the hangar was a solid place, but there were no bars on the windows or steel doors. The carpet was plush, and a comfortable lounge area offered an array of supple chairs. Instead of a bent steel tray pushed through a slot, Davis was looking at a catered spread with a good selection of meat, cheese, and crackers. There was a veggie tray too, with a nice avocado-based dip, and sweet rolls on a platter shaped like Air Force One. The bottles of water had come all the way from Fiji, and there was an assortment of soft drinks, all the standard products of the Coca-Cola company. No, not a holding cell at all. This was the place Stuyvesant had waited out their arrival. Now it was Davis' turn to wait.

Comfort aside, he was anything but free. They'd removed the cuffs from his wrists, but around the large room he counted eight Secret Service agents, all with unwavering eyes. They'd started with a contingent of four, until whispers began to circulate about a china shop in Bogotá, and the number magically doubled. He didn't much care. Jen was on her way home, delivered safe and sound. He had done what he'd set out to do, from beginning to end.

He was standing behind a seemingly bottomless coffee pot when the only door to the room opened, and the lead Secret Service man he'd met earlier came through. He was followed by Larry Green.

Green stared at him with exasperation, like a football coach eyeing a player whose foolish penalty had lost the big game. It was the third time in a week Davis had been in someone's custody, and he was sure Green had the tally marks to prove it.

Davis held out his palms in a *what's a guy to do?* gesture.

After a brief discussion with his escort, Green walked over while the Secret Service man stayed at the door. That brought the count to nine agents. Davis sank into one of the wide lounge chairs. Green took the opposing seat.

"You'll never learn, will you, Jammer?"

"How is he?"

"Stuyvesant's in surgery—the best maxillofacial surgeon in town is trying to reconstruct his lower mandible."

"I missed the upper?"

Green eyed him severely.

"Are you here to bail me out?" Davis asked.

"Actually, I don't have to. For reasons I cannot imagine, they've decided not to file charges. Any idea why?"

"Maybe . . . but it's a long story. And I'm not supposed to talk about it."

Green gave him a tormented look.

"I'll tell you about it later . . . that is, if you can keep a secret. And if you buy me a beer."

A sigh from Green, then, "I checked on Jen—she made it home."

"Thanks."

"I'll bet she sleeps for a week," said Green.

"I might join her. By the way, thanks for setting me up with those DEA guys. They were good, a first-rate crew. None of them will get in trouble, will they? You know, with what happened to the drone and all?"

"That's something else I wanted to bring up. Why is it that every time I send you to investigate an accident, you end up crashing another airplane?"

Davis only shrugged. "McBain and Jorgensen?" he asked again.

"They'll be fine. It was *you* who turned that drone into a weapon. General Jammer T. Davis? God help us."

"What? You don't think I'm flag-grade material?"

Green ignored the question. "Your co-conspirators were operating under some kind of emergency authority. It's not exactly a get-out-of-jail-free card, but the seniors at DEA seem pretty happy with the way things turned out. Rumor I heard was that nine paramilitaries were killed in the crash, including the guy who ran the whole operation—Echevarria, I think, was the name. Apparently he was a busy guy, a major on the Bogotá police force who operated a paramilitary squad on the side. He's been sabotaging government operations for years to support his trafficking and extortion sideline. I also heard something about a former TAC-Air pilot who got caught trying to leave the country on a false passport."

"Reyna?" Davis asked.

"Yeah, that's him. What they nearly got away with down there was madness. But somehow . . . " Green paused for emphasis and leaned closer, "*somehow* this is all getting swept under a carpet."

Davis said nothing.

Green looked pointedly around the room at a sea of somber faces. "Then there's the fact that you and I are sitting right now in the hangar they use to stow Air Force One. Surrounded by Secret Service agents. What the hell did you get into, Jammer?"

Davis flexed his right fist, squeezing the fingers open and shut. Two knuckles were sore. "*You* put me on this inquiry, Larry. But, like I said, buy me a beer later and I'll explain everything."

Green heaved a long sigh. "Anyway, I'm supposed to tell you that somebody is going to stop by your house tomorrow and take statements from both you and Jen. Otherwise, for reasons I can't imagine, you're free to go. I'll give you a ride home."

Both men got up and headed for the door. None of the special agents flinched. They were two steps from leaving when the head of Stuyvesant's security detail stepped in their path and held up a palm.

They paused, and the agent stared at Davis. His face was stone as he said, "I'm not sure how you got away with what you did in that hangar. And I really don't like that it happened on my watch. It makes for a hell of a lot of paperwork." Then a barely perceptible smile edged one corner of his mouth, and he leaned close to whisper, "That was a nice shot, though. A few of us around here have been wanting to do that for a long time."

Davis grinned back. "My pleasure."

FIFTY-ONE

It was the second Sunday of November, the most spectacular day in an unusually mild autumn. The air was crisp, the lake like glass, and Davis regarded the end of the dock with the pride of a new father written on his face.

"That's what you brought me to see?" said Jen. "You got a new toy?"

"It's not a toy, baby. You're looking at my new line of work."

"A seaplane? What are you going to do with it? Run drugs to South America or something?"

Davis watched close, saw the smile, and decided it was good that she could joke about her ordeal. Jen had spent four days as a hostage in a remote corner of the globe, yet she'd come out unscathed. At least in the physical sense. He'd been watching closely for the other kind. He had insisted she take the semester off school, and she'd countered by agreeing to move home only if she could sign up for online courses. Another positive sign—moving forward. The deal was struck and it kept Jen busy. It also kept her under his paternal eye. There were moments when he could see her contemplating what had happened, reflecting on the dark days. But only a few.

Because it had been, at least in part, a common experience, he tried to keep things light. They compared notes on the finer points of Colombian jails; *like father, like daughter*. When more difficult days intruded, Davis went for distraction. They took in a movie or went out to fly. In the intervening months Jen had twice met with Kristin Stewart, who seemed a decent kid, if a bit wayward in the boyfriend department. Indeed, Davis took heart that his own daughter had learned a lesson in the avoidance of greed-smitten, faux-revolutionary young men.

The bottom line—both girls seemed to be recovering. Healing and moving on.

A brisk gust of wind swirled leaves along the shore, and as he guided Jen down the dock he briefed her on the airplane. "It's a Lake 250 Renegade."

"Renegade? How fitting is that?"

He maintained a father's enduring patience. "I've got a buddy down in Florida who runs a charter business, fishing trips and sightseeing. He can't keep up with the demand."

"What about the NTSB?" she asked. "Are you still going to do investigations?"

"Larry has my number. I was always more of a consultant, anyway. Wait until you see how smooth she flies. There are six seats, although the two in back are a little cramped. Three customers and all the fishing gear they can pack, I'm thinking."

At the end of the dock Davis began his preflight, checking the fuel level and flight controls. As he went about his chores, Jen said, "Did I mention that I voted last week?"

She'd been showing a temperate interest in politics lately, an affliction that caused Davis to revisit her mental state.

"Did you? That's great! Your first presidential vote."

"I'm not a Republican, but I had to vote for Paulson."

"Well, yeah—I can definitely understand that. Have you talked to Kristin? Who did she vote for?"

"Are you kidding? She and her mom have been volunteering at the Paulson campaign for a month."

Davis stopped working a docking line long enough to smile at his daughter. "Now that's just perfect."

"The whole election seemed so weird," Jen continued, "the way Stuyvesant fell down that flight of stairs and shattered his jaw at such a critical time in the race."

"What are the chances?" he replied, untangling a knot. His moment of madness in the hangar had been completely covered up—he hadn't even told Jen. He didn't like keeping things from his daughter, but in this case he made an exception.

She said, "The guy is scum, no doubt about it . . . but I almost felt sorry for him. The way he had to back out of the debate and so many campaign appearances. That one interview he tried to give was comical, mumbling through a jaw that was wired shut—you couldn't make out a word he said."

"Heck of a way to campaign." He was holding the Lake close with a hand on the wing.

"What about you, Dad?" she asked. "Did you vote?"

Jammer Davis took his daughter's hand as she stepped into the seaplane. He said, "Well, it wasn't last week . . . I sort of voted early this year."

Jen looked at him suspiciously, a hauntingly familiar expression. Then he made the connection—it was the same look that had so often visited her mother's face.

"Come on," he said, "let's go fly."

Davis pushed off the dock at noon that Sunday. His daughter was at his side. It was one of the best days of his life.

ACKNOWLEDGMENTS

Thanks to all those who helped bring this story to life. The brilliant staff at Oceanview Publishing, Lee Randall, David Ivester, and Emily Baar. To Bob and Pat Gussin for their support over the years.

To my agent Susan Gleason, whose expertise, not to mention sense of humor, is always appreciated.

And of course, to my family for their primary editing and unfailing encouragement.